Praise for *The Dark at the End*

"Refreshingly unpredictable . . . This thriller fittingly concludes one of the most consistently entertaining series in modern fantastic fiction."

—*Publishers Weekly*

Praise for the Repairman Jack Series

"Repairman Jack has got to be one of the greatest characters ever. . . . When all things start pointing to the end of humanity, Jack's the guy to turn to."

—*RT Book Reviews* on *Fatal Error*

"Repairman Jack is one of the most original and intriguing characters to arise out of contemporary fiction in ages. His adventures are hugely entertaining."

—Dean Koontz, bestselling author of *Whispers*

"Readers who like fast-paced, dark urban fantasy from a master storyteller will find this a thrilling journey. Get on board now, 'cause this train is moving fast, folks. Strongly recommended."

—*SFRevu* on *Ground Zero*

"Jack stand[s] out from the supernatural pack. . . . The books are about an ordinary guy doing whatever it takes to protect the innocent, and that's a story that always has resonance."

—*Chicago Sun-Times* on *By the Sword*

"A canny mix of sci-fi paranoia and criminal mayhem . . . *Bloodline* starts fast, keeps the accelerator down, and defies you to stop reading."

—*Entertainment Weekly*

BOOKS BY F. PAUL WILSON

REPAIRMAN JACK*
The Tomb
Legacies
Conspiracies
All the Rage
Hosts
The Haunted Air
Gateways
Crisscross
Infernal
Harbingers
Bloodline
By the Sword
Ground Zero
Fatal Error
The Dark at the End

YOUNG ADULT*
Jack: Secret Histories
Jack: Secret Circles
Jack: Secret Vengeance

THE ADVERSARY CYCLE*
The Keep
The Tomb
The Touch
Reborn
Reprisal
Nightworld

OTHER NOVELS
Healer
Wheels Within Wheels

An Enemy of the State
Black Wind*
Dydeetown World
The Tery
Sibs*
The Select
Virgin
Implant
Deep as the Marrow
Mirage
    (with Matthew J. Costello)
Nightkill
    (with Steven Spruill)
Masque
    (with Matthew J. Costello)
The Christmas Thingy
Sims
The Fifth Harmonic
Midnight Mass

SHORT FICTION
Soft and Others
The Barrens and Others*
Aftershock & Others*
The Peabody-Ozymandias
    Traveling Circus &
    Oddity Emporium*
Quick Fixes*

EDITOR
Freak Show
Diagnosis: Terminal

* See "The Secret History of the World" (page 419).

F. PAUL WILSON

THE DARK
AT THE END

A REPAIRMAN JACK NOVEL

TOR®

A TOM DOHERTY ASSOCIATES BOOK
NEW YORK

This is a work of fiction. All of the characters, organizations, and events portrayed in this novel are either products of the author's imagination or are used fictitiously.

THE DARK AT THE END: A REPAIRMAN JACK NOVEL

Copyright © 2011 by F. Paul Wilson

All rights reserved.

A Tor Book
Published by Tom Doherty Associates, LLC
175 Fifth Avenue
New York, NY 10010

www.tor-forge.com

Tor® is a registered trademark of Tom Doherty Associates, LLC.

ISBN 978-0-7653-6281-0

First Edition: October 2011
First Mass Market Edition: October 2012

Printed in the United States of America

0 9 8 7 6 5 4 3 2 1

ACKNOWLEDGMENTS

Thanks to the usual crew for their efforts: my wife, Mary; David Hartwell and Stacy Hague-Hill at the publisher; Steven Spruill; Elizabeth Monteleone; Dannielle Romeo; and my agent, Albert Zuckerman. And, as always, thanks to copy editor extraordinaire Becky Maines.

AUTHOR'S NOTE

You hold the final installment in the Repairman Jack series.

As I've mentioned in the past few books, I'm ending the series with number fifteen (though Jack will appear in *Nightworld*), and *The Dark at the End* is it.

I've always said this would be a closed-end series, that I would not run Jack into the ground, that I had a big story to tell and would lower the curtain after telling it. The major arc—the cosmic conflict between the Ally and the Otherness—has accrued critical mass and it's time to pay off on everything I've been building toward. Drawing it out further will do nothing but add excess verbiage and vitiate the series's punch.

Let's end on a high note, okay?

The Dark at the End picks up two weeks after *Fatal Error*. I hope you've read the Adversary Cycle by now. The two story tracks—Jack's tale and the Cycle—have merged here. (See "The Secret History of the World" at the end of this book for how everything fits together.)

From *The Dark at the End* we'll move on to the extensively revised *Nightworld*. Jack is a major player there, but only one of many. *Nightworld* is an ensemble novel with characters from across the Secret History. It ends both narrative tracks, as well as the Secret History. More stories remain to be told, but the timeline stops there. I will set no stories after *Nightworld*.

However . . .

In response to cries of agony from readers, I've agreed to write three more Repairman Jack novels from the period between his arrival in NYC and *The Tomb,* just to fill in those gaps. They'll trace how he gets to know Abe and Julio, and how he becomes the guy you meet in *The Tomb.* After those books, it's *over.* You will then know all I know about Jack and I'll have nothing left to say. I need to move on.

—F. Paul Wilson,
the Jersey Shore

WEDNESDAY

I. "Sir!" the cabbie said in heavily accented English as Jack slammed the taxi door shut behind him. "Those people were—"

"Drive!"

"They were there first and—"

Jack slammed the plastic partition between them and shot him his best glare. "Drive, goddammit!"

The guy hesitated, then his dark features registered the truth that he wasn't going to win this one.

"Where?"

"There!" Jack pointed uptown, where the cab was facing. "Anywhere, just move!"

As the cab pulled into the bustling morning traffic on Central Park West, Jack twisted to peer through the rear window. The couple he'd shoved out of the way to commandeer the taxi stood at the curb, huddling against the March wind as they stared after him in openmouthed shock, but they seemed to be the only ones.

Good . . . as if anything about this could be called good.

He faced front again and checked his arm. His left deltoid hurt like hell. He noticed a bullet hole in the sleeve of his beloved beat-up bomber jacket. He reached inside, touched a *reeeally* tender spot. His fingers came out bloody.

Swell. Just swell. This was *not* how the day was supposed to go.

It had begun serenely enough: shower, coffee and kaisers with Gia, then a trip to Central Park West to drop in on the Lady. He knew certain forces wanted to rid the world of her, and had almost succeeded a couple of weeks ago. But he'd never expected an armed ambush.

After finding the Lady's apartment empty, he'd taken the stairs one floor up to Veilleur's floor.

Even though he could call him Glaeken now, he'd trained himself to think of him as Veilleur and Veilleur only for over a year, so shifting to his real name was going to take a little time.

He knocked on the steel door at the top step. "Hello?"

"Come in, Jack," said a voice from somewhere on the other side. "It's open."

Inside he found Glaeken slumped in an easy chair in the apartment's great room, sipping coffee as he stared out at the morning sky through the panoramic windows.

Jack slowed as he approached, struck by his appearance. He was as big as ever; his shoulders just as broad, his hair as gray, his eyes as blue. But he looked older today. Okay, the guy *was* old—he measured his age in millennia—but this morning, in this unguarded moment, he looked it. Jack hadn't been by since the Internet mess. Could Glaeken have aged so much since then?

"You okay?"

He straightened and smiled, and some—but not all—of

the extra years dropped away. "Fine, fine. Just tired. Magda had a bad night."

His aged wife's memory had been slipping away for years and was little more than vapor now. Glaeken radiated devotion to her, and Jack knew he'd hoped they'd grow old together. The *old* part had worked out, but not the *together*. Glaeken was alone. Someone named Magda might be in a bedroom down the hall, but the mind of the woman he'd fallen in love with had left the building.

"Didn't the nurse—?"

"Yes, she did what she could, but sometimes I'm the only one who can calm her."

Jack shook his head. Like the old guy needed more stress in his life.

"Have you seen the Lady? I stopped in to check on how she's doing but her place is empty."

She occupied the apartment just below. Couldn't say she *lived* here, because the Lady wasn't alive in the conventional sense.

"You just missed her." Glaeken gestured to the window. "She went for her morning walk in the park."

"Really? When did she start that?"

"Almost a week now."

Jack stepped to the glass and stared down at Central Park, far below. A little to the left, ringed by winter-bare trees, the grass of the Sheep Meadow showed brown through patches of leftover snow.

"I take it she's recovering then?"

"Still weak but feeling a little stronger every day."

"Well, I guess after being wheelchair-bound and damn near dead a couple of weeks ago, that's not bad."

"Would that I had a fraction of her resilience."

Jack scanned the park but couldn't pick her out. Even though the park was relatively empty due to the cold, the strollers looked too small from up here. All his uncles looked like ants, as the joke went.

"Can you spot her?"

Glaeken rose and stood beside him, leaning into the sunlight as he squinted below. "My eyes aren't what they used to be."

"What's she wearing?"

"One of those house dresses she favors lately. It's yellow today."

"That's all? It's freezing—" He caught himself. "Never mind."

Glaeken shot him a quick glance but said nothing.

Right. He knew. The Lady didn't feel cold. Or heat. Or pain. And her clothes weren't really clothes, simply part of whatever look she was presenting to the world. She'd worn the form of Mrs. Clevenger before her near-death experience and seemed to be stuck in that form ever since.

Glaeken said, "You know how she likes to be out among her 'children.' "

Jack spotted a bright yellow someone strolling in the near half of the meadow.

"Got her." He turned away from the window. "I'll catch up to her."

"She'll be back soon."

Jack shook his head. "Got things to do. Today's the day I start looking for the R-Man."

"You can say his name now."

"I know. But it's geekier to have code names for him."

Glaeken looked at him. "Geekier?"

"Don't worry about it. Just me running at the mouth."

"I hope it doesn't indicate that you are in any way taking him lightly."

"Believe me, I'm not. I've seen what he can do."

Just my way of coping, he thought as he headed for the elevator.

Glaeken's elevator had two buttons—one for the top floor and one for the lobby. One of the perks of owning the building.

At street level, Jack waved to the doorman and stepped out onto the sidewalk. Central Park loomed just across the street. He strode to the corner of Sixty-fourth and waited for the light.

He'd developed enormous respect, maybe even a sort of love for the city's traffic signals after they'd gone down during the Internet crash. Days of pure hell followed. They were back in working order now, though not all in sync yet. The Internet, however, still had a ways to go before it could call itself cured. The virus that had brought it down—and the city's traffic and transit systems along with it—was still replicating itself in unvaccinated regions of the Web. Cell phones were back up and running, much to everyone's relief, though local outages were still a problem.

He adjusted the curved bill of his Mets cap lower over his face. Working lights meant working traffic cams. Designed to catch red-light runners, they recorded tons of pedestrians every minute. Couldn't go anywhere these days without some goddamn camera sucking off a bit of your soul.

He crossed with the green and trotted a block uptown to one of the park entrances. He stopped at the edge of the fifteen-acre field known as the Sheep Meadow. In the old days it had lived up to its name, with a real shepherd and his flock housed in what was now a visitor center. Nowadays, in warmer weather, hordes of sun worshippers littered the grass. None of those on this blustery

March day, making the Lady's yellow dress easy to pick out.

He spotted her ambling along the tree line at the northern end. Gray-haired Mrs. Clevenger had been a fixture in his hometown when he was a kid, but she'd always worn black. To see her in any other color, especially yellow, was jarring.

As he started toward her, he noticed the stares she was attracting. People had to think she was a little off in the head, strolling around in this temperature wearing only a thin, sleeveless housedress.

He was about fifty yards away, and readying to call out, when four men stepped out of the trees, raised semiautomatic pistols, and began firing at her.

Jack froze for a shocked instant, thinking he had to be hallucinating, but no mistaking the loud cracks and muzzle flashes. He yanked the Glock 19 from the holster at the small of his back and broke into a run.

The Lady had stopped and was staring at the men firing nearly point-blank at her head and torso as they moved in on her. She didn't stagger, didn't even flinch. They couldn't be missing.

As he neared and got a better look, she seemed to be unharmed. No surprise. Her dress was undamaged as well. The bullets seemed to disappear before they reached her.

One of her assailants looked Jack's way. As their eyes locked the man shouted something in a foreign language and angled his pistol toward him. Jack swiveled his torso to reduce his exposure and veered left, popping three quick rounds at the gunman's center of mass. Two hit, staggering him, felling him. He landed on his back in a patch of old snow. The third bullet missed but winged his buddy behind him. Another of the attackers shouted something and fired just as Jack changed direction. He felt an impact and a stinging pain in his left upper arm. He dropped to a knee and began pulling the trigger, firing two-to-three rounds per second in a one-handed grip. This was going to run his mag in no time, but he had only one man down and couldn't allow any of the three still standing to get a bead on him.

Relief flooded him as they grabbed their wounded pal and ran back into the trees. He stopped firing and didn't follow. He'd counted thirteen rounds fired. That left two in his magazine and he wasn't carrying a spare—a firefight had not been on the morning's agenda. He did have his Kel-Tec backup in an ankle holster, but that was useful only at close range.

The Lady was staring at him. "They tried to kill me."

"Ya think?"

Jack looked at the downed attacker. His face matched the shade of the dirty snow cushioning his head. Ragged breaths bubbled the blood in his mouth. His pistol lay by his side. A Tokarev. Jack had seen a lot of Tokarevs lately—too many—and its presence pretty much nailed who'd sent him and his buddies.

The Order.

Drexler had sent out a hit team on the Lady. What was he thinking? Nothing of this Earth could harm her, and lead slugs were of this Earth. Drexler knew that. So why would he try? Unless he thought he'd come into some special super bullets.

As Jack holstered his Glock, he grabbed the Tokarev and felt a jab of pain in his left upper arm. Yeah, he'd been hit. Worry about that later. People were pointing their way, some already on cell phones. Too much to hope for one of the random phone outages here and now, he supposed. And even if they couldn't get their calls through, they could use the phones as cameras. None of the callers was too close but that could change. Cops would be here soon.

He shoved the Tokarev into his jacket and grabbed the Lady's arm.

"We've got to get you out of here."

In the good old days—as in, before last summer—she could simply change into someone else or disappear and reappear somewhere else. But nowadays she was stuck in old-woman mode and had to travel like a human.

She wasn't very spry but Jack moved her along as fast as she could go. He pulled his cap even lower and kept his head down, not exactly sure of where he was taking her— out of the park, definitely, but after that? Couldn't take her straight back to her apartment. Her damn yellow dress made her stick out like a canary at a crow convention. Needed to get her off the street, then figure out what to do.

As they reached the sidewalk he saw a taxi pull to a stop before a late-middle-aged couple—he wore an *Intrepid* cap and she carried a Hard Rock shopping bag. Tourists. They stood a few feet ahead. He knew his next step . . .

The Lady sat beside him in the rear of the cab and stared at the blood on his hand.

"You're hurt."

"Yeah. Looks that way."

Jack wiped his fingers on his jeans and moved his left arm. Pain shot up and down when he flexed the elbow. He checked the sleeve and found the exit hole in the leather. He wondered how bad it was but wasn't about to remove the jacket here in the cab to find out.

The Lady gently touched his sleeve over the wound, her expression sad.

"Not so long ago I could have healed you."

"I know." What he hadn't known was that she no longer could. "You've lost that too?"

She nodded. "I have lost so much. But at least I am still here."

"Yeah, that's the important part. But there *is* something you could do that would help things."

"Tell me."

"Can you change into someone else?"

She shook her head. "I am not able. I am still fixed as Mrs. Clevenger."

"Well, how about switching that dress to something less noticeable?"

"That I can do." Suddenly she was wearing a drab cloth coat. "Better?"

"Much."

He marveled at how he'd come to take these things as a matter of course. The workaday world remained blissfully unaware of the secret lives and secret histories playing out around them. As he once had been. As no doubt their cabbie was.

He checked their driver. The Lady was seated directly behind him and he gave no sign that he'd witnessed the transformation. If and when he did notice the coat, he'd assume she'd carried it in with her.

Jack spotted Seventy-second Street approaching. The light was green. He rapped on the plastic partition.

"Take a right up here—into the park."

The cab turned into the traverse and headed across Central Park. Where to now? Couldn't head straight back to Glaeken's. He'd left a dead guy behind in the park. NYPD would be all over the area, collecting witness accounts, checking the traffic cams. They might end up talking to . . . he checked the operator license taped on the other side of the partition: *Abhra Rahman* . . . they might track down Abhra and want to know where he'd dropped them. Jack needed a diversionary stop.

He pictured the city. They were heading east. What was landmarky in this area of the East Side? Of course—Bloomie's down on Fifty-ninth and Lexington. Get out there, then downstairs to the subway station, hop a downtown N, R, or Q two stops to West Fifty-seventh, then cab back to Glaeken's.

Yeah. That would work.

He rapped gently on the partition. "Drop us at Bloomingdale's, please."

He'd make sure to give Mr. Rahman a good tip.

2. "Who the hell are you?" Jack said as he spotted the guy sitting in the Lady's front room.

He already had the Glock half out of its holster when the Lady touched his arm.

"A friend of Glaeken's."

The guy rose and extended his hand. "You must be Jack. Glaeken sent me down. I was visiting him. He's told me a lot about you. I'm Bill."

"Told me a little about you," Jack said as they shook. "Very little."

Jack had seen him from a distance before. This was the first time close up. Long hair pulled back into a ponytail and a full beard, both generously salted with gray, a scarred forehead and bent nose, eyes almost as blue as Glaeken's. The face put him in his sixties, but his lean, muscular six-foot frame seemed younger. Jack felt thick calluses on his shake hand.

Bill shrugged. "Not a whole lot to tell."

"You were in North Carolina with him. Heard things went sour down there."

Till that moment, Bill's eyes had been closed off, showing nothing. The shutters opened for an instant, releasing an almost palpable flash of pain and anguish. This guy had been through hell—a number of hells. Then they snapped shut again.

"You could say that." He cleared his throat. "Glaeken said you might need help with an injury."

Jack checked his jacket sleeve. Blood had soaked his arm and begun to drip during their trip back from the park. He'd kept his arm inside the jacket and phoned ahead to see if Glaeken had any bandages. He knew the Lady sure as hell didn't. Glaeken kept that nurse around for Magda, but Jack didn't want her involved. She might recognize it as a bullet wound and get all good-citizeny and report it.

"You a doctor or something?"

He smiled. "I've been a lot of things, but not a doctor. I used to take care of a bunch of boys who tended to hurt themselves or each other on a regular basis." Another, briefer flash of pain.

"Sleep-away camp?"

"Nope. Orphanage. Here . . . let's take a look at that arm."

Jack laid the Tokarev on the table and shrugged out of his jacket. The lining of the left sleeve was soaked. Same with the long-sleeved tee he was wearing beneath it. The tee he could throw away, but the bomber jacket was an old friend. Maybe he'd take it downtown to Tram's place and see if he knew a way to clean it up. Couldn't bring a bloody jacket just anywhere.

Bill was staring at the gun. "Do you carry that everywhere?"

"Not mine. But one just like it did this."

Bill stared a moment longer, then pulled a pair of scissors from a paper bag on the Lady's table. He pointed them toward the torn sleeve of Jack's T-shirt.

"That's got to go."

"Do it."

He cut over Jack's shoulder and around and under his armpit, then rolled the bloody fabric down and off. He shook his head as he inspected the wound.

"That's going to need stitches, which I can't help you with."

Jack took a look and winced at the sight of the open, two-inch-long gash running across the skin at the lower end of his deltoid. The bleeding was down to an ooze.

"I know someone who can."

He hoped Doc Hargus was around and available.

"I can butterfly it until you get to him."

"Sounds like a plan."

The Lady helped Jack wash the blood off his arm in her shower. The barest woman's bathroom he'd ever seen. Not one cream or lotion, not even a toothbrush or toothpaste.

"Where do you keep the towels?" he said after the blood had swirled down the drain.

"I'm afraid I don't have any. I don't bathe."

Of course she didn't. She didn't need to. He made do with the rest of his T-shirt.

As Bill was cutting strips of adhesive tape, Glaeken walked in with Weezy. After calling Glaeken, Jack had let Weezy know about the attack on the Lady. He wanted her input.

Glaeken dropped into a chair next to Jack and glanced at the wound. He didn't seem impressed, or even sympathetic. After all the wounds he'd no doubt collected over his thousands of years, this probably qualified as a scratch in his book.

Weezy was another story. Concern tightened her features as she went down on one knee next to him and closely inspected his arm.

She'd been a skinny, goth type during their childhood together, but on the chunky side and living in sweatsuits when she rocketed back into his life last year. These days she'd slimmed some and dressed in fitted jeans and sweaters. Her dark hair was longer and tied back in a simple ponytail. No trace of the heavy eyeliner she'd worn as a teen.

"Does it hurt?" she said, and chewed her upper lip.

"Not as much as you'd expect."

Bill dabbed it with something that foamed the blood and made it feel like a nest of hornets was attacking it.

Jack squeezed the chair's armrest with his free hand and said, "Okay. Make a liar out of me. *Now* it hurts."

"Sorry," Bill said. He dabbed again. "Needs to be done."

Weezy bounced up and stepped around to the other side of the table where the Lady stood watching in silence.

"Are you all right?"

The Lady nodded. "Not the slightest harm done."

Weezy turned to Glaeken and Jack. "I don't get it. What happened?"

Jack didn't get it either. He hadn't wanted to get into the details over the phone, so he gave them a quick runthrough now.

When he was done Weezy turned to the Lady and said, "It sounds as if they knew just where you'd be."

"No question," Jack said. "They jumped out directly

in her path and began firing." He looked up at the Lady. "Do you take the same route every day?"

She nodded. "Since I began walking again."

Weezy turned to Jack. "You're sure they were from the Order?"

"Sure as I can be without seeing a sigil brand." He pointed to the Tokarev. "They used that and spoke a foreign language. Drexler seems to favor Eastern Europeans for the rough stuff and Eastern Bloc types favor Tokarevs and Makarovs."

Glaeken frowned. "But the Order wouldn't attempt such a thing without clearance from the One. And Rasalom knows very well that bullets can't hurt the Lady."

Jack grabbed the pistol and ejected the magazine, then popped out the 9mm rounds one by one.

"I thought he might be using some supersecret Lady-killing ammo, but these are standard jacketed hollow-points."

"If they are of this Earth," the Lady said, "they cannot harm me."

"Maybe he was making sure that was still true," Weezy said. "You've been damaged, you've been weakened, you can't change your looks, you can't hop around the globe like you used to. If you lost those abilities, he had to wonder if maybe you'd lost the invulnerability as well. Even you weren't sure right after you survived the Internet outage."

Jack remembered that. To test herself, she'd thrust a knife blade into her hand. To everyone's relief, the wound had closed instantly.

Glaeken was nodding. "Yes, that makes sense."

"You know what this means, don't you?" Weezy said, looking around at them. "Rasalom has been watching us, clocking and tracking our movements."

Something tightened in Jack's chest. He didn't like the idea of anyone tracking him, especially Rasalom.

"Maybe not yours or mine," he said. "But obviously the Lady's—especially the Lady—and probably Glaeken's too."

Weezy turned back to the Lady. "Is there a way we can hide you?"

"I cannot hide. The purpose of my existence is to proclaim this world's sentience."

"Hide you from Rasalom, not the Ally."

"I don't think there's a way to do that," Glaeken said.

The Lady thought a moment. "There might be. I am not always aware of what the One and the Otherness are doing. Perhaps there is a way to keep them unaware of what I am doing. I shall consult the noosphere."

"Consult?" Weezy said. "But you're a part of it."

"Not anymore. I am still its creation, but no longer its appendage, no longer directly fed by it. I must reconnect regularly now."

She closed her eyes and stood still and silent. Utterly. She didn't need to breathe and did so only to speak.

Bill stared at her, then at the three of them. "At the request of my new friend here," he said, gesturing to Glaeken, "who's some fifteen thousand years old, I'm patching up a man with no identity who got wounded protecting a woman who's not really a woman, or at least not a human woman, and is even older than my friend, and for whom the Internet was crashed in an attempt to kill her. What happened to the world I used to know—or thought I knew? I've gone through bizarre, life-changing experiences, but they take a backseat to what I've seen and heard the past couple of weeks."

Jack knew how he felt. Weezy had always known there was a Secret History. Jack had learned gradually, piecemeal, over a period of years, and was still adjusting. He gathered Bill had been thrown headfirst into the Secret History. And the cosmic shadow war that fueled it.

Two nameless, unimaginable forces in a tug-of-war for control of the sentient realities across the multiverse. Earth occupied one of those universes, and was one of the prizes. Not the gold medal, just another piece of the sentient mosaic the forces were assembling. Without sentience, a world had no value, and had no place in the mosaic.

That was why the Lady was so important. As the avatar of humanity's collective consciousness, a product of the noosphere, she was the beacon that announced this world's sentience to the multiverse. Extinguish that beacon and this world, this corner of reality would appear worthless.

Earth was currently the possession of a force known to those aware of the Secret History as the Ally—a misnomer. It didn't have humanity's back, cared nothing for it, and valued it only for its sentience. Indifferent was the best description, but considering the alternative, indifference seemed downright benign. The alternative was the other half of the cosmic yin and yang, the Otherness— unquestionably inimical, and determined for countless millennia to add Earth to its own mosaic. But the Otherness's mosaic was toxic to humanity, and life here would be hell under its influence.

An immortal named Rasalom—or the One—led the Otherness's forces here. Glaeken had once led the Ally's, had once been immortal, but had been released and allowed to age. He was now as mortal as Jack. Rasalom's lifelong mission was to clear the path for the Otherness. All that stood between him and that goal now was the Lady. Extinguish her and this world would no longer appear sentient. The Ally would discard it and the Otherness could grab it for its own.

"Welcome to the Secret History of the World," Jack said.

"Thanks. But in this case, knowledge isn't power." He positioned himself closer to Jack's arm. "Hold still. Time for the butterflies."

Jack put a whine in his voice. "Please don't hurt me."

Bill gave him a concerned look, then smiled. "For a moment there you almost had me."

"You'd be amazed how many times that has come in handy."

"I can't imagine how, and I'm not going to try."

He began applying the homemade butterflies, using them to bridge the wound edges and hold them together.

Glaeken said, "So now that the One has established that the Lady still cannot be harmed by anything of this Earth, including him, what does he do with that information?"

"He looks for another way to make an end run," Weezy said. "The *Fhinntmanchca* failed, so did the Internet meltdown. He'll need to find something else."

Glaeken frowned. "Is there anything left to find?"

Jack shrugged. "I'm sure there is. Maybe Dawn's baby."

"Dawn's baby," Weezy said, shaking her head. "She's out looking for him as we speak."

"Any way you can help her find him?"

"I can try, but I'm still working on the *Compendium*."

The ancient *Compendium of Srem* . . . Weezy had been collating its uncollated data since last year and still wasn't finished. Its pages could be photographed, but the language would no longer be English. And so, with her faultless memory, she was probably one of the few people in the world who could wrestle it to coherence.

Jack felt like standing and pacing, but had to sit still for the butterflies. "Maybe it's not the baby. Maybe that's a red herring to distract us while he's looking for something else. Whatever, we need to bring the battle to Rasalom before he finds something. But I've got to *find* him first."

Glaeken's intense blue eyes bored into him. "And should you find him, then what?"

"He goes down."

"Don't be so sure. At the risk of being a bore, I must remind you once again that he will not 'go down,' as you put it, easily. As the One, he has been gifted with extraordinary recuperative powers. As once was I."

Glaeken had become kind of a broken record on that.

"How extraordinary?" Bill said.

"Wounds heal much more quickly than you'd imagine." He pointed to Jack's arm. "A scratch like that would heal almost immediately."

"Scratch?" Bill said. "This is no scratch."

Glaeken shrugged but said nothing.

Jack checked out the scars on the backs of the old guy's gnarled hands. "But the wounds still left scars?"

He nodded. "Oh, yes."

"What about penetrating wounds?"

"They take a little longer; they take a toll, but they heal."

"Even the heart?"

"Even the heart. My body spat out a dozen or so bullets shortly before the Ally cut me loose to join you mortals."

"Spat them out?"

Glaeken nodded. "More of a slow extrusion, I would say, but I hope you're getting the picture."

He was, and not liking it.

"How about amputations?"

"The bleeding will stop quickly, the stump will scar over, but what's gone is gone."

"No regeneration?"

"He remains human, and humans do not regenerate limbs."

Bill was shaking his head. "How did I get myself into this?"

"You know very well how," Glaeken said. "Your virtue nearly killed the One."

Jack looked at the gentle, ponytailed, hippie-type guy patching up his arm. Almost killed Rasalom?

"Really? How—?"

"That's for another time," Glaeken said. "How do you plan to put him 'down,' as you say?"

Jack considered this a moment, then said, "Sounds like beheading will work."

"It will, but you'll never get that close."

Jack knew that. "I guess that leaves kablooie."

Glaeken frowned. "Kablooie?"

"Blow him to pieces."

Glaeken's expression became grim. "Yes, that will work. But it had better work the first time. You won't get a second chance."

"There won't be a first time if I don't find him."

"How do you plan to do that?"

"Start at the last known sighting."

"The Osala apartment?" Weezy said.

Jack nodded. "I'll see what the doorman can tell me and go from there."

"Be careful."

"You sound like Gia."

"Neither of us wants to see you hurt. Or worse."

That makes three of us, Jack thought.

Bill had finished his butterflying and bandaging.

"That oughta hold you until you find a real doctor."

Jack rose and extended his hand. "Thanks. Nice meeting you. We'll have to talk about your set-to with Rasalom sometime."

Bill gathered up his tape and bandages. "It won't help you."

"Don't be so sure."

"I'm pretty sure. He wasn't born yet."

Before Jack could ask for an explanation, Glaeken rose.

"I must get back upstairs."

They would have said good-bye to the Lady but she was still in her trance, communing with the noosphere, so they all followed Glaeken out into the hallway. Bill started for the stairway, but Glaeken didn't follow.

"Coming?" he said, stopping and turning.

Glaeken shook his head as he pressed the elevator button. "I don't feel up to the stairs today."

Weezy put a hand on his arm. "Are you okay?"

"I'm fine. Just a little tired."

Jack looked at Weezy and read the concern in her eyes—not much different from his own, he imagined. Was Glaeken failing? He seemed as solid and steady as ever, but this was a new twist. He'd been shuttling back and forth to the Lady's apartment via the stairs since he'd moved her in. Why couldn't he manage them now? His heart? His knees?

He was an old man, had been aging since his mortality was restored on the eve of World War II. His chronological age was mind-boggling. But what was his body age? That was what mattered. One day his body would give out, just like everybody else's.

And then Jack would step into his shoes—or so he'd been told.

Hang in there, Glaeken, Jack thought. You keep on being the Defender, and I'll stay perfectly happy being the Heir.

Bill too looked concerned. "Okay. See you upstairs."

The elevator arrived and Glaeken pressed the Lobby button once the three of them were aboard.

"Kind of a roundabout way to go," Jack said for lack of anything better.

Glaeken sighed. "I don't have my key."

The building had two elevators: Glaeken's private express to his penthouse, and the local that required a key to reach his floor.

He turned to Weezy. "How is Dawn searching for her baby?"

"She tracked down one of the doctors at her delivery—a pediatrician—and she's haunting him in the hope the baby will show up at his office. I'm worried about her. She's become obsessed with finding that baby. It's all she talks about anymore."

Motherly concern infused the descending cab. Still in her teens, Dawn had awakened Weezy's maternal instincts. Not surprising. The girl was young enough to be her daughter—Weezy would have had to deliver her as a teen herself, but it was biologically possible. She'd never said so, but Jack suspected Weezy's subconscious saw Dawn as the child she'd never had and most likely never would.

Glaeken turned to Jack. "Perhaps, when you're not in active pursuit of the One, you might help her."

Jack had been thinking about that.

Rasalom, posing as a Mr. Osala, had hidden Dawn away during her pregnancy under the guise of protecting her from the baby's father. He arranged for prenatal care and for a skilled delivery team . . . which promptly whisked the newborn away to parts unknown.

Obviously the child—which according to Dawn had some pretty scary deformities—meant something to Rasalom. And if it meant something to Rasalom, maybe it could be used as a lure.

"Yeah. Not a bad idea."

The elevator arrived at the lobby. Weezy said good-bye and walked toward the entrance, but Glaeken grabbed Jack's arm and held him back.

"What do you plan for the baby if you find it?" he whispered.

Jack shrugged. "Not sure."

"I know what you *should* do."

Glaeken put his fists together and gave them a sharp twist. The meaning was clear and it shocked Jack. So unlike Glaeken . . .

"What?"

"Too much is at stake—*humanity* is at stake. Nothing good can come of that creature. Only evil."

With that he turned away and pressed the button on his private elevator. Jack stared a moment, then slipped back into his bloody jacket.

"What did he say?" Weezy said as he joined her on the sidewalk.

"He wants the baby found too."

"I'm glad he's on board with that. Maybe then Dawn can find some peace."

Don't count on that, Jack thought.

3. "Doctor Heinze?" Dawn Pickering said as he approached her stalking spot.

That was what she called this stretch of hallway in the McCready building where she'd set up watch on Kenneth Heinze, MD. She'd totally memorized his office hours and had made a point of being in the building whenever he was. Sooner or later Mr. Osala or Gilda or Georges would appear with the baby, bringing him in for a checkup.

Or so she hoped. He'd been present at the delivery. Didn't it stand to reason that whoever had the baby would follow up with Dr. Heinze? At the time she'd been impressed at how Mr. Osala had totally thought of everything, even going so far as to have a pediatrician on hand to check out her newborn.

She'd had no idea what they had in mind. She'd been whisked in and out of a surgicenter she could not identify. She'd tried contacting Dr. Landsman, the obstetrician, but he said he'd never heard of her and had left instructions with his office building's security that she was not to be allowed in. During her pregnancy he'd examined her in his office during off-hours and done his own ultrasounds. She'd thought she was getting VIP treatment but now she realized no one on his staff would remember her. And Mr. Osala and his entire household had vanished.

Her only link was Dr. Heinze. She remembered thinking of "fifty-seven varieties" when she'd first heard his name. But when she looked she found only one pediatrician named Heinze in the five boroughs. She'd thought she was on the wrong track when she learned he was a pediatric *surgeon*. Why had they thought they needed a surgeon? But one look at this tall, fair-haired man with the round, apple-cheeked face totally dispelled all doubts. He was the one.

But still . . . why had they wanted a surgeon who specialized in children on hand?

Maybe they'd expected problems. After the quick glimpse she got of her child she wasn't surprised. The black body hair, almost like fur, the clawlike hands—nobody had prepared her for that. But the most horrifying of all was the tentacle springing from each of his armpits, writhing in the air like little snakes.

And then they'd said he'd stopped breathing and they whisked him away. The next day they told her he hadn't survived. She'd been so not ready for that. And since she'd already signed him away for adoption, they never let her see him.

But she didn't believe he was dead. Neither did Jack. And so she was totally determined to find him. She'd let her baby down before—tried to abort him, signed him away to be raised by strangers—but things had changed. She was so not going to let him down again.

Dr. Heinze walked past. He either hadn't heard her or was ignoring her. She had a chance to back off. And maybe she should. Confronting him was dumb. She needed to hang back and keep lurking. She'd made a point of dressing in business casual and staying on the move so she looked like she belonged here. The research wing of the McCready Foundation's headquarters had restricted access, but the outpatient areas were open to the public.

Patience, she told herself. Sooner or later the baby would show.

But her patience had thinned, and now it tore. Totally. "Doctor Heinze?" she repeated.

He stopped and gave her a pleasant smile. "Yes?"

"Remember me?"

He stared at her with no hint of recognition. "Should I? Were you once a patient?"

"My name's Dawn Pickering and you stole my baby."

His eyes widened and the apple in his cheeks faded. *Now* he recognized her.

"I-I did no such thing."

"Then you helped. Where's my baby, Doctor Heinze? Where's my baby?"

He pushed open his office door. "I have no idea what you're talking about. Please leave."

She followed him inside.

"Where's my baby, Doctor Heinze?" She felt herself losing it. No turning back now. "Where's-my-baby-where's-my-baby?" Startled looks from parents and little patients in the waiting area as her voice rose in pitch and volume. *"Where's-my-baby-where's-my-baby?"* The receptionist grabbing the phone and calling someone, had to be security, but Dawn was screaming now and it felt so good to scream. "WHERE'S-MY-BABY-WHERE'S-MY-BABY- WHERE'S-MY-BABEEEEE?"

4.   "Well, well," Mack said with a smile as he admitted Jack to the foyer of Rasalom's former residence. "If it isn't the hit man."

Like Glaeken, "Mr. Osala" had occupied the top floor—in this case, *floors*, since the penthouse was a duplex. Jack had come looking for him, not knowing he was Rasalom, only to learn that he had moved out just a day or two before and taken everything with him.

"Hey, Mack. Osala or any of his staff been around?"

Mack shook his graying head. He had deep brown skin,

a Sammy Davis Jr. build, and a Redd Foxx beard. *McKinley*—his first name—was engraved into the brass name tag that graced his gray uniform.

"No sign, not a word from them."

No surprise.

"Too bad," Mack added.

"Yeah? Why?"

"Because I looooove his ride. A black 1980 450SEL 6.9."

"An old Mercedes? I had him figured for a Maybach, or maybe a Bugatti."

Mack shook his head. "Uh-uh. That ain't just an 'old Mercedes.' Don't you dare call it that. It's one of the greatest saloons ever built."

Jack knew Mack was baiting him with the term. He knew what he was talking about but bit anyway.

"Saloon? I thought we were talking about a car."

Mack's eyebrows rose. "We are, my man. That's the British term for sedan. But that SEL is a *saloon*."

"More like a tank."

"Got that right."

Jack pushed the conversation back on target. "Okay, so when Osala moved out, did you happen to notice who did the actual moving?"

Mack gave him an annoyed look. "You take me for some kinda fool who's gonna let a bunch of yahoos come in here and clean out a tenant's apartment without knowing who they are and making sure it's cleared with the tenant ahead of time? Course I did."

Jack knew from their previous run-in that Mack took his job very seriously.

"Was there a name on the truck?"

"There was."

Compared to Mack, a rock was garrulous.

"What was it?"

"Don't remember."

"Crap."

"But I do have a work order."

Bless you, Jack thought as he followed the bantam of a man to his cubbyhole of an office. Mack pulled open a drawer, fished around, and came up with a yellow sheet of paper.

"Here it is."

Jack reached for it but Mack pulled it away. Jack snagged it on his second try. The name on the header came as a shock, but only for an instant, replaced by an I-should-have-known feeling and accompanied by a Bernard Herrmann cue.

Mack snatched it back. "Don't you go grabbing my papers."

Wm. Blagden & Sons, Inc.

A year and a half ago, in South Florida, a Blagden & Sons dump truck had been stolen—supposedly—and used to run down his father, leaving him in a coma. A couple of months later, Jack had followed Luther Brady to the Blagden & Sons' concrete plant in Jersey . . . a bad memory there.

And now the name pops up again. He had known back then the Blagden company was connected to the Order, and that the Order was connected to the Otherness and Rasalom. So not a huge surprise that when Rasalom needed his stuff moved, Blagden & Sons showed up. After all, they had trucks galore. But mostly dump trucks and cement mixers.

"What kind of truck was it?"

"Typical box truck."

"Like a moving van?"

Mack glanced ceilingward. "A moving van *is* a box truck."

"Okay, okay. Jersey plates?"

"How'd you know?"

"Lucky guess. You don't happen to remember the plate number."

"Don't have to. Wrote it down. You don't think I'm going to let them drive off without me knowing that, do you?"

He jotted the number on a scrap of paper and handed it to Jack.

"I suppose it would be too much to ask if they happened to have a delivery address on that work order."

Mack nodded. "It would."

"Then I guess I'll have to ask them."

"You really think they'll tell you?"

"I can be very persuasive." He clapped Mack on his upper arm. "Thanks for your help."

As he turned to go, Mack said, "Don't you want the address?"

"Don't need it. Been there a couple of times already."

On his second trip he'd discovered the plant's awful secret.

5.   Ernst Drexler hung the jacket of his white suit on a hanger in his office closet, then adjusted his vest before seating himself behind his desk. He had to look cool, calm, and most of all, in control. He could not reveal the rage and—yes, he admitted it—fear and uncertainty roiling through his gut.

The man who would knock on the door any minute now could not be allowed to see any of that. Ernst was an actuator, one of the long arms of the Order's Council of Seven. The man arriving was a tool for that arm . . .

A tool who had acted on his own.

Or had he? That was the unsettling part.

He rubbed his hands together. Chilly in here. Maybe he should have kept his jacket on. The thick granite walls of the Order's Lower Manhattan Lodge kept it cool in the summer but made it hard to heat in the winter. And he wasn't getting any younger. He'd passed sixty years ago. One felt the cold more in one's seventh decade.

Or was it just his mood?

A knock on the door.

"Come."

Kris Szeto entered in his beloved black leather jacket. He had black hair, swarthy skin, and always appeared to need a shave, even when he didn't. He had been living in America for years but maintained a Eurotrash look. His face still exhibited faint reminders of the severe beating he'd sustained two weeks ago. The bruises had cleared but a couple of fresh scars remained.

"You wished to see me?" he said in Eastern Bloc–flavored English as he came to a stop before the desk.

Control . . . keep the voice steady.

"Yes. It has come to my attention that Claudiu Ozera is dead."

The incident was all over the news. Four men had opened fire on an elderly woman in Central Park this morning. A fifth gunman came to her aid, killing one of her attackers before whisking her away. The dead man had not been identified to the public, but a brother of the Order who was also a member of the NYPD had reported it to the Council. The news came as a shock. Ozera had been assigned to Szeto. Szeto was assigned to Ernst. The Council was in an uproar over it: Why was a member of the Order involved in a public shootout? Why hadn't the actuator informed them?

For a very good reason: Ernst had known nothing about it. But he was about to find out.

"Yes. Most unfortunate. An unforeseen circumstance." Szeto's tone was flat, matter-of-fact, as if explaining a spilled quart of milk. "My team engaged target as instructed—"

As instructed? Ernst let it pass for now.

"—and fire many times, make many hits, but she does not go down. Then other man appears, firing. He kills Claudiu and wounds Filip. I am watching from side. Since Lady is not going down, I order retreat."

Ice shot through Ernst's veins. No . . . it couldn't be.

"'Lady' . . . do you mean *the* Lady?"

"Yes, of course."

"But she cannot be hurt by bullets."

"I know this. But if the One wishes to have her shot, then I must shoot her, yes?"

Ice was fire compared to the interstellar cold exploding within him now. He couldn't help himself—

"*The One?* How would you know what the One wishes?"

Szeto's bland expression finally changed. "He came to me and told me."

"You idiot! That was not the One. You've been duped!"

Szeto's face darkened. "I know the One. Is my mother not his housekeeper?"

Yes. Yes, she was. The connection had slipped Ernst's mind. Women weren't allowed in the Order, of course, but the Order supplied the One with staff, and traditionally any woman supplied would be related to a brother.

"But the One knows better than all of us that the Lady can't be shot."

Szeto shrugged. "He tells me shoot Lady, I shoot. I do not question the One."

No one questioned the One.

Szeto's eyes narrowed. "Why is it you do not know of this?"

Ernst had been dreading the question, but was prepared for it.

"I have been out of town on Council business. Most likely he did not want to wait until I returned. The One is not known for his patience. And since he knows you are my right-hand man, he went directly to you."

Szeto nodded slowly as he stared at Ernst. "Yes. That must be it."

Ernst hoped Szeto swallowed the lie. He hadn't been anywhere but here and home in his apartment. The One could have contacted him any time.

Yet he hadn't. He had bypassed Ernst the actuator and gone straight to Szeto the enforcer.

The One had been furious when the Internet meltdown Ernst had engineered failed to remove the Lady. Had he given up on Ernst because of that?

He took a breath and looked at Szeto. "I have not spoken to the One recently. Did he say why he thought bullets might harm the Lady?"

"No. He tells me where she will be and when, and says to gun her down. So that is what I do."

"Of course. And no effect, I assume."

"None."

"And the man who came to her defense? Was he a bodyguard?"

"We observed before we acted. She was walking alone, no sign of anyone following. And besides, Lady does not need bodyguard."

No, of course she doesn't. I'm not thinking straight. How could he with his world turning upside down?

"Did you recognize him?"

Szeto shook his head. "He was wearing hat and had pistol held before face. And I was helping Filip escape. But he took Claudiu's gun. We have seen this happen before."

Yes . . . last summer, when Max and Josef were gunned down at the hospital, and just a couple of weeks ago when Fournier was killed.

"Do you think it's the same man who was protecting Louise Myers and Edward Connell? That would mean he has collected three of your guns in the course of killing half a dozen of your men."

Ernst put the slightest emphasis on each *your*.

Szeto spoke through clenched teeth. "If it is same man, I want him. The Myers woman can lead me to him . . ."

"But the One says she is to be left alone. Remember that?"

"I remember. But no matter. I will find him, I will catch up to him one day, and then he will curse his mother for giving him birth."

"Yes, well, good luck on that. Now, if you don't mind . . ." He shuffled assorted random papers on his desk. "I have some of the Council's business to attend to."

Szeto left without another word. As soon as the door closed behind him, Ernst shot from his seat and began pacing his office. He could not sit still, not after what he'd just heard.

Bypassed! The One had bypassed not only him but the High Council as well, and gone straight to one of the Order's enforcers.

Memory of Ernst's last encounter with the One, here, on this very spot, flashed through his brain. He could still feel the pressure of the One's hand on his throat as he'd lifted him off the floor, the heat of his breath as he'd spoken so close to his face.

You still might prove useful, otherwise . . .

Otherwise *what* he hadn't said. He hadn't had to. Ernst hadn't been able to breathe.

"At last I can take direct action. I may call on you and your Order for minor logistical support, but now that I am free to act, I will take matters into my own hands. I will finish this myself."

And then he'd hurled Ernst across the office.

Ernst rubbed his throat. The bruises had faded away only recently, but the fear hadn't.

I may call on you and your Order for minor logistical support . . .

But he hadn't called on Ernst. He'd called on Szeto.

Have I been marginalized?

The possibility brought a surge of bile. Like his father before him, he had devoted his entire life to the Order, to helping the Otherness become ascendant in this world. The Otherness would bring about the Change, and elevate its loyal helpers to allow them not only to survive unscathed in the remade world but to oversee it as well. To be Movers among the Moved.

His father hadn't lived to see the Change, but Ernst fully expected to. He could sense its imminence. And the One would choose those who would be part of the Change rather than merely subject to it. Ernst had fully expected to be among the chosen . . .

Until now.

He had failed the One and the One had turned against him. No . . . not against him. Simply discarded him.

He had to find a way back into his good graces. If he couldn't, it meant all his years in the Order had been wasted. After the Change he would be just another face in the hordes of oppressed humanity . . . looking up to the likes of Szeto for mercy.

No. He would die first.

6. Now what? Hank Thompson thought as he strolled the hall of the Lodge that served as Kickerdom head-quarters.

He was bored out of his skull. Worse than that, he was still pissed that the Internet was rebounding so quickly from the meltdown. His Kickers had busted their asses blowing up the infrastructure while Drexler and his Order attacked from the inside. The one-two punch was sup-posed to cause a KO.

But no. A couple of days of chaos, and then things started getting back to normal. Amazing how fast they'd come up with a fix for the Jihad virus, disrupting the bot-net. Even more amazing was how fast they'd repaired those blown fiber-optic cables. He'd wanted the 'Net down for good. Without all that constant networking, people would be forced to realize that their so-called intercon-nectedness was a trap. And that would push them one step closer to dissimilation, one step closer to him and joining the Kicker Evolution.

But the 'Net hadn't been down near long enough for that. In no time their chat rooms and facebooks and myspaces and all that crap were back up and running. Still lots of glitches and bandwidth problems, but pretty much business as usual.

Fuck 'em. Fuck 'em all.

"Hey, boss," said a passing Kicker, a burly guy named

McGrew. He carried a red toolbox emblazoned with a Kicker Man.

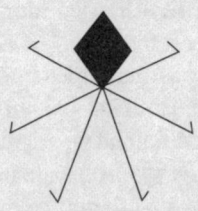

A tattoo of the same figure adorned the web between his thumb and forefinger.

Lots of Kickers had asked Hank why he'd never got himself inked with the symbol. He always gave the same answer. *Because I* am *the Kicker Man.*

Hank nodded and kept moving, thinking about the Kicker Man. He was more than a symbol to Hank. Years ago the Kicker Man had appeared in one of his dreams and led him to write *Kick*, the book that had put him on the map and started the Kicker Evolution. He'd appeared from time to time to guide him.

Maybe his frustration in real life was behind that weird dream he'd been having the past few nights, wherein the Kicker Man seemed to be in trouble—attacked by a flock of birds. At least they looked like birds. Hard to tell because it was happening in the dark. Hard enough to see the Kicker Man in the dark, let alone what was attacking him. Whatever they were, they swarmed him, buzzing him from all sides. He couldn't seem to drive them off.

What the hell did that mean?

He knew it meant something, because the Kicker Man never appeared unless something was in the offing.

Sometimes it was good, sometimes not. This didn't look good.

Hank needed a little distraction. Maybe Drexler was in. Been a while since he'd hassled him. The uptight dick-head was always good for a laugh. Couldn't tick him too much, though. He was the Order's head honcho around here, and the Order let Hank use this Lodge as Kicker HQ. Push Drexler too far and he might kick them all out.

He entered Drexler's office without knocking—Hank knew he hated that—and found the man standing at one of his windows, looking out at the street. The Kickers who hung out at the Lodge called him the Ice Cream Dude because of the white suit he wore year in and year out.

When Drexler didn't turn, Hank said, "How goes it?" When Drexler still didn't turn, Hank raised his voice. "Hello? Anybody home?"

Finally the guy turned and Hank felt a little jolt of surprise when he saw his face. He couldn't put his finger on it, but it had changed somehow. The swept-back black hair with the widow's peak and the bits of gray at the temples were the same. So were the hawk nose and thin-lipped mouth.

The eyes . . . that was it. As blue as ever, but the Master of the Universe look was gone. Their usual ice had melted, leaving just . . . eyes.

"Yes, Thompson? What is it?"

His itty-bitty German accent hadn't changed, but what happened to "Mister"? Ever since they'd met he'd called him *Mister* Thompson.

Hank shrugged. "Just stopping by to see what's new in the world of the Ancient Fraternal Septimus Order."

Drexler's eyes widened as he took a quick step for-ward. "Why do you ask? Have you heard anything? What have you heard?"

Whoa. His face was all uncertainty and hunger now. What the hell was going on?

"Nothing. Just sort of wondering if you folks have any more Internet tricks up your sleeve. One that'll last a little longer. Like maybe permanent."

"It wasn't a '*trick*.' And it wasn't designed to be permanent, just long enough . . ." His voice trailed off.

"Yeah, just long enough for what? At first you said the Internet was all that was standing between the One and the Change. Then you mentioned some lady. Which was it?"

"It didn't work. That's all that matters."

"No, it's not. Not by a long shot. Things are pretty much back the way they were. My Kickers are just hanging around instead of going out and gathering up converts who don't know what to do with themselves without the Internet."

"Your precious Kickers," Drexler said, looking like he'd just bitten into a lemon. "They're just tools. As are you."

That stung—maybe because it hit a little too close to home.

"Watch it. We don't answer to anyone, especially your lame Order."

"We all answer to someone. And we expect at least a modicum of loyalty in return. But sometimes it turns out to be a one-way street, and expectations aren't met."

What was he talking about?

"You mean the Change?" Bringing the Internet down was supposed to clear the way to start the Change. But it hadn't. "You telling me there's gonna be no Change?"

That would mean all that Internet business had been for nothing. The Change was supposed to be bad news for everyone except those who helped bring it on. Like

Hank and Drexler and the high-ups in his Order. They were supposed to be the One's right-hand men when he took over.

Drexler's thin smile was pure condescension. "Oh, the Change will come. There's no stopping it. It will take all of humanity by surprise." He took a step closer. "And you, Hank Thompson, might be the most surprised of all."

Hank felt like he'd been punched.

"What? What are you talking about?"

Without replying, Drexler turned away and removed his white suit coat from the closet. He shrugged into it, grabbed his black rhino-hide cane, and strode to the door. Hank grabbed his arm as he passed.

"Hey, I asked you something—"

Drexler batted his wrist with the silver head of the cane, sending a shock wave up to Hank's shoulder. Hank released his grip and stood rubbing his arm as Drexler stepped out into the hall and disappeared without a backward glance.

But his final words hung in the air.

And you, Hank Thompson, might be the most surprised of all.

What the *hell* did that mean?

7. Jack stopped at Tram's laundry off Canal Street and showed him the bomber jacket. Tram squinted against the smoke from his unfiltered Pall Mall as he inspected the ruined lining of the sleeve. He was on the far side of sixty and as a younger man had lost the lower half of his right leg to a Viet Cong finger charge. He'd hired Jack a while back to help him with a mob problem he'd been pushed into.

"Much blood."

"Tell me about it."

He poked a finger through the bullet hole and eyed Jack. "Yours?"

Jack nodded. He'd gone home, found an insulated Windbreaker, then trained down here.

"Can't clean," Tram said, shaking his head. "But can fix hole and sew new sleeve liner."

"Okay on the liner, but leave the holes."

His eyebrows lifted. "Eh?"

"A reminder."

Tram's smile revealed a mouth crowded with canary-yellow teeth. "Yes. Reminder is good." He pointed down to where his right leg was steel and plastic. "Makes one more careful."

From Tram's he walked up to Canal Street and caught a cab over to Doc Hargus's place. He'd called from home and the doc was in. Doc's office was his apartment, a third-floor walk-up. He'd had a little substance abuse problem back in the day. Okay, a big problem and he'd lost his license before he'd cleaned up. His only vice now was beer, and that in moderation.

He still practiced on the QT, treating injuries and overdoses and things people didn't want part of the public record. Too bad, because his portly physique, deep voice, and Wilford Brimley mustache inspired trust and confidence.

"What're you running on me?" he said after Jack had stripped to the waist and he'd removed Bill's dressing.

Odd question.

"Not running anything. What're you talking about?"

Doc pulled on a pair of latex gloves and removed one of the butterflies, peeling both ends at once toward the middle.

"Didn't I tell you over the phone I couldn't stitch up any wound over twenty-four hours old?"

"Yeah."

"And you told me this happened just this morning, right?"

"Right."

"Bullshit."

Jack tensed, feeling a niggle of annoyance. "What do you mean?"

Doc pointed to the wound. "I can't suture this. It's already started to knit."

Jack craned his neck and looked. The wound still looked bloody and angry to him.

"That's just the butterflies holding it together."

Doc looked at him over his glasses. "I think I've seen a few more of these than you, Jack."

"Okay, no argument there, but Doc, I swear: I got grazed at around ten o'clock this morning. Why would I lie?"

Doc looked at him, then adjusted his glasses and leaned closer to the wound. He studied it for a few seconds, then straightened, shaking his head.

"Yeah. Good question. Why would you? But Jack . . . that's at least two days old—" His hand flashed up as Jack opened his mouth to protest. "I'll rephrase: It's got at least two days' worth of healing there. If, as you say, this happened this morning, well, you tell me what vitamins and herbs you're taking because you've suddenly developed some super healing powers."

Jack went cold as he heard Glaeken's voice echo in his head.

Wounds heal much more quickly than you'd imagine . . . a scratch like that would heal almost immediately.

Jack's wound hadn't healed "almost immediately," but Doc said it was already days into the process, though only hours had passed.

"You okay?" Doc said. "You don't look so hot. Never known you to mind the sight of blood—even your own."

"I'm okay."

Big lie.

Glaeken seemed to be failing, and here Jack was developing the healing powers the old guy had once possessed. Pretty obvious that Jack, as the Heir to the Defender post, was being prepared to step into Glaeken's shoes. How long had this healing thing been going on? If Jack hadn't been hurt, he still wouldn't know about it. It could only mean Glaeken's demise was imminent. How long did the old guy have?

"I'll replace the butterflies," Doc was saying, "even though it hardly needs them at this point. Pretty good job of closing that wound. Who did it?"

"Some guy."

I don't want this, Jack thought. I do *not* want this.

But no one had asked. No one had given him a choice.

8.   "Oy. You're trying to start the next world war?"

"Call me the rovin' gambler."

Abe glanced up from the wish list Jack had handed him and offered a puzzled look. "Nu?"

"Were you ever a Dylan fan?"

Abe shook his head. "Neither Thomas nor Bob."

Jack waved him off. "Never mind then. Take too long to explain."

He took a bite of his cheesesteak. He'd brought two of them from Vinny's pizzeria off West Houston. Vinny was a Philly transplant and knew his way around the classic cheesesteak. Jack confessed to being a purist and a minimalist where cheesesteaks were concerned. Razor-thin slices of steak, provolone cheese, fried onions on a sub roll. No peppers, no gravy, and Vinny might do violence to anyone who added mustard or catsup. Jack would help him.

Jack and Abe had laid the torpedo-shaped packages on the scarred rear counter of the Isher Sports Shop, spreading the greasy wrapping paper to reveal the treasured contents, then chowed down. Parabellum, Abe's powder-blue parakeet, hopped around on the hunt for scraps. The seedless rolls made for slim pickings, so Jack tossed him a sliver of meat. He pounced on it.

Abe, already finished with his first half, had the second clutched in his pudgy fingers, which in turn were attached to pudgy arms connected to a pudgy body. He needed a cheesesteak like he needed herpes, but Jack had given up nannying Abe's health. Eat, drink, and be merry, for tomorrow we die. The last part was likely if Rasalom got his way.

Abe closed his eyes and groaned softly as he chewed.

"Why is *traif* so good?" he said around a mouthful.

"Because forbidden and flavor both start with *F*?"

"In her grave my mother would turn if she knew what I was eating."

"Could be worse."

"How?"

"She could find out about that Taylor pork roll and cheese with egg on a kaiser you had last week."

Abe rolled his eyes. "Oy. That might return her from the dead."

"I'll never tell." Jack nodded at the list. "What can you do for me?"

"All right already. What I've seen so far is not for everyday home protection. The first thing here, an MM-1 . . . you really want an MM-1? You been watching—what's that film?"

"*Dogs of War*?"

"That's the one. With that meshuggeneh actor . . ."

"I prefer 'quirky'—Christopher Walken."

"Him, yes. You've been watching that movie?"

"No. Not lately."

But Jack remembered it well. The MM-1 had been the film's iconic weapon. It looked like a sawed-off shotgun with a huge rotating drum that held a dozen 40mm grenades.

"Then why an MM-1 already?"

"I may have a need for grenades and I want to be able to use them at a distance greater than I can throw."

"Fine. But this throws a dozen in rapid succession."

"I'm after a tough bastard."

"Well, I don't have one sitting downstairs. I'll have to call around."

"Fine, but please get on it ASAP."

"This is a rush job?"

Jack looked at him. "It's a long overdue job."

Abe understood. "That mamzer whose name, like God's, we shouldn't say?"

"It's 'Rasalom.' Say his name anytime you feel like it now. I want him to come looking."

"Not for me, thank you." He scratched his stubbled chin. "Like I said, the MM-1 itself I don't have, but rounds to feed it I do. You want HE, I assume?"

Jack nodded. High-explosive grenades, yes—the higher, the better.

"What's the kill zone?" Jack asked.

"Five meters."

"Perfect."

"*But* . . . the HE rounds won't detonate within thirty meters of the launcher."

Well, he couldn't allow himself to get close to Rasalom anyway. But just in case it happened . . .

"Understood. What've you got for close range? I've heard of Beehives—"

"With the flechettes?" Abe waved his hands. "Those you don't want."

Jack had thought shooting a round that held forty or fifty darts might come in handy.

"Why not?"

"Unless you're very close, the flechettes don't necessarily land point first. Skip the Beehive. You want the buckshot round. Filled with number-four pellets. Does a nice shredding job close in."

"Okay. I'll take four HE and eight shot."

Abe jotted that down on the list, then went to the next item. His head shot up.

"LX-14? You're going to trigger a nuclear bomb?"

"Nooo." Jack had heard it had been used in nuclear weapons but, although he'd have loved to be able to hit Rasalom with a tactical nuke, he didn't have one. And Abe wasn't going to find him one. "I just want max of everything—detonation velocity, brisance, everything. And I'm told this is powerful stuff."

"It is. But as far as I know, it's made only at Livermore in this country. I'll see what I can do." He gave Jack a sidelong look. "You're changing your last name to Kozlowski, maybe?"

Jack laughed. "Please, no."

The Kozlowski brothers, Stan and Joe, had been demolition experts, really got off on blowing things up. Damn near blew Jack to smithereens a couple of years ago. But Jack had learned a few things from them . . . before he blew them up.

Abe squinted at the last item on the list. "If I didn't know better I'd say this says 'Stingers.'" He looked up and smiled. "But you couldn't want—"

Jack was nodding. "Yup. Two of them."

Abe threw his hands—and the list—in the air as he gestured to the leaning shelves and crowded aisles running toward the front of the store.

"Gevalt! This is a sport shop."

"What about the armory in the basement? Or did you forget?"

"Small arms I sell. *Small.* Stinger missiles are not small arms."

"I figure if one guy can carry it and fire it, it's a small arm."

"That's *your* definition. Others—like yours truly—would disagree." He picked up the list and read it again. "You're sure about this?"

"Absolutely."

Abe shook his head. "I should maybe not complain about you saving the world, but . . ."

"But what?"

He didn't correct him about the saving-the-world bit. If that happened, fine. But he was out to save Gia and Vicky and Abe and Weezy and Julio and Eddie and a few others.

"This isn't your style."

"Why? Because of all the firepower?"

"Yes. With you it's always up close and personal. This . . ." He shrugged again.

"I don't have a choice, Abe. Get too close to this guy

and he can freeze you with a look, paralyze you so all you can do is watch. I'm not giving him that chance. I have to operate from a distance."

"But surface-to-air missiles?"

"Well . . ." Jack paused. He'd never told Abe this.

"Well, what?"

"He can fly."

Abe's eyebrows lifted halfway to his far-receded hairline. "Like a bird, you mean? Like Superman?"

"No . . . but he can float. I've seen it. I don't intend to give him a chance to do that. But if he does . . . he gets stung."

Abe sighed as he resettled himself on his stool. "I know the world is not what I once thought it to be. Seeing that thing that came out of the Hudson and cut up your chest— how long has it been?"

"Three years this coming summer."

If summer came. Word was it might not.

Abe shook his head. "Like a lifetime it seems. Anyway, seeing that happen made it abundantly clear that the world is keeping secrets. Not just the kind I thought it was—and is. Currencies and economies and governments are being manipulated, but that's *gornisht* compared to what's really going on, right?"

"'Fraid so. It's cosmic, dude."

"Since when you're a hippie?"

"But it *is* cosmic."

"And how do you find this Adversary, as you call him?"

"I hope to pick up his trail tonight."

"Where? In the cosmos?"

"Nope. New Jersey."

9. "They kicked you out?" Weezy said.

She'd run into Dawn Pickering in the lobby downstairs and they'd rode the elevator up together. They now stood outside their respective apartment doors across the hall from each other. A blue-eyed blonde, Dawn had lost some baby weight in the weeks since she'd delivered, but was by no means slim.

"Totally. Not just out of his office, out of the *building*." She glanced away. "I sort of lost it."

This wasn't good. Weezy, Jack, and Glaeken all wanted to know the baby's fate. Rasalom had personally involved himself in protecting Dawn during its gestation. He wouldn't have done that out of the goodness of his heart—he had no goodness anywhere in him, especially his heart. So the baby had to be useful to him. Or potentially so.

And if it was useful *to* Rasalom, it might be useful *against* him.

"You really think stalking Doctor Heinze is the best way to find your baby?"

Dawn shrugged. "If you can think of a better way, I'm all ears."

"Wish I could."

Weezy and Jack had tried, but besides the obstetrician—who seemed to have washed his hands of Dawn since the delivery—Heinze was their only link to the baby.

"So do I. But until we do, this seems the only way. But it just got harder now that I'm persona non grata at the McCready building. I mean, they won't even let me through the front door anymore."

Weezy had to smile.

Dawn caught it and frowned. "I hardly think it's funny."

Touchy, touchy, Weezy thought. Dawn was becoming more and more strung out in her quest for her baby.

"Neither do I. It was 'persona non grata.' You don't hear that too often in daily conversation."

"Don't you mean *quotidian* conversation?"

"Um, yeah. That too."

Finally Dawn allowed a faint smile. "You know, just because I'm still in my teens and say 'totally' a lot doesn't make me dumb. I aced my SATs, especially the verbal parts. I'd be in my second semester at Colgate right now if I hadn't . . ."

Her smile crumbled as her throat worked and she blinked back sudden tears.

Weezy's heart went out to her. This poor kid had been through more heartache in the past year than many people see in a lifetime.

"It's okay."

"It's *not* okay. If I hadn't gotten involved with that . . . that monster, I'd be a college freshman instead of an unwed mother, and my own mother would still be alive." She shook her head. "She used to fine me every time I said 'totally' and 'like.'"

Weezy fought an urge to hug her. Dawn was too brittle right now. No telling how she'd react.

Aw, hell with it, she thought and slipped her arms around her.

"I'm so sorry. I wish I could say something to make you feel better."

Dawn hesitated, then, with a soft sob, returned the hug. She clung to Weezy a moment, then eased away.

"Just having you to talk to keeps me sane."

"You worry about staying sane?"

"Not really. Well, maybe. The baby's all I can think about. Sometimes I wish I could turn it off, but it won't stop."

Weezy knew how that was. She'd been diagnosed as manic-depressive as a teen—they called it bipolar now. She didn't know if the diagnosis was accurate, but she'd been medicated and it had helped . . . some. She still hadn't been able to turn off the thoughts, but she'd been able to slow them. Having a memory that wouldn't allow her to forget anything, ever, was no help either.

Dawn wasn't bipolar, though, just post-partum and obsessed.

"Want to come in for some coffee?"

Dawn shook her head as she turned toward her apartment door. "I know you need to go back to reading your bizarro book, and I need to crash. Haven't been sleeping much and I need to catch up if I'm going to be fresh tomorrow."

"What's tomorrow?"

Dawn pushed open her door and stepped inside. "Back to the McCready building."

"But you're, as you say, persona non grata."

Her smile was grim. "They can keep me out of the building but they can't keep me from watching it. Thanks for being a friend."

She closed the door, leaving Weezy alone in the hall, wondering how long Dawn could keep going like this.

In her own apartment, Weezy headed directly for the kitchenette and her coffeemaker. She'd invested in a Keurig personal brewer—named it Katy, of course— and immediately it had become her favorite appliance. Pots of coffee went stale after a while. Her beloved Katy was always ready to brew a fresh cup for her.

She unlocked the kitchen cabinet where she hid the

Compendium of Srem, the "bizarro book" Dawn had mentioned. Almost as old as Glaeken and Rasalom, and virtually indestructible, Torquemada had tried to destroy it during the Spanish Inquisition but couldn't, so he buried it and built a monastery over it. It wouldn't stay buried, however, and after a torturous journey through many hands—Hank Thompson's and Jack's among them—it wound up here in Weezy's apartment.

She laid it on the kitchen table and opened it to the leather marker she had left against the last page she'd read. As usual it did not open to that page. The book had this maddening, frustrating tendency to change pages on its own. Nobody knew the exact number of pages in the *Compendium*—the book was designed to have a finite number of sheets but a virtually infinite number of pages. But something had gone wrong and all the pages were out of order. What you found when you turned the page rarely had anything to do with the page before. And when you turned back, the original page might have changed as well.

She flipped to a random page, just to see what she'd find. When she saw the header, she caught her breath. *The Other Name* . . . she'd seen that mentioned in the past but had never encountered a whole page devoted to it. Glaeken had mentioned something about each of the Seven who championed the Otherness back in the First Age having a secret name. This could be it. But the text that followed caused her to slam on the brakes.

It wasn't in English.

One of the many miraculous things about the *Compendium*—and what Torquemada must have considered the most Satanic—was its ability to present its text in the reader's native tongue. Someone born and raised in Riyadh would see Arabic; from the Congo, Swahili; from Johnson, NJ, English.

Yet this was in some mishmash of symbols and characters that Weezy had never seen. She had a feeling this was important—so important that she couldn't risk losing the page. She pulled out her cell phone and began snapping photos. As expected, what she saw as English reverted to the Old Tongue in the photos, but the gibberish remained the same.

She couldn't wait to show Glaeken.

10. The dashboard clock in the Crown Vic read a little after eleven P.M. as Jack exited the Garden State Parkway and began to wind his way along rural back roads in northern Ocean County. The twisting pavement led him along hilly curves until the road crested. He knew what was coming up on his left: an opening through the trees with a concrete skirt abutting the road's asphalt. The skirt seemed to end at a cliff, but Jack knew better. He turned onto it and descended a steep concrete driveway into a former sandpit, a huge excavation maybe seventy or eighty feet deep, with a hodgepodge of buildings backed up against the near wall.

All the buildings were dark. He passed a small fleet of cement-mixer trucks and haulers of various shapes and sizes, all lined up and facing front like grunts awaiting inspection. No moving van in sight.

He pulled up to the office door of the biggest, tallest building. A sign above it showed a stylized black sun that looked like a sunflower, and the words *Wm. Blagden & Sons, Inc.*

Yep. They still ran the place.

He got out and banged on the door, shouting, "Anybody there?" a couple of times.

If anyone answered, he'd ask for directions.

No one did. He flashed his penlight on the lock. A Schlage. Good.

He parked the Vic behind the mixers. Its black color blended nicely into the shadows. He pulled out his Schlage bump key set and returned to the door. Found one that fit the lock, tapped it with the butt of his Glock, and he was in. The place hadn't been alarmed on his last trip and didn't appear to be now. After all, what was there to steal? Sand? Loose cement mix?

Jack flashed his light around the office. Pretty bare bones: a couple of desks, chairs, computer monitors, filing cabinets. His plan was to find a work order for the date Osala was moved and maybe a delivery address to go along with it. A picture window looked out onto the big building's wide, open floor. Jack aimed his flash through and the beam picked up . . .

A truck.

He stepped out onto the floor and played his beam over it as he approached. A box truck with the Blagden logo on the side. Jack froze as the light picked up something else beyond it. Something big and long and metallic.

Forcing himself back into motion, he passed the truck and stopped before a large metal tube, maybe twenty feet long and five in diameter, its flanks embossed with odd symbols. Jack knew it well. A year and a half ago he'd come here looking for someone. He'd peeped through the window as this cylinder—standing upright then—had been filled with concrete, unaware that the person he'd come to find was bound inside, and had drowned in the wet mix while Jack watched.

A wave of sadness rippled through him as he returned to the truck. He grabbed the handles on the rear door and heaved. As it rolled up, he flashed his light into the truck's bay, revealing stacks of gleaming furniture protected by thick mover's pads.

He stepped back and checked the license plate. It matched the numbers Mack had given him.

So . . . weeks after loading, Osala's—Rasalom's—furniture still hadn't been delivered.

He hopped into the truck's cab—it stank of cigarettes—and hunted for papers. None on the seat. In the glove compartment he found maps, matches, and a work order that matched Mack's copy, but no delivery address. Instead, someone had scrawled *Hold until further notice* across the bottom.

Jack had a feeling the "further notice" might never come. But even if they eventually unloaded all this at Rasalom's new digs, when would that be? More weeks? Months? Jack had no way of knowing. And no way to know about the move if and when it happened.

He couldn't set up a stakeout. Not while Rasalom was skulking about, planning who knew what.

He returned to the rear of the truck and climbed in. Rasalom's *stuff* . . . maybe it would give some clue to the guy.

He began inspecting things, then throwing them out—pushing them off the edge of the bed to crash on the concrete floor. Chairs got an immediate heave-ho. Dressers and bureaus first had their drawers pulled out and inspected—all empty—then were dumped.

Empty, empty, empty.

Nothing, nothing, nothing.

When he'd finished, he eased himself down amid the splintered remains of the furniture and found himself facing the cylinder. A rush of anger burned away his frustration.

The Dormentalists had been behind the ritual murder

in that tube. The higher-ups behind it had paid, but others hadn't. William Blagden was a Dormentalist and had been involved, yet life was still business as usual for him. Maybe Jack should do something about that.

He knew his next step.

He retrieved the matchbook from the glove compartment and then popped the truck's hood. Took him a moment to find the fuel line, took only a second to cut it. The sharp smell of gasoline spread as it spilled onto the floor. He waited for a good-size puddle to form, then struck a match, lit the book, and tossed it.

The gas went up with a *woomp!* and Jack headed for the door. Outside, he started his car and waited until the truck's gas tank exploded, blowing out a number of windows. He watched a little longer, to be sure the building was catching. When he was, he put the Vic in gear and drove away.

Not at all what he'd come for, but at least the trip hadn't been a total waste.

11. Gia zeroed in on the gauze as soon as Jack pulled off his T-shirt.

"What's this?"

He pulled off the dressing and saw it had further healed to the point where it had stopped oozing. He'd forgotten about it because the pain was gone. This was scary.

"Just a scratch." At least it was now.

Slim, with short blond hair and sky-blue eyes, Gia sat next to him on her bed. Vicky was asleep and they were enjoying a little private time.

"When? I don't remember this yesterday."

She removed her top and unfastened her bra as he gave her a quick rundown of the incident in Central Park. Her pink-tipped breasts weren't large and weren't small. A handful each . . . just right.

Her blue eyes were wide. "That shoot-out in the park? That was you?"

"I was just walking by—"

"How do you manage to get involved in these things?"

"I was minding my own business."

He was reaching for one of her breasts but she pushed his hand away and leaned close, studying the wound.

"The news said a man was killed. That could have been you." She frowned. "This looks almost healed."

"Told you it was just a scratch. Doc Hargus said it hardly needed the butterflies." To prove his point, Jack pulled them off. "There."

He stared at the wound. No way the healing should be this far gone.

"You do heal fast."

Jack opened his mouth to tell her, but closed it again. Why try to explain what he didn't know for sure, what he only suspected? He'd talk to Glaeken first and see what he thought.

She ran a finger lightly along the line of the wound. "That other bullet scar is round."

"That was a direct hit. This was a graze."

"Looks like something a knife might make." He'd expected her to be repulsed, and maybe if the wound looked fresher, she would be. But she seemed fascinated. "Or a sword."

"Sword?" He laughed. "Where'd that come from?"

"I guess I have swords on my mind," she said as she slipped out of her jeans. "I mean, since Vicky asked if I thought you'd mind if she brought your katana into school for show and tell."

"The Gaijin Masamune?"

"Whatever."

"How does she know about that?"

"Well, it's visible on the top shelf of your front closet. Every time we hang up our coats—"

"Okay, okay. But how does she even know what a katana is?"

"A combination of things. They're studying Japan in school, and today she happened to catch some of *The Seven Samurai* on TV."

"But she hates black-and-white films."

He remembered how he'd had to bribe her to watch the original *King Kong*.

"Well, she didn't watch for long, and I'm pretty sure she would have flipped right past if they hadn't been studying Japan. But she lasted long enough to recognize the swords in the samurais' belts as just like the one in your closet."

"And she wants to bring it to class?"

She slipped out of her panties.

"Don't worry. I've already told her it's not going to happen. Not with the schools' zero-tolerance policy."

He couldn't take his eyes off her.

"Right. They get freaked about toy light sabers. Imagine something that can *really* lop off limbs and heads. Besides, it's pretty messed up."

Gia kissed his wound. "Not like your other sword."

"What other sword?"

She kissed his chest. "The pretty one. The one that only I see."

"Oh . . . that one." His skin tingled at her touch.

"Yes, that one. How's it doing?"

"Ready for battle."

She pushed him back and trailed her lips down along his abdomen.

"I sure hope so . . ."

THURSDAY

1. Jack yawned as he closed and locked his apartment door behind him.

One A.M. Long day.

But he couldn't call it quits yet. Gia's mention of the Gaijin Masamune had set him to thinking, and he didn't like where his thoughts were going.

He pulled open the door to his closet and brought the scabbarded katana down from its high shelf. He pulled on the handle and unsheathed the blade. Vicky would be disappointed if she saw it, because it looked like a piece of junk. The blade was Swiss-cheesed and mottled with a random pattern of a hundred or so holes and pocks— not eaten or rusted out, *melted* out.

The story went that in the fourteenth century a gaijin warrior commissioned the legendary swordsmith Masamune to make a sword for him using metal that had fallen from the sky. It turned out to be the strongest steel Masamune had ever encountered, but he had enough for only a short kodachi. When the gaijin failed to return, Masamune melted down the kodachi and added more steel— Earth steel—but the two metals never fully blended. The resultant katana's mottled finish embarrassed the swordsmith, and so he didn't sign it. Instead he carved the two symbols for "gaijin" on the tang.

The so-called Gaijin Masamune became a legend—supposedly stronger and sharper than anything Masamune had ever made. Somehow it wound up at ground zero in Hiroshima on that fateful day. The atomic heat supposedly melted out the Earth steel, leaving only the metal from the sky, pocked and riddled with defects.

Jack angled the blade back and forth, watching the light play off the mottled surface. The edge and the undulating temper line that bordered it, however, were unmarred.

A lot of people had died by and for this sword. He wondered if it was cursed. Used to be Jack didn't believe in curses. Used to be he didn't believe in a lot of things he took for granted now.

Holding the katana safely away from his body—he'd seen what that blade could do—he wound through the Victorian oak furniture that cluttered his claustrophobic—Gia's term, not his—front room. He occupied the third floor of a West Eighties brownstone that was much too small for all the neat stuff he'd accumulated over the years.

When he reached the old fold-out secretary at the far end of the room, he angled it out from the wall and removed the lower rear panel. His collection of saps, knives, bullets, and pistols hung on self-adhering hooks or cluttered the floor of the space. By far the largest weapon was the huge Ruger Super Redhawk revolver chambered for .454 Casulls. He had no use for it here in the city, but it always made him think of his dad. Maybe that was why he couldn't let it go. He wasn't good at letting go of stuff anyway.

On the other hand, something in the compartment wouldn't let go of him—a ten-by-twelve-inch flap of human skin. He'd buried it three times but it always returned to his apartment.

He unfolded the rectangle, as supple as suede, with no hint of decomposition. The pattern of pocked scars crisscrossed with fine, razor-thin cuts used to confound him. Later he learned it was a map of Opus Omega, the pocks indicating places where concrete pillars—some of them fashioned in the recently razed building on the Wm. Blagden & Sons grounds—had been buried around the world.

Everything was connected . . . everything.

Another thing he'd learned about the skin was that he couldn't cut it up. He'd tried to slice it into pieces to get rid of it, but it wouldn't allow itself to be cut. Or rather, wouldn't allow itself to *stay* cut.

He wondered if that was still true.

He pulled out his Spyderco Endura and flipped out the curved blade. He pierced the skin with the point near a corner and sliced downward.

The blade parted the skin, which promptly sealed itself closed behind it. Just as before. Good.

As the Lady had said of the bullets fired at her yesterday: *If they are of this Earth, they cannot harm me.* Nothing of this Earth could harm her.

The Endura's blade was of this Earth.

But Gia had started Jack thinking about the blade of the Gaijin Masamune. It had "fallen from the sky." Which meant it was not of this Earth. Could it harm the Lady?

He picked up the katana and stretched the flap against the point. His gut clenched as he saw the pierced edges of the skin glow a ghostly blue as it poked through. But only briefly. Taking a breath, he sliced downward. Again the glow along the cut edges—which stayed cut and separate, even after the glow faded. No self-repair when cut by the Gaijin Masamune.

His saliva evaporated as he stared at the blade.

This could do it . . . this could kill the Lady . . . cause her third death . . . end her existence.

At least that was the way it looked.

Only one person would know for sure.

2. The other three members of what Jack had come to call the Ally's Gang of Four were seated around the table in the Lady's front room when he arrived. Weezy was leaning toward Glaeken where he sat at the head of the table, shaking his head as he stared at the *Compendium*.

"I've never seen anything like it."

Weezy looked shocked. "But-but-but you must have."

Glaeken shrugged. "I—"

"Can I interrupt?"

Jack didn't know what was going on, but whatever it was, the contents of the blanket-wrapped bundle under his arm took precedence.

Weezy looked annoyed as she tapped the open page in the *Compendium* before Glaeken. "This could be important."

Jack unrolled the blanket, revealing the katana and the rectangle of skin.

"Not as important as these."

"We've all seen them before," Weezy said.

He held up the sliced piece of skin and wiggled the cut flap. "Not like this."

He pulled out his Endura and held it up. "Of this Earth."

He made a quick cut, showing everyone how the skin healed itself. Then he unsheathed the katana.

"Not of this Earth."

He made a cut—again the blue glow along the edges, again no healing.

Weezy's face had gone white, Glaeken looked concerned, but the Lady seemed unperturbed.

"That skin is not me," she said.

"But it used to be yours."

She used to be able to appear in many guises. Jack had known her as Anya when she'd been stripped of this piece of skin—or rather, stripped of everything *but* this skin.

That had been her first death . . . caused by creatures not of this Earth.

Then her second death, caused by the *Fhinntman-chca*, also not of this Earth.

And now the Gaijin Masamune . . . would that cause her third and final death?

"Still, it is not me." She held out her hand. "I know this sword. You showed it to me."

"Yes. Last year." He handed it to her. "Remember what you said?"

"Of course." She held the katana by the handle and studied the pierced, pitted blade. "I said I sensed something significant, something of great import about it . . . that it would be a means to a momentous end."

Jack raised his eyebrows. "*Your* end?"

She shook her head. "I don't believe so."

Without warning, she held out her left arm and slashed at it. Blue light flared and her cry of pain mixed with Weezy's cry of alarm as the blade sliced through her wrist and embedded itself in the tabletop.

But the hand remained attached.

"Jeez," Jack whispered. "What the hell?"

"The blade can cause me pain," the Lady said. "But it cannot damage me."

Jack leaned in for a closer look—not even a line to mark the blade's passing.

"Swell. But how about a little warning before you pull something like that?"

"Th-that was your wrist," Weezy said, still visibly shaken. "What if it pierces a vital organ?"

The Lady rose. "Like this?"

Before Jack could stop her, she turned, placed the butt of the handle against the wall, and impaled herself on the blade. She yelped in pain as pale blue light flashed and the point emerged from her upper back.

She turned and faced them, her expression pained as she looked down at the sword protruding from her chest.

"Could someone help, please?"

Jack was already halfway there. He stepped up to her, gripped the handle and, after a heartbeat's hesitation, yanked it free. No blood, not even moisture on the blade.

"Thank you," she said.

Jack couldn't help but be angry. "Are you crazy? That could have killed you."

But the Lady was looking at Weezy. "No fear of piercing my vital organs, dear. I have none. I am all of a piece."

Weezy opened her mouth but couldn't speak.

Jack could. He held up the sword. "Remember what else you told me about this?"

"I believe I said it might be used for good or ill."

"No, I mean what you told me to do with it."

She nodded. "I said to throw it into the sea."

"You went further than that. I believe you suggested getting on a boat and dropping it into the Hudson Canyon."

She nodded. "Yes, I did."

"Well, that's exactly what I'm going to do." He glanced at Glaeken. "Unless you object."

The old man frowned. "Why would I object?"

"Well, it's sort of yours. You supplied Masamune with the original 'metal from the sky.' I figure you should have some say."

Glaeken shook his head. "I lay no claim to that blade."

"Then it goes."

"Thank God," Weezy said. "When?"

"ASAP."

"Good or ill," the Lady said. "You never know."

"I know the ill it can do. That's enough." He turned to Weezy. "How deep is the Hudson Canyon?"

She shrugged. "Depends on how far out you go. It's four hundred miles long. Go out about a hundred and the canyon floor is probably a mile from the surface."

"A mile sounds good."

"Hire a tuna boat captain to take care of it for you on his next trip."

He shook his head as he sheathed the sword in its curved scabbard. The Gaijin Masamune was a collector's item. Couldn't risk somebody finding out and getting greedy.

"This needs the personal touch."

He'd take it back home, then see about hiring a boat to ferry him out over the canyon. When they reached a point where the depth finder read a mile, he'd discard the scabbard, unwind the handle, and drop the blade over the side.

Not even Rasalom would be able to find it in the muck a mile down.

"Need some company?" she said.

"Not if you get seasick."

"I was thinking of Eddie. We're having lunch later. Wants to talk to me. He hasn't got much else going on."

Jack thought about it a sec. "Sure. Why not? I'll see if I can set it up for early tomorrow."

She smiled. "Great. We done with the sword?"

"Yeah. I'll—"

The Lady held up a finger. "One minor thing."

"Yes?"

"I wish the return of my skin."

The request startled him. Since it didn't seem to want to leave him, he'd come to think of it as his skin, his memento of Anya—a grisly one, but a memento nonetheless. Then again, Anya had been simply another manifestation of the Lady.

"Of course." He held it out to her.

She touched it—immediately the two slices Jack had made with the sword sealed up—but she did not take it.

"I wish it returned to my person."

With that she turned and her housedress split, revealing an identical map on her back. Jack would never get used to her clothes not being clothes, but part of her. As she said, *I am all of a piece.*

The split also revealed the two tunnels running back to front through her flesh, scars of her first two deaths.

"Lay it against my back but please align it properly."

Jack handed it to Weezy, who was closer, but she backed away, shaking her head. But finally she took it. Gingerly, she aligned the pattern on the Lady's back with that on the flap, and pressed it against the Lady. It blurred, then melted into her. The Lady's back was unchanged, but the flap was gone.

3. "My turn again," Weezy said when the Lady had reseated herself.

She watched Jack lean the wrapped katana against a wall, then return to the seat directly opposite her. She wondered at his almost feline grace. When, how had he developed that? He'd been such a gangly kid as a teen.

She shook off the questions and pointed to the *Compendium*, still before Glaeken. "Still on the same page?"

He nodded. "Yes."

That was weird, but fortunate. Weezy had come prepared for the opposite. She'd expected the *Compendium* to lose that page, so she'd uploaded jpegs of last night's photos to her laptop.

Turned out to be wasted effort. She'd brought the laptop and the *Compendium* over to the Lady's place, but when she arrived, the book opened to the same page. A virtual miracle, since the *Compendium* never showed you what you wanted most to see. And it had stayed on the same page.

She'd been counting on Glaeken to translate the gibberish.

"I still can't translate this," Glaeken said, staring at the page. "I recognize some of the Old Tongue, the language we spoke in the First Age, but that gibberish in the middle is not any language I've ever seen."

Weezy said, "The section I can read talks about 'The Other Name,' but why can't I read the rest? I mean, you've told us about the Seven Other Names and all, but what's this page talking about?"

Glaeken shrugged. "I wish I could tell you. Each of the Seven had three names, two of which were given, and one chosen. The first given was from their parents and, like everyone else, they had no control over that. The second was one they chose when they aligned themselves with the Otherness. They had to discard their old name as a symbolic way of renouncing everything they were before. The man we know as the Adversary or the One chose 'Rasalom.' "

Jack said, "So 'Rasalom' didn't come from the Otherness? He actually *chose* that? You'd think he'd come up with something better."

"Like what?" Weezy said.

"Like Mordan . . . or Omen . . . or Dethlok." He smiled, but it had a sour edge. "Or Stimpy."

Glaeken didn't seem amused. "He chose Rasalom—which is why he can't seem to let it go. His third name, his Other Name, was, like his first, also given—by the Otherness. Each of the Seven received an Other Name when they were elevated to the group. Each Other Name consists of the same seven characters in a unique arrangement."

Weezy tapped the table. "Seven times six, times five, times four, times three, times two, times one gives us five thousand forty permutations."

Jack shook his head. "You just did that in your head?"

Yeah, she had. Without even thinking about it. Just the way her mind worked.

"It's a gift. And that's a *lot* of names."

"Especially if you don't know the seven characters. And I can guarantee none of them is from our alphabet."

Weezy remembered something . . . from 1983. "Remember that little pyramid we found as kids?"

"Sure. The little black thing with six sides."

"Seven if you count the base. And each of those seven faces was carved with a symbol."

Jack straightened from his slouch. "Hey . . ."

Weezy looked at Glaeken. "Do you know the symbols we're talking about? The same ones were on the big pyramid on your property in the Pine Barrens."

"I do," he said.

"Could they be the seven characters in the Other Names?"

"Who can say? I never saw or heard the One's Other Name or any of the Seven's. But it seems a possibility."

Other possibilities flashed through her head as she grabbed a pen and a sheet of paper from her backpack and began drawing. She held up the result and showed it to the other three.

"That's what they looked like."

Jack was staring with an awed expression. "You remember? After all these—" Then he shook himself. "What am I saying? Of course you remember."

"So . . ." she said, "if Rasalom's Other Name is composed of these seven characters, we can arrange them in the five thousand forty possible sequences, and know that one of them is his."

"So? What does that get us?"

"Well, if people saying his 'Rasalom' name used to get him worked up, think what saying his Other Name will do?"

Jack shook his head. "You're talking five thousand possibilities. And even if we do find the right one, how would you pronounce it?"

That brought Weezy to a screeching halt. "Oh, right. Didn't think about that."

"And even if we could antagonize him by spreading his Other name around, what good would it do?"

"It might bring him out in the open where you could get a bead on him."

The smile broadened. "I like the way you think. Make him come to us."

"How's the search going, by the way?" she said. "Any luck with the moving people?"

Jack's smile faded as he shook his head. "Dead end."

The Lady pointed to the *Compendium*. "May I see this mysterious writing that no one knows?"

She'd fully intended to show the Lady, but she'd been so quiet, Weezy had forgotten she was there. She placed the book before her and pointed to the middle section.

"That gobbledygook there. Does that make any sense to you?"

The Lady stared little more than a heartbeat, then nodded. "Of course. I know all the languages of Earth for all time."

Of course you would, Weezy thought, chagrined that she hadn't figured that out on her own.

"Well?" Jack said, sounding more impatient than usual. Weezy guessed he didn't realize that the Lady's responses were very literal at times.

"What language?" Weezy said, almost as curious about that as the translation.

"It is the original language of the small folk."

Glaeken's eyes lit. "The smithies."

Weezy leaned forward. "'Small folk.' I've seen them mentioned in the *Compendium*. Like gnomes, elves?"

"I'm sure they're the source of those tales," Glaeken said. "Tiny people skilled with metals. As soon as I could afford their services, I allowed no one else to make my weapons." He looked at the Lady. "So this is their tongue.

I'd heard them talk among themselves but never saw it written down."

"That is because they rarely committed words to paper," the Lady said. She frowned. "If Srem used their tongue for this, she must have wanted it kept secret."

A secret passage in a book full of secrets—Weezy could barely contain herself.

"What does it say—read it, read it, read it."

"I already have. It details the ritual of the Other Naming Ceremony."

The excitement died—fell off a cliff—and Weezy dropped back into her chair.

"Oh. Well, that's no help." She sighed. "I mean, I don't see any of us being given an Other Name soon, so I can't see any use in knowing the naming ceremony."

Jack swiveled to face her. "Then why write it down in a language that's effectively code?"

Good point.

"Perhaps it has something to do with what Srem added here at the end: *'No two humans may have the same Other Name. The First-named shall be powerless as long as the Second-named lives. The First-named shall hear the Name within the Second and thus be able to resolve the duplication.'*"

"What's *that* mean?" Jack said.

Glaeken looked baffled. "I've never heard of any of this." He glanced at the Lady. "You?"

She shook her head. "Many things originating with the Otherness are hidden from me. It does, however, offer a reason why they so jealously guarded their Other Names."

"'No two humans may have the same Other Name,'" Weezy recited. "We'll probably never know why, so let's just accept that that's the way the Otherness wants it. But the next part is interesting: 'The First-named shall be powerless as long as the Second-named lives.' Powerless how? Does that mean no longer connected to the Other-ness?"

Jack's eyes lit. "Could mean he's mortal and normally vulnerable while someone else has his name."

Weezy could almost see the wheels turning in Jack's head, and guess what he was thinking.

"The last part's a little scary, though: 'The First-named shall hear the Name within the Second and thus be able to resolve the duplication.' I've got a pretty good idea what 'resolve the duplication' entails, but what does 'hear the name within the Second' mean?"

Jack said, "Rasalom knows whenever someone speaks his self-given name, so it makes sense he'd know when someone speaks his Other name. But this sounds different."

"Right," Weezy said. "'Hear within' doesn't seem quite the same. 'Within' what?"

"Within the mind," the Lady said. "I recall tales of this. The First-named will know when someone else has ad-opted his Other Name, because that name will live in the mind of the Second-named. The Second-named need not speak it, merely be conscious of his Other Name for the First-named to be able to home in on it—and 'resolve' the problem."

"What if the Second-named forgets the name?" Jack said.

The Lady gave him a look. "I believe that is unlikely."

Weezy shook her head. Jack . . . always looking for a workaround.

"You know . . ." he said slowly, "this has possibilities. If we figured out his Other Name, you could put me through the naming ceremony and give it to me."

Weezy's stomach twisted. "He'd hunt you down and kill you."

"He'd try. But I'd be ready for him. Especially since I wouldn't have to waste a lot of time looking for him—he'd come to me. I could choose the battlefield."

"Speaking of wasting time," Glaeken said, "you're doing that now. We don't know his Other Name, so there's no point in discussing it."

"You could christen me with all of them."

"'Christen' is a Christian term," Weezy said. "I don't think that applies here. And we're talking five-K-plus possibilities."

The Lady said, "Whether it applies or would work is irrelevant. Only I can read the text, therefore I am the only one who can perform the ceremony, and I will not—not with one name, not with five thousand."

Jack looked offended. "Why not?"

"It would be tantamount to pronouncing a death sentence. I would not do that to you or anyone else."

"It might be *Rasalom's* death sentence."

The Lady folded her arms with grim finality. "I have spoken."

And that's that, Weezy thought, relieved.

"Can we move on to something a little more pressing?" she said.

Jack said, "What's more pressing than taking out Rasalom?"

"Protecting the Lady from him."

A pause, then a nod. "Well, yeah. There's that. After yesterday, there's no doubt she's still his focus."

"Speaking of yesterday," Weezy said, "how's your arm?"

Jack got a funny look in his eyes. "Coming along fine.

Just fine." He turned to the Lady. "Did the noosphere come up with a place you can hide from him?"

The Lady nodded. "A possibility."

"Where?"

"Very near where the two of you grew up."

A shock zapped through Weezy. "Johnson?"

Jack too looked surprised. "I know there's a nexus point in the Barrens—"

The Lady shook her head. "Not there." She looked at Glaeken. "There is a structure on your land—"

"The pyramid?" Weezy said.

She nodded. "There is a good possibility I will be shielded from his awareness if I stay there."

Weezy tapped the *Compendium*. "I found something once—of course, I can't find it again—that mentioned a pyramidal structure and hinted it had some sort of 'power of occultation.' And typical of Srem, she didn't explain."

"Occultation," Jack said. "Fancy word for hiding. How? It's not even enclosed."

"Srem said."

"That was once a cage, wasn't it?" Jack glanced at her. "At least we figured it was."

Glaeken nodded. "Yes. Once a very famous place in the world of the Ancient Fraternal Septimus Order when it wasn't quite so ancient. They built it to house the last q'qr."

Weezy pounded a fist on the table. "I knew it!" She pointed at Jack. "That thing that chased us in the lost town—that was a q'qr. The last q'qr." She looked at Glaeken. "Is that possible?"

He shrugged. "Well, after all, they live until they are killed, so I suppose it could be."

Weezy had been finding references to q'qrs in the *Compendium* and Glaeken had filled in the gaps: Q'qrs

were created by the Otherness back in the First Age—
genetically retrofitted from humans—as savage soldiers
in its war against the Ally. Dark, hairy bipeds with two
arms and two tentaclelike appendages sprouting from
their armpits.

"But why New Jersey, of all places?"

"I believe the cage—or pyramid, as you've called it—
was erected in the late Archaic period. The Order had
preserved a good deal of knowledge after the cataclysm
that ended the First Age, but never shared it. The 'New
World' was not the least bit new to them. They penned
the last q'qr near their first Lodge in North America."

"The one in Johnson?" Jack said, his expression baffled. "Why?"

"The Pine Barrens, in what would eventually become
New Jersey, were convenient to the coast via rivers and
streams, and even more isolated then. The woods presented a good buffer against the natives."

"But why not someplace warmer—like the Caroli-
nas?"

"The location of the Johnson lodge isn't random. It lies
on a convergence near a particularly powerful nexus point.
A settlement sprang up around it long before Columbus
or even the Vikings found this continent, and eventually
became the Old Town section of Johnson. You probably
can't pronounce its First Age name, but because of the
presence of the last q'qr, it was referred to as Q'qret—
which translates as Q'qr Home. As English became the
dominant local language—"

Weezy saw where he was going. "Q'qret was bastard-
ized into Quakerton."

Glaeken nodded. "Which remained the town's name
until President Andrew Johnson decided to spend the
night there. Members of the Order had largely moved on

by then, leaving only the Lodge as a permanent holding. I knew the cage was empty and assumed the last q'qr was dead, but I bought the land around it to prevent development. Who knew what trouble people might unearth if they started digging?"

Weezy remembered what she and Jack had uncovered when they'd dug on his land—Glaeken had been known to the locals back then as Old Man Foster—and it had led to a ton of trouble.

She looked at the Lady. "But you're saying that old stone cage would be a safe place for you?"

"Wait," Jack said, holding up a hand. "We're just going to forget about this Other Name thing?"

Glaeken said, "I think it's a dead end, Jack."

Jack shook his head. "I'm not so sure. There's an opportunity there. I don't know what, exactly, but something's there."

"Not if I do not perform the ceremony," the Lady said.

Jack leaned back, looking frustrated. Weezy had a feeling he wasn't going to let this go.

The Lady turned to Weezy. "To answer your question: Yes, I think that ancient cage might offer a hiding place."

Jack frowned. "How? It's got open sides. I think you'd be more exposed."

"But it was built in a way that honors the Otherness. If I stay within its confines, its walls might deflect the One's awareness of me."

Glaeken said, "It's obvious he has no way to harm you—at least at the moment—otherwise he would have used it yesterday. But we can be just as sure that he is leaving no stone unturned looking for a means to extinguish you. So I see no downside to trying the cage."

"Well, who knows?" Jack said. "If you drop off his radar, he may waste time and resources locating you instead of hunting up ways to off you." He looked at Weezy. "Somebody's going to have to drive her."

Right. The *Fhinntmanchca* encounter had robbed her of the ability to zap herself around, appearing anywhere on Earth whenever she pleased. Until she regained her full strength, she had to travel like anyone else.

Weezy raised her eyebrows. "Road trip?"

He sighed. "I guess so."

He couldn't have sounded less enthused.

"Today?"

He shook his head. "Something I need to do. Tomorrow is better."

"Then we head home tomorrow."

Home . . . so many memories back there, good, bad, and awful.

4. Dawn stared through her windshield at the Mc-Cready Foundation building from her quasi-legal parking space. Senator James McCready had died last year but his foundation lived on. Part of the building was rented office space—mostly to the private practices of the physicians associated with the foundation—but the rest was devoted to research.

And that totally bothered Dawn. Dr. Heinze was a pediatric surgeon—it still bothered her that Mr. Osala had called in a surgeon—associated with a medical research facility. Were they doing research on her baby? Were his birth defects so unusual that he had to be hidden away and studied?

She didn't care about his defects, she wanted him back.

But where was he?

She hadn't named him, and he certainly wouldn't be

listed anywhere with her last name. *Baby Boy Pickering.*
Totally unlikely. But he had to be somewhere.

Banned from the building, she'd had to set up watch
out here. Not an easy thing in midtown Manhattan.

She stepped out of the car—a used Volvo V70 wagon—
and stretched her legs. Jack had helped her buy it. She
glanced through the side window into the rear where the
infant seat was securely strapped in. She'd wanted a Volvo
because she'd heard they were safe, and if she was going
to be driving her baby around, she wanted a safe car.

She'd parked where she could see not only the front
entrance to the office section of the building but the ramps
in and out of the attached garage as well.

She was suddenly on alert as a silver Lexus pulled out
of the garage. Dr. Heinze drove a silver Lexus—

And yes, that was him behind the wheel.

She jumped in and started the car. She'd never before
been able to follow him after he left his office. Now she'd
know exactly what he was up to. And, eventually, where
he lived.

5. After arranging a time to meet here at the Lady's
and drive her into the wilds of the Jersey Pine Barrens,
Weezy left to meet Eddie, and Jack stayed behind.

As Glaeken rose and started for the door, Jack said,
"I want to show you something."

He pulled off the long-sleeved T he was wearing and
angled his wounded left arm toward him.

"Remember that from yesterday?"

The butterflies were gone and the wound had further
healed. No dressing necessary.

Glaeken peered at the arm, then looked at Jack with concern in his eyes.

"You're healing . . . quickly."

"Too quickly. What gives?"

"It's obvious, isn't it?"

"It's obvious in a direction I don't want it to be moving, so tell me something else. Please."

"I wish I could, but the answer is clear: As I begin to fail, you are progressing."

"Toward what?"

Jack knew the answer but needed to hear Glaeken say it.

"Toward what I used to be. You are the Heir, after all. And as you well know, upon my death, you assume my old place as Defender."

Jack did know.

"Swell."

Glaeken looked at the wound again and heaved a sigh. "I can only assume this means I haven't much time left."

That saddened Jack. Yeah, he wanted Glaeken to live forever for his own selfish reasons—so he wouldn't have to take on the Defender mantle. But he had others. He'd grown attached to the old guy. Glaeken had a quiet nobility that appealed to him. He was a walking trove of arcane knowledge. With his passing, humanity would lose someone unique and infinitely valuable.

"How much do you think? I mean, this is all new to me."

Glaeken smiled. "It's new to me as well. I've never died before, so I have no idea." The smile faded. "But I'd hoped to outlive Magda. Without me . . ." He looked at Jack. "May I ask you a favor?"

Jack sensed what was coming. "Look after her? Sure.

Gia and I will see she's well taken care of. And you know Weezy will pitch in."

"Thank you. That's a comfort. I want her to stay right where she is. Any change in her surroundings worsens her confusion. If she was moved to another apartment, it would upset her terribly. I don't want her upset."

Jack slipped back into his T-shirt. "Don't worry. I'll see to it."

"Good. I knew I could count on you." He turned toward the door, then swung back. "Oh, and don't worry about paying for her care. I—"

"I've got plenty of money stashed away."

"You won't need it. I've left everything to you."

"What do you mean, 'everything'?"

"All that I own. You are the Heir, after all, so you will be my heir as well—my sole heir."

"You don't have any kids?"

"Hundreds. But they're all gone. And Magda and I never had any, so you're it. You'll own this building and all my other holdings, including the Foster tract in the Barrens."

Jack shook his head. Me . . . owning a building on CPW—

"Wait. I can't inherit anything. I don't exist. No Social Security number, no property, never paid taxes."

He'd run into this problem when Gia was pregnant. Without an official existence, he couldn't be a child's legal parent.

Glaeken smiled again. "I'm aware of that. And I've been aware of *you* for a long time. I knew this day would come, so, maybe a dozen years ago I had someone create an alter ego for you. You, as you are now, have a corporeal life but no legal existence. This other entity has a legal existence but no life. He draws a salary from me and pays all proper taxes on it. He has your face and your fingerprints. He is named in my will and you will assume that identity whenever you need to access the assets I will leave to you."

"But I don't need—"

"A few billion dollars? Of course you don't. No one does. But it's got to go somewhere."

Jack swallowed. "Billions?"

Glaeken shrugged. "Give or take. I'm not sure of the exact figure. I've had a long time to accrue treasures and property, and they all tend to increase in value over time."

Billions . . . the responsibility was daunting. But then . . .

"This is all working under the assumption that there'll be anything to inherit. People who've had a peek at the future say it all goes dark sometime in the spring. That's not far off."

Glaeken nodded gravely. "Yes. If Rasalom gets his way, if he succeeds in bringing about the Change, this conversation becomes moot. Ironic in a way. He's wanted me dead for all these millennia. But now that he has the upper hand, now that he's so close to succeeding, he wants me to live—so he can rub my nose in the Change before he destroys me. And in a way, I will deserve that."

That startled Jack. "Deserve? How?"

"Because I could have ended the One back in the fifteenth century when I trapped him in the Keep. But I didn't. I thought our existences were linked, and if I destroyed him, the Ally would have no further use for me, and would destroy me in turn. So I locked him away for what I thought was forever. Well, not forever, just until I tired of the world. I wanted the decision to make my exit to be my own, and to choose the time of that exit. When

I was ready I would return to the Keep and end him. But the German Army ruined that plan."

"You couldn't have known."

He shook his head. "Pure selfishness on my part. I'd lived for thousands of years. I could have risked it. So now, if we lose, I deserve whatever happens to me."

Jack found the thought intolerable.

"Not if I find him first."

"But should I die before anything happens, promise me you'll use some of the inheritance to keep Magda comfortable."

"Of course. Absolutely. Anything and everything she needs."

He clapped Jack on the shoulder. "Good. Good."

Glaeken headed for the hall and the elevator, leaving Jack alone with the Lady.

"I have sensed you undergoing a change for a while," she said.

She hadn't moved from her place at the table. Her gaze was serene, her voice low.

"Really? Why didn't you tell me?"

"I know you do not want it. The realization has caused you only pain. What purpose would telling you serve?"

Good point. He was glad he hadn't known. He cocked his head toward the door where Glaeken had exited.

"And him? Any idea how long he's got?"

"Not long. His heart is failing—not his will to live on and fight. Those will never fail in that one. But the pump itself is old and it is tired. He will not see midsummer's eve."

"When's that?"

"In the latter half of June."

Shaken, Jack pulled out a chair and dropped into it. One thing to say he hasn't got much time left, but to hear

it narrowed down like that. Early March now . . . that
meant . . .

"Glaeken's got less than four months to live?"

The Lady nodded. "I cannot say the exact day, but the
way his light is fading, it cannot last too long."

Jack felt his throat constrict. He'd bumped into
Glaeken—as Mr. Foster—once as a kid, but had come to
know him only last May, not even a year ago. Yet he felt
as if he'd known him all his life.

"I'm going to miss him."

"*You're* going to miss him!" the Lady said. "He's been
my friend since the First Age. We've been the only con-
stants in each other's lives over these many millennia." She
pointed at Jack. "It rests in your hands to see that his few
remaining days are not reduced to even fewer by the One."

Right. Eliminate Rasalom first.

"Any sense of where he might be?"

She shook her head. "I sense him most often to the
east, but he seems ever on the move."

"To the east . . . Monroe?"

"Where he was conceived . . . perhaps. Perhaps farther. Perhaps Europe."

This was no help.

"Well, tonight I'm going to meet with someone who
might know the One's whereabouts."

"Someone who knows is not likely to tell you."

"Oh, if he knows, he'll tell me."

6. "Are you really going to eat that?" Weezy said,
eyeing Eddie's thick pastrami on rye. "All of it?"

He smiled. "Every freakin' bite."

Weezy shook her head. If the meat wasn't stacked a

full two inches, it was close. She looked around at the
Lower East Side kosher deli Eddie had chosen—Moishe's
on Second Avenue.

"How'd you find this place?" she said as he took a
great-white bite. He had a sublet in the West Village, on
the opposite side of the island.

He chewed, swallowed, and sipped his Pepsi One.

"I wander the city most of the day. I mean, nothing else
to do. I wandered in here for breakfast once and liked it."

"Youse folks okay here?" said a high-pitched, cigarette-
scorched voice with an aggressive Brooklyn accent.

Weezy studied their waitress. She looked seventy and
was built like Olive Oyl, but with a widow's hump and
hair the color of a caution light. She seemed to have a pot
of coffee grafted to her hand. Her name tag read *Sally*
and her eye makeup was a wonder—a rainbow of blue
hues applied like spackle.

"We're doing great," Weezy told her.

"You ain't touched your lox. Eat up. You never know
when you're gonna get to eat again."

As Sally wandered away in search of needy coffee
cups, Weezy forked a piece of the salmon into her mouth.
She wasn't particularly hungry. Not after seeing the
Lady pierce herself with that sword.

She nodded at Eddie who'd just taken another huge
bite. "I don't think you'll have to eat again for a week."

She noticed he'd gained some weight since she'd last
seen him, though nothing like the Pugsley pudginess of
his teen years. He was either letting his sandy hair grow
longer or hadn't bothered to get it cut.

"Still working out?"

He shrugged. "What's the point?"

"Same point as before, I guess."

"For what?" he said with some heat. "I played by all

the rules, Weez. I slimmed down, I got in shape, I worked hard, gave good value to my clients. And where did it get me? I had to abandon my business, I'm afraid to go back to my house, I'm subletting a roach-infested apartment. What went wrong?"

He'd never been the type to feel sorry for himself. Maybe he was simply bored and frustrated. Either way, she would let him answer his own question.

"I think you know what went wrong."

He sighed. "Yeah. I joined the Order."

Bull's-eye.

They'd discussed this before but she'd never gotten a satisfactory answer.

"Why, Eddie?"

He shrugged. "At the time it was, 'Why not?'" He raised a hand as she opened her mouth to reply. "I know, I know. You always categorized it as one of the sinister forces in the world, one of the powers guiding the Secret History. But do you know how that sounds to the average person?"

"Yeah. Crazy. Plus I did have my emotional problems, and I was diagnosed as manic-depressive, so I don't blame you one bit for dismissing what I said."

"It went beyond dismissing, you know. I got to the point where if you said something was black, I'd assume it was white."

She felt her throat tighten and her eyes fill. She blinked back tears.

Eddie reached across and covered her hand. "I'm sorry, Weez. I didn't mean—"

"No-no. It's okay. It wasn't just you. Mom and Dad were the same, and the kids in school. Every time I opened my mouth, eyes would roll. Finally I simply shut up. And now . . ."

"Now you know you were right all along."

"And wish I weren't. I wish this were all the product of a mind careening out of control due to a screwed-up soup of neurotransmitters." She squeezed his hand. "But Eddie, it's worse and more fantastic than I ever suspected."

He frowned. "More fantastic? How—?"

"Trust me?" She squeezed his hand harder. "I'm saying it's black."

He hesitated a heartbeat, then nodded. "Then black it is. *How* black?"

Weezy closed her eyes and swallowed a sob of joy. Breakthrough. Her brother believed her . . . finally believed her.

"Black-hole black."

He shook his head. "That book of yours—"

"The Compendium of Srem."

"Yeah, that. There's nothing else in the world like it. That was a clue. And then the Order turning against me."

"They were never *for* you."

"Pretty obvious now, but they come on so benign, with such a seductive line. All the movers and shakers belong, and you can belong too—*if* you qualify."

Weezy nodded. "That's the grabber."

"Damn right it is. Appeals to the elitism in all of us. And it's not a marketing tool. You really do have to qualify. They put you through a rigorous vetting that lots of people don't pass."

" 'Many are called but few are chosen.' "

"You're quoting Jesus now?"

She shrugged. "Whatever fits."

"Well, whatever their criteria, I was chosen. I look back and can't believe I let them brand me. That's how seductive it is. I spent six years in blissful ignorance until . . ."

"Until I upset the apple cart."

"Turned on the light is more like it." He shook his head again. "The Order was going to kill me."

Right . . . bad enough Eddie had learned something he wasn't supposed to know, he'd mentioned it to the wrong person.

He added, "They would have if Jack hadn't interfered."

Weezy had to smile. "He's very good at interfering."

Had it been only two weeks?

"You should have seen him, Weez. He beat the crap out of some guy named Szeto, then killed the guy who was driving me on my one-way trip. I mean, killed him like you or I would swat a fly."

"Well, the driver *was* trying to shoot you."

"I know that." He barked a brittle laugh. "Don't get me wrong. I'm not being the least bit critical. You'd told me he'd killed to protect you, but the image wouldn't stick. Then I saw him in action and he was . . . the best way I can put it is coldly efficient. It was like someone else had taken over."

Weezy nodded. "He's able to do that. It's like he has a switch that can turn off every emotion and allow him to do what has to be done without hesitation."

"Well, I don't have that, but I do want to get involved."

"In what?"

"In getting in the Order's way. They've made a mess of my life, so I'd like to return the favor."

A part of Weezy immediately disliked this. The last time he'd been proactive hadn't turned out so well.

"I don't know, Eddie . . ."

He leaned forward. "Why not? You don't think I can be useful?"

"You're maybe a little too emotionally involved."

"I'm an actuary, Weez." He tapped a temple. "A numbers guy. I can be dispassionate, especially about probabilities."

"But you have no idea of the scope of what we're up against. The Order is just the tip of the tip of an unimaginable iceberg. Meanwhile, humanity, existence as we know it, is sunning itself on the decks of the *Titanic*."

He frowned. "'Humanity' . . . 'existence as we know it'?"

She sensed a reflexive doubt.

"Listen to me, Eddie: It's *black*."

He hesitated, then nodded. "Okay. Black. I accept that it's black because I trust you. But *you* never take things simply on faith, so don't expect me to. You need to educate me."

She wished he could have been at the Lady's just a little while ago. Seeing that flap of skin melt into her back . . . that would have been a combination education and big-time doubt eraser.

She tapped her backpack. "I've got the *Compendium*. I'm going to give you a crash course in the Conflict."

"The Conflict?"

"With an uppercase *C*." She looked around. "But not here. Eat up and we'll go to your apartment. We'll start with the First Age."

He frowned. "That little black pyramid you found as a kid . . . you said it was from some First Age."

"It was, Eddie. It's all connected. Everything is connected."

Wait till she told him about the Otherness and the Ally and the Lady—he'd grown up knowing her as Mrs. Clevenger—and all the rest. The big question: Would he be able to handle the fact that he and the rest of humanity were property?

7. Hank Thompson popped into Drexler's office to see if he'd calmed down from yesterday. And to see if maybe he'd explain his "you might be the most surprised of all" remark. It had bothered him yesterday, but after last night's dream . . .

The Kicker Man in trouble again, worse this time. Just like the past few nights, he'd been under attack by a flock of birds or things that looked like birds—like in that movie where the birds turned on people. Just like before, they swarmed him, but this time they knocked him down and wouldn't let him get up. And at the end he'd just lain there as they pecked at him.

Gave Hank the creeps.

Annoying Drexler would take the edge off.

But instead of Drexler he found his enforcer, Szeto, in the office. Not just in the office, but seated behind Drexler's desk. The Kickers had their fair share—some said *more* than their fair share—of scary guys, but Hank had always found Szeto even scarier. Everything about the guy was black, from his eyes to his hair—Hank had always wanted to ask if he dyed it—to his clothes. He looked better than he had a couple of weeks ago when someone worked him over real good. Anyone who could put that kind of hurt on Szeto had to be one tough mother.

"Where's the boss?"

"Mister Drexler not in today," he said in English warped by an Eastern European accent. Russian? Romanian? Hungarian? They all sounded the same to Hank.

Then he raised his black-booted feet and plopped them on the desk.

"Don't know if the boss would like that."

"Do I look worried?"

Hank noted the smug tone. What was going down here? A little palace revolt in the works?

Szeto smiled. "Is something I can help you with?"

Hank was about to say no, then remembered a little research Szeto had been assigned last month.

"Remember those guys you were supposed to look into? The one who'd been a kid when Drexler met him—the friend of the brother and sister you were hunting—and John Tyleski, the one who stole something from me?"

Stole the *Compendium of Srem* . . . Hank couldn't believe he'd allowed that to happen. He still lay awake some nights dreaming of strangling that son of a bitch.

Szeto shook his head. "Both are dead ends. The boy disappears during college. No record, not of taxes or even Social Security number. Your man, Tyleski, he lives only on paper. Has credit card and Social Security but address is mailbox."

Hank wandered around the office. The news was hardly a surprise. About a year ago—in fact, next month would make it exactly a year—this asshole Tyleski had presented himself as a reporter from the Trenton *Times* who wanted to interview him about his book and the growing Kicker movement. Back then, Hank would ramble on to anyone who'd listen. The guy had asked all the wrong questions—hell, they almost got into a fight. Hank ran a check and found out the Trenton *Times* had never heard of John Tyleski. And then he went and robbed Hank of what was unquestionably the most valuable book on Earth—mugged him and snatched it in broad daylight.

Hank couldn't report the theft, of course, because the book had been stolen from the Museum of Natural History by one of his Kickers.

But wait . . .

Certain tidbits began to circulate in his head, bouncing off each other, looking for ways to fit together.

"Check this out: We've got a real person—personally known to our good buddy Drexler—who grows up and disappears. Later on there's a person who uses the name of a man who exists only on paper." He turned to Szeto. "Could the first guy have become the second?"

Szeto looked mildly interested. "Possible. But not probable."

"Tyleski knew more about me and other things than anybody should know." That had become apparent to Hank during the interview. "And then last summer up pops this guy who Tasers your boss and me while we're trailing the *Fhinntmanchca*. Only Drexler got a look at him."

Szeto smirked. "No. You must have seen him as well. I understand he was posing as Kicker and was in and out of here many times."

Hank had been down with a zillion Taser volts in him and not noticing a whole lot of what was going on in his immediate vicinity. The guy had been wearing a beard so it was hard to sync up memories of Tyleski with Drexler's description of the Taser guy. No point in getting sidetracked into the possibility that Tyleski could have grown a beard and been right under Hank's nose for who the hell knew how long.

"According to Drexler, the Taser guy had brown hair and brown eyes, just like Tyleski, and he *also* knew all sorts of stuff no one outside the Order should know. So, couldn't he and Tyleski be the same person?"

Szeto looked a little more interested. "Possible."

"But still not probable?"

"I do not know."

"Can we agree on still improbable, but less so?"

Szeto shrugged. "If you wish."

"Good. Then, as I recall, last summer you were looking for a woman who knew lots more than she should."

Szeto's eyes flashed. "Louise Myers, yes. We know where is bitch but the One does not wish her touched."

"But what if we—?"

"The One has spoken."

Hank sighed. The One, the One, the One.

"Okay. Be that as it may, I recall that she had a protector who killed just about every man you sent against her. A man you never saw and could never find. And the Myers gal comes from that same town as the man Drexler knew as a boy, the one who vanished without a trace."

Szeto dropped his feet from the desk and leaned forward. "You really think . . . ?"

"All I'm saying is we've got three guys messing with us—'Tyleski,' the Taser guy, and the killer—and no one knows who they are or where they are. They're untraceable."

"But you mention boy."

"Yeah. The boy—a *fourth* guy we can't find. A circle is a perfect shape, and I see things circling back to a certain boy in that small town in Jersey. Could all four mystery men turn out to be just one guy?"

Szeto pounded his fist on the desk. "But we do not know where he is!"

"The boy's got to have family—"

"All dead or disappeared."

"Then we're left with Louise Myers, who you're afraid to touch."

Szeto smiled like a snake. "You are free to approach her. Do not let me stop you."

Going against the One . . . uh-uh.

"Well then, looks like we're stuck, amigo."

"No. Not stuck. He has been to high school and to university. We can get picture—"

"Right-right-right. Yearbooks." Hank hadn't thought of that.

"And you can see if face is same as Tyleski."

"Well, that'll answer some questions about *who* he is, but we won't be any closer to knowing *where*. Let's just hope that if the One changes his mind about the Myers babe, he lets your people know. Because she can point us to him, and I sorely want to get my hands on that fucker."

Szeto rose to his feet and puffed up behind the desk. "The One speaks to me. He will tell me first."

Hank stared at Szeto as the implications of that remark sank in.

First?

"I thought he spoke to your boss—"

"No. Speaks to *me*. He comes to *me* for solution to problems. If he does not wish Myers woman disturbed, okay. I am in her hometown many times. I can find other way perhaps."

"In Jersey? What for?"

"Is not your concern. The One gives me many things to do and I am taking care of them all."

Many things to do?

"Like what?"

That smirk again. "If the One wishes you to know, I am sure he will tell you."

Had Drexler been taken out of the loop? Hank didn't like that. Not one bit. Because if Drexler had been booted aside, Hank might be next.

. . . You might be the most surprised of all . . .

Hell, he might have been given the boot already and didn't even know it.

8. Dawn followed Dr. Heinze through the Midtown Tunnel onto the Long Island Expressway. Her stomach totally knotted when he turned off on Woodhaven Boulevard and headed south into Rego Park. She'd grown up in this area. He continued on to Forest Hills where he eventually parked his car in the driveway of a two-story brick house with a manicured lawn and shrubbery that probably looked beautiful in season.

Home again, home again, jiggety-jig.

Now where had that come from? Oh, yeah. Her mother used to recite that nursery rhyme line every time they pulled into their driveway.

Dawn's throat tightened. God, how she missed her.

She shook it off and stared at the house. Well, Dr. Heinze, I now know where you live.

What she was going to do with that information, Dawn hadn't a clue, but she tucked the address away, just in case . . .

She wound her way back to Queens Boulevard and Rego Park, and slowed as she passed the Tower Diner where she used to wait tables . . . where she first met Jerry Bethlehem or whatever his real name was . . . where he started spinning the lies that led her into his bed and got her pregnant with the child she was now chasing.

Full circle.

Her hands seemed to have a life of their own as they turned the wheel, taking her off Queens Boulevard into the confusing local residential streets. She headed for 68th Drive, which paralleled 68th Road and 68th Avenue. She slowed before an older, stucco-walled house with high-peaked gables and an attached two-car garage. On impulse she pulled into the driveway.

Home again, home again, jiggety-jig.

Mom's house. The house Dawn had left to move in with Jerry. She remembered it being better kept, then realized it had been almost a year since her mother had died in there, leaving a huge hole in her life.

A sob burst from her as she saw the foreclosure sign. Mom had loved that place, had worked so hard to earn it, and now . . .

She stared at the darkened windows.

What would you do, Mom? Would you tell me to find my baby or let him go?

Dawn realized her mother might very well tell her to let him go. She'd warned her against Jerry from the get-go, but Dawn wouldn't listen. And Dawn was totally sure she'd tell her now that nothing good could ever come from something that came from Jerry.

And maybe she was right.

But I can't let it go, Mom. I can't.

A car pulled out of a driveway two doors down—the Schanz house. It turned this way and slowed as it approached, the driver probably wondering about a car parked outside the deserted Pickering place. Dawn's pulse picked up as she recognized Mrs. Schanz behind the wheel. Couldn't be seen here by that old busybody—not when she was a "person of interest" in her mother's death.

She turned her head, praying the biddy wouldn't recognize her in the failing light.

After Mrs. Schanz moved on, Dawn backed out and gunned away. She headed back to Manhattan, but she'd be back in the morning to trail Dr. Heinze from his house to the foundation—just to make sure he didn't make any stops between.

She shook her head, realizing how this had totally become a sickness. But she couldn't let go. She couldn't.

9. A voice had invaded Hank's head. A cut from his conversation with Szeto kept playing and replaying as he walked up from the Lodge toward Allen Street.

"The One speaks to me. He will tell me first."

"I thought he spoke to your boss—"

"No. Speaks to me."

Couple that with how distracted Drexler had seemed the last time he'd seen him—

No, more than distracted—upset. Drexler was pretty damn near the most together, focused guy he'd ever met. But not yesterday. Yesterday he looked like he was being held together by spit and baling wire.

Had something gone wrong at the Order? Their High Council had an inside track on everything connected to the Change, and Drexler was Hank's connection to those bozos. Hank was counting on riding with them to Mover-Shaker status after the Change.

But then Drexler had made that "the most surprised of all" remark.

Hank had to get all this straightened out, and the only guy he knew who could do that was Drexler.

But he wasn't answering his phone. Hank had left half a dozen messages.

Only one thing to do. Go over there and get some face time, whether Drexler liked it or not.

Hank reached Allen Street and found it at a standstill. Something must have happened on the outward-bound Williamsburg Bridge around the corner. He'd planned on taking a cab but Drexler's place wasn't all that far away. He decided to walk.

10. "Hello, Mister Drexler."

Ernst had just stepped into his dark and supposedly empty apartment. He fumbled with the grocery bag he was carrying, almost dropping it in shock at the sound of the voice.

The One would occasionally surprise him by suddenly appearing in his office or apartment. But this was not the One's voice. Ernst almost wished it were. It would mean . . .

"Who are you?"

"An old acquaintance."

Ernst felt for the wall switch, found and flipped it. The light revealed a nondescript man in his midthirties relaxing in a chair on the far side of the room. He looked like someone off the street: jeans, baseball cap, sweatshirt. He was clean shaven, with brown hair, brown eyes . . . and was that one of Ernst's Grolsch lagers in his hand?

Something about his face ignited a spark of familiarity, but not bright enough for recognition.

"You look familiar . . ."

"Remember your little sojourn at the Lodge in Johnson, New Jersey?"

And then it all came crashing back.

"Jack."

The man nodded. "Your former groundskeeper."

Controlling his initial shock, Ernst walked across his front room and set the bag on the counter. As the answers to a number of long-running questions began to flash through his mind, he realized he might be in mortal danger.

Might be. Jack certainly had changed from the skinny teenager Ernst had known. He'd filled out but remained wiry instead of bulky. He didn't look the least bit threatening. In fact, he appeared perfectly innocuous.

But if what Ernst suspected were true, he was anything but. Hard to believe, looking at him now, but no one knew better than Ernst how appearances could deceive.

Talk . . . get him talking.

"How did you get in here?"

"The door."

"And how did you reach the door?"

"The stairs."

Ernst clenched his jaw. The building was supposed to have excellent security. He'd have to have a talk with the management.

"I have armed guards from the Order who routinely . . ."

Jack was shaking his head. "No, you don't. Weeks ago I followed you from the Lodge and I've been watching this place on and off since. You don't have any extra security. And why should you? No one outside the Order knows who you are."

True. He had no enemies. Except perhaps the man seated before him.

Stay cool and keep him talking.

"Rather ironic, don't you think, that while you've been stalking me, I've been looking for you?"

"I assumed that," Jack said.

"Am I so predictable?"

"After you learned that Weezy Myers was Weezy Connell of Johnson, En-Jay, and her brother Eddie was a member of the Order, I figured it wouldn't take you long to start wondering what had happened to the third musketeer."

"Yes, it was idle at first. Then I learned that you had seemingly dropped off the face of the Earth."

"Still on Earth, just off the radar."

"But now you're here. Any particular reason?"

"A little conversation."

"Nothing else?"

"That depends."

"On what?"

"On how the conversation goes."

That had just enough of an ominous ring to bunch the muscles at the back of Ernst's neck.

"Will we be a while?"

"Depends."

Ernst didn't ask again on what. Instead he pointed to the green bottle in Jack's hand.

"I could use one of those. Shall I get you another?"

"Thanks. I'll come with you."

He realized it had been too much to hope for Jack to leave him alone in the kitchen, but it had been worth a try.

"I need to put some food away as well."

A few months ago he'd found a wonderful German butcher, a man who made superb bratwurst. Brats had always been a comfort food for him, but over the years he had avoided too many of them for health reasons. After yesterday he didn't see much point in worrying about his health, and he was in desperate need of comfort.

Jack hovered as he placed the perishables in the refrigerator, and Ernst thought about that term.

Perishable . . . we're all perishable, but am I about to perish?

He removed a pair of bottles.

"Hope you don't mind that I helped myself," Jack said. "Not too many people stock Grolsch. Hard to resist."

Keep him talking . . .

"Yes, the Dutch make excellent lagers, but not quite up to my favorite—Märzen."

He found an opener and popped the caps. He handed a bottle to Jack and grabbed a Pilsner glass for himself—he didn't drink from bottles. They returned to the front room where Ernst made a show of searching for coasters. He knew exactly where they were but opened two wrong drawers first. He pulled a Taser from the second and palmed it, thumbing the *ON* switch before quickly slipping it into his suit coat pocket as he pretended to discover the coasters in the third.

Now he felt a little safer. He had no idea how this might turn out, but at least he could protect himself.

He handed Jack a coaster and they settled into upholstered chairs, facing across a glass-top table.

"If I may ask," he said, keeping his tone light, "how did you, as you phrase it, drop off the radar so completely? After a cursory search found no trace of you, I put some very skilled people to work looking for you. They came up with nothing."

He shrugged. "I was never on the radar. Never bothered applying for a Social Security number, always worked for cash." A quick smile. "You always paid me cash, remember?"

Ernst nodded. He remembered. Petty cash.

"A long time ago." Half a lifetime.

"Why were you so intent on finding me?"

"You were a blank space that needed filling in. A mystery man. Brother Connell said you were a repairman, but I began to wonder if you might be related to another mystery man."

"Really? And who might that be?"

How did he phrase this? Should he choose his words carefully? Why? Jack's appearance here pretty much confirmed his suspicions, although he still found it hard to believe.

Might as well simply come out and say it.

"Someone involved with the Connells was using deadly force against the Order."

Not a trace of surprise in Jack's eyes as he said, "Now why would anyone do that? I mean, considering the caliber of people you sent against them."

Ernst felt his saliva began to evaporate. Jack had just admitted to being that man. One thing to suspect, but to have it confirmed in such a matter-of-fact tone . . .

The skinny, innocent kid who had mowed the Lodge's lawn had grown into a cold-blooded killer. Granted, he had been facing equally cold-blooded killers, but he had proved just as ruthless and much more efficient.

Ernst was trapped here with a very, very dangerous man. Was he armed? Of course he was.

Keep him talking.

He forced calm and shook his head. No need to fake bafflement. "How did that boy pulling the lawn mower behind his bike wind up . . . ?" He shook his head again.

"Necessity."

"What could—?"

He held up a hand. "I didn't come here to tell my life story."

"Then why *did* you come?"

"I've got a question, and you've got the answer. At least I'm assuming you do."

Only "a" question? That was a relief. But what would happen if he couldn't answer it?

"You seem awfully sure of that. Let's see if you're right. Go ahead: Ask."

Jack spoke and the question seemed to hover in the air between them. Clear, succinct, to the point. He could almost see the words floating before him, but he couldn't quite grasp their meaning. It sounded as if he'd said . . . but no . . . he couldn't have.

"Pardon?"

"How do I go about finding the One?"

Ernst's muscles seized, freezing him in place. His first impression had been correct. He'd truly asked about the One. But . . . impossible. He couldn't know about him.

And then Ernst flashed back on a conversation with the One, perhaps a month ago. He had appeared in Ernst's office and asked what he knew about the Order's Lodge in Johnson, New Jersey. He'd made Ernst recount his stay there in excruciating detail. Ernst hadn't perceived it at the time, but in light of what was transpiring at this moment, it occurred to him that the One had seemed especially interested in the young groundskeeper and his girlfriend who had invaded the Lodge one night with near disastrous consequences. Ernst had thought he was interested in the event, but now it was clear he'd been interested in Jack.

An unexpected symmetry: the One asking about Jack, and now Jack asking about the One.

"The one?" Ernst fought to maintain a neutral, mildly curious expression as he took a sip of his beer. He noticed the glass shaking in his hand. "The one what?"

Jack looked annoyed and the mild brown eyes hardened. "No games. I asked you a straight question. I expect a straight answer. You know exactly who I'm talking about: the One . . . the point man for the Otherness . . . Rasalom."

Ernst choked and spewed beer across the table.

"Don't speak his name!"

But a bigger shock than hearing the name said aloud was the realization that Jack knew it. Only the High Council of Seven and precious few others were privileged with the One's name. Even Ernst wasn't supposed to know it, but he'd heard it from his father shortly before he died.

Jack merely stared at him, waiting.

Ernst stared back as other connections formed. Jack knew something only a few in the Order were aware of. So had another man . . . the bearded man who'd accosted him in Central Park. He'd known about the One and the *Fhinntmanchca*. He'd pressed a good Austrian pistol under his chin and asked him questions.

And then Tasered him.

He remembered the feel of the current jolting through him, running from the back of his neck down his spine and limbs, coursing through his chest. Pain and helplessness— his useless muscles felt as if they'd melted.

He remembered the humiliation.

He imagined a beard on Jack and—yes . . . no question. Ernst had never seen the adult Jack, so he hadn't recognized him through the beard. No doubt about it.

In a burst of anger he slid his hand toward the pocket where his own Taser hid. He'd bought it after the incident, hoping someday he'd have a chance to return the favor when he caught up to the mystery man. His fingers brushed against the comforting lump, then withdrew.

He was too far away. He'd bide his time till Jack was closer. Then . . .

"Last summer," Ernst said. "In the park. That was you."

Jack nodded. "I was in a rush chasing that *Fhinn*-thing, and neglected to introduce myself. Sorry."

"The man I was with—"

"Hank Thompson."

No surprise there. If he knew the One's taken name,

he probably knew as much about Thompson as Ernst did.

"Yes. He didn't see you but is under the impression that you've met before."

Jack nodded. "We have."

"You do get around."

"Not by choice."

Ernst wasn't sure what that meant, but didn't want to waste time pursuing it when he had another question burning to be asked.

"How do you know about the One? How do you know his name?"

"We've met—a couple of times, in fact."

The words struck like a blow. "Met? I don't believe you. How could you have met the One? And if you really know him, why do you need me to find him?"

"We're not on the best of terms."

And then it became clear.

"You're aligned with the Enemy."

That was the reason for the One's interest in him.

Jack frowned. " 'Enemy'?" Then nodded. "Oh, right. From your end, I work for the Enemy. From mine, *you* do."

Ernst remembered secretly testing him for the Taint as a teen.

"How does someone so rich with the Taint come to oppose the Otherness?"

Jack shook his head. "Only the Ally can answer that. But you tell me: How does anyone with half a brain—and you've always struck me as an intelligent man—come to work for a force that is out to put some serious hurt on humanity?"

"Because the Otherness is going to *win*. I have no

doubts about that and neither should you. Those who help it win will not, as you put it, have the hurt put on them."

Jack gave him a lopsided grin. "You really believe that? You really think you can trust something like the Otherness?"

"As much as you trust your so-called Ally."

Something flickered across Jack's features. Pain?

"I don't trust the so-called Ally. Not a bit. It keeps the Otherness at bay. That's all it's good for. And not for our sake. It has its own agenda. I learned that the hard way."

Interesting. The Enemy—Jack's Ally—was reputed to be as ruthless as the Otherness.

"Really? How?"

Instead of answering, Jack said, "You don't strike me as a man with many illusions, so why do you think you'll be spared if the Change comes?"

"*When* it comes," Ernst said, "the One will ascend to power, and those who aided him will ascend with him."

"Right. You and your buddies in the Order will be seated at the right hand of God." Jack laughed. "At the risk of sounding like John McEnroe, you can*not* be serious."

"The multimillennial existence of the Septimus Order has been devoted to that. Our lore confirms it."

He laughed again. "And you're basing this on what— the word of a guy who feeds on pain and misery? Not exactly what I'd call an ironclad guarantee. After the Change he won't need you or your Order anymore, Drexler. He'll be top dog and all bets will be off. New rules will be in place and he'll be the one making them."

The words cut to the heart of Ernst's own misgivings. He'd taken it as a matter of course that if the Change occurred during his lifetime he would be part of it. But would he?

Jack wouldn't stop.

"What kind of leverage will you have, Drexler? Do you even have a promise? Did he ever say to you, 'When I take over, you'll be one of my lieutenants'?"

"Enough!"

Jack ignored him.

"I'll take that as a no. But think about it: Even if he did promise, you'd have only moral leverage, and we know what kind of moral code this creep lives by. We're talking about the guy who convinced Vlad that impaling people was an entertaining hobby."

"That's quite enough."

"Face it, Drexler: If the One gets his way, you'll be as screwed as the rest of us."

Ernst felt something snap within him. With a cry he leaped across the room, pulling the Taser from his pocket as he moved. When Jack raised an arm to ward him off, Ernst rammed the prongs of the Taser against it and pressed the button.

Nothing happened.

He pressed it again with the same result.

Still seated in his chair, Jack stared up at him, his smile almost sad as he shook his head.

Ernst felt a pressure against his throat and angled his gaze downward. He realized with a start that the pressure originated from the muzzle of that same Austrian pistol.

Where had that come from?

"Drop it and get back to your seat."

Ernst did just that, and watched as Jack rested the Glock on his lap and took a sip of his beer. He shifted his gaze to the Taser on the floor. What had gone wrong? It had been turned on, had had plenty of time to build a charge . . . It should have reduced Jack to twitching helplessness. What sort of man was this?

Jack looked at him. "Hit a nerve, huh?"

Ernst didn't answer.

What is happening to me?

Where was the icy control that had been his lifelong pride? His father would be ashamed of him for letting someone—his former teenage groundskeeper, of all people—goad him like that. And it was clear to him now that Jack had been doing just that.

Was that what this visit was about? To demonstrate that Ernst was not in control—not of who entered his home, not of his own emotions?

"Where is he?" Jack said.

That question again. Was *this* his true reason for coming?

"The One? I don't know."

Jack stared at him. Ernst tried to read his face. What next? Torture. Ernst didn't see Jack as a torturer, but he was rich with the Taint, and someone with so much of the Otherness in him might be capable of anything.

"It's true," he added. "The One answers to no one and has never felt the need or obligation to keep the Order informed of his whereabouts. Communication with the One is, fittingly, a one-way street. When he wants something from us, he contacts us. We do not contact him."

Jack kept staring in silence. He was beginning to make Ernst uncomfortable. Finally he broke it.

"When was your last contact with him?"

"Weeks ago."

"After your Jihad virus failed?"

How did he know that? Did he have a contact inside the Order? Oh, yes. Edward Connell. It must have been him.

Ernst saw no use in playing coy.

"Yes."

"Is that when he put out the hit on the Lady?"

Ernst stiffened and tried to hide it. "Yes."

Jack frowned. "You hesitated."

In truth, he didn't know when the One had ordered the attack. Szeto never mentioned it.

Ernst dodged that. "May I inquire as to why you wish to know his whereabouts?"

"I'm going to kill him."

Ernst barked a laugh. He couldn't help it. He waved a hand. "I apologize. Kill the One? Your hubris borders on the surreal."

Jack seemed unperturbed. "You think he's invulnerable?"

"Well, no. But he's so much older and wiser than you. If you know his taken name, then I'm sure you're aware that he's survived countless attacks over the thousands of years of his life, many of them launched by one of equal longevity who is far more capable than you. And yet he is still standing."

"So is the one who made those attacks."

"Ah, yes. The so-called Defender or Guardian or Paladin or whatever he's called these days. But where is he?"

Jack rose from his seat. "That was my question to you: Where is the One?"

"I told you: I don't know."

Jack closed the distance between them and stood over him, reaching into the pocket of his jacket.

Now what? Ernst wondered. A knife? A bullet?

No . . . something small and metallic in his hand. Ernst flinched as it landed in his lap.

"Your little gizmo will work better with that."

Ernst glanced down and saw the Taser's battery, then looked at Jack's retreating form.

"That's it?"

Jack turned at the door and pulled the hood of his sweatshirt up over his baseball cap. "That's it."

"But . . ." Ernst didn't know what to say.

"You say you don't know where he is or how to find him, and I believe you."

He was baffled. "Why?"

"Because if you knew, you'd tell me. Right?"

It hadn't occurred to Ernst until this moment, but if he did indeed know the whereabouts of the One . . .

"Yes . . . yes, I believe I would."

"Because you think I don't stand a chance against him, and you'd like to see me get my just deserts for thinking I can take him on. Right?"

"Exactly." This was uncanny.

He shrugged as he opened the door. "So there's no point in continuing this conversation."

He stepped into the hallway and closed the door behind him, leaving Ernst alone.

11. Ernst rose and locked the door. He felt a little safer after he slid the surface-mounted bolt into place, but not much.

What a jarring experience. But it had answered a slew of questions, solved some nagging mysteries.

Jack and the One had met . . . and the One had wanted to know more about Jack.

The man who had killed all those operatives Szeto had sent after the woman, stolen Thompson's *Compendium*, Tasered Ernst in Central Park, and done who knew what else . . . all were the same person . . . all were Jack the lawn-cutting teen.

And Jack was working for the Enemy. Not only working, but looking for the One . . . to kill him.

And that raised another question.

Why wasn't the Defender looking for the One? Why had an immortal sent a mortal to kill a fellow immortal?

It made no sense unless . . .

Ernst remembered his bizarre last meeting with the One. He had been enraged that the Jihad virus had not had the desired effect, and yet quite literally giddy—had actually laughed—about an unspecified event. He could hear his voice again as if he were in the room . . .

. . . *something* wonderful *happened yesterday. Something I should have suspected, but never dreamed possible . . . something that changes* everything *. . . at last I can take direct action . . . take matters into my own hands. I will finish this myself.*"

Two obstacles had stood in the path between the One and bringing about the Change: the Defender and the Lady.

No question that the Lady remained—Szeto's failed attempt on her life proved that.

. . . *At last I can take direct action . . .*

In all the One's moves against the Lady, he had stayed out of the picture, kept his hand hidden. Even with the *Fhinntmanchca*, he had remained in the background, orchestrating the attack through the Order and the Dormentalists and the Kickers. He had never taken direct action.

Now he felt he could.

What had changed?

The Defender? Had something happened to him? That might explain why Jack was so openly searching for the One.

If the Defender was out of the picture—and really, that

was a question being asked with increasing frequency over the years in the upper echelons of the Order: *Where was the Defender?*

During the months since the *Fhinntmanchca* debacle, it had become an incessant buzz.

Why hadn't the Defender stepped in—if not in time to stop it, then at least making himself known afterward? The incident should have goaded him into *some* sort of action.

But no . . . nothing.

The Defender hadn't been heard from since the dawn of World War II when it appeared he'd slain the One. No need for him to do anything after that. But then came the One's reincarnation in 1968. He could have— *should* have—acted then. Countless opportunities to snuff out the One for good must have presented themselves during the years he was growing to manhood.

But again . . . nothing.

Was it possible he'd been killed in the war? Caught in Dresden during the firebombing, perhaps? In the wrong place when a V2 smashed into London during the Battle of Britain?

Whatever the reason, the Defender had been conspicuous by his absence. And now Jack was taking on the task that should be the Defender's.

As Americans liked to say: What's wrong with this picture?

Everything.

. . . *Something I should have suspected, but never dreamed possible . . . something that changes* everything . . .

That "something" could only be that the Defender was no longer around. Which would indeed leave the One free to take direct action.

So . . . all that stood between the One and the Lady now was a lone mortal.

Jack didn't stand a chance.

Or did he?

Was that why the One had been asking about him? He couldn't possibly fear Jack . . . could he?

For some reason Jack seemed to think he could bring it off. Ernst had gathered from their brief conversation that the intelligent boy he'd known as a teen had not grown into a fool, so why did he think he could win? Did he know something Ernst didn't?

If he did succeed, the Change would be forestalled . . . indefinitely.

And that possibility brought back other things Jack had said, frightening things that had struck home . . .

12.   Hank had kept up a brisk pace on his trek and found himself puffing a little by the time he stopped at the corner across the street from Drexler's apartment building.

Out of shape. Back in the day before he became a best-selling author, he earned his pay through hard physical labor—and every so often he missed the simplicity of his slaughterhouse job. But, despite all the pain-in-the-ass picayune bullshit it entailed, being the King of Kickerdom was better. He had a purpose now, something he'd lacked before.

As he waited for the light to change he saw a guy in a hoodie come out the front entrance and signal an approaching cab. Hank gave him a casual glance and was turning away when the cab's headlights caught his face.

He knew that face. Where—?

Him! Shit, it was *him!*

Tyleski—the guy who stole the *Compendium*.

A burst of rage pushed Hank off the curb but he reined it in after two steps and stopped. The guy was getting into the cab and Hank would never reach him.

But he couldn't let him get away again. No fucking way.

He looked upstream and saw a couple of cabs barreling his way. He waved an arm and the one in the lead swerved across three lanes to stop in front of him. Hank jumped in and pointed to Tyleski's departing taxi across the street.

"Follow that cab!" he said, realizing how the words sounded as they spilled out.

But no wisecrack from the driver. He just hit the gas and followed.

Now what? Think.

Follow the guy home, find out where he lived, then arrange payback.

Wait. Shit happened. What if traffic snarled and he got away? This was a precious opportunity. Couldn't let chance screw it up. He needed backup. He could call Kewan and—

No. Szeto—call Szeto. Good chance this was the same guy he was looking for. He'd be more aggressive than Kewan. Tons more. He had a real hard-on for this guy.

He found his number and punched SEND.

"Yes."

"Hey, it's me. You know that guy we were talking about today, the guy you've been looking for? I'm following him in a cab as we speak, but I'm afraid I might lose him, so—"

"Do not lose him! I will call you right back."

Szeto was gone.

Hank looked at his phone and said, "'Do not lose him'? Well, fuck you."

Ahead, the guy's cab stopped at a light. Hank's pulled up right behind it. As they idled, waiting for green, Hank watched the silhouette of the guy's head. And wondered what the hell Szeto was planning. Had to be up to something. He wanted this guy.

The light changed and they started moving again. Hank drummed his fingers on his leg. Well, so far so good. Maybe he wouldn't need backup. Maybe—

His phone rang.

"Where are you?" Szeto said. His voice echoed like he was in hands-free mode or using the speaker on his phone.

Hank gave him the intersection.

"Going uptown?"

"You got it."

"What side he is seated?"

Wondering why that mattered, Hank double-checked the silhouette ahead.

"He's on the right."

"Good."

"Why is that good?"

"Just stay on phone and keep me posted."

Hank felt his steam rising.

"Hey, look. I brought you in as backup. I don't need—"

"Just stay with him. I will handle this."

Hank bit back a remark and let it go. Maybe better to let Szeto call the shots. That way, if they came up empty-handed, he'd have no one to blame but himself.

So he kept Szeto informed of their uptown progress, wondering what the enforcer had in mind, and wishing he'd get to it before—

A bright yellow Hummer roared through a red light

and T-boned the right side of the cab ahead of Hank, knocking it a good half dozen feet sideways. Hank's own cab screeched to a halt. A second later Szeto, carrying a pistol, jumped out of the Hummer. Hank watched, stunned and slack-jawed, as he ran around to the undamaged side. He pulled open the rear door and looked inside, then shoved the pistol into a shoulder holster and signaled to Hank to come help him.

Hank shook off his paralysis and jumped out. By the time he reached the damaged cab, Szeto was dragging an unconscious guy in a hoodie out the door. A van screeched to a halt beside them and the side door slid open. Hank helped load the guy into the van, then jumped in behind Szeto. They roared off, leaving the cab and the Hummer behind.

13.   Every jounce and bounce rammed a spike of pain through Jack's head. Vaguely familiar voices, one accented, echoed through cottony air . . .

". . . about the Hummer? . . . Stolen. This is he? . . . Yeah, that's him. Think he's your guy? . . . We will find out . . ."

Lying on his back. Where? What happened? He remembered leaving Drexler's, grabbing a cab, and then . . . what?

Seemed to be moving. Still in the cab?

No. Hard floor against his back.

God, his head. And his stomach felt ready to hurl.

Tried to open his eyes but the reluctant lids allowed him only a brief glimpse of blurred figures before losing strength and collapsing.

Tried to move but couldn't. Seemed to be—alarm shot through him as he struggled to move his arms. They'd been tied or taped.

The lump of his Glock was missing against the small of his back.

And then the cab or whatever he was in hit a pothole or a curb and took a big bounce and the world faded away . . .

14. Kristof stared at the man blinking up at him from the chair. He was securely taped into it. His Glock and backup pistol had been removed.

He turned to Thompson. "You are absolutely sure this is man who rob you?"

"Sure as shit." He flung the man's wallet across the room. "All his ID backs that up. John Fucking Tyleski." He leaned closer to the man, almost nose to nose. "Ain't that right?"

Tyleski looked up at him. Kristof was quite sure that was not his real name, but it would do for now. They would know his real name before this night was over. He had seemed confused before but his eyes had cleared and he appeared more alert now.

He blinked at Thompson. "Who are you?"

"You know goddamn well who I am."

"Never saw you before in my life."

Thompson bared his teeth as he cocked his right fist. Kristof grabbed his arm before he could strike.

"I do not want him knocked out again."

"I owe this guy, Szeto. So do you."

"I want him to talk. He cannot talk if he is unconscious."

"Talk, huh? You want talk? I saw a hardware store down the block. How about I pick us up a few tools to loosen him up?"

Kristof nodded. The Order had owned this top-floor loft and the one below it since the days before the meat-packing district became trendy. Thompson had kept his distance while Dieter and Erich were dragging Tyleski up the stairs from the street. But he'd gained swagger and confidence once the man was secured to the chair.

Just then Dieter and Erich returned from hiding the van.

Dieter stared at Tyleski. His English carried a thick German accent. "Kristof! I thought he looked familiar before, but now in the light, I am sure: This is the man from the park yesterday, the one who killed Claudiu and wounded Filip."

"Is he now?" Erich said with an equally heavy accent as he pulled out his pistol.

The revelation triggered an explosion of rage within Kristof but he managed to contain it. He raised a hand and stopped Erich.

"No. We have time for that later."

He pulled his own pistol from its holster and a three-inch suppressor from a side pocket. He made a show of screwing it onto the threaded end of the barrel.

"How much later?" Dieter asked, looking equally itchy to inflict damage on this man.

"After I have learned what I want to know, we shall play Last Shot Loser, the three of us—and Mister Thompson too, if he wishes."

"What's that?" Thompson said.

"We take turns shooting Mister Tyleski with one bullet each."

Thompson smiled. "Count me in. How do I win?"

"By not losing. You lose by killing him. The one who fires the kill shot must pay each of the other players one thousand dollars."

Thompson's grin broadened. "Oh, I'm definitely in. The way I see it, even if I lose, I win."

"But first, your suggestion about hardware store is excellent. Get whatever tools appeal to you, but for me . . . you are familiar with something called X-Acto knife?"

"Course I am."

"Get me one, or something quite like it."

"Planning a little cosmetic surgery?"

"In a way. First thing I do is cut off eyelids so he must watch whatever we do to him."

Dieter and Erich slapped palms as Thompson turned to Tyleski. "You are soooo fucked!"

Tyleski didn't react. Szeto hadn't expected much from him. A man like this would know better than to show fear, even if he were quaking inside. And the prospect of losing his eyelids should cause deep quaking. Kristof had seen men broken by that alone. Not so much because of the pain, but because of the finality of the mutilation, the realization that even if he survived, his life was changed, horribly and forever.

Thompson turned at the door. "Hey, we forgot about Drexler. Think he might be in on—oh, shit. You think he might have hit Drexler?"

That had occurred to Kristof, but he hadn't had time to check on it. Not that it would be such a terrible loss. Ernst Drexler had been bypassed by the One. That meant that the High Council might decide to elevate someone else to Actuator status. And since the One was dealing directly with Kristof Szeto, who better to choose?

But until that happened, Kristof would have to play the game.

He pulled out his phone. "You go," he told Thompson. He pointed to Dieter and Erich. "You two wait outside."

He didn't want them overhearing his conversation with Drexler. And he wanted a little time alone with the prisoner.

When the door closed behind them, he speed-dialed Drexler's number. Kristof couldn't help a stab of disappointment when he picked up on the third ring.

"Yes, Szeto?"

"You are aware that man we have been looking for was seen leaving your apartment building?"

A long pause, during which Kristof was certain that Drexler was wondering if he was being watched and whether to ask about it.

Instead he said, *"Jack from Johnson, New Jersey. Yes."*

"He visits you often?"

"Never before. He was looking for the One."

That took Kristof by surprise. He glanced at the man before him. Looking for the One? Was he mad?

"Why would he—?"

"Never mind that. Did you follow him?"

"Yes, of course. He is now guest at meatpacking place. He will soon be telling us many things we wish to know."

Another long pause, then, *"Don't do anything until I get there. I have a score to settle with that man."*

"Many have scores."

He ended the call and turned to the man.

"So . . . you are called John Tyleski. Another name for John is 'Jack,' yes? Are you called Jack?"

The man said nothing, merely stared at Kristof.

Kristof said, "I am making conversation. I know answers. I know you are Jack from Johnson, New Jersey. I have come to know your hometown very well lately. I know you grew up with Louise and Edward Connell.

I know you have killed many of my men." He lifted the man's Glock from the floor. "Probably with this very gun."

He wanted to smash the barrel across his face but held back. Men who had just recovered consciousness were too easily knocked out again. He needed him awake. Instead he leaned closer and pointed to the healing scars on his own face.

"And even though I did not see you, Jack, I know you were one who did this to me."

Still no response.

"You are looking for the One, yes? It is sure now that you will never find him, so you can tell me: Why do you look for him?"

Instead of continuing his impassive stare, Jack seemed to consider this. Finally he shrugged.

"I'm going to kill him."

Kristof couldn't help but laugh. "You are quite mad, you know."

"You won't think so when he's dead."

"Why do you want him dead?"

"I think you know."

Kristof realized he had finally met someone directly related to the Enemy. Almost everything he had done for the Order was intended to weaken the Enemy, but the men and women he had run up against along the way had not been directly connected to the Enemy, merely impeding the One's ascent. Here, at last, was someone with a direct connection.

"It is too bad you work for Enemy. You would have been strong fighter for Order."

"Not much of a joiner, Mister Szeto."

He knows my name, Kristof thought. How—?

Well, of course he would.

Jack said, "My turn for a question: Why work for a guy who's going to wreck the world if he wins?"

Kristof laughed again. "This is Enemy propaganda. 'The end of world as we know it.' Is like Church telling children they go to hell if they do not follow rules. When the One wins, *we* make rules."

Jack shook his head. "You're dealing with a guy who has one agenda—himself. You, Drexler, Thompson, the high-ups in your Order, you're all going to be left out in the cold with the rest of us when he changes the world to his own brand of hell."

Kristof kept his expression impassive, not wanting this man to know that he'd struck his most secret fear. Not that the world would be changed into a place of pain and terror—those were the laughable fantasies sold by the Enemy—but that he would not be elevated to a position of power. That fear had receded since the One had turned directly to him for assistance, but it had not vanished.

"I would love to prove you wrong, but unfortunately, you will not be around to see it."

"When does your master arrive?"

"Master?"

Kristof bristled at the comment but feigned confusion. He would so much enjoy making this man scream.

"The man in the wonderful ice cream suit."

"Oh, you must mean Drexler. No, I answer only to the One. In fact, soon I may be Drexler's master. The One comes to me now. In fact, he has engaged me for special project in your hometown. Isn't that interesting?"

Finally a reaction from the man—surprise . . . concern. "What project?"

Just then Kristof heard the door open. He turned and saw Drexler, wearing a long, dark herringbone overcoat over his white suit. He stepped in and closed the door behind him.

"Well, well," Drexler said, smiling at Jack. "We meet again. But this time I have the advantage."

15.   This Washington Street hardware store was tiny but it had everything. He found an X-Acto number two knife with a long, slim aluminum handle and a sharp-pointed number eleven blade.

Perfect for cutting off eyelids.

At least Hank thought it would be perfect. He shuddered at the thought of it happening to him. Something like that would never even have occurred to him. But Szeto seemed pretty comfortable with it. Like maybe this wouldn't be his first eyelidectomy.

Be the first for Hank. He was kind of looking forward to it. He'd never tortured anyone. Before becoming King of the Kickers, he'd earned his daily bread alternating between a knocker and a sticker in a slaughterhouse. The former involved shooting a steel bolt into cows' heads to knock them out; the latter meant slitting the cow's throat as it hung by a back leg from an overhead rail. So blood and guts were no problem.

Especially this guy's blood and guts. The son of a bitch had stolen his *Compendium of Srem*. But worse than that, he'd made a fool of Hank while doing it, right out in public on the streets of New York. Nothing too bad could happen to this guy.

But the thing was, Hank didn't want the guy to die before he told him where he'd stashed the *Compendium*. Or if he'd sold it, who to.

He found a pair of needle-nose pliers. Might be good for yanking off fingernails. He added that to his shopping basket and moved on till he came across some Drano Kitchen Crystals. Sprinkle some of that onto lidless eyes . . . oh, yeah.

He kept shopping . . .

16.
Szeto, Thompson, the Katzenjammer Killers who'd ambushed the Lady, and now Drexler.

Party time.

Jack wasn't sure if his nausea was from the concussion or the certainty of impending torture. Probably a little of both. He wondered how he'd hold up.

And he wondered how he'd landed here. He'd watched Drexler's apartment for a number of nights—no guards, no surveillance. Drexler hadn't had time to contact anyone to tail him, so how had he been set up?

Not that it mattered now. Barring a miracle, he was done. He wouldn't mind dying so much if it didn't mean leaving Gia and Vicky to fend for themselves in the coming Change. He did mind dying in agony. And worse, whoever found his body wouldn't be able to identify him—he had no identity. He'd wind up in Bellevue with a "John Doe" tag on his big toe.

Still smiling at him, Drexler reached into the pocket of the overcoat and pulled out his Taser.

"I replaced the battery."

"We have more interesting plans," Szeto said.

"Yes, but this is direct payback. He Tasered me in Central Park last summer and I am going to return the favor . . . many times."

Jack steeled himself. This wasn't going to be fun.

"Well, this is all right, I suppose," Szeto said. "It will soften him up for main event."

"By the way, how did you manage this?"

"Thompson was on his way to visit you when he spotted him leaving your building."

So that was it—one of those random events that screws up the most careful plans.

Drexler's eyebrows lifted as he looked around. "Thompson? Really? Where is he?"

"He returns soon with tools."

"Then we have no time to waste."

He turned and jammed the Taser against Szeto's neck.

Jack figured the shock on Szeto's face had to mirror his own as the man's muscles turned to overcooked spaghetti and he dropped to the floor. Jack watched him twitch, then looked at Drexler standing over him.

He knew he had a bad concussion. Did hallucinations go with it? If so, this was a doozy.

"All right. I give up. What was that all about? Not that I'm protesting or anything."

Drexler—Jack had to assume he was real—said nothing as he pulled a jackknife from his pocket, opened it, and cut the duct tape fastening Jack's right wrist to the chair. As Jack pulled it free, he handed him the knife.

"Finish yourself."

Jack went to work on his other wrist and realized his right shoulder hurt like hell. What had happened to it? But more important . . .

"What's going down here?"

Drexler didn't answer. Instead, he zapped Szeto again, then reached inside the man's leather coat. He removed the Tokarev and held it up, staring at the suppressor.

"Perfect."

He stepped back and pointed it at Szeto. The pistol went *phut-phut* as Drexler, with about as much ceremony as a carpenter tacking up wallboard, double-tapped the supine man in the forehead.

"Jeez," Jack whispered.

He finished freeing his left wrist and hurried on to his ankles. He didn't know what was playing out here but wanted all his limbs available for the next act.

Drexler turned and raised the Tokarev toward him. Jack was already making a move to deflect the barrel when Drexler flipped it so the grip was turned his way.

"Take this and hide it and be ready to use it."

"What?"

He opened the door and called out in what sounded like German. "*Sie zwei! Schnell kommen!*"

Some hurried footsteps and then the Katzenjammers arrived. They gasped, "Kristof!" in unison when they saw their boss.

A lot of things began happening at once. Drexler was behind the Germans. He slipped out the door and closed it behind him as they went for their weapons. They were facing Jack, half a dozen feet away. Raising and extending his arm reduced the range to four feet. He shot each once in the chest. He didn't know what sort of ammo Szeto had loaded, but it proved damn effective. The lights instantly went out in the Katzenjammers' eyes and they hit the floor in unison.

Drexler came back through the door and held out his hand for the pistol. But Jack wasn't about to give it up. He pointed it at Drexler.

"For like the third or fourth time: What's this all about?"

"I'll explain later." He snapped his fingers. "Come-come. I want to be out of here before Thompson returns."

"Maybe I don't."

Thompson had been so into the prospect of torturing him. Be kind of fun to see his face when he walked in with his tools and learned the tables had been turned.

"It's important. Please."

Drexler saying *please* . . . Jack would have thought the word long expunged from his vocabulary.

Fact: He'd already had plenty of opportunities to shoot Jack but hadn't. Still . . .

"Back up."

When Drexler complied, Jack quickly finished cutting the tape on his ankles, then rose. The room did a spin and he thought he'd either hurl, collapse, or both, but he locked his throat against a surge of bile and widened his stance. Room and stomach settled.

Moving carefully, he stepped over to where his Glock and backup lay on the floor. Only after he'd reclaimed them did he hand back the Tokarev.

Drexler turned and, keeping his distance, administered a coup de grâce to Hans and Fritz, or whatever their names were. Then he pulled out a handkerchief and wiped down the pistol. He dropped it on Szeto's belly and turned to Jack.

"We have no time to waste." He pointed to the chair Jack had just vacated. "Help me remove this tape, then we'll go. I'll explain outside."

As much as Jack wanted to wait for Thompson, he wanted that explanation more.

17. "I'm sure you're thoroughly confused and have a million questions," Drexler said. "But I can answer them all with one simple statement."

They stood in a shadowed, recessed doorway across the street from the loft building, watching the entrance. The fresh cold air was like a tonic for Jack. The nausea had receded and his head felt clearer.

"Hit me."

"I wish to prevent the Change."

Jack almost laughed. "As the saying goes, 'I may have been born at night, but not last night.'"

"I don't understand."

"You really expect me to believe that?"

"I was hoping that what just transpired in that loft would add credence to my statement."

Jack digested that, looking for the angle.

Rasalom knew Glaeken was powerless, leaving only the Lady blocking his path to the Change. He knew too that Jack was the Heir. So how could Drexler's approaching him with this off-the-wall change of heart work to Rasalom's advantage?

Jack couldn't see the trip wire—at least not yet.

Nor could he see how this could have been set up. No one had known he'd be visiting Drexler tonight. No time to set up a big-store type scam like this. Especially since it involved the deaths of three members of the Order, including Drexler's right-hand man.

"Let's just say I buy that. Why?"

"That is not something I care to discuss. Take it or leave it."

Wait . . . something Szeto had said tonight . . .

I answer only to the One. In fact, soon I may be Drex-ler's master.

Was a palace coup in the offing? Or threatened? Was that why Drexler had executed Szeto?

Jack tried to read Drexler's expression in the shadows as he replied.

"You think the One is going to abandon you when the Change comes. Is that it?"

Drexler didn't react. "I repeat: I want to stop the Change. Take it or leave it."

"You think killing off the Order's enforcers is the way to do that?"

"The only way I know to stop the Change is to stop the One. You told me tonight that you are set on doing that. Therefore our goals are confluent. I will help you make the attempt."

Jack shook his head. "'Attempt.' Not exactly a vote of confidence."

"I am nothing if not a realist and a pragmatist. And you . . . you are not a fool. You must know you face a daunting challenge."

Jack sighed. "Yeah. I do. But if I find him, I'm gonna hit him with everything."

"You must. It must be your personal Armageddon."

"But the key word is *find*. If I can't find him, I can't take him out. You've no idea where he is?"

Drexler shook his head. "None. But I haven't been looking. That changes as of tonight. I will work with you. Only you. No one must know of my involvement. Are we agreed?"

Jack hesitated. This was the weirdest damn turn of events. Working with Ernst Drexler against the One. Sur-real. So surreal, he couldn't fully buy into it. Blagden seemed a dead end. Rasalom and the Order were connected, so tapping into the Order's datastream seemed a good way to go.

But he'd keep one eye looking over his shoulder.

Jack extended his hand. "Agreed."

They shook.

Drexler looked about to say something when his gaze fixed over Jack's shoulder.

"There he is."

Jack turned and saw Hank Thompson fast-walking along the sidewalk, carrying a paper bag. Containing an X-Acto knife, perhaps? To remove a man's eyelids?

Jack fought the urge to start after him . . . and failed. But Drexler grabbed his arm as he stepped from the doorway.

"No. I have need of him."

Jack stepped back.

As they waited for Thompson to enter the loft building, Jack said, "One last question: When you let Hans and Fritz through the door—"

"Hans and Fritz?"

"The two German guys. Why did you step out and close it?"

"Obvious, I should think: I didn't want to risk blood spatters on my suit or coat."

"Right. Obvious."

As soon as Thompson was through the entrance, Drexler handed Jack the balled-up remnants of the duct tape that had bound him, then hurried across the street.

Jack watched him go. So weird. Could he trust Drexler to hold up his end of the bargain? Well, at least as long as their goals remained—to use his term—confluent. Jack harbored no doubt that if Drexler got a better offer, their deal would be as dead as Szeto and the Katzenjammers.

18. Ernst caught up to Thompson just as he was entering the big, open elevator.

"Mister Thompson. Hold that."

Thompson smiled. "Well, well. Look who got invited to the party. I didn't know if Tyleski had got to you or not."

"Tyleski?" The name threw Ernst for a second, then he remembered. "Oh, yes. That was the name he gave you."

"Bogus as all hell." He raised the paper sack he was carrying. "But these will bring out the truth. Before the night is over, we'll know everything about this guy."

Ernst removed the Taser from his pocket and held it up.

"This will help too."

"That's way too tame, man."

"But if he is the one who Tasered us last summer, it is only fair, no?"

Thompson grinned. "Well, maybe for appetizers."

The elevator stopped at the top floor and he let Thompson lead the way across the foyer.

"Hey, everybody," he said as he opened the door to the loft. "It's party ti—"

He stopped dead one step inside the threshold. Ernst was expecting that but purposely ran into him from behind, pushing him farther into the room.

"Oh, shit!" Thompson cried. "Oh, fuck!"

Ernst put on a suitably shocked expression and pushed past him. Perhaps only partially put on. It always surprised him how much blood the human body contained. And when it ran out through multiple large exit wounds, it formed pools of remarkable size. These three pools had merged into a crimson lake. Clotting had begun.

Thompson seemed mesmerized by the blood, but he tore his gaze away and focused on the empty chair.

"He's gone!"

"Yes, I can see that," Ernst said.

"But how? Szeto and I taped him into that chair ourselves. No way he could have gotten out."

Ernst stepped around the pool of blood and inspected the chair.

"Tape? What tape? There is no tape here."

"There's gotta be!" Thompson's eyes looked ready to pop from his head. "What the fuck's going on?"

"Szeto once told me he thought he was a ninja."

"A ninja? Naw, he was just some American guy, but this—this is like supernatural!" He looked around. "We better get out of here."

"I think that is wise."

"What about the bodies?"

This encounter had served its purpose. The Order would want answers. Ernst would say he arrived and found them all dead. Thompson would back that up. But Ernst would wonder aloud about Thompson . . . the last to see the three men alive . . . or *had* they been alive when he'd left? He claimed to have taped the stranger into the chair, but no tape was evident when Ernst arrived . . . could he be working with the stranger?

The Order would find no evidence of that, but the questions would focus attention on Thompson while Ernst searched for clues to the One's whereabouts.

Even better, the One might contact him. Since he could no longer go to Szeto for "minor logistical support," as he'd called it, would he turn again to Ernst Drexler? Ernst hoped so.

If that happened, and if Ernst regained the One's trust and favor, the deal with Jack would be null and void.

19. A sharp intake of breath hissed between Gia's teeth as she parted the hair on the right side of Jack's head.

"Oh, Jack, your scalp's all bruised."

He knew. He'd felt the squishy blood under the skin there earlier. Not the first time he'd been knocked cold, but the first time in years. Doc Hargus had called it a hematoma back then—not subdural, subcutaneous.

He pressed his fingers against the area now. Odd . . . no squish. The last one had lasted a week.

And his headache. Last time he'd been knocked out his head had pounded for days.

More proof that he was being changed in preparation for Glaeken's impending demise.

She dabbed at the area with a cold, wet washcloth.

"You've got a little dried blood here from these little tiny scratches."

Which were probably bigger an hour ago.

"Oh, and look. Here's a teeny piece of glass."

"I can shower all that away."

"No, let me help."

Normally this kind of attention would make him claustrophobic. If she were a nurse in an ER, he'd be pushing her away. But injuries, even minor ones, brought out Gia's nurturing side. With every passing year Vicky needed less and less nurturing, so she had a lot stored up.

Gia never made him claustrophobic. The closer the better.

"Two injuries in two days," she said as she picked at the glass. "I hope you're not going to be making a habit of this."

He smiled at her. "If tonight ends like last night . . ."

"Don't count on that. You've got me worried now. I mean, you seem to be getting hurt lately. First your arm and now this. You never used to get hurt. Are they connected?"

"In a way."

"What way?"

"Long story. All part of a bigger problem. But this particular part of the problem has been solved."

She stopped dabbing at his scalp. "Solved . . . do I want to know the details?"

"Probably not."

She sighed. "Okay. No details. But just tell me: Is the person responsible for these injuries in a position to cause more injuries?"

"No."

"Okay. Good. That's enough." She slipped her arms around his shoulders and hugged. "I worry about you, you know."

"I know."

Her attitude had switched a hundred and eighty degrees from last night. The arm wound had seemed old then, well on its way to healing. But this one was fresh. And he could feel her trembling inside.

Still holding him, she said, "Don't you feel it's all unraveling?"

" 'All'?"

"The world."

"What makes you think it was ever truly raveled?"

"You know what I mean."

"Yeah, unfortunately I do."

Was she sensing Rasalom's ascent? Ever since her coma she seemed sensitized to the Conflict. She'd seen what she interpreted as a landscape of the future while she was out, and it had ended in impenetrable darkness this coming spring.

And spring was only weeks away.

Her hug tightened. "I'm worried."

"I know."

"Not for myself, so much. I'm worried for you. But most of all I'm worried for Vicky. There's so much I want for her. I want her to fall in love, I want her to have a chance at motherhood, I want her to . . ."

"Live long and prosper?"

She laughed softly. "Exactly, Mister Spock. Actually, that's the least of what I want for her. I want *everything* for her, or at least a chance at it."

"I'll do my damnedest to see that she gets that chance."

No more needed to be said.

FRIDAY

1. Dawn was going crazy with boredom.

Mind numbing. The only way to describe it. She didn't know how long she could keep up the surveillance on Dr. Heinze before totally losing it and committing mass murder.

She'd been up since before sunrise, arriving at the doctor's house and watching it until he'd left. She'd followed him to the hospital where she assumed he made morning rounds. She didn't know because she'd stayed outside in the visitor lot with a view of his Lexus in the doctors' lot.

After an hour and a half or so in the hospital, he'd returned to his car and she'd followed him to the Mc-Cready Foundation offices.

Was all this worth it? She had to wonder if this would ever pay off, if she'd *ever* see her baby. She could be wasting her time on a total wild-goose—

Wait. A silver Lexus pulled out of the parking garage, and Dr. Heinze was behind the wheel. Leaving early today. Maybe things were slow at the office. Maybe he had a golf game—no, wait . . . too cold for golf.

She followed him toward the east side. When he got in line for the Midtown Tunnel, she wanted to scream. She was so not in the mood for the LIE and another trip to Forest Hills. But she hung in, following him through the tunnel and onto the Long Island Expressway. But instead of turning off onto Woodhaven Boulevard like he had yesterday, he kept heading east.

And farther east.

Soon they were out of Queens and into Nassau County. And still he kept speeding east.

Dawn followed. This was something different. This could prove to be nothing, or might be the break she'd been waiting for.

2.   "Hey, I've got an idea," Jack said with all the gosharooty enthusiasm he could muster as he, Weezy, and the Lady cruised south on Route 206. "Let's sing 'Ninety-nine Bottles of Beer'!"

He'd awakened early feeling pretty decent, considering what he'd gone through the night before. Maybe too decent. His bruises were already fading.

He'd tried to fall back to sleep but began imagining what he *would* have gone through if Drexler hadn't gotten cold feet about the Change. The possibilities had made sleep impossible.

Later he'd rented a Jeep Cherokee for the Jersey trip and now had the wheel. Not the cushiest ride, but this one had a high suspension that would come in handy once they hit the Pine Barrens.

He thought about their destination, the pyramid. He still couldn't imagine how that fifteen-foot construct of standing triangles with open spaces between them—he remembered Eddie describing it as half a dozen Godzilla pizza slices standing on end—could hide anyone from anything. But real life had been leaving his imagination in the dust lately, so why not?

" 'Ninety-nine Bottles of Beer'!" Weezy said with equal faux glee from the passenger seat. "My favorite! You take the first ten verses by yourself, and then the Lady and I will sing harmony on the rest."

"I do not sing," the Lady said from behind him.

Jack wasn't sure why, but he was glad for that.

"Neither does Weezy," he said.

Weezy looked offended. "You don't know that."

"You used to howl in the shower when you were staying with me."

"I didn't *howl*."

"Caterwaul, then. Whatever it was, you can't call it singing. And 'Hungry Like the Wolf,' of all things. What happened to Bauhaus?"

She reddened. "I had a closet crush on Simon Le Bon."

Jack checked his phone. No missed calls.

"You keep doing that," Weezy said.

"I'm waiting to hear back from a couple, three charter boats I contacted."

Earlier he'd made a few calls to fishing boats in the Coney Island area. No one had answered, so he'd left messages about chartering the boat for a day trip.

Weezy nodded. "Oh, right. Disposing of the katana. No responses?"

"March isn't exactly charter fishing season. Gotta be colder than hell out there."

"Obviously you left your number. We'll be back by early afternoon."

Back from Johnson . . . he hadn't been back *to* Johnson since his father's funeral, and that had been—what?—a year and a half or so ago. Dad and Mom were buried side by side.

Weezy turned in her seat. "I've got something serious to discuss."

Jack said, "Uh-oh."

"It's about Eddie. He wants to join the fight."

"Against what?"

She shrugged. "The Order, the Otherness, whatever we're fighting."

"Since when does he know about any of that?"

"Since yesterday when I spent half the day educating him."

"And he's convinced?"

She nodded. "Pretty much. It's a lot to swallow, but the *Compendium* is an excellent persuader."

Jack hesitated. He didn't want to offend her. "Don't take this wrong, but . . . what's he bringing to the table?"

"A new way of looking at things, maybe?"

"Good enough." He couldn't see a downside. He turned to the Lady. "Any objection?"

She shook her head. "Not at all."

Jack had to smile. "To tell the truth, I can't wait to see his face when we seat him at a table with Mrs. Clevenger."

Weezy laughed. "That makes two of us."

They passed through Tabernacle and now farms lined the highway.

"Nothing changes much around here," Weezy said. "I haven't been back in forever and it's like I never left."

"Big change up ahead," Jack said.

"What?"

"You remember the blinker at 206 and Quakerton Road?"

"Of course. Johnson didn't rate a full stoplight."

"It does now."

And it was red when they reached it. As they waited to hang a left, Weezy pointed out the window.

"Look. The Krauszer's is still here, and Burdett's is now an Exxon."

"Well, it *is* the twenty-first century."

Joe Burdett had kept up his Esso sign for decades after the company changed its name. What had once been Sumter's used-car lot was now a discount furniture store.

Quakerton Road split the north and south halves of Johnson and sported a couple of new stores. USED, where Jack had worked as a kid, was a mom-and-pop drugstore now. Mr. Rosen, his old boss, had died back in the 1990s. The bridge over Quaker Lake was wider but otherwise Old Town looked pretty much the same as it had when they were kids. The two-story stucco box of the Lodge remained unchanged.

"There's your old place," he said, swinging by the rickety Victorian house where the Lady had lived as Mrs. Clevenger during their childhoods.

"It needs painting," she said.

Weezy stared at it as they passed. "We all thought you were a witch."

"By most standards, I was."

"Wonder who lives there now."

"The Meads," the Lady said. "Tom and Alice, and their daughters Selena and Emily."

"Can you tell where anybody is at any given time?" Jack said. "I mean, do you keep track of all of us?"

She shook her head. "The noosphere is a unified consciousness. No identities there. However, when I am near enough to individuals here, I know identities. After all, they help keep me here."

Jack noticed with a start that the lightning tree was still standing—how had it lasted so long?—and then they entered the Pine Barrens, the million-plus acres of mostly uninhabited woodland sitting in the belly of New Jersey. Jack steered onto one of the firebreak trails that crisscrossed the area. He experienced the same creepy sensation he'd get when riding his bike into the trees as a kid. The forty-foot scrub pines got thicker and thicker, their crooked, scraggly branches leaning over the path as they crowded its edges. He remembered imagining them shuffling off the path ahead of him and then moving back in to close it off behind.

Dumb question, but he asked Weezy anyway: "You remember the route?"

"I think so."

He hadn't expected that. "*Think* so?"

She smiled. "Just kidding. I remember it exactly." She tapped her forehead. "The map's right here."

He followed her directions on which way to turn as the firebreak trails forked left and right. The NO FISHING / NO HUNTING / NO TRAPPING / NO TRESPASSING signs posted along the way confirmed that they were on land owned by "Old Man Foster," known to them now as Glaeken. But that was about all he knew for sure. He was thoroughly lost by the time she told him to stop.

He scanned the surrounding trees, which looked pretty much like all the myriad others they'd passed.

"You sure this is the place?"

"You remember it as burned out. That was decades ago."

The Lady had already stepped out of the car and was starting into the trees. Jack and Weezy hurried after her.

"You know where you're going?" Weezy said.

"Of course."

Yeah, well, of course.

Somewhere in all the revived undergrowth—winter bare now—lay the remnants of a burial mound he and Weezy had explored as kids. What they'd found had set a whole deadly chain of events in motion. Sometimes secrets were better left secret.

The Lady, wearing only a housedress, forged ahead, moving easily through the brush, with nothing snagging her clothing that wasn't clothing. Clouds had moved in and the temperature had dropped, but as usual she didn't appear to notice.

Then they broke into the pyramid's clearing and Jack had to stop and take it in, just as he had the first time he'd seen it at age fourteen.

Six huge, elongated triangular megaliths stood in a circle, their bases buried in the sandy soil with their pointed ends jutting skyward and leaning toward each other.

Godzilla pizza slices . . .

One had broken off halfway up, but the points of the other five met at the pyramid's apex, fifteen feet above the ground.

The Lady's new home.

3. Dawn checked her gas gauge. Getting low. She'd never guessed she'd be driving all the way out to Long Island's South Fork. But no way she could stop. She'd lose Dr. Heinze and never find him again.

If she'd had unlimited funds she could have bugged his car—was "bugged" the right word?—with some sort of transmitter that would have allowed her to follow him on a GPS map.

She wondered if he was at all concerned about being followed. He didn't seem to be. No big deal on the LIE, but here on the narrower, slower Montauk Highway, he might notice the same Volvo behind him mile after mile. So she kept a car or two between them.

She followed him through all the Hamptons—West-, South-, Bridge-, and East—and Amagansett as well. She was wondering if he was going all the way to Montauk Point when his left blinker started flashing and he turned off at someplace called Nuckateague. She started to follow him into the hairpin turn but stopped herself. No. Too, too obvious. She had to be totally careful now because hers was the only other car in sight.

It killed her to keep driving but she did. But only for an eighth of a mile or so, then she made a U-turn and raced back. Her heart thumped out a dance beat. She'd never heard of Nuckateague and had no idea how big it was. Couldn't be too big because the South Fork was so narrow out here, but Dr. Heinze could be checking on a summer place he owned and have his car garaged before Dawn caught up to him. Then what?

She turned off at the Nuckateague sign and raced up a narrow blacktop called Nuckateague Drive. She slowed as she came to a street that ran off to the left—Bayberry Drive. Nothing moving there. She pushed on and stopped when her street ended at a T intersection with Dune Drive. She looked right and left—again nothing moving in either direction. She tossed a mental coin and turned right.

Her tension increased as she ran the length of the waterfront homes with no sign of a silver Lexus. She reached the east end of the road and raced back to the intersection. Only a few houses on the west end of Dune Drive, one of them dominating the waterfront with its own lagoon cut in from the bay. The houses she'd seen so far were just that—houses. This was totally a mansion.

She drove past it and spotted a silver Lexus with MD plates, parked near the lagoon by what was either a garage or boathouse.

Gotcha.

Either pediatric surgery was a very lucrative specialty or Dr. Heinze had some rich friends or relatives.

Or—hope-hope-hope—he was making a house call.

Dawn kept moving, then made a quick left into the driveway of a house two lots west and across the street. She twisted in her seat and checked out the mansion. She had a clear view of the front door, the lagoon dock, and the Lexus from here. Perfect.

Now . . . if she could only stay here.

She checked out the house before her: a two-story saltbox clad in weathered cedar shakes. It looked empty.

She left her car running and stepped to the front door where she rang the bell and waited. If someone answered, she'd ask if they knew where so-and-so lived.

No answer, so she rang again.

Still no answer.

Cool.

She tightened her coat around her against the buffeting wind off the bay—they kept talking about a big storm coming—and checked out the neighbors. Only half a dozen houses down here on the west end of the street, and they all looked deserted. The Lexus was the only car in sight.

No surprise. Some of these were summer homes, some were year round. But if you could afford to live out here, you probably spent the winter months someplace warm. Like Key Biscayne or Naples, or the Keys.

She returned to her car, pulled out, then backed in close to the garage so she was half hidden but still had a view. She turned off her engine—save that gas—and settled down to watch.

Not ten minutes passed before she saw movement around the far side of the house.

A boat was bobbing down the lagoon toward the dock, moving backward. A small white cabin cruiser, twenty-five feet long, with a couple of fishing rods poking up from the rear and a lone man at the helm. As it eased against the dock, the driver—captain? pilot?—hopped out and grabbed the lines. A big man, bundled up and wearing a slicker against the cold and wet. Something familiar about him . . .

After he'd tied the lines, he went to a compartment by the transom and pulled out a string of four flat fish. He'd had his head down or turned away since he arrived, but now he raised it. He wore a satisfied grin on a face Dawn knew all too well.

"Oh . . . my . . . God!" she said aloud.

Her mouth went dry as her heart doubled its rate.

Georges . . . Mr. Osala's driver and general gofer.

If he was here, and Dr. Heinze was here, that could only mean her baby was here too. Probably inside with that bitch Gilda. And maybe Mr. Osala as well.

What should she do? What *could* she do?

She fumbled for her phone. Call Weezy. No, call Jack. He'll know what to do.

4. Hank stood at the window of his second-floor bedroom and thought about birds. A big, double-hung window. The room sported two of them. Thick, old-fashioned glass with faint ripples through it. But one large bird or a bunch of smaller, determined birds might break through it.

He had birds on the brain because he'd had that dream again and it was worse than ever.

He'd expected to dream about Szeto and his Eurotrash

enforcers with bullets through their heads. Those three dead bodies tangled on the floor, all staring eyes and punctured foreheads and blood, so much blood . . . he couldn't get the image out of his head.

The death and blood didn't bother him in the least—really, who gave a shit about Szeto and company? What did bother him was knowing that the guy he'd been looking for all these months had done it. Killed all three—single-handed. Hank was glad now that he'd never found him. Still couldn't figure out how he'd got free. But the guy was back on the streets now, and he knew Hank had gone out to find some tools to mess him up, so it was a good chance he'd be coming for Hank.

Bad enough, but then the new Kicker Man dream. Not completely new—it started like the others with the K-Man being attacked in the dark by birds or something like birds, unable to fight them off, and finally knocked down and repeatedly buzzed. But it hadn't stopped there. The birds had left the Kicker Man laid out on the ground. As soon as they flew off, worms slid out of the ground and crawled all over the K-Man . . . eating him. They didn't quit till they'd devoured his diamond-shaped head, leaving behind a decapitated stick figure.

Hank didn't need any gypsy to interpret that dream. The K-Man was Kickerdom, and Hank was its head. Someone wanted Hank's head. And that someone could only be the guy known as Jack.

Well, Hank Thompson's head was staying right where it was, and the rest of Hank Thompson was staying right here. Neither that Jack guy nor anyone else was going to scare him off.

Hank was going to take steps.

5. Jack helped the Lady step over the three-foot-high wall of rectangular slabs—they still reminded Jack of headstones—ringing the pyramid. The three of them stopped and stared at the structure.

Odd glyphs had been carved in the outer surface of each megalith, and remained faintly visible. He could make out three from this angle:

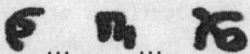

Eddie had also called it a giant stone teepee, and that wasn't too far off. But it looked ancient, *felt* ancient . . . and alien.

Everything was exactly as he remembered it. No sign of vandalism or evidence that anyone else had discovered it. The absence of litter confirmed that.

Weezy must have been thinking along the same lines. "Nice to know that some secrets remain secret," she said.

The Lady approached the pyramid. She stopped at the opening between a pair of the megaliths and stuck her head through.

"I believe Srem was right," she said as Jack and Weezy came up behind her. "This does have a power of occultation."

"Great," Jack said. "Then we won't have to worry about anyone sneaking up on you."

She pulled her head back and turned to face them.

"It might have had the power to hide me completely when it was whole." She pointed to the broken megalith. "But it is not."

Weezy frowned. "But then—?"

"It will, however, reduce awareness of me, and *diffuse* what seeps through. If you have a sensitivity to me, you will know that I exist, but you will not be able to pinpoint my location."

Jack grinned. "Perfect."

The Lady thrust her arm through the slit. "Let us waste no time then."

She turned sideways and squeezed through the opening, easing herself down to the sunken sandy floor within. She strode to the stone column, maybe a foot in diameter and four feet high, that stood in the exact center of the space, then turned to face them.

"I will stay here."

Jack didn't know what to say. He glanced at Weezy, close beside him, and she seemed at a loss for words too.

"Go," the Lady said, making a shooing motion. "You both have more important things to do than stand here and stare at me."

"Just . . . leave?" Weezy said.

"Yes. Go."

"You'll be all right?"

"Perfectly fine."

"Won't you be lonely?"

"How can I be lonely when I have all of you—when I *am* all of you?"

Good point.

"Do you need—?"

"I need you to go about your business."

Jack took Weezy's arm and gently pulled her away.

"You heard her, Weez."

"Yeah, but . . ." She came with him, but kept looking back over her shoulder. "Walking away and just leaving her there—with a storm coming, no less—seems so . . . wrong."

Jack looked back and saw the old woman standing alone in the cold within the confines of the megaliths. He knew how Weezy felt.

"Yeah, it does, because we keep thinking of her as an old woman. But that's simply the avatar she's stuck with. She's not an old woman. And she doesn't feel cold or hot, rain and snow don't bother her, she doesn't eat, she doesn't sleep, and she doesn't feel lonely. Ever."

They made their way back to the Jeep and headed back to Johnson, driving in silence until they reached Old Town.

"Do we have time to swing by our old places?"

Jack nodded. "Tons of time."

Back over the bridge and then onto North Franklin up to Adams Street where Weezy used to live. He slowed as they passed and let her stare at her place.

"Want me to stop?"

She shook her head. "No. Seen enough." She leaned back. "I don't know why people have such nostalgia for their childhoods."

"Was yours so bad?"

"I remember the grammar school years as being pretty good—at least I don't remember anything bad. But high school . . ." She shook her head again. "As soon as I stopped being the Stepford child and started thinking for myself, it all went to hell."

"You went goth."

"I didn't *go* anything."

He smiled. "Oh, right. Black shirts, black jeans, lots of eyeliner, Bauhaus, Siouxie . . . you were a disco queen."

"Okay, okay, I fit a type. But I didn't go around thinking, 'Look at me, I'm a goth.' It was what I liked. And what my folks hated, unfortunately."

"Yeah, your dad . . ."

"I still remember that disapproving look on his face every time he'd see me. Every time. I was on an emotional seesaw as it was, with my moods all over the place, and he made it ten times worse."

Jack remembered her ups and downs, wild swings sometimes.

She sighed. "Even after the doctors came up with a drug cocktail to even me out—well, I never evened out, but the amplitude of the swings lessened. Even so, high school was hell."

Not for Jack. He remembered having a pretty good time. But he wasn't about to say that.

She reached over and rubbed his shoulder. "Except for you, Jack. You were my rock. You never rejected me, even at my nuttiest."

Jack was wondering what he could say that wouldn't sound lame. The ringing of his cell phone saved him.

"I'm calling from the Easy Peasy," said a male voice. *"You left a message about a charter?"*

"Yeah. Thanks for calling back. First thing: you have a depth finder?"

A snort. *"Course I do."*

"Can you take me out to the Hudson Canyon where it's a mile deep?"

"Yeah." He stretched the word. *"We are talking fishing here, right?"*

"No. Scientific experiment."

Weezy gave him a look and he shrugged. Couldn't very well tell the guy he was dumping a sword overboard.

"How many people?"

"Two. Just me and my assistant."

Another Weezy look.

He pressed the mute button. "Eddie?"

She nodded.

"Easy Peasy's built to hold up to twenty. Kind of expensive for just two people."

"Money's no object. I've got oceanography grants."

Weezy rolled her eyes and put a hand over her mouth to stifle a laugh.

"Whatever. When do you want to go?"

"This afternoon."

"No way."

"Why not?"

"Don't you listen to the news? Heavy weather coming. Big nor'easter heading up the coast. Ten-foot swells out there already."

Jack hadn't been paying much attention to the weather. He'd heard some mention of snow.

"Tomorrow, then?"

The master of the *Easy Peasy* couldn't hide his exasperation with this landlubber. *"It hits tomorrow. I'll call you next week."*

Jack didn't want to wait that long.

"I'll pay extra."

"Look, you can't pay me enough to take my boat out into what's coming. Talk to you next week."

He hung up.

"Crap," Jack said. He told Weezy about the nor'easter.

"It's been all over the news," she said. "Where've you been?"

Abducted . . . taped to a chair . . . threatened with torture . . . shooting people . . .

"Preoccupied, I guess. Maybe one of the other boats—"

"Maybe the *Andrea Gail* will take you. Look, that katana's been in your closet for months. It can stay there a few more days. No sense in risking your life just to—"

Now Weezy's phone rang. She dug it out of her pocket.

"Hello?" she said. "Oh, hi. Yeah, he's right here. What—?" She frowned and handed Jack the phone. "It's Dawn. She sounds a little worked up. Says she's *got* to talk to you."

6. "Nothing?" Dawn said, her voice rising in pitch and volume. "We do *nothing*?"

Jack noticed a couple of people in the deli/sandwich shop glancing their way and made a calming gesture.

"Let's keep this between just the three of us, okay?"

"Okay," she said at a lower volume. "But my baby's in there. I can totally feel it."

Jack watched her. Dawn looked more animated than he'd ever seen her. After her call, he and Weezy had driven directly from Jersey to Long Island by way of the Verrazano and Brooklyn. They'd stayed in touch much of the time, with only a few cell dead spots along the way. When Dawn had called to say Dr. Heinze was leaving the beach house, Jack had told her to follow him as far as the nearest town and find someplace like a coffee shop where she could wait for them. She'd resisted at first, preferring to stay where she was, but had finally agreed.

She'd found a Citarella with a view of a windmill, and waited. The three of them occupied a rear table, with Jack facing the two women.

Jack decided she looked more than animated. She looked wired. Not the state of someone who'd be easy to convince that slow and steady was going to win this race. So he'd have to let her convince herself.

He said, "I agree a hundred percent: Everything points to your baby being in that house. What do you think we should do?"

She shrugged as if the answer was too obvious. "Go in and get him."

"Really? How many people are inside?"

From her spot beside Dawn, Weezy gave him an almost imperceptible nod of approval.

"Well, I know Georges is there, and I assume Mr. Osala and . . . Gilda."

Lots of poison in that last name. From what Jack had gathered, Osala's housekeeper had given Dawn a pretty hard time while she was a not-so-voluntary guest at the Fifth Avenue digs.

"Can't assume. You do a home invasion, you'd damn well better know what you're getting into."

She lowered her voice further. "Well, you have a gun—I've seen it. You could use it to make them give us the baby."

"They could have guns too, and things could get ugly, endangering us and your baby. But let's say they're unarmed. What if they refuse to give up the baby? Who do I shoot?"

She didn't hesitate. "Gilda."

"Really? Shoot her dead or just wound her?"

She looked away. "All right . . . I guess not."

"Okay. But let's assume we do cow them and they hand over your baby. Where do you take him? They know where you live. Reprisals could follow. Not only that, you signed him away for adoption. Maybe Mr. Osala adopted him. You have no legal right to that baby, so they could send the police after you—and Weezy and me, as well—for kidnapping."

She leaned back, looking defeated. "Okay, okay, okay, but I can't believe there isn't *something* we can do."

Weezy put an arm around her shoulders. "We talked about this on the way here and we think we've come up with a plan."

He was glad she'd sat next to Dawn; that way it didn't seem like the two adults against her. Jack had to keep reminding himself that she was only nineteen.

"Right," Jack said. "A full frontal assault is a last resort. We need to determine exactly what we're dealing with and find a way to spirit your baby out of there without being seen. But before we try that, we need to set up a way for you to drop out of sight afterward. You'll be their prime suspect, but if they can't find you . . ."

Jack had no idea if he could pull this off. Really . . . how do you hide a woman who has a baby with a tentacle growing out of each armpit? But he was going to try his damnedest.

The only way he could see even a glimmer of hope of success was to take out Rasalom first. Do that and Georges and Gilda would lose their center, their purpose for staying with the baby. They might be glad to have someone take the child off their hands. But even if they weren't, grabbing the baby would be much easier with their Mr. Osala out of the picture. In the aftermath of his death, Jack could very likely swoop in and snatch the child from right under their noses.

A plan began to form . . .

"First thing we need is an observation post. You say you found a house that's a good vantage point?"

Dawn nodded. "But I don't see how we can camp out there very long without someone noticing."

Jack agreed. "It has a garage?"

Another nod.

"Okay, we need to find out who owns it and—"

"It has an oar over the door carved with 'The O'Donnell's'—that's with an apostrophe s."

"Perfect. Time to learn all about the O'Donnells."

7. It took longer than expected. Not because the O'Donnells were particularly secretive, but because the Internet still wasn't up to snuff after the crash.

First thing after leaving the coffee shop, the three of them drove to the county seat and looked up the lot and block number of the property jointly owned by Francis and Marie O'Donnell who were listed as residents of Riviera Beach, Florida. From there to the local library where they used a computer to track the couple. Bits and pieces from multiple sites sketched out the details Jack needed. Francis: seventy-six and a former stockbroker who retired from Bear Stearns well before the meltdown. Marie: seventy-four and a former high school teacher.

Jack made the assumption that, barring a family emergency, a couple in their midseventies with a primary residence in South Florida would keep their distance from the bitter cold of Long Island in March.

So he decided to move in.

He left Weezy and Dawn in the Hamptons and made the long trip to his apartment to retrieve his break-in kit and a few other goodies.

Darkness had fallen by the time he returned. Weezy dropped him off at the end of the street and he walked the rest of the way. He had a bad moment when he reached the place and found lights on in the front room and an upstairs window. But a few cautious peeks inside showed no signs of life: he spotted a timer in the socket feeding the light in the front window. No doubt the same story upstairs. A good policy for the owner: The place looked occupied to anyone driving by.

He used a bump key to enter the house through the rear door into the utility room. The place felt delightfully warm to Jack after the frigid wind off the bay, but still a little cool for the comfort of a couple of septuagenarians. A good sign, but he needed to be absolutely sure the place was empty. He hurried through the first floor, then through the bedrooms upstairs. All empty.

Back on the first floor, he used quick flashes of his penlight to find a thermostat. They'd left it set on fifty-five. He upped that ten degrees and heard a furnace go on. He tried a faucet. No water. Took him a few minutes to find the shut-off valve; he turned it back on.

He called Weezy and gave her the all-clear, then went out by the garage—a one-car garage, unfortunately. But they'd found a spot in the trees down by the highway, not a hundred yards from the O'Donnells' back door, to stash the SUV. A padlock on the simple gate latch held the garage's old-fashioned double doors closed. He shimmed it open and waited.

A few minutes later a car appeared with its headlights out. Jack swung the garage doors open and held them until Dawn's Volvo was inside, then closed up and replaced the padlock without securing it. Weezy and Dawn emerged from the garage's rear door with the bare-necessities groceries they'd picked up in Amagansett. Weezy had her backpack with her precious *Compendium* slung over her shoulder.

"Okay," he said as they unpacked the bags in the kitchen. "We've got heat, water, and power."

The backwash of light from the front room provided

enough illumination to allow them to see what they were doing.

"All the comforts of home," Weezy said.

"Not quite. We need to stay out of the front room while the light is on. Same for the lighted room upstairs. The owners may have hired some security people to drive by now and then, or they may have some sort of neighborhood watch. We don't want to risk someone spotting movement in a supposedly empty house."

The women nodded.

"I'll find a blanket to drape over the bathroom window, so we can at least put that light on when we need it, but otherwise no lights."

Dawn looked at him. "Sounds like you think we're going to be here a long time."

"I don't know. I hope not."

She looked from Jack to Weezy. "I've got a feeling there's another agenda here."

No dummy, this girl.

Weezy said, "I want you to get your baby back. But . . ."

Dawn turned to Jack. "But what?"

"Mister Osala is important too," he said.

She frowned. "Why?"

Okay. Time to lay out as much as he could for her. He gestured to the kitchen table.

"Maybe we should sit down and discuss this."

They pulled out chairs and seated themselves in the near dark.

Jack said, "Where do I begin, Weez?"

She cleared her throat. "I think we should keep this on as mundane a level as possible."

Explain it without mentioning the Otherness and the

Ally? Not easy, but it would keep them from looking like head cases.

"Worth a try."

She leaned toward Dawn. "There's a war going on. It's being fought behind the scenes. Mister Osala is a very big player in that war. He's not a detective, your mother never hired him to protect you—in fact, your mother never met or even heard of him. Everything he told you is a lie."

"Then why—?"

"He leads a cult. You saw their symbol on the back of your obstetrician's watch. They think they can take over the world."

Dawn slapped her hands on the table. "Oh, I don't believe this!"

Jack saw where Weezy was going.

"*You* don't have to believe it," he said. "What's important to know is that *Osala* believes it. And he believes your baby is the key to that takeover."

Jack didn't know if that was true—he had no idea what Rasalom had planned for the baby—but it might be. And even if he was wrong, it sounded good. Whatever it took to widen Dawn's focus from just her baby to a bigger picture.

"But that's crazy!"

Weezy said, "No argument. But crazy or not, the baby is why he took you in during your pregnancy and dumped you as soon as you delivered. That's why he spirited the baby away."

"And that," Jack said, tapping the table, "is why he's got to figure into what we do here."

"But I just want my baby back."

Jack hit her with an angle he thought would lock her in.

"Do you want to keep your baby once you find him?"

"Of course!"

"Well, you can depend on Osala to do his damnedest to get him back. So unless we deal with Osala here and now, you and your baby could spend the rest of your lives on the run."

Dawn leaned forward. "What do you mean by 'deal' with him?"

"Leave that to me."

A pause, then, "You're a little scary, you know that?"

"Scarier than the guy who locked you away in his apartment for months on end and then stole your baby?"

Another pause. "Score one for you. But how does this affect what we're doing here?"

"Okay," Jack said. "We're working with only two facts right now: Osala's driver is over there, and the pediatric surgeon present during your labor has paid a visit. Everything else is assumption. We can assume your baby is there but we need to establish that as a fact. And even if we do, we can't move until we can establish beyond a doubt that Osala is there."

"But why?"

Jack thought he'd made that obvious but Dawn's tunnel vision persisted.

"So that when you take the baby and leave, I can make sure no one hounds your trail."

Weezy rested her hand atop Dawn's. "Larger issues than you and your baby are at stake here, Dawn. You don't need to know the details, but you were right: We have another agenda. But it dovetails perfectly with yours. We'll help you get and keep your baby, but you've got to promise us you'll play it Jack's way and let him decide the timing. That way we'll all walk away with what we came for."

"Do I have a choice?"

"Of course you have a choice," Jack told her. "But if you do something rash, we could all come away empty-handed."

"Rash?" She sounded offended. "Like what?"

"Like going over there and peeking in the windows to see if you can spot the baby."

She didn't reply.

"On target?" Jack said.

She sighed and he saw her nod in the dim light. "Yeah."

He'd figured if she hadn't already thought of that, it wouldn't be long before she did. Might as well get it on the table.

"Just promise me, Dawn, that the only window you'll peek through is one of those upstairs, okay?"

A reluctant tone: "Okay. But somebody needs to look in that house."

"I agree. And that would be me. Dark is the best time. In fact, I'll take a look right now."

8.   The bayfront mansion occupied an oversize lot—at least triple, maybe quadruple. The excess land on either side had been left untended and filled with a tangle of wild bayberry. The leaves had dropped in the fall and the bare branches scratched and tugged at Jack as he made his way toward the west side of the house.

Before approaching the mansion, he'd done a quick reconnoiter of the neighborhood. Half a dozen houses occupied this end of the street. He already knew about the mansion and the O'Donnell house, so he checked out the others. All four were empty. Still had to be careful, though. Never knew who was going to drive by.

When he reached the yard proper, he encountered an expanse of three-quarter-inch gravel that substituted for grass out here.

Good thing it was March instead of summer. No way to cross those stones in silence. If the windows were open, he'd be busted. But even though they were all shut tight against the cold, he moved as carefully and silently as he could.

The icy wind off the bay cut at him as he peeked through a lighted side window that looked in on the house's great room. Probably should have been called a *huge* room. It had a high, raftered ceiling and took up the entire waterfront side of the first floor. An unbroken line of sliding-glass doors faced the water; the stained plank walls were bedizened with all the standard beach house paraphernalia: framed seascapes, sailboat-racing pennants, mounted fish, and an assortment of nets and buoys suspended among the rafters.

Two people—a heavyset gray-haired woman on the sofa and a big guy in an easy chair—watched an appropriately large flat-screen TV.

And off to the side . . . a white bassinet.

Isn't this cozy. Just a down-homey, Norman Rock-welly domestic scene.

Okay, the guy had to be Georges, and the woman fit Dawn's description of Gilda, the housekeeper. The baby himself wasn't visible and no tentacles coiled in the air above the bassinet. But after Dr. Heinze's visit today, the mere presence of the bassinet was enough.

Only one thing missing: the Master of the house. Where was—?

He stiffened at the sound of a high-pitched screech from within. Not human, and not like any animal he'd ever heard. Something between, that tickled the hairs on the back of his neck.

He saw Georges jump in his chair—the screech had to have been much louder in there—but he didn't rise. He looked like he'd heard it before. The woman, however, bounced her thick body off the couch and hurried in Jack's direction. Another screech sounded as she approached and he saw her press her hands over her ears. He ducked back as she neared. When he peeked back in, Georges was still in his chair, eyes on the screen, and Gilda was nowhere in sight.

That noise . . . had to be Dawn's baby. But what kind of baby had a cry like that? Jack had spent some time with Gia down in the St. Vincent's pediatric AIDS ward before the hospital shut down. He'd heard a lot of distressed babies but never one that sounded like that.

The sound didn't repeat. Jack watched until Gilda reappeared from a side room. He'd hoped to see her carrying a baby but she was empty-handed. She returned to the sofa where she and Georges had a brief conversation before fixing their gazes on the screen again.

Lowering to a crouch and stepping carefully, he moved around to the south side to what he estimated would be the window into the room she'd visited. He couldn't stay here long because it faced the street where he was exposed to anyone driving past, but he felt compelled to peek. The streetlight behind him cast a skewed quadrangle of light across the floor within, ending at the legs of a crib. He saw the shadow of his head moving within the light, but the crib lay beyond it, sheathed in darkness.

He spotted two bright points behind its railing—not glowing, merely reflecting the light from the window. Little eyes? But they seemed too high in the crib to belong to the baby. He'd have to be standing upright for them to be at that level. Jack's knowledge about babies was on a par with his grasp of quantum mechanics, but he was pretty damn sure infants couldn't stand at only two weeks of age.

But then again, this was no ordinary baby. This little guy was full of oDNA, damn near a q'qr. Maybe . . .

No way. But damn, they looked like eyes, and they seemed trained on him . . . but they didn't blink.

He ducked away for fear of triggering another screech.

He shook off a chill. The previous Norman Rockwelly scene had taken an Addams Family turn.

He returned to the great-room window and the really important question: Where was Rasalom?

What did he do in his downtime, when he wasn't plotting the end of the world? Hang upside down from a rafter? Jack couldn't help a glance up to check among the junk up there.

The rest of the house was dark, so he had to assume that Rasalom was either sleeping or absent. Jack couldn't buy sleeping, so he'd have to go with his being somewhere else.

But where? When was he coming back? Did he *ever* visit?

The presence of his driver was a good indication that he did. But hell, he could be a couple of continents away on some extended jaunt. If so, how long could Jack keep Dawn reined in?

Dawn . . . she worried him. She was the weak link here. He wished he could send her back to the city and tell her to wait while he took care of everything. But that would never fly.

That infant seat in the back of her car spoke volumes: She wasn't leaving here until she had a baby in it.

The question now was how much to tell her? Mention the bassinet? Would that send her flying across the street?

He needed more info on Rasalom's whereabouts and knew of only one place to get it.

9. "I'm glad you called," Ernst said when he recognized Jack's voice. He meant it. "I have uncovered some information and didn't know how to contact you."

"I'm all ears."

"I proceeded in a circumspect manner, pretending to look for one thing while really looking for another."

"And?"

Impatience was already creeping into Jack's tone. Well, too bad. Ernst's information could not be fully appreciated without the details of the quest.

He glanced around his apartment. Hard to believe that only twenty-four hours ago Jack had invaded his home and threatened him. In the ensuing hours Ernst had become responsible for the deaths of three of his brothers in the Order and had joined forces with Jack against the One. An almost unthinkable turnaround in any length of time, but a *day*?

All the One's doing, of course. He had deserted Ernst, not the other way around.

"Do you know the name of the One's housekeeper?"

"Gilda."

Ernst felt his eyebrows lift. Odd that Jack would know. Only the very upper echelons of the Order were aware of that. Well, here was something he would not know . . .

"Are you aware of her last name?"

"Not a clue."

That was a relief, in a way.

"The Order has supplied logistical support and personnel to the One for millennia. His current driver/assistant—"

"Georges."

"Yes . . . correct."

Did Jack have a source high up in the Order? His friend Edward Connell would be privy to none of this. Who then?

"Georges is a member of the Order. When the One needed a female to deal with a certain matter—"

"That matter being Dawn Pickering, right? Does this train have a caboose?"

Of course—the pregnant Pickering girl had lived in the One's house and was no doubt in touch with Jack now. She was the source.

He felt better.

"Since the Order does not admit female members, a relative of one of the brothers was recruited for the housekeeper position. Gilda's son's name was Kristof . . . Kristof Szeto."

"Ah. Like mother, like son, I gather. But so what?"

"Well, I could not very well draw attention to myself by going to the High Council and inquiring directly as to the One's whereabouts. Instead I asked about Kristof Szeto's mother so that I might offer my condolences, seeing as how her son and I had such a close working relationship."

"Pretty close dying *relationship too."*

"Yes, well, be that as it may, I learned her location but I was instructed not to approach her. She's still being used by the One and has not been informed of her son's demise because it might distract her from her duties."

A short, bitter laugh. *"You guys are all heart."*

"Never mind that. She will be told at a later date. The

important thing is that locating her is the same as locating the One."

"Not necessarily. I've been to the Nuckateague place—she's there, but he's not."

The words shocked Ernst.

"You know about Nuckateague? How can you possibly—?"

"Vee haff vays."

If that was supposed to be a German accent, it was terrible.

Ernst felt unaccountably crushed. He thought he'd been quite clever in ferreting out the location without allowing the slightest hint of what he was really looking for. And here Jack had found it without him.

"So if he's not at the house," Jack said, *"where is he?"*

Ernst wanted to say, You mean there is something you do *not* already know?

"I do not know."

"Then what good—?"

"But I know where he *will* be."

"Where?"

"JFK Airport at six P.M. tomorrow evening. Georges is scheduled to pick him up then and drive him to the Nuckateague house."

During the ensuing silence Ernst thought of how fortuitous it was that the High Council required Georges and Gilda to log in regarding their duties. Gilda was apparently taking care of the Pickering baby now, while Georges had what could only be described as a cushy assignment—few duties in luxurious surroundings. With the One away—no one knew where—he quite literally had nothing to do.

"Six o'clock tomorrow night," Jack said. *"You're sure?"*

"I'm sure that is what Georges told the Council. Whether or not it will change, I have no idea."

"All right. Thanks."

And then he was gone. Ernst laid his phone on the table.

Thanks . . .

No . . . thank *you* . . . if you succeed.

Would Jack make his move tomorrow? He seemed impatient to have this done with, but he also seemed very cautious . . . a careful planner.

But even the most carefully laid plan could go awry, usually because of the simplest little thing. Some unpredictable mishap, some unforeseeable variable completely outside the plan could change everything.

If Jack succeeded, excellent. If he failed, Ernst would stand ready to assist the One in any way humanly possible.

Yes, though he foresaw little chance of success, from the depths of his heart Ernst wished Jack luck. The best of luck. Eliminating the One would save the entire world from a terrible fate.

But most important, it would save Ernst Drexler.

10. Jack pocketed his phone.

Tomorrow at six . . .

That didn't leave much time. He had the huge trunk of his Crown Vic stocked with the special ammo Abe had supplied, but it was garaged a couple of hours away in the city. He needed to get back to Manhattan, and hoped Abe had acquired the final items on his shopping list.

Dawn's Volvo sat in the O'Donnells' garage and would stay there. Weezy had hidden the rented SUV off road in the trees down by the highway and driven in with Dawn. Round trip from way out here to the city this time of year took about four hours. On a crowded summer weekend it could take that long just one way. Weezy could drive him in and head right back, but that would mean leaving Dawn out here alone for four hours. Not a good idea.

Then he remembered: The Hampton Jitney ran between Montauk and the city. Probably a limited schedule this time of year, but he could hop one of those early tomorrow morning and make it to the city without leaving Dawn unattended.

He took the steps to the second floor two at a time and slipped into the darkened front bedroom. Two figures sat by the window, silhouetted against the glow from the streetlight outside. Dawn stared out at the night, Jack's Leica Ultravid binocs pressed to her eyes. Weezy turned at his entrance.

"The lights are going out over there," she said. "Looks like they're calling it a night."

"Are you *sure* you didn't see my baby?" Dawn said, still peering.

"I've a pretty good idea what a baby looks like, and I didn't see one."

But I'm pretty sure I heard one.

He'd told her about seeing Gilda but hadn't mentioned the bassinet or the screech. He wasn't sure of the best way to play this, but that seemed like the way to go. The screech might get her all upset, thinking the baby was in distress or being mistreated, making her a wilder card than she already was.

She lowered the Leica. "Damn."

"Hey, Dawn, it's late," he said. "Only the great room was lit. The baby was probably asleep in one of the dark rooms. Add Gilda's presence to the doctor's visit and it's almost a sure thing he's there."

"I hope so."

Weezy looked at him. "Just as you're almost sure Ra—" She cleared her throat. "Mister Osala is not?"

He glanced at her. She'd almost slipped there. Dawn knew nothing of Rasalom.

"I just got it on good authority that he'll be returning tomorrow night."

"Excellent," Weezy said. "Then all the pieces will be in place and we can start to plan our moves."

Jack already had a plan forming. If it worked out, Rasalom would never reach the house.

Weezy was rubbing Dawn's shoulder. "Won't be long now, Dawn."

Jack took the glasses and checked out the mansion. All dark now. Early to bed and early to rise?

He focused on the window to the baby's room, re-membering those two points of light in the crib. Could it have been standing at two weeks old?

He'd promised Dawn he'd help her get her baby back, but what exactly would she be getting? She'd had only a glimpse of the child right after delivery. Would she still want it when she saw it close up in the light of day?

The memory of its screech still rattled him.

SATURDAY

1. Weezy guessed this was what cops called a stake-out. How did they stand it? Boredom had her ready to scream.

She was sick of watching that place on the far side of Dune Drive but they had to track anyone coming or going—especially Rasalom or the baby. Rasalom—had to remember to call him Osala when Dawn was around—wasn't due in till tonight, and she hardly expected to see the driver or the housekeeper taking the baby for a walk in a stroller. Not in this wind and cold.

Still . . .

She trained Jack's Leica on the place anyway. She didn't know what these binoculars cost, but knew they were pricey. Worth it, though. She felt she knew every cedar shake on the house's siding, every shingle on its hipped roof. Even found a few that needed replacing.

After checking all the windows, she aimed the binocs at the yard. This window in the O'Donnell house offered a view of the west and south sides of the place, plus some of the bulkheaded yard along the bay. With a waterfront house, which was the front yard—water side or street side?

She tracked right to the bulkheaded lagoon that ran

along the far side of the house. The cabin cruiser bobbed in the water, moored to the pilings of the small planked dock.

Farther right she came to the detached garage that sat at the end of the lagoon. Its siding and roof were identical to the house. Weezy hadn't looked, but assumed Rasalom's Mercedes rested within.

She angled her view up and left to the stormy water beyond the house. Out there among the whitecaps, maybe three miles off shore, sat Gardiner's Island—privately owned and big enough to have its own airstrip.

Lots of money out here. Some of it old, some of it new. But if Rasalom had his way, none of it would be of any use, no matter what the amount.

She lowered the glasses and stared at the gray clouds flowing over the bay. Comin' up a storm, as they said down south. Indeed it was. And that was where the nor'easter lay—to the south.

She glanced over at the bedroom's fourteen-inch TV where the Weather Channel's reporters were salivating over the storm roiling up the coast. D.C. and Baltimore were getting snowed in; Delaware, Jersey, and New York were next in line.

She hoped Jack got back before it hit too hard.

They'd left Dawn asleep in the downstairs bedroom and walked to where Weezy had parked the SUV. The short drive into Amagansett gave them a chance to talk. While they waited by the school for the jitney to show, Jack had told her about his conversation with Drexler.

"Can you trust him?" she'd asked.

Jack had shrugged. "As long as our agendas overlap, maybe. My agenda is stopping the One. Drexler's only agenda, now and forever, is Ernst Drexler. At the moment, stopping the One seems good for Drexler. He told me about the Nuckateague house, which we already knew to be true, so I think I can believe that Georges is scheduled to pick up the One at JFK tonight."

" 'The One' . . . I thought we were going to use his name—not around Dawn, of course, but between us."

"That's okay back at Glaeken's place, but I'd like to avoid it out here. Even if he's no longer paying attention, he might still be aware of it. I don't want him to have the vaguest hint of what I'm planning."

"But what *is* the plan? Dawn's going to be asking me."

"It's still forming, but I can tell you I'm going to do my damnedest to hit him before he reaches the house. He'll be much harder to take down once he's inside. Plus, making a move on him in the house could endanger the baby. I promised Dawn I'd get her baby back, and that sort of implies alive and well."

Something in his tone . . .

"And if you hadn't promised?"

He looked out the side window. "Let's not go there."

It seemed to be a moot point anyway, so, okay, she wouldn't go there. But his attitude started a knot of concern in her chest.

"Where do you plan to 'hit' him?"

"On the road . . . target his car."

"What about the driver?"

"What about him?"

"Are you going to 'hit' him too?"

"Not on purpose, but I intend to reduce R's car to molten slag. And if this guy Georges is in it, well . . ."

"That's kind of cold. He's just his driver."

He turned to her, his expression grim. "He's more than 'just his driver.' He's a member of the Order. You remember them, don't you? The ones who expended all that effort last year trying to kill you?"

She remembered. She found herself shuddering under the covers some nights with the memory.

"Touché. Just reflex, I guess. I'm new at this sort of thing."

Jack didn't seem to be listening. His eyes blazed. "He's made a choice as to whose side he's on. Serve the One, you take your lumps with the One."

He was frightening like this.

"What's happening to you?"

"What's happening?" His voice rose. "Something! We've been sitting around doing nothing. Finally *something* is happening. This is the end game, Weez. We've come to the point where we either win it all or lose it all. I'll get one shot at this guy. If I blow it, there'll be no second chance. So I've got to make that first shot count. No more Mister Nice Guy."

"Does that mean no niceties like worrying about collateral damage?"

He sighed and stared through the windshield at the empty school.

"I always worry about that, Weez. And I think I've got a way to do this with zero collateral damage. But the driver won't be collateral. He's part of the package."

The jitney pulled up then. He turned to her.

"Keep an extra close watch on Dawn. Do your mother-hen thing with a vengeance and keep her out of sight and away from the mansion. Gilda and Georges know her. If they spot her, even a passing glimpse, it will blow everything. Just tell her to sit tight. Because if things go according to plan, she'll have her baby tonight."

"You're so sure?"

"I'm not sure of anything. I'm not even sure she'll still want the baby once she sees it."

"Why do you say that?"

"Claws? Hair? *Tentacles?* Sounds like it might have a face even a mother can't love."

Something in his eyes . . .

"Do you know something I don't?"

"No. Just a feeling. But we can deal with that later. If things work out, without Georges and the One around, we can sashay in, tie Gilda to a chair, and waltz out with the baby."

"And Gilda?"

"When we're well on our way, we'll call the local cops and give them her address."

"Well, at least she won't be collateral damage. But what if she were in the car?"

"Good-bye, Gilda."

A crazy thought leaped from her brain to her lips.

"And what if I were in the car?"

He stared at her. "Now you're getting stupid. You're one of the reasons I'm doing this."

And there it was. This was all personal for Jack. He wasn't acting on behalf of humanity or the Ally, he was doing it for the people he knew and loved and cared about. He didn't look beyond that circle. He didn't wish the masses any harm, but they simply weren't on his radar.

Knowing she was in that circle sparked a warm feeling that somewhat relieved the chill of his new cold-bloodedness.

He'd kissed her lightly on the cheek and ran for the bus like a commuter heading for his job in the city.

Weezy had reparked the car in the trees and walked back here to find Dawn still asleep. Poor kid was knocked out.

Weezy checked out the mansion again. Nothing moving over there. She rose and stepped back from the window to stretch her aching back. Not the most comfortable chair.

She realized what she needed to make this bearable: the *Compendium of Srem*.

Yeah, that would do it. Sit by the window with the *Compendium* on her lap, leafing through it, looking up and checking across the street, then back to the *Compendium*. Multitasking.

She'd kept coming across that page about the Naming Ceremony, and the more she thought about it, the more she saw it as a possible back door to weakening or even neutralizing Rasalom.

That wouldn't matter if Jack succeeded today. But if he failed . . .

And best of all, the *Compendium* was across the hall. She'd brought it along on the Jersey trip to quiz the Lady on a few points but had never got around to it.

But first: more coffee. As she headed downstairs to refresh her cup, she peeked in on Dawn and found her sitting on the edge of the bed, yawning.

"Hey, sleepyhead."

Dawn gave her a little smile. "My mom used to call me that." And then the smile faded.

Weezy understood: *My mom . . .*

She wondered at her feelings for this woman-child. In less than a year Dawn had weathered the murder of her mother, the loss of her home, months as a fugitive and virtual prisoner, pregnancy, childbirth, the abduction of her child and yet . . . she was still a vulnerable teenager.

Jack teased her about Dawn, about how she became all motherly whenever she was around. She supposed it was true.

Supposed? No. Don't kid yourself. Own it: She's some

sort of surrogate daughter, the child you never had, never will have.

Weezy had always assumed she'd be an inept mother. Her emotions had become untethered during her teen years and never fully grounded since; plus she saw herself as too involved in her own little world to give herself fully to a child. Now she wasn't so sure. Now she wished she'd taken the plunge, because she could have been a damn good mother. And she would have been proud to have a daughter like Dawn. Yes, she'd made some terrible mistakes, some awful decisions that had left her bruised, battered, chipped, and dented, but she still was functioning. That girl had steel in her core.

But she still needed some guidance, some mothering.

Weezy could provide that.

"How about we make some breakfast together?"

Dawn made a face. "You don't want anything I cook."

"You can't be worse than me. Come on. It'll be fun."

She glanced toward the front of the house. "Shouldn't we be watching the mansion?"

"I've been watching it all morning. Nothing shaking over there. We'll whip up something and eat it by the window. Fair enough?"

Dawn smiled. "Okay. Let's do it."

When they reached the kitchen, Weezy poured Dawn a cup of coffee.

"Hope you like it strong."

"Like a black hole."

"Meaning?"

"Milk disappears when you pour it in."

Weezy beamed at her. "Black-hole coffee. I like that."

Dawn looked around. "Where's Jack?"

"Took the jitney into the city."

"What for?"

"To gather the means to remove the obstacles between you and your baby."

Could she phrase "murder" any more obliquely than that?

"How is he going to do that?"

"He's not saying. But he *is* saying that if all goes according to plan you should have your baby back tonight."

Dawn fumbled her coffee cup, nearly dropping it.

"You're kidding! Tonight?"

"That's what he said."

"Does he really mean it?"

"Obviously, you don't know Jack."

2. "Oy, such powerful stuff," Abe said, gently placing the gallon paint can atop the scarred counter. "I'll be glad when you take it off my hands."

"Why? LX-14 is stable." That was why Jack had ordered it.

"That's just it. I couldn't get LX-14—at least not near the quantity you wanted."

"Aw."

Abe patted the can. "Octol will do the job."

"Octol . . . what's the mix?"

"Seventy-five/twenty-five."

Hmm. Three quarters HMX, one quarter TNT . . . LX-14 was 95 percent HMX. Not quite the same.

"Detonation velocity is ninety-one hundred," Abe added.

Well, okay, yeah, that would get it done.

"Cool. And the paint can is a nice touch."

Jack spotted a letter opener nearby and used it to pry

loose the lid. A chemical odor wafted out as he lifted it. He made a show of sniffing the air.

"I love the smell of aliphatics in the morning."

Abe was shaking his head. "If you're ever caught with this . . ."

"I know. They'll think I'm some homegrown jihadist. Especially when they find my Koran."

"That way at least you'll get special treatment, not to mention a special diet."

"Kosher?"

Abe shrugged. "Either way, no more pulled-pork sandwiches for you."

"I could handle that. Don't know how long I can go without a beer, though."

"Then you should go kosher if you can."

Jack shook his head. "I suppose they'll be even more upset if they find my copper cones."

Abe's smile faded. "Shaped charges?"

Jack nodded. "Roadside IEDs. A matching pair."

When Jack got back to Nuckateague he planned to pack the claylike octol around the copper cones, insert a detonator connected to the receiver of a garage-door opener, then fit each into its own little open-ended container.

Abe said, "How big are these cones?"

"Eight inches across at the mouth."

Abe winced. "You're taking out maybe a tank, an armored half-track?"

"No, a Mercedes."

"Gevalt! All that for a car?"

"Well, it *is* a classic SEL."

"Seriously, Jack—"

"One on each side, Abe. Simultaneous detonation."

"Do you realize—?"

He nodded. Two high-pressure plasma jets of molten metal penetrating each side of the car at eight thousand meters per second, heating the interior to ten thousand degrees and igniting the gas tank to add to the party.

"I'm not taking any chances with this guy."

"Then why the Stingers?"

"Insurance. Backup."

"Because turning the car into a supernova isn't hot enough already?"

"Because things can always go wrong. Detonators fail, he might change plans. I don't have a team of observers along the route, I don't have time to experiment, I don't have an expert to help me set it up. Just little old me. If the IEDs are placed at the wrong distance, the molten copper in the plasma jet will solidify into a slug that will punch a hole in the car but can't be counted on to disable it, and certainly not turn it into the inferno I need to make this work."

"And this will happen where? Not on the LIE, I should hope."

Jack shook his head. "Much closer to his home. In fact, home will be in sight when I hit him."

He waggled his pudgy fingers in a "gimme" move. "Run it for me."

"I got up extra early this morning and checked out the road leading to the mansion."

"Sandy?"

"I wish. They're too damn civilized out there. Too damn rich to want to get their tires dirty. Would've loved sand. Then I could dig a hole and set the charges to blast straight up through the floor of his car as it passed over."

Abe was nodding. "But . . . ?"

"But it's paved with asphalt—cracked and buckled, yeah, but still too tough to break through without a jackhammer. So I've got to make do with roadside—two big mean, opposing charges flanking the road just east of the mansion."

"And it has to be tonight? Isn't that pushing?"

Maybe it was, but Jack didn't see that he had a choice.

"It's too good to pass up. I know he's being picked up at six. I know it will take him about two hours to get there. The neighborhood's deserted. And I need to hit him before he gets into that house."

"Why?"

"Because once he's in there, who knows when he'll leave again? When will I get another chance to know his schedule in advance? It's got to be tonight."

"What about this strange baby? You want him, right?"

"Not for myself. No way. But Dawn does. And she's another reason I need to strike sooner than later: I don't know how long I can hold her in check."

"You shouldn't have involved her maybe?"

"No choice. She found the place. I can't very well ship her out. But here's the scenario: Georges leaves around four o'clock to head for JFK. After he's gone, I set up my roadside IEDs about fifty yards east of the mansion. At six o'clock Georges picks up his boss and heads back. Around seven, Weezy, Dawn, and I invade the mansion. We tie up Gilda and relieve her of the baby. Weezy and Dawn head back to Manhattan with the kid. I wait in the bushes with my remote detonator. When Rasalom's Mercedes passes between the charges, I set them off and he becomes a piece of the Colonel's Extra Crispy recipe. Then I get in my Vic and ease on down the road to the city."

"And that's it? Humanity will be saved?"

Jack shrugged. "Saved from the Change, not from itself."

"Well, *that* would be too much to ask anyone."

"That's the plan, anyway. But just in case . . . just in case he somehow gets out of the car and is staggering around in flames, I'll finish him with a Stinger. I'm assuming you were able to get *them*."

"You doubt? Delivered yesterday."

"Excellent. And the MM-1?"

Abe heaved a deep sigh and shook his head. "Haven't found one yet."

Jack couldn't hide his disappointment. "Abe . . ."

"Such short notice you give me." He waved his hands in the air. "You think they grow on trees? These are not the low-hanging fruit of the arms world. How many do you think are around already? And finding someone who has one and wants to part with it—you should be so lucky. They're all maybe fans of—what's his name again?"

"Christopher Walken?"

"That's it. They're Christopher Walken fans, maybe, and want to snuggle it close to their bosoms. Who knows? If I had a little more time . . ." He gave one of his shrugs.

"Tonight's the night."

"Well, I did track down a modified thumper."

"An M-79?"

"Shoots the same grenade or a forty-millimeter round."

"But it's single shot. And it's break action. I might need to get off a few shots real quick like."

"Hit close with one of those HE rounds and there won't be a pupik's worth of him left."

"That's the idea."

"Nu? Needing a second shouldn't be a concern." He held up a finger. "But not to worry, because your uncle Abe has solved the problem. He has found you an M-79 with the China Lake modification."

"The what?" That was a new one.

"A naval research station designed a four-round pump-action version of the M-79 for SEAL use. Only thirty were made. Unless I should rob a museum, those are impossible to find. But a fellow I know in South Dakota makes working replicas, mostly for collectors and gun pornists, and they're lighter and more reliable than the China Lakes. He shipped me one."

"Four shots?"

Abe nodded.

Well . . . not the twelve rounds the MM-1 offered but . . . He drummed his fingers on the counter.

"All right, I'll take it. I'm already stocked up on the grenades and ammo, so I might as well." He looked around. "And the Stingers are . . . ?"

Abe pointed behind Jack. "Right there."

He turned and saw a golf bag with half a dozen clubs jutting from it. Two carpet-wrapped bundles lay on the floor next to it.

"Really?"

"The golf bag is home for the M-79. Like a glove it fits."

Jack had to smile. "You knew I'd go for it."

"Like you said, the ammo you've got, why waste it? The clubs I added for authenticity. No charge."

"But I hate golf."

"This is the Isher *Sports* Shop, bubbela. I should send you out the door carrying a grenade launcher? And each of those rugs holds an FIM-92 Stinger—no case, just the rocket and launcher."

"Nice. I can squeeze those into the Vic's trunk along with the golf bag."

"It's big enough?"

"Will be after I evict the immigrant family that's renting it now." He turned back to Abe and leaned on the counter. "So, what do you think of the plan?"

Abe pouted, furrowed his brow, then said, "It's simple, direct, and to the point. It should work like a charm, but . . ."

Jack didn't want to hear a *but*.

"Meaning?"

"Something is bound to go wrong."

His own gut had been telling him the same.

"Exactly what I'm thinking."

3. "Let me spell you," Dawn said.

Weezy rubbed her eyes. Focusing and refocusing between the *Compendium* on her lap and the house across the street had given her a headache.

"Gladly." She took one last glance at the mansion as she began to rise. "Nothing doing over there any—" The front door flew open and a man dressed in a yellow nor'easter and jeans stepped out. "Hang on a sec."

He started across the yard toward the detached garage.

"That's Georges!" Dawn said, pressing against Weezy's back for a better view. "Has he got the baby with him?"

From the way his arms swung at his sides, Weezy knew he couldn't, but she raised the glasses anyway.

"Nope. Empty-handed."

She bit her lip as she watched him enter the garage by the side door. Was he going somewhere simple and mundane—like the grocery store? Or had plans changed and Rasalom was coming in early? No way she could know. She was going to have to call Jack.

But then Georges emerged carrying a pair of fishing poles.

"Going fishing," Dawn said. "He must do that every day."

"What do you mean?"

"Shortly after I got here yesterday I saw him pull the boat into the dock and get out with a bunch of flat fish."

"What did they look like?"

Weezy didn't really care, just something to talk about as they watched him board the boat and set the rods in holders near the stern.

"One side was white and the other was medium brown with dark splotches."

Weezy nodded. "Winter flounder. Good eating."

"You fish?"

"No."

"Then how do you know?"

"I just . . . know."

It's what I do.

"Nice cozy little life they've got out here," Dawn said, her tone bitter. "Big house, beautiful view, fresh fish daily . . . and my baby."

"Not for long, Dawn. Not for long."

Weezy kept the glasses trained on him as he opened the engine hatch—to release fumes, maybe?—then started the engine. He fussed with the rods while the engine warmed.

She said, "He must really love fishing if he's going out in this weather."

The bay teemed with whitecaps, but the water here was relatively sheltered. She wondered what the surf looked like on the ocean side of the South Fork. The Atlantic had to be pretty wild right now.

Dawn said, "Maybe Gilda's planning a welcome-home fish fry for Mr. Osala."

Weezy glanced at her, sensing fuming sulfuric acid when she said "Gilda."

They watched Georges cast off the lines and head out into the bay until the boat disappeared behind the house.

"Take a break," Dawn said. "My turn."

Weezy rose from the chair and handed her the Leica. "I'll make some fresh coffee."

"No more for me, thanks. I've had more than enough."

More than enough coffee? Weezy found that an alien concept.

"This from the girl who likes 'black-hole' coffee?"

"I'm wound up enough as it is."

Yeah, she probably was.

"Hang in there. This should all be over by tonight."

Down in the kitchen, as Weezy filled the carafe with water for the O'Donnells' Mr. Coffee, she glanced out the back door and saw flashing lights. Not good. When you'd invaded someone's home, flashing lights were not good. At least they weren't blue-and-red police lights. These were orange. Still . . .

She put the carafe down and stepped to the door for a better look. Yes, flashing orange lights visible between the houses on the next street, down by the highway . . .

. . . where she'd parked the Jeep.

"Oh, Christ!"

She dashed back into the front room, grabbed the keys and her coat, then called upstairs.

"Gotta go down to the Jeep! Be right back!"

She didn't wait for a reply as she dashed out the back door. Only a hundred yards or so. She'd make it in no time.

She ran across the O'Donnells' backyard into the scrub that buffered their property from the houses behind. She cut through a neighbor's yard—again, nobody home—and onto Bayberry Drive, the street parallel to Dune.

No doubt about it. Those lights belonged to a tow truck. Aw, no. She'd parked the SUV on a sandy path within the trees. It wasn't bothering anybody there, and it hadn't been visible from the road. How—?

She angled onto Nuckateague Road and raced down toward the highway. She reached it just in time to see a flatbed truck pull out with a Jeep Cherokee on its bed— *her* Cherokee. Or rather Jack's.

She increased her speed, shouting and waving her arms as she chased it. Whoever was driving either didn't look back or ignored her.

What on Earth?

She'd caught a glimpse of the writing on the driver's door. She stuttered to a stop and called up the image: *Neumeister's Towing and Auto Body* . . . with an Amagansett address and phone number below.

She reached into her coat pocket. She'd call those sons of—

Where was her phone? She searched through all her pockets. Damn! Back at the O'Donnell place, charging.

Puffing from the unaccustomed exertion, she turned in a small circle, stamping her feet in frustration.

So now what? Walk back to the O'Donnell place just to tell Dawn she'd be delayed, and then walk back here and beyond to get to Amagansett?

Didn't make sense. And she couldn't have Dawn drive her to town in the Volvo. That would mean leaving the mansion unwatched. Besides, Dawn's car had to stay hidden. Best to just head into Amagansett and call her from there.

Wouldn't take long to hitch into town, pay whatever fine was due for whatever ordinance they'd broken, then return.

She began heading west along Route 27—labeled the

Montauk Highway out here. She walked backward, ready to stick out her thumb when a car approached.

Something wet hit her face. Then another. White flakes began to swirl from above.

Snow.

She shook her head with chagrin. Could it get any worse?

4.   Dawn noticed the flurries and leaned back from the window to check the Weather Channel. Yep, the Doppler map showed the first green bands of the storm hitting Long Island's South Fork.

She wondered about getting snowed in. Wouldn't that mess up Jack's plans? She'd worry about that when the time came. Nobody seemed totally sure of how much was going to fall anyway.

As she turned back to the window, she thought she saw movement near the house. She grabbed the binoculars and scanned the property through the scattered flakes.

There—in the yard, on the bay side, a gray-haired woman in a coat was crouched by the bulkhead. Dawn adjusted the focus to sharpen her features and confirm what she'd already guessed. She knew that hatchet face, totally recognized that toadlike body.

Gilda.

Her hands tightened on the binoculars. Gilda . . . how happy she must be. She hated Dawn, and taking charge of Dawn's stolen child must have given her incalculable pleasure.

But what was she doing?

Dawn focused on her hands as they pulled bits of greenery from the stones in the yard.

Weeding?

But why would she be out weeding? And in the blustery snow? Had she totally lost her mind? She had a two-week-old baby inside.

An awful thought struck like a blow: What if she didn't? What if they didn't have the baby over there? What if there was no baby? What if he'd died, just as Dr. Landsman had said?

The what-ifs filled her head, reverberating across her brain until—

Wait-wait-wait. Dr. Heinze . . . only one reason a pediatrician would visit that house: a child.

But then why, if she had a baby inside under her care, was Gilda out in the yard, pulling weeds in the snow?

Something totally wrong here.

And if Dawn and Weezy and Jack were all wrong, and there was no baby in that house, they were all wasting their time.

She focused again on Gilda, still crouched, still weeding. She tracked over to the dock. Empty. Back to Gilda: weeding. Then to the front door: The glass-paned storm door was closed but the paneled inner door stood open. Georges hadn't closed it on his way out.

She fought a terrible urge to go over there and check it out.

Call Weezy.

She grabbed her phone and called Weezy from her contact list. She heard a strange ring tone coming from downstairs. She hurried down and found a phone charging on the kitchen counter. Its display read *Dawn*.

That did it.

Dawn ended her call and hurried for the front door. She didn't stop to find her coat, simply pushed out and trotted across the street through the wind and cold and swirling flakes toward the mansion.

She wasn't going to do anything stupid like take the baby. That would upset all of Jack's plans. He'd made it clear that if Dawn was ever going to be able to keep her baby in peace, Mr. Osala had to be stopped—she hadn't asked for clarification on exactly what he'd meant by "stopped." She hadn't really wanted to know.

Jack had totally wanted her out of sight for fear she'd be recognized. But Georges was out fishing on the bay and Gilda was out in the yard on the far side of the house. Nobody around to recognize her.

No . . . nothing so stupid as taking the baby, but she wanted—needed—to make sure the baby was *there*. Once she established that, she'd totally run back to the O'Donnell place and let Jack work his plan.

She was almost to the front door when the possibility of a third adult in the house slowed her. But even if it were true, what were the odds of him or her recognizing Dawn? Only Gilda and Georges knew her.

She picked up speed again and bounded up the two steps to the front door. She cupped her hands around her face as she leaned close and peered through the storm glass. The central hall ran directly into the great room Jack had mentioned. Looking straight ahead she could see all the way to the window wall and the churning bay beyond.

She was about to rap gently on the glass to see if anyone responded when she heard a piercing shriek from within. It jolted her. She'd never heard anything like it—high-pitched and thin, like it came from a little throat.

The baby?

Another shriek.

It had to be the baby. Was it in pain? Had that bitch

been mistreating him because he was Dawn's? She had to know.

Steeling herself, she tested the latch. It moved.

Okay, she had to do this. Just a look—just one look. She pulled open the door, slipped inside, and eased it closed behind her. She stood there listening. Somewhere a television was playing. She tiptoed forward toward the great room and peeked in.

Empty.

She looked through the window wall and saw Gilda, still outside, still pulling weeds.

Yes!

Now where—?

The screech startled her, almost buckled her knees. So loud!

It came from behind her and to the left. She backed up and found a door ajar. She pushed it open . . .

. . . and froze, staring, not sure of what she was seeing.

A crib with a child . . . a small child wearing a dark blue, sleeveless onesy . . . very small . . . only two feet tall, if that . . . but standing in the crib. *Standing.* Should a child that small be able to stand?

And yet there he stood, gripping the bars, staring at her with his black eyes. He had wild black hair shooting straight out from his scalp, a flat nose and nearly lipless mouth.

Those eyes . . . she recognized those eyes.

And then he opened his mouth and loosed an ear-splitting shriek that rocked Dawn back on her heels.

But only for a second. She moved closer, slowly, so as not to startle him. His eyes never moved from her face. She looked at his sturdy little legs. They seemed covered with black stubble. And his hands where he gripped the rails of the crib—his fingernails looked more like black claws, and might have been sharp but they'd been trimmed back. He opened his mouth and shrieked again—a nerve-wracking sound—and Dawn thought she saw glimmers of white along his gums.

Teeth? Already? Whoever heard of a baby teething at two weeks? And yet . . . was that why he was shrieking?

My baby.

This was her child. Dawn knew it as surely as she knew her own name.

He's alive. My baby is alive!

But where were the tentacles she'd seen? She leaned left and right for a look at what little she could see of his armpits, but no sign of a tentacle in either.

Okay. Maybe she'd been wrong about the tentacles. She'd been sure she'd seen two little tendrils like wriggling garter snakes right after she delivered, but she'd been pretty stressed out then, and frankly, being wrong about the tentacles was totally okay.

He continued to stare at her, as if she were the most fascinating thing he had ever seen. She had to smile. With no one else to look at but Gilda and Georges, maybe she was.

Yes, this was her baby, but . . .

She'd expected this totally overwhelming surge of maternal love when she saw him, but it hadn't come. She felt more curiosity than anything. And she had to ask herself: Did she really want him back? She knew she should, and she *wanted* to want him, but she couldn't help it: The maternal urge wasn't there. He was like some creature . . . the result of combining all the bad DNA that had been bred into her and into the baby's father. Her baby was alive, he was well—already standing, for God's sake—and looked like he was being well treated. Could she do better? Should she try?

She backed away. She'd assumed the decision would be easy, automatic, but it wasn't. She'd have to give this some thought. No, more than some—a *lot* of thought.

As she turned away toward the door, she heard a whimper. She looked back and saw him still standing there with his little arms stretched out toward her. Did he recognize her as his mother? Could that be possible? She felt a sudden impulse to rush to him but fought it off.

"Sorry," she whispered. "Can't. See you later maybe."

She heard another whimper as she stepped out the door into the hallway but kept moving. A third whimper, louder, more drawn out, turned her around and forced her to take one last peek at him.

As she watched, he turned away, head hanging, and curled up on his mattress facing the wall.

The forlorn dejection tightened her throat and damn near broke her heart. He *had* recognized her as his mother and she'd turned away from him, rejected him. And with those looks, he was probably facing a lifetime of people turning away.

Something crumbled inside her.

God help her, she couldn't leave him like this. She hurried over to the crib. He turned over at her approach, crawled to the railing, and pulled himself to his feet. His arms went out to her.

"Come on, baby," she whispered. "I'm taking you home."

She pulled him into her arms—heavier than he looked—and grabbed the blanket from the crib, then she retraced her steps to the door. She peeked out. No sound other than the TV. She stepped to the edge of the great room and peered through to the bayfront yard.

She didn't see Gilda.

Her heart twisted in her chest. Oh, God, where was Gilda?

And then Dawn spotted her at the other end. She'd switched sides to pull weeds over there.

The baby saw the older woman and shrieked, a truly ear-splitting sound this close.

Weak with relief, her heart still thumping, Dawn turned and hurried for the front door. She paused long enough to wrap the baby in the blanket, then she pushed open the storm door and pulled the inner door closed behind her.

She ran for the O'Donnell house.

The baby loosed another shriek as the chill wind and snowflakes swirled around him.

5. Gilda straightened and cocked her head.

What?

That cry . . . it almost sounded like the little one. But that baby, that awful, ugly little baby couldn't be heard in the yard. Which was why she was out here. She couldn't stand that cry. It set her teeth on edge. It scraped her nerves raw. And the little monster kept doing it, over and over.

Not a hunger cry. Nor was it a distressed cry because it needed changing. She'd feed it its formula—such an enormous appetite—but even when finally sated and changed into a fresh diaper, still it shrieked. All through its waking hours. Gilda had come to the conclusion that it *liked* to make that noise. Almost as if it knew it disturbed her and it cried out just to torture her.

Sometimes she needed all her strength and loyalty to the Master to keep from holding a pillow over its wretched little head to stop it forever.

But the Master had plans for the baby. He had not shared them with Gilda or Georges, but he had made it clear he wanted the baby kept well until the time when he had use for him.

Gilda had had only one child of her own, and Kristof had been nothing like this one. Her Kristof had been headstrong, but a good boy. She hadn't heard from him lately, but that wasn't unusual. Sometimes his work for the Order did not allow easy communication. But he would call when he was able. Kristof was a good son.

But that child inside—a devil child from a devil girl. That Dawn Pickering was no good, and she'd given birth to a child just as bad. Gilda almost wished the mother had been allowed to keep the child. Let her deal with that awful sound.

There. She heard it again. It seemed to come from the other side of the house. But it couldn't be the child. Probably some seagull.

Time to go inside anyway. Her hands were stiff from the cold, almost frozen. But the discomfort was nothing compared to the sound of that child.

The Master could silence him. The Master would step into the child's room and stare at him. And thereafter the child would remain silent—for as long as the Master stayed in the house. As soon as he left, as he had last week, the screeching resumed. For six days straight now. Gilda was so glad the Master was returning.

The Master . . . he frightened and fascinated her. Her Kristof feared him and said she must obey him at all times or suffer grave consequences. She had taken that with a grain of salt until Georges's predecessor, Henry, had deviated from the Master's instructions regarding that little trollop, Dawn. He disappeared. Gilda never saw or heard from Henry again.

She opened the door at the side of the great room and stepped in. She pulled it closed behind her and tensed as she stood listening, waiting. But the sound didn't come.

She waited longer. Still silence.

Could it be . . . could the little monster have fallen asleep? She found that almost too much to hope for. After screeching all day, the child would fall asleep at night, but rarely for more that two consecutive hours. Then he'd be up, waking the house with his cries. But never since the day he was born had he taken a nap.

She tiptoed across the great room and approached the center hall. She stopped at its entrance. Still silence, glorious silence. She had no idea how soundly he slept—deep, like her Kristof in his baby days, so that almost nothing awakened him, or very lightly, so that the slightest sound would rouse him? If the latter, she needed to sneak that bedroom door closed, or run the risk of waking him with the simple rattle of a pan in the kitchen.

She glanced farther down the hall at the front door to the street side and noticed it closed over. Hadn't that been open? She couldn't be sure. The child's racket was so distracting it was a wonder she remembered her own name.

She slipped out of her shoes and edged up to the nursery door. Anyone watching her exaggerated caution might think she was sneaking up on an unsuspecting victim, but this opportunity for peace and quiet was too rare and precious to ruin with carelessness.

When she reached the doorway she peeked through the narrow opening between the frame molding and the hinged side of the door. She had a view of the foot of the crib but no sign of the child. He must have fallen asleep at the other end.

Gilda took a breath before peeking around the door.

The last thing she wanted to see was that ugly little face staring back at her through the bars. Because sure as the sun rose in the east, a screech would be quick to follow.

She poked her head past the edge of the door for a full view of the crib and—

Empty!

Mouth dry, heart pounding, she rushed into the room and gripped the top rail as she stared at the rumpled sheets.

No! This could not be!

Wait. The child could stand long, long before it should have been able. Could it have climbed out?

She dropped to her hands and knees and was crawling about the floor when she remembered something. She popped her head back up to the level of the crib mattress.

The blanket. Where was the blue blanket she kept in the crib? Even if by some miracle the baby could have climbed out, it would not have taken the blanket.

And the front door—Georges had left it open when he'd gone fishing. And now it was closed.

Someone had taken the baby!

Who? The mother? Dawn? No. She was too self-centered to even worry about her baby, and too stupid to track him here and take him.

Dr. Heinze? He'd visited only yesterday. He was interested in the baby, yes, but more as a specimen than a child. She couldn't see him involved in a kidnapping.

She ran to the front door and pulled it open. She stood there, panting with terror as she scanned the empty yard. The Master . . . no telling what he would do if he returned tonight and learned that Gilda had allowed the baby to be taken. Not even her Kristof could save her.

A random passerby? Saw the open door and investigated? Took the child for ransom or perversion?

But where was he? No sign of a car, or another living soul. She'd have heard car tires on the stones.

She ran back to the great room, slipped back into her shoes, then raced out to the bayside yard. She searched the churning waters but saw no sign of Georges. The misty, snowy air hampered visibility.

Back to the house, this time to the kitchen where she yanked open a drawer and grabbed a carving knife. She would search, go from house to house if she had to, until she found that child. And if anyone interfered . . .

Out again into the cold, the street side, this time. She went to the garage and kicked open the side door. The Master's car sat within. She checked inside, around, and under. No sign of that miserable little child.

She stepped back into the yard and slammed the door behind her. Where next? Maybe—

She heard something . . . a high-pitched shriek. Like she'd heard before and written off as a seagull. But this was no seagull. She knew that awful cry like the sound of her own name. No sign of anyone about, but it seemed to originate from somewhere to her left.

She headed in that direction and had reached the middle of the roadway when she heard it again.

She could swear it came from that garage across the street . . .

6.   Oh, that sound. It pierced her like a knife.

"Come on, little guy," Dawn said as she fitted him into the infant seat in her Volvo. "Cool it, okay? Somebody'll totally hear you."

Carrying the baby wrapped against the weather, she'd run straight back inside the O'Donnell house, just long enough to grab her keys and her phone. The display informed her that she'd missed a call from a number she didn't know. Weezy? Where was she, anyway? And how could she call without her phone? Not important right now. Dawn would get back to her once she was on the road.

She'd hurried out to the garage, entering by the side panel door and leaving the two big doors closed. And they would stay closed until the last minute. Jack had left the padlock in the latch but unlocked. As soon as the baby was strapped into his seat, she'd open those doors and get out of here.

She knew she was probably messing up Jack's plans, and probably even screwing herself. And if she had to do it over again, maybe she could have resisted grabbing her baby. But when he'd turned his face to the wall like that, she'd lost it.

And now this little genie was out of the bottle and she saw no way of putting him back.

But maybe if she got out of the neighborhood without leaving a trace, Jack could still make his plan work.

As she fitted the child's arms beneath the seat straps, she couldn't resist a quick, closer look at his armpits. No . . . no tentacles. But she could have sworn—

Wait. Were those little scars in his armpits? Had they removed his tentacles?

Dr. Heinze . . . a pediatric surgeon. She'd always been curious as to why a surgeon had been present rather than a plain pediatrician. Now she knew. They'd cut them off. She noticed a bump beneath the surface of each of the scars. Were the tentacles trying to grow back?

And what happened to all the hair she'd seen? She felt his arm . . . bristly. Had they—? Yes! They'd shaved his arms and legs. What the—?

And then she heard the squeal of the side-door hinges behind her and the garage filled with daylight. She turned and saw a squat silhouette rushing toward her, screaming.

"You! You-you-you-you-*you*!"

She knew that voice—Gilda!

Something glinted in the older woman's raised hand, then slashed toward her. Dawn tried to duck and turn away but was trapped against the car door. The blade cut through her sweater, and a blaze of pain, like nothing she'd ever felt in her life, lanced into her chest near her left shoulder. She spun away with the knife still in her and stumbled, landing on her hands and knees, worsening the pain. She'd heard of seeing stars and now she really did.

Meanwhile Gilda had moved to her side and was kicking her, screaming in fury.

"You! Will I never be free of you?"

Dawn gasped as she felt a rib crack. The old bitch was going to kill her . . . kick her to death.

She grabbed the handle of the knife and pulled. The blade came loose from her chest with a slick wet sound and another burst of agony. Nearly overwhelmed by the pain, Dawn slashed out blindly, connecting with her first swing. She felt the knife sink into something—had to be flesh because she heard Gilda's screams change tone from rage to shock and pain.

She yanked the knife free and turned on her knees in time to see Gilda falling backward, clutching her bleeding lower leg. Dawn heaved to her feet and stumbled over to her. Gilda kicked at her but missed. Dawn felt her legs turn to taffy as she moved in. They gave way and she landed knees first on Gilda's abdomen, knocking the wind out of her with a whoosh. Nearly blind with pain and panic, Dawn raised the knife and drove it into Gilda.

She didn't know where she struck but Gilda screamed louder, so Dawn struck again, and again, and again . . .

"Take my baby?" said a barely audible voice she recognized as her own. "*My* baby? You? No! Never! Especially you. *Especially* you!"

Soon the screaming stopped, but Dawn kept stabbing. Her arm seemed to have a life of its own, and it seemed to be thinking that Gilda was somehow connected to Jerry, the foul scum who'd seduced her and fathered the baby, and who'd later killed her mother. Everyone who'd ruined her life seemed to be connected. Not that she hadn't played a part in the ruin, but she was the one who'd suffer for it until her last breath. She couldn't reach those others, but she had Gilda and Gilda was going to pay for all of them.

And then the strength ran out of her and Dawn dropped the knife and looked at the bloody piece of butchered meat splayed before her. Gilda's eyes stared roofward from a blood-spattered face. Red still oozed from the ruin of her throat into the sandy floor of the garage.

Oh, God! Did I do that?

Dawn felt her stomach heave but the morning's coffee stayed down. Clinging to the rear fender of the car, she pulled herself to her feet with her right arm—the left seemed useless—and checked the baby. He hadn't made a sound. And now he stared at her with wide black eyes. His arms thrust out to her, his hands opening and closing as if squeezing some invisible toy.

"We'll play later," she gasped as the garage tilted around her. She grabbed the edge of the door to steady herself. "First we get you out of here before Georges gets back."

She looked at the closed garage doors. Somehow she was going to have to find the strength to go outside, walk around to the front, remove the lock, and swing them open.

Every breath hurt like a new wound. She didn't know if she could make it.

She had a thought: Maybe she wouldn't have to.

The doors were wood—old wood—held closed by a little lock in a simple gate latch. And she had a car.

It took nearly all her strength to slam the rear door and open the driver's. She dropped behind the steering wheel and found the keys. Somehow she got her door closed—not easy without her left arm, and not completely, but at least latched. She started the car, put it in reverse, and stomped on the gas. The car lurched into motion and hit the doors. With a crash and a clatter they blew wide. The passenger-side mirror caught the edge of one and ripped off with a crunch.

Worry about that later. No, she wouldn't worry at all. Didn't matter. Getting out was all that mattered.

She backed to the middle of the street, shifted into drive, and began the laborious process of turning the wheel with one hand. It seemed to take forever. Finally she got it turned and gently hit the gas. As the car began to move forward, the road swam before her. She clenched her teeth and kept a death grip on the wheel with her good hand.

She coughed, spurring a fresh jab of agony and spraying blood all over the dashboard. She watched in horror as it dripped onto her legs and the floor.

Oh, God, what did that mean? Had Gilda punctured her lung?

Everything went blurry. She blinked, trying to focus. Gravel crunched under the tires. The ringing of her cell phone brought her back, her vision cleared—and she saw she was rolling across the mansion's front yard to-ward the boat dock and the lagoon.

Taking her foot off the gas she hauled the wheel to the right. The car came to a rest, still in gear, engine running, nosed against the mansion's garage. She had to back up.

The world went blurry again, but instead of clearing, it faded to black, taking the sound of her phone with it.

7. "What the hell?"

Anxiety nibbled at Jack as he jabbed the END button and tossed the phone onto the passenger seat.

Where *was* everybody? No answer from either Weezy or Dawn. Not good. Not good at all. All they had to do was sit tight in that house and watch from the window. What was so hard about that? Had the goddamn O'Donnells come back from Florida and found their home invaded? What? *What?*

His phone rang. He grabbed it. The display showed a number he didn't recognize. He thumbed SEND. He'd take a call from anyone right now.

"Yeah."

"Jack, it's me." Weezy's voice. *"Where are you?"*

"Just about to the Nuckateague turnoff. Where are you?"

"In a garage in Amagansett."

"What? How the hell—?"

"Long story. The Jeep got towed. I can't get it back because it's rented under your name. A complete mess."

Well, rented under his Tyleski name. He'd been ready to deep-six that identity anyway. No arguing about the mess, though. He looked ahead for a place to make a U-turn.

"I'll come get you and—"

"No. Check the house first. I can't get hold of Dawn."

"Neither can I."

"I'm worried."

"Makes two of us. I hope she didn't do anything stupid. You were supposed to keep an eye on her."

"I know, I know. But I saw the lights of the tow truck. I figured I'd be right back—"

"I'm turning into Nuckateague. Stay by that phone."

"I'll keep trying Dawn."

He hit the END button and made the turn.

Okay, how to play this? His initial plan had been to find another empty garage farther down the street to hide the Crown Vic and its armamentarium. To reach that house, whichever one it was, required him to drive by the O'Donnell place.

So that was what he'd do . . . and hope everything was as he'd left it. He shook his head as foreboding thickened around him like a fog.

Fat chance.

This was why he worked alone.

8. As was his custom, Georges reversed the boat toward the dock. The lagoon wasn't wide enough to turn it around without a whole series of forwards and reverses, so he always backed in and docked it nose-out toward the open water. Today he'd have to secure the boat to the dock with an extra mooring line against the storm.

A waste of time going out. Too rough. He'd spent more time fighting the wind and waves than fishing. And then the snow had come. But he'd known this would be his last chance for a while, so he'd given it a try.

Well . . . almost fishing was better than no fishing at all.

He'd tied the first stern line and was about to add a second when he noticed the car.

Immediately he was on alert, senses humming, muscles tensed. He reached for his pistol but his hand came away empty. Of course. He never took it fishing. The salt air was poison for a fine weapon like his SIG Sauer. He grabbed a rusty knife from his tackle box and hid it, palmed against his wrist, and assessed the situation as he approached through the thickening snowfall.

A Volvo . . . the engine running . . . someone slumped forward in the driver's seat . . . a young woman . . . blond . . . something familiar—

He froze when he recognized the Pickering girl. What was she—?

No need to ask. It could only be the baby. But how had she found them? No matter. What was she doing now?

He started forward again, but more cautiously. She made no move. Had she passed out? When he reached the driver's door he peered through the glass and saw blood on her and on the dashboard. Knife held at ready, he opened the door.

Her left arm moved toward him and he went into a defensive stance, ready to make a backhand slash. But her blood-soaked arm had been resting against the door and had merely fallen when he'd opened it. She made no further movement. He felt her throat. Still a pulse.

What had happened here? She'd been wounded—shot or stabbed, he couldn't tell.

He edged around the rear of the car and opened the passenger door. Still in gear. He put it in park and turned off the engine, taking the keys. A cell phone started to ring—

A sudden nerve-shattering shriek so startled him that, had he been holding his pistol, he was sure he would have fired it.

There, in the backseat, the monster baby, staring at him.

Blood on Dawn . . . the baby here . . . Gilda would not have given up without a fight.

He was starting toward the house when he caught movement to his left. One of the doors to a garage across the street was swinging in the wind and . . . was that someone on the floor inside?

He couldn't make sense of this whole situation, couldn't come up with a scenario to explain it. The street and the neighborhood looked as deserted as they had every other day—the very reason the Order had offered this location for the One. Georges had a terrible premonition about the figure on the floor of the garage.

He hurried over and gaped at Gilda's corpse. He'd seen damaged human flesh before—had inflicted a good deal of damage himself—so he felt no physical repulsion. But this wasn't anything like what he'd expected. He'd seen damage inflicted by design, and damage inflicted by emotion. And this . . . someone had relieved an enormous burden of rage upon Gilda.

Georges felt nothing for the woman, but he feared for himself. He had been appointed guardian of the household in the One's absence, and he had failed—miserably. When the One returned—

He heard the baby shriek. He turned.

Her baby's screech brought Dawn to. She opened her eyes. Her phone was ringing.

Where—?

It all came back to her in a rush. The baby . . . Gilda . . .

Her door was open. So was the passenger door. She reached to start the car but the keys were gone. Someone was here. Georges? She had to keep the baby from him. Couldn't let him take the baby.

She slithered out of the door. Her legs barely supported her but somehow she managed to pull the rear door open. The baby looked at her and screeched. The sound was almost sweet over the roaring in her ears. As she reached out to undo his straps, she realized that she'd never be able to get him out with just one arm. How—?

Someone grabbed her roughly from behind. Her left shoulder and chest screamed as she was whirled around but she hadn't enough breath for a single sound as she saw Georges's livid face. His teeth were bared and clenched.

"You killed her!"

His big hands went around her neck and his thumbs jabbed into her throat.

"You whore! You killed her and I will pay the price! But so will you!"

The pressure on her throat was unbearable, unrelenting. She couldn't breathe and didn't have the strength to fight him, not even with her good arm. She felt like a rag doll in his hands. She heard a *crunch* as something in her throat gave way. The roaring increased as the light faded, leaving only blackness.

And then even the roaring stopped.

Georges knew she'd never breathe again through her crushed larynx, but he kept squeezing her throat because it felt so good. So damn good. The little trollop had most likely ruined his life. Well, he'd just ended hers, but it wasn't enough. Not nearly.

He heard tires screech in the street. He looked up and saw a big black sedan skidding to a halt. He tossed Dawn back into the rear compartment atop her ugly baby as a man leaped from the sedan.

What now? He hadn't seen a single car on this street in over a week, and one had to pass by now?

Wait—he had a pistol in his hand. A Glock. And his expression was fierce as he raised the pistol and fired twice.

Georges's thighs—first the left, then the right—exploded in pain. The second hit spun him half around as he felt his femur shatter. The pain brought tears to his eyes, but he bit back the scream that rose to his lips. He would not scream.

What was happening? Who was this? Georges had never seen this man before. He hadn't asked what was going on, like any normal passerby. He'd simply looked at Georges and started firing.

The man stared into the car, then reached inside. Georges couldn't see his hand but imagined he was checking for a pulse. Clenching his jaw against the pain, Georges reached into his pocket and pulled out the rusty knife. Not a throwing knife, but the only weapon he had. He had to try something.

He hurled it at the stranger—

Who turned and batted it away with his pistol. But he cut his hand in the process. He switched the Glock to his left hand and sucked on the side of his index finger as he approached Georges. His expression was furious . . . and frightening.

"Why'd you kill her? No reason on Earth to do that. She's just a teenager trying to get her kid back."

Georges jutted his chin toward the garage across the street. "She killed Gilda."

The man glanced over his shoulder, then back to Georges. "Yeah, well, you guys stole her baby." He looked at his wounded finger. "You trying to give me tetanus? Cause that was a piss-poor toss."

Georges spat at him. "May you die in agony."

The man waved his pistol at Georges's legs. "Doesn't look like you'll be picking up your boss tonight."

Georges felt as if he'd been slapped. How could he know that? It could only mean he wasn't here by accident. Who was he?

"No worry," the man said. "I'll sub for you. What airline?"

"Fuck you."

He looked at his finger. "Well, whatta ya know?" He thrust it toward Georges. "All better."

It was true—the cut had already stopped bleeding.

"Just like your master. We're old buddies. So tell me: What airline?"

"Fuck your mother!"

The man looked at the sky, then back to Georges.

"I haven't got time for this."

He pointed the Glock at Georges's chest.

"No!"

9.   Jack double-tapped Georges's heart and put one through his forehead for insurance.

Then he heard his phone ringing back in the car. He holstered the Glock and went to retrieve it. The same number as before. He thumbed SEND.

"Weezy?"

"I've been calling Dawn but she doesn't answer."

Jack glanced back toward the Volvo. "Yeah . . . well . . ."

"What? What, Jack?"

He was on a cell, the signal going who knew where.

"Remember that movie with Bruce Willis?"

"Die Hard? Listen, Jack, I don't want to play movie trivia. Dawn—"

"Remember what Haley Joel Osment's character could see?"

"Ohmigod! You mean—?"

"I'm seeing three . . . and a really ugly baby."

"Dawn? Is she—oh, God, no!"

"Pull it together, okay? I—*we* need you to stay together. We've got big trouble. What street are you on?"

"Ju-just off twenty-seven."

"Any landmarky place nearby?"

"I can see a farmer's market across the street but it's closed."

"I think I saw the place on the way in. Forget the car and get over there and wait. I'll pick you up ASAP."

He cut the call before she could say anything else and looked around. Had to get these bodies out of sight. He wasn't worried about anyone hearing the shots in this wind and weather. What few people were within earshot were inside.

He emptied Georges's pockets and found nothing but a cell phone and the Volvo keys. He grabbed him by the wrists and dragged him around to the far side of the car where he loaded him into the passenger seat. Heavy son of a bitch. Then he moved to the rear compartment to deal with Dawn.

Poor kid. If she'd just done what he'd told her she'd

still be alive. He tried to imagine what had happened since he'd left. She'd been with Weezy, and Weezy had walked down to the car . . . and then what?

He leaned in and went to grab her shoulders to pull her farther into the car when the baby's deafening screech stopped him. He looked at the child—the Marty Allen hair and the scrunched-in features gave him a troll-doll look without any of the cuteness. Fury lit his beady little black eyes and Jack thought he was angry for taking his mother from him.

"Don't worry, little guy. I'm not gonna—"

But then he saw the red smears on his face.

As he watched, the kid dipped his fingers into the blood welled in Dawn's shoulder wound and then stuck them in his mouth, sucking greedily.

10. They had a litany going . . .

"We can't just leave her there," Weezy said for what seemed like the thousandth time.

And each time Jack gave the same reply: "We don't have a choice."

They stood inside the door to the O'Donnell house, looking out on Dawn's Volvo, collecting snow as it sat in the yard.

After Weezy's call from the garage, Jack had moved Dawn and Georges into the O'Donnell garage, where they joined Gilda on the floor. He'd arranged them along its west wall, Dawn supine, covered by a sheet from the house, the other two facedown. Then he'd eased the Crown Vic in beside them—a tight fit even if the garage had been empty—and closed the damaged doors. Their hinges had been loosened and twisted a bit, and the latch was broken, but he'd managed to jury-rig them so they stayed closed.

Then he'd taken the Volvo and its little passenger into Amagansett to pick up Weezy. Snow had begun to accumulate on the asphalt, but the Volvo handled nicely.

He'd tensed himself during the ride, waiting for one of those screeches, but it never came. A glance in the rearview mirror showed the kid asleep. Good thing, too. He'd pitched a fit when Jack had taken his mother away, screeching like the proverbial banshee. Jack hadn't known whether it was maternal attachment or removal of his snack. He'd been chowing down on Dawn's blood with lip-smacking gusto. Jack had wiped the blood off the dashboard before heading for Weezy, and now realized he should have cleaned up the baby's face as well. But he'd had more important things on his mind.

Like how to salvage this clusterfuck.

He'd found a snow-dappled Weezy rubbing her hands and stamping her feet in front of the empty produce stand.

"Sorry to take so long," he said, turning up the heat as she got in. "Cleanup took longer than I expected."

Shivering, she slid into the passenger seat and held her hands over the dashboard vents.

"'S-s-s'all right."

She glanced at the baby in the backseat and grimaced.

"Was I right?" he said.

"Not so bad."

She had to be kidding. Then again, this baby belonged to Dawn, her surrogate daughter, and so maybe Weezy was seeing the child with different eyes.

She looked at him again. "Does he really have . . . ?"

"Tentacles? I didn't check."

Time had been tight and he was in no great hurry to find out. Plenty of time for an anatomy check later.

She gave him a quick rundown of seeing the tow truck flashers and running out to stop it.

"How did anyone find it?"

"The guy at the garage told me it was reported to the police and the police called them to pick up an abandoned vehicle. That's all he knows."

Jack shook his head. "Murphy's law rules the goddamn universe."

"The *multi*verse," Weezy said.

Unasked questions about Dawn layered the air within the car. Finally Weezy took a deep breath and looked at Jack.

"Dawn . . . she's really . . . ?"

He nodded.

Her features twisted as tears began to roll down her cheeks. "How?"

Jack described the scene as he'd found it, then, "The best I can come up with is somehow she got hold of the baby, Gilda came after her with a knife, wounded her, but Dawn fought back and killed Gilda. Then Georges killed Dawn."

Weezy buried her face in her hands. "Oh, God. It's all my fault!"

He sighed. "Somehow I knew you'd say that."

"Well, it is. I never should have left her."

"You saw the flashers. I'd have hauled ass down there too."

"But if I'd stayed—"

"This never would have happened? Okay, probably not. But just because you could have stopped her if you were there doesn't make you responsible for her bad decisions. And she made a whole series of them, one right after another: leaving the house, going to the mansion, entering the mansion, taking the baby. At any point along the way she could have made the opposite choice, but she didn't."

She raised her head and looked at him. "That's awfully cold."

Yeah, it was, wasn't it. But anger was leaving him feeling pretty damn cold at the moment.

"Sorry, but that's the way I see it."

"She was a young mother, her baby had been taken from her, she wasn't thinking."

"Exactly. This wasn't all about her. There's a bigger picture. We explained that. But in the end none of that mattered to her. Dawn-Dawn-Dawn—that was it."

Weezy was staring at him with a worried expression. "What's happening to you?"

"What's happening to *me*? How about what's happening to *us*—as in the whole world? How about she's blown this primo chance—a near-perfect setup—to stop this guy."

"How can you say it's blown?"

"Well, Georges isn't going to be waiting at JFK to pick him up tonight. And neither Georges nor Gilda will be answering the phone—death tends to create something of an impediment to that. He's no idiot. When Georges doesn't show and he can't contact either of them, don't you think he'll suspect that maybe, just maybe something's amiss? And when he does, he'll head elsewhere. Maybe turn around and catch the next flight to Timbuktu or anywhere far from here. We're losing our last chance to stop the Change. And when the Change happens, how many deaths will be laid on Dawn's doorstep?"

"There'll be other chances."

"Not like this one."

She gestured toward the backseat. "We have him."

"Yeah, there's that—assuming the kid is crucial to his plans. If not . . . then, as Abe would say, we've got bupkes."

She reached out and patted his arm. "You can salvage this."

"Oh, really?"

"Yes, really. I have faith in you."

"Swell."

He didn't tell her that he hadn't a clue as to how to accomplish that.

He'd turned into Nuckateague and sensed Weezy pulling into herself as they neared the house. Dune Drive was quiet as, well, a tomb—and would be sort of functioning as one for a while. As he approached the mansion and the O'Donnell house he couldn't find a clue that all hell had broken loose here less than an hour ago.

She'd insisted on seeing Dawn's body. He'd warned her it was bloody and she'd suffered an ugly death, but she'd insisted. And when he'd pulled the sheet down, she lost it.

She'd recovered somewhat now, but was keeping up the how-can-we-leave-her-there-like-that? litany. The most rational woman he'd ever known had surrendered all her critical faculties.

"You're not thinking, Weez. Where can you take her?"

"I don't know, but we can't just—"

He raised his hands. "Please. Stop. You're talking about driving around with a dead body in your car. Not just dead—*murdered*. So you can't take her to a funeral home or even an ER without winding up being asked a lot of questions you do not want to answer."

"But—"

"Think of it as cold storage."

"But rats . . . mice . . ."

He realized he had to give her something.

"Okay, here's what I can do: Before I clear out, I'm going to wipe this place down—everything we might have touched. After I'm gone I'll call the East Hampton police and report bodies in the O'Donnell garage on Dune Drive. I'll even give them Dawn's name so she can be buried with her mother."

Weezy thought about this for a moment, then nodded. "Okay. I guess that's the best we can do. It means she won't be out there for long. I'll help you wipe down and—"

"No. You take the baby and head for the city."

"The baby?"

"Well, yeah. You've just become his unofficial guardian."

"But I don't know the first thing about babies." Her hand shot up as Jack opened his mouth. "And please, no Butterfly McQueen references."

How had she guessed? Was he that predictable?

"You mean there's something you don't know?"

"I never found babies very interesting."

"Better start reading up on them because you just became Aunt Weezy."

Her expression reflected mild panic. "This is serious, Jack. I've never had contact with children, especially babies, and this is no ordinary baby."

"That's for sure."

"I mean, what does he eat? Formula? Cereal? Were they feeding him Jell-O or jelly or something?"

"What?"

"He's got red smears on his face."

"Oh, um . . ." He decided not to burden her with that detail. "I have no idea what Gilda was feeding him."

"Jack, what'll I do?"

"You're the smartest person I know. You'll figure it out."

Weezy looked ready to cry again. Jack couldn't help it. To do what he needed to do, he needed her and the baby gone.

They packed up Dawn's things and Weezy's things, and within half an hour she and the baby were on their way, leaving Jack at the door staring across the empty yard at the equally empty mansion on the far side of the street.

Dawn had deep-sixed his original plan. Had to be another way to salvage this opportunity. He'd have to improvise.

Jack hated to improvise.

II. After wiping down the O'Donnell place as best he could, he went to the garage and opened his trunk. He stared at all the ordnance he'd acquired and might never get a chance to use.

The octol and the copper cones—what good were shaped charges now? The double-whammy roadside IEDs were out. Even if Rasalom decided to return to the mansion on his own, Jack would have no idea how he was arriving. If he rented a car, Jack wouldn't know what it looked like. He couldn't simply incinerate the first car that passed between the charges. And if he took a taxi, he'd have somebody driving—Jack had had no qualms about Georges, but he wasn't about to kill an innocent cabbie.

He grabbed the golf bag and checked inside: the M-79 nestled among the clubs. Easy enough to use. He leaned that against the wall and pulled out one of the two carpet-clad Stingers. He unwrapped and inspected it. The missile and its launcher ran about five feet long and weighed north of thirty pounds. Not exactly a conceal-able weapon. He'd never fired one, but Abe had included instructions. He'd have to read up on the procedure if he was going to use it.

A big if.

He leaned the Stinger next to the golf bag and stared at the makings for his shaped charges. He'd had big plans for those—taking out Rasalom before he made it to the house. Now, if he showed up at all, Jack would have to try to take him down on his own turf.

He stepped out the side door and stared at the man-sion. Launch a grenade and missile attack on the place once he was inside and reduce it to rubble? A possibility.

But first Jack had to get him out here. How to do that? How to explain Georges's no-show at the airport without arousing suspicion? Couldn't send a stand-in driver—he'd never go for that. Had to be a way.

Jack made a mental list of the elements he had to work with—all the people and things that involved Rasalom's life in Nuckateague: Gilda, Georges, the baby, the car, the house. Some combination of those might provide the key.

First thing he needed was a plausible reason for Georges not to show up at JFK . . . and for both him and Gilda to be incommunicado. And he needed a way to get that information to Rasalom.

Did Rasalom carry a cell phone? Well, why not? Glaeken carried one, no good reason Rasalom wouldn't.

He ducked back into the garage and made a beeline for Georges. He'd left the guy's phone with his corpse. Yep, there it was. Jack flipped it open, found the address book, and began going through it. He tried "Osala," "Boss," even "Rasalom," but no luck. He did find "One." A New York City code. Pretty good chance that was it. But just to be sure . . .

He had to roll Gilda over to check her pockets. He'd placed her facedown to hide her gory front from Weezy. He'd found only one knife, and he doubted that Dawn had stabbed herself, so the most logical scenario was that Gilda had found the baby gone, grabbed a knife, and run over here to stop Dawn. Dawn had somehow disarmed her and given her a dose of her own medicine. Many doses.

He shook his head at the butchery. Dawn had continued stabbing long after Gilda was gone. Weezy wouldn't want to believe that her Dawn was capable of that.

He found Gilda's cell in a pocket of her coat. He searched for "One" first this time but came up blank. No luck either with "Osala," "Boss," or "Rasalom." While searching he noticed a number of texts from "Kris" and a reply to each. So, the murderous old broad liked to exchange texts with her equally murderous son. How sweet. The family that kills together, what?—chills together?—heads for the hills together?—stomps anthills together? He wondered if they discussed their favorite blades for cutting off eyelids.

Gilda didn't seem to have many names in her address book so he went through them one by one. He stopped when he reached "Master." That number matched the one in Georges's.

Got it.

A phone number for Rasalom . . . how weird that seemed.

But then he remembered Glaeken's warning of a few

weeks ago: Rasalom was human. He had a few enhancements that weren't standard equipment in the off-the-rack members of the species, but he wasn't a god—not even a demigod. Another thing he wasn't was telepathic, so he had to resort to prosaic methods to stay in contact with his minions.

The number glowed on the displays of the two phones. Great.

Now what?

An idea, barely formed, began to tickle his brain. He didn't jump on it. That might scare it away. Better to leave it alone and let it develop on its own.

He'd need some luck—the good kind. Plenty of bad luck today . . . he was due for some good. Yeah, with a little luck and a lot of fancy footwork, there might, just might be a way.

12. A man who was something more than a man, who was known as the One to many and as Rasalom to a few, who had numerous names, the most important known only to him, strode through the airport toward the baggage area.

The solid floor of the terminal felt good beneath his feet. Such a relief to tread solid ground again—ground that would soon be *his*. He was not one for anxiety, yet he'd experienced a few moments of concern during the flight, especially when the plane had dipped and yawed in the rough weather toward the end. The pilot had mentioned something about an East Coast storm. He could survive far more trauma than any of his fellow passengers, but he had limits.

How ironic, after all the dangers he'd survived across

the millennia of his life, to die in a plane crash when he stood on the brink of his ultimate victory.

He had been to China where he stood atop Minya Konka. The planet's largest nexus point is located there. He had stood naked within it, his feet resting upon a buried pillar, communing with the Otherness, preparing for the Change.

For the time was near . . . close, so close he could taste it. So could the Otherness. It hovered, poised to re-enter this world, slavering to engulf this reality.

It knew of his plan and approved. No more surrogates, no more underlings doing his bidding. He would handle this entirely on his own, because he could act freely now, without fear of retribution from Glaeken.

Glaeken . . . He shook his head with chagrin. He had spent the entire time since his last rebirth looking over his shoulder, wondering when Glaeken would strike. The man had fooled Rasalom before, lulled him into believing he had wearied of his role in the Conflict and retired from the field of battle. Rasalom had let down his guard and, as a result, had spent half a millennium languishing in a stone prison in a remote pass in the Transylvanian Alps.

And when he'd thought he'd found a way free, Glaeken had shown up and slain him with that cursed sword.

But now the sword was gone, as was its hilt, and Glaeken had been stripped of his immortality—aging since he'd slain Rasalom at the keep. He was now an impotent, doddering old man who could do *nothing* to stop the Change. He had his Heir working for him, but the Heir was no Glaeken. He carried not an iota of his predecessor's experience or cunning. He was no threat. After the Change, Rasalom would tear him into tiny screaming pieces, and make Glaeken watch. And then he would move onto his wife, and take even longer with her.

How different things would be now had Rasalom known all this upon his rebirth. All that wasted time . . .

But now he was poised to end this battle. All the pieces were in play. He merely had to wait for the proper alignment, and that wouldn't be long.

He drank in the emotions oozing from the cattle around him. Normally an airport did little to ease his hunger. Too many of the cattle were headed for vacations, filled with pleasant anticipation about their destination—rest, relaxation, fun activities, good food, good drink, good sex. Occasionally he'd come across one in a near panic about flying, and that was a pleasing hors d'oeuvre, but he rarely found enough of them to qualify as even a snack.

This evening was different. The air was redolent of anxiety over the weather and the safety of flying and whether or not their precious flight would be canceled. And even better: the crushing disappointment of those whose flights had already been canceled—especially the children. The young ones' emotions were so intense. Their joy was like a knife in his heart, but their anger, sadness, fear blended into a splendidly potent cocktail.

But the emotions here, now, were nothing compared to what the Change would precipitate. Grief and fear would reign at first, but would devolve into hate and rage and violence as resources became scarce and the cattle gouged and maimed and killed for scraps of food and sips of water.

He looked at the passing faces and smiled. Yes, after the Change these average humans will engage daily in actions they presently consider unthinkable. The fragile mental constructs the herds call civilization will crumble, their rational veneers will flake away to reveal the beast lurking just below the surface.

Fear . . . fear was the gateway to debasement—of others, of the self—and debasement was ambrosia, the pièce de résistance. Fear was the key to everything that empowered the Otherness and, consequently, Rasalom.

Fear will rule as their mortal world is transformed, as the very rules of nature shift and twist into tortured parodies of everything they once relied upon. Their sun will go out, and in the ensuing nightworld, every shadow will hide the threat of agony, the very air will scorch their skin and scald their eyes, and they'll pray that every searing breath will be their last. But it will not. They'll live on and on, and the Otherness will feed and feed.

As will I.

For he would undergo his own Change—into a new form adapted to the new Earth . . . the Other Earth.

When the Change was ready to begin, he would return to the summit of Minya Konka to be imbued with the seeds of his own Change.

All that stood between him and that day was the Lady.

But she would not be standing too much longer.

He arrived at the baggage area but saw no sign of Georges. Had the snow slowed him? No excuse. He should have left earlier.

He pulled out his phone. He'd shut it down during the flight and hadn't yet turned it back on. The display lit with the date and local time, plus a little envelope at the bottom. A message? As wonderful as these little devices were—how different the First Age wars might have turned out had these been available—he felt they had too many options. He did not like text messages, and apparently he had one.

He toiled through the menu and discovered he had

two, both sent while he was in flight. And both from Gilda. He knew she frequently texted her son. Perhaps she thought a text was the best way to leave a message while he was in the air.

He opened the first:

> The child is ill. We must take him to hospital.

He frowned. Ill? He did not like the sound of that. The child had become integral to his plans—delicate plans, easily thrown off. It wouldn't do for it to become seriously ill. But hadn't that doctor, that surgeon who had excised his tentacles—Heinze, wasn't it? Hadn't he been out to the house just yesterday and pronounced him in excellent health?

Good thing the tentacles were gone. Dr. Landsman, who had delivered the child, had lobbied for the amputations, saying that if the child ever needed inpatient care, the tentacles would cause a tremendous stir—headlines in the tabloids, reporters, medical specialists, geneticists, TV camera crews. A circus.

He now was glad he had listened.

He glanced at the message again. No mention of which hospital. Perhaps in the second message. He noted it was sent almost three hours after the first.

He opened it:

> He is very sick. They are admitting him. My phone does not work in hospital. Georges will fill you in when he picks you up.

. . . *very sick* . . . not good at all. This could ruin everything.

Still no mention of which hospital. Had they taken him someplace in the Hamptons or to the city? Probably the latter. Dr. Heinze would most likely want to be involved in his care.

He tried calling Gilda but her voice mail came on immediately. Had she turned off her phone or was the hospital jamming it? He'd heard that some hospitals did that. Well, he would have to depend on Georges.

Speaking of whom, where was he?

He speed-dialed Georges's number but was shifted to his voice mail immediately too. Was he still at the hospital with Gilda? That was no excuse.

He turned and saw his bag riding the carousel. He refused to walk over and pick it up. That was Georges's job.

And Georges had better have a very good reason for not being here.

13. Dark had fallen extra early due to the storm. Jack debated turning on the mansion's lights. Would Rasalom be more comfortable entering a lighted house? Most definitely. Jack had done his best to leave everything looking as close as possible to the way he had found it—*exactly* was not an option. Would the lights increase the chances of Rasalom picking up telltale signs of his handiwork? Certainly, but only incrementally.

He decided in favor of lights, but only a few, judiciously chosen.

He made his final walk-through. Everything looked good. Had this been the original plan, and had he had time, he would have photographed every area before starting work, to make sure he'd returned it to its original condition. This was why he hated to improvise.

His phone rang. He checked the display: Weezy.

"Everything okay?"

"Well, no. The roads are bad and getting worse, but I made it."

"Then what—?"

"This baby. I don't know what to do with him. How much—?" A screech in the background. *"Oh, God. He's awake. I gotta go."*

The call ended. He closed his phone and checked the display: 6:35. He pulled out Georges's and Gilda's phones. He'd turned both off after sending the text messages. Now he turned on Gilda's for a quick look at the call history. Two missed calls in the past half hour, both from "Master." He powered hers down again and turned on Georges's. *Four* calls from "One." He resisted the impulse to listen to Rasalom's voice mails, which he assumed would ascend in irritation and anger as they progressed. Didn't want to risk Rasalom getting through. So he turned off that phone as well.

Yes, sir . . . ol' Rasalom oughta be royally pissed by now.

14. Where *was* that man?

Rasalom could understand Gilda being incommunicado with the baby. But Georges . . . no. Possibilities, none of them good, cascaded through his mind: accident, arrest, death, something catastrophic with the child. While devastating to contemplate in relation to his plans, the last should not be a factor in Georges's absence.

He made up his mind. The snow continued and road

conditions were no doubt deteriorating. If he was to entertain any hope of returning to Nuckateague tonight—and he did not wish to stay in one of these dreary airport hotels—he would have to act now.

He signaled to one of the loitering skycaps to remove his bag from the carousel. The man found him one of the limousines that cruised the arrival areas like sharks, and stowed the bag in the trunk while Rasalom seated himself on the leather upholstery.

"Good evening, sir," the driver said, putting the car in gear and beginning to roll. "Where to?"

"Nuckateague."

The driver braked. "Out past the Hamptons?"

"Correct. Is there a problem?"

"I'm afraid that's too far, sir. Especially in this weather. It's a long ride out and probably even longer back with no fare."

Rasalom had kept his wallet out after tipping the skycap. He'd anticipated this. The driver had probably expected to hear a Midtown or Westchester address. He pulled out five hundred-dollar bills and tossed them over the backrest onto the front seat.

"Sufficient?"

The man's eyes lit. "Yes, *sir*!"

He was certain he could have bought him off with less, but didn't care to bargain with his sort. Over what? These pieces of paper that people chased after with such unseemly fervor? He had access to a virtually limitless supply, but so what? They lacked even the slightest intrinsic value and were leaking what little fiat value they still retained. After the Change they might be useful as toilet paper, but little else.

"Proceed," he said. "But with caution."

15. The intercom buzzed and Weezy fairly ran to it. She jammed the talk button.

"Gia?"

"That would be me."

Oh, thank God, thank God, thank God! she thought as she hit the button to buzz her through the front door.

"Seven-C. Come on up."

And please hurry.

Once again she complimented herself on the simple brilliance of her solution to the problem of the baby: call Gia. Gia had firsthand baby experience—Vicky was proof of that. But she'd offered more than just advice, she'd volunteered to come over and give hands-on help.

Weezy restrained herself from doing a Snoopy happy dance, but even if she'd given in to the urge, the piercing shriek that shot through the apartment at that moment would have brought it to a screeching halt.

It originated in the spare bedroom she had turned into an office, but now served as a bedroom again—the baby's. She'd put him there because she didn't know what else to do with him. And she sure as hell didn't know how to stop those shrieks.

She admitted she was frazzled. No, *frazzled* didn't quite cut it. How about at her wits' end?

Nothing she did would stop his shrieking. She might have been able to stand the sound if it hadn't been so loud. Already her next-door neighbor had knocked on the door and asked if everything was all right. She'd have management calling if this went on all night.

She paced her front room, waiting for Gia's knock. When it came she didn't even bother checking the peephole—something she never skipped. The door swung open to reveal Gia and Vicky, red-cheeked from the cold, in snow-sprinkled knit hats and puffy coats.

"Come in! Come in!"

"Hi, Weezy," Gia said, giving her a quick hug. "Good to see you again."

Weezy had roomed with Jack most of last summer into the fall. Another woman might have made it impossible, or at the very least, terribly awkward. But Gia and Jack had such trust and confidence and regard for each other, simultaneously deep and casual, that it never became an issue between them. Not surprising, considering what they'd weathered together.

Weezy, on the other hand, couldn't deny that it had been tough on her at times, especially on certain lonely nights when she felt the need to snuggle up to a warm body, and the best friend from her past and now the best friend of her present was in the next room . . .

"Hi, Weezy!" Vicky said with a grin. "Remember me?"

Vicky . . . if Weezy ever had a daughter—and she didn't see that ever happening—she'd wish for one like Vicky.

"Of course I do." They hugged. "How could I ever forget—?"

Another shriek.

Gia winced and stiffened. "What . . . ?"

"That's the baby," Weezy said, taking her coat.

"Is something wrong?"

"I don't know. I don't think so. He's . . . different."

Gia nodded. "Jack told me about him back when he was looking for her mother. Something about genetics. But—"

Another shriek.

Vicky put her hands over her ears. She looked frightened.

"How long has he been doing that?" Gia said.

"Since I brought him in and he woke up."

"Is he—?"

A shriek.

"I've fed him—or tried to, anyway—and changed him and held him and rocked him and . . ." Weezy was afraid she'd break down in tears of frustration. "Nothing works. I don't know what's wrong. He just stands there and screams."

"Stands? On the phone you said he was only two weeks old. He can't—"

Another shriek.

"He is."

Gia looked dubious as she began moving toward the spare room. "And you said you 'tried' to feed him?"

"He sort of wrecks the nipples on the bottles."

"Wrecks?"

Another shriek.

"I'll show you in a minute."

As they stepped inside the room, Weezy found the baby right where she'd left him: Dressed in a diaper, standing in the crib, and holding on to the side rail. He went a little crazy at the sight of Gia and let out a series of back-to-back ear-splitting shrieks that went on and on. Both Weezy and Gia pressed their hands over their ears. And then—

—the shrieks stopped as if somebody had turned an off switch.

Weezy saw the child's wide-eyed stare directed past them. She turned to see what he found so interesting.

Vicky had entered the room.

Weezy looked back and forth between them. The baby seemed fascinated . . . couldn't take his eyes off her.

"Vicky," she said. "Do me a favor . . . leave the room for a second, will you, please?"

Looking confused, Vicky glanced at her mother.

Gia nodded. "Go ahead, honey."

Vicky backed out and turned the corner. As soon as she was out of sight, the shrieks resumed.

"Okay, come back in."

The baby immediately went silent at her return.

"I think he likes you, Vicky," Weezy said.

Vicky's wary look said she wasn't so crazy about that idea.

As the baby stared at Vicky, and Vicky stared back, Gia stepped up to the crib and gave the child a closer look.

"Back in Iowa," she said in a low voice, "when I was growing up, the ladies of Ottumwa used to have a name for little guys like this. They called them 'I'm-sorry' babies."

"What do you mean?"

"The mother would be asked, 'Is this your baby?' When she said, 'Yes,' they'd think, *I'm sorry.*" She glanced at Weezy. "Tough crowd, that Ottumwa bunch."

Vicky stayed back, looking unsettled. The baby's stare seemed to bother her. "He scares me, Mom."

Gia reached out and stroked his stiff black hair. "He's just a baby, Vicky. And I think he's had a bad day. A very bad day. So we have to cut him a little slack, okay?"

"But he looks so—"

"Remember what we talked about? People can't help the looks they're born with, so we never make fun of them for that. We never hurt their feelings, right?"

"I guess." Vicky looked at Weezy. "What's his name?"

"I . . . I don't know." Gia's puzzled look spurred her on.

"If Dawn ever came up with a name for him, she never told me. To tell the truth, I don't think she had one."

Gia frowned. "How could she not have a name for her own baby?"

Weezy hesitated, unsure of how much Gia might want her to say in front of Vicky.

"Well, the circumstances were unique. Dawn couldn't be sure her baby was even alive, so I got the impression she was afraid to name him until she found him and got him back."

"And did she?"

Weezy's throat constricted. "Yes, poor kid. Briefly. Very briefly."

Gia was studying her. "You and Dawn were close?"

"She . . . I was all she had." A sob built. "I—"

She couldn't speak. Gia stepped close and put her arms around her.

That did it. The dam burst and Weezy lost it. All the grief, the anguish, the sense of loss she'd been holding in since she'd heard, since she'd seen Dawn's pale, lifeless body, broke loose and flooded from her. She clutched Gia, leaning against her as she sobbed on her shoulder like a child.

It felt so good to let it go. The pressure of it . . . she'd been afraid she'd explode. She hadn't dared let go on the ride home—not with a sleeping baby in the backseat and the roads so awful. And once here, when he woke up and the screeching began, and she'd been trying to feed him and wash him and get him settled . . .

She regained control and eased herself away from Gia.

"I'm sorry. That's not like me. I just . . ."

"It's okay. Really."

Weezy studied her. From the day they'd met last year,

she'd sensed a steely core in Gia. And when the Lady had told her what she and Vicky and Jack had been through—coma, brain injury, miscarriage—she realized Gia had needed that core to survive. But she hadn't appreciated until now how her steel was cushioned within an envelope of serenity.

"Thanks for understanding. How did you know?"

"I've been there."

She took a deep breath. "I feel so much better. Thank you."

Gia smiled and nodded as she ran her hand over the top railing of the crib.

"You must have been expecting him."

"What do you mean?"

"How else would you get a nursery set up so quickly?"

"Actually, they're Dawn's things." Dawn had given her a key, so Weezy had used it to enter her apartment. "I brought them over from across the hall."

That was when Weezy had come closest to losing it. Dawn had been all set for motherhood: the crib, baby clothes, bottles, formula. She hadn't been sure her baby was even alive, but she'd been ready to take on the role of mother if she found him.

Gia nodded. "That's right. She lived across the hall. I remember Jack being very concerned about that."

"He still is, I'm sure."

"And you're not?"

"Well, we'd feared there might be a plan to use Dawn and the baby against us, but we could never figure out what. It all seems moot now. They put a lot of effort into separating Dawn and her child, and hiding the child from her, but now Dawn's gone"—that tightening in her throat again—"and the baby's here."

"Could that have been the plan all along?"

A shocking possibility, but . . .

"Somehow I doubt it."

Gilda and Georges dead, and Jack at this very moment lying in wait, ready to blow the One to hell . . . no way that could have been Rasalom's plan.

Gia bent for a closer look at the rail. "This is all gnawed. Almost like he's teething. But that can't be. He's too young."

"That's what I'd have thought, but he's doing more than teething." She glanced around and spotted one of the plastic bottles she'd used to try to get formula into him. She grabbed it and handed it to Gia. "Here."

Gia stared at the torn end of the nipple and shook her head. "I don't . . ."

"He has teeth."

She stared at Weezy. "What? Teeth . . . at two weeks?"

"See for yourself."

Weezy carefully lifted his upper lip—at any other time he might have fought her, but whatever level of concentration he possessed was fully focused on Vicky. Light glinted off four white points poking through the upper gum and four through the bottom.

"My God," Gia whispered. She glanced at the ruined rubber nipple on the bottle in her hand. "I can't imagine nursing him."

"That's why he's dressed in just a diaper. His teeth are pointed and sharp. He starts sucking, then chewing, and it spills all over him."

"Maybe that's why he's screeching like that. They must hurt."

"They don't seem to be hurting him now." Weezy watched Vicky crossing the room to look out the window. The baby followed her every move. "But I think they were bleeding earlier today."

She'd assumed the red on his face and his clawlike fingers was Jell-O or the like, but it had turned out to be blood. She'd learned that when she'd cleaned him up. The only source she could think of were his gums.

"We need to get him teething rings," Gia said. "The kind you can freeze."

"But what about bottle nipples? I've just about run out."

"Plastic sippy cups—with the hardest plastic we can find."

"Why didn't I think of that?"

"You never babysat as a kid?"

Weezy shook her head. "No. Never."

As she'd told Jack, babies had never interested her.

Gia smiled. "I did a lot of it. Loved babies then, and still do." She turned and headed for the door. "Show me what you've got and I'll run out and stock you up with what you're missing."

Weezy followed, with Vicky bringing up the rear. But as soon as the little girl left the room, the baby renewed his screeching.

Weezy gave Gia a pleading look.

"Honey," she said, leaning close to Vicky, "would you mind staying in there with the baby?"

She shook her head. "He's scary."

"But he likes you—he likes you best of all."

"But it's boring."

"Well, you brought a book. Why don't you sit in there at Weezy's desk and read?"

"Even better," Weezy said. "Maybe you can read to the baby. I think he'd like that."

She brightened. "Okay."

You wonderful child, she thought as the baby screeched and screeched again. But please hurry.

"What are you reading?" Weezy said as Vicky bee-lined for her backpack.

"*Nocturnia*. I'm on book three."

"She just discovered the series," Gia said. "Loves it."

"She's ten, right?"

"Ten and a half next month," Vicky said.

"I remember reading lots of Judy Blume as a kid."

Gia smiled. "Me too. And Beverly Cleary. Loved those books."

Vicky stopped by the table in the front room where Weezy had left the *Compendium*. "Hey, that's Jack's book."

"Hay is for horses," Gia said and rolled her eyes. "I hated when my mother would say that, and yet here I am . . ."

Weezy smiled at Vicky. "Well, hay *is* for horses and yes, that's Jack's book. He lent it to me."

Vicky opened it, scanned a page, and shrugged. "Weird as ever."

A particularly loud screech prompted her to return to the baby's room and the result was . . .

. . . silence . . . blessed silence.

She glanced and noticed Vicky had opened the *Compendium* to the naming ceremony page Weezy had come across not too long ago. A lot had happened since then.

Faintly from within the baby's room she heard Vicky begin to read aloud.

"She's a gem," Weezy said. "Do you rent her out?"

Gia laughed. "She loves to read. Getting paid for it would be her dream job." She spread her arms. "Peace."

Peace here, Weezy thought. But she imagined it soon might be a different story tonight in a mostly deserted hamlet near the east end of Long Island.

16. Jack blinked and rubbed his eyes.

Sleepy.

Concerns, contingencies, and uncertainties about to-day had made for fitful slumber last night. The confinement of sitting at the watch window and waiting for the Otherness's Godot were dulling his consciousness. He couldn't afford that.

He stood and began walking around in as wide a circle as the tiny room would allow.

Considering what lay immediately ahead, how could his brain and body even consider sleep? He'd run a dozen or more mental checks on all his setups in the mansion. He'd studied the Stinger manual and had the pair set up and ready to rock. He wished he could have test fired one, but no way . . . no way.

Nothing left to do but wait . . . and watch the snow pile up . . . and know that each inch of accumulation further increased the odds of a no-show by Rasalom.

He might have decided to stay in town and wait out the storm. Or he might have become spooked and lit out for parts unknown.

And then what? Jack had three bodies in the garage and his car could be snowed in by the time it became certain Rasalom wasn't coming tonight. How long did he wait before aborting? A day? Two?

Damn. He felt like kicking a hole or two in these walls. Maybe three or four. But it wasn't the O'Donnells' fault. He—

A glow outside.

He leaped to the window and saw headlights working their way down Dune Drive. He watched as they passed the spot where he'd planned to set up the shaped charges.

A click of his remote and *kaboom!*—game over for the R-man.

Same for the hapless bastard driving him.

Jack suddenly wished he'd set the charges as planned— and let the chips fall where they may. That was Rasalom out there. Nothing was more important than stopping him, and as for anyone who happened to wander into the line of fire . . . sorry, Charlie. A little collateral damage was a small price to pay for—

Whoa! Where'd all this come from?

He pushed back against the alien homicidal regrets and concentrated on the here and now.

He found the field glasses and focused them on the car as it pulled into the mansion's front yard. Looked like a late model Lincoln Town Car. Typical rental limo. The driver got out and opened the rear door, then hurried to the trunk where he removed a suitcase. As he lugged it through the snow to the front door, another man slid from the rear of the car. Jack trained the glasses on the second's head as he passed in front of the headlights on his way to the house.

He felt his lips pull back from his teeth when he recognized the face.

Rasalom.

The One.

Godot.

He hurried downstairs to where a number of remotes sat on the coffee table next to the M-79 thumper. He picked out the one labeled FRONT DOOR and held it ready.

He'd rigged the front door with a tripwire. He'd wanted to position one of the shaped charges six feet inside the door, set to go off when the door was opened. The blast would pretty much vaporize whoever had his hand on the knob. Trouble was, Jack didn't know who would step through, so he'd scrapped that plan.

Good thing too as he watched the driver push open the door and set the bag inside. He waved to his passenger and scooted back to the warmth of his car. No money exchanged hands. Probably a prepaid fare.

As Rasalom entered and closed the door behind him, Jack pressed the remote. The door's tripwire was now armed for a different kind of surprise. Same with the back door.

A welcome-home gift for the One.

Soon to be the None.

17.
He stood in the front hall and stamped the snow off his feet.

The house was warm, lights were on, but . . .

He didn't have to call out. He knew the house was empty. He sensed no other presence. Like everyone else, Gilda and Georges had their own unique, emotional signatures. Neither was evident. Nor was anyone else's.

But . . .

Something was different. A residue of high emotion. He couldn't identify it, but it had been intense at the time. Gilda discovering the child was sick?

Perhaps.

He knew she loathed the child and it provided a constant source of amusement to him to sup on that loathing while she cooed over it and pretended to love it. He was certain she would not harm it. But something had happened here—sickness or injury—and she probably feared she would be blamed for negligence and face punishment.

A not unreasonable concern.

Yes, that would explain the residue.

He strode to his office to see if Gilda or Georges had left a message for him before departing. No . . . nothing. He'd called each of them a number of times during the long trip from the airport, and had watched his cell phone display for return calls, but nothing.

What happened? What is wrong with my baby?

My baby . . . what an odd, singular thought.

In all his years, he had never fathered a child. But he had taken possession of this one, so in the most practical sense it was indeed *his* baby. And central to his plans. If it died, he would have to scrap his carefully constructed timetable and chart a whole new course.

He considered calling the hospitals, one by one, but discarded that. He had no idea under what name Gilda would have presented the child.

He would wait. He was good at waiting.

He realized he was thirsty. After the Change he would have no bodily needs, but until then . . .

He realized he didn't know where Gilda kept the glasses. Attending to himself was a new experience. As he moved to the kitchen he considered how pampered he'd become. He simply asked for something and someone served it up.

Glasses . . . one of these cabinets over the counter, he assumed.

The refrigerator-freezer was a side-by-side model. As he opened a cabinet door in search of a tumbler, he reached over and tugged on the handle of what he assumed to be the refrigerator side—

—and found himself on the floor . . . across the room . . . a room full of roaring smoke and flaming debris. The refrigerator was gone. A remnant of one of its doors lay across his legs. The kitchen table and chairs that had sat before it were gone as well, reduced to flaming splinters.

And then he noticed his coat was on fire. He went to slap at the flames and searing agony shot up his left arm. He looked at it and cried out when he saw no hand. No bleeding—the stump was charred—but nothing beyond his left wrist.

And then the rest of his body announced its survival with screams of agony. Ignoring the pain, he rolled over to douse the flames, trying to orient himself, trying to remember what had happened. He'd been opening the refrigerator . . .

Flashes returned . . . the door swinging open . . . a white-hot blast of light and sound . . . the door disintegrating as a jet of flame spewed from within, catching his hand, vaporizing it . . . and then being hurled backward across the kitchen to slam against a wall.

Had he not happened to be looking for a glass he would have been standing before the refrigerator when he opened that door, and his entire body would have suffered the fate of his hand.

A trap.

Too obvious to need stating, but the buzzing hornets in his brain were drowning out his already jumbled thoughts, and he needed orientation. He clung to the word.

A trap . . . the child was not sick . . . Georges and Gilda had taken him nowhere . . . Georges and Gilda were dead, floating in the bay, perhaps . . . and someone was bent on destroying him.

Mind working frantically, he struggled to his knees.

He had been beyond lucky. And yet, even if by some chance the refrigerator contained the only bomb, he had to escape this burning house.

To where?

Outside could be just as dangerous. Odds were the assassin was waiting to confirm his kill, or to finish the job.

Thoughts congealed. Trade places: Where would *he* wait?

Out front, on the street. With the frigid, storm-tossed bay blocking retreat to the rear, that was the place to cut off escape.

Go out the rear, then. Sneak into the unlandscaped brush that flanked the property. Hide there until safe to move on.

Staying low, he threaded his way around the flaming furniture in the great room toward the back door. Snow gusted through the blown-out windows. He peered through the shattered glass of the back door. No sign of anyone about. He turned the knob and pulled—

—and the world lit up around him.

Jack saw the flash of light from the rear of the mansion. A faint boom echoed through the night, muffled by the wind and snow.

Shit.

He'd made only one shaped charge—for the refrigerator. He figured sooner or later everyone winds up at the refrigerator, right? Even Rasalom.

He had used the rest of the octol for other booby traps, mainly the front and rear doors.

The rear door had just blown. Could have been secondary to the pressure wave from refrigerator explosion, but somehow he doubted it. Not the way his luck was running.

How could anyone, even Rasalom, survive the refrigerator? No question it had been tripped—the inside of the house had lit up like a mini nuke had gone off and then most of the windows had blown out. The plasma jet from the shaped charge sitting on the shelf inside should have apocalypsed his ass. Whatever part of him escaped being sublimated to red vapor should have been reduced to charbroiled meat confetti. Glaeken had said he was tough, but no one was that tough.

Something had gone wrong.

Well, he'd prepared for that. If the shaped charge misfired, Rasalom would know he was in a trap and flee the house. Jack would have gone out a window, but he was pretty sure in all the millennia Rasalom had lived, he'd never set a bomb, so he'd probably choose a door. He had come in the front, so he'd assume it was safe to exit that way. But it was no longer safe—not after Jack had used the remote. For some reason Rasalom had chosen the back. No matter. Jack had lined its frame with octol as well.

Trouble was, that sort of bomb tended to be chaotic, with no direction, no reliable kill radius. In a word: unreliable. Especially where an immortal was concerned.

Looked like he was going to have to get closer—but not too close—to make sure he'd done what he'd come to do.

He checked his watch. He'd marked the time of the first detonation: just over thirty seconds ago. He had only so much time before the explosions were recognized for what they were and called in.

He reached for the modified M-79. He'd loaded it with

M406 40mm high-explosive grenades—one chambered, three in the tube—each with a fifteen-foot kill radius. He stuffed a variety of rounds into his jacket pockets—just in case—and headed out to the garage where he had the Stingers ready.

He swung the right door open and stepped inside. The Vic's trunk lay open with the two Stingers waiting in their launchers. He leaned the M-79 against the wall and grabbed one of the rockets. He shoved the coolant unit into the handle and let the argon gas do its work. The IFF antenna was unfolded but wouldn't be needed. He rested the launcher on his shoulder, centered the front door in the sight, and pulled the trigger.

The missile flew from the launcher. The ejection charge took it across the street before its solid fuel rocket flared to life and shot it toward the house. It wouldn't have time to reach its top speed of Mach 2, but its acceleration was awe inspiring.

He groaned and rolled over. He looked down at himself. The surrounding flames revealed a dozen wounds on his limbs and torso—all bleeding. Pain told him he had more in his back.

Another bomb. Was the whole house booby-trapped? He had to get out of here before he tripped another.

He blinked to focus on the back door—or rather where it had been. A charred, smoking, ragged opening had replaced it. Rasalom forced himself to his elbows and knees and crawled toward it. He had just reached the threshold when another explosion ripped through the house. The blast flung him through the opening and onto the snow outside.

What was *that*? The biggest explosion of all. Whatever glass had survived the first two blasts cascaded into the yard with that one. He had to put some distance between himself and this doomed house. If he could reach the brush he'd—

Rasalom froze as he saw the piling a few feet ahead of him, blocking his way. He'd exited on the east side of the house—his dazed, pain-fogged brain had forgotten that the mini lagoon and dock lay this way.

But not too far to his right . . . the garage. If he could reach that, he'd have a place to hide, out of sight and out of the elements.

Another explosion from within. The house would be a smoking ruin before long. He had to move now.

As yet another blast shook the house, he forced himself to his feet and stumbled toward the garage, praying to the Otherness that its side door wasn't locked.

The Stinger had blown a gaping hole in the front of the house, but Jack wasn't through. He dropped the launcher and picked up the M-79. He wished he could move across the street and pump the grenades into the house at closer range, but the high-explosive rounds were equipped with a safety feature that prevented detonation within a hundred feet of the launcher. He'd have to fire from here.

He settled the thumper's stock into his shoulder and sighted to the left of the former door, on the front bedroom where he'd peeked in and seen the baby last night.

Last night . . . seemed like days ago that he'd watched Georges and Gilda in their domestic bliss. They lay stretched out a few feet away. As did Dawn . . .

He pulled the trigger and heard the *thump!* that had

earned the M-79 its nickname. Surprisingly little recoil for such a big round, but nothing little about the explosion that ripped out the bedroom wall. If Rasalom had thought that might be a safe place to hide—*wrong*.

He pumped another HE grenade into the chamber and took aim at the room to the right of the door. Another *thump!* Another ruined wall.

He fired two more for insurance, emptying the weapon. As he bent to pick up the empty casings, he caught motion on the east side of the mansion. A dark figure, limned by the flames from the house, moving toward the garage.

Jack watched, stunned, as the man leaned against the side door and fairly fell inside.

How could it be? How could anyone, even Rasalom, survive all Jack had thrown at him? He looked hurt—he'd definitely taken some damage—but the fact he was moving at all was a miracle.

Jack pulled the extra 40mm ammo from his pockets and inspected them. Two more HE grenades, and a couple of buckshot rounds. He loaded them up—the HEs first, followed by the shot. He might not need either type, but he was ready to finish this in any number of ways.

In fact, if things went right, Rasalom might end it himself.

He closed the door behind him and slumped against the black hood of the Mercedes. The metal was cold. No surprise there. He wondered how long Georges had been dead. No matter.

He needed a place to rest, time to heal. His recuperative powers were vast. The bleeding would stop soon, the pain in his wrist stump would ease, and then the healing would begin. He could not grow a new hand, but all his other wounds would mend. He would need nourishment, though. And warmth.

He would contact Szeto, or better yet, that fool Drexler. Let him think he was still of value, let him provide shelter in the hope that it would return him to the One's good graces.

No chance of that.

But the first thing to do was remove himself as far from here as possible. He'd need the car for that. He'd only recently learned how to drive. He'd left home as a child—a very wealthy child who could afford a chauffer—and so he'd never had a need until his sojourn in North Carolina. But he'd never driven in snow.

How hard could it be? The roads were filled with idiots.

He opened the driver door and slipped painfully behind the wheel.

Jack watched the garage blow open its doors and belch flame.

The car had been an afterthought. Insurance of a sort. What if Rasalom had checked the garage and found the car there? He'd have known that Gilda and Georges were not at the hospital with the baby. He might have skipped going in the house, jumped in the car, and hauled ass out of there.

Might have . . .

An unlikely scenario, to be sure. Considering his hubris and his special abilities, he'd think himself capable of handling any situation mere mortals could toss at him. But Jack was taking no chances.

Georges, good chauffeur that he was, had kept the gas

tank full to the brim. Jack hadn't had enough octol left over to do a proper car bomb, but enough to make sure the tank went up and fried anyone inside. He'd thoughtfully left the keys in the ignition.

He checked his watch. Only a minute and ten secs since the first blow. Seemed a lot longer. Had to get a move on. But first and foremost, he had to *end* this.

He raised the thumper to his shoulder again and sighted on the garage. Time for the coup de—

A figure, engulfed in flame, broke from the side door in a staggering run, weaving back and forth, and then careening toward the lagoon. It tumbled over the edge and into the water.

Jack pulled the trigger, a too-quick shot that demolished the rear corner of the garage. He worked the pump and chambered the second grenade. He fought the impulse to run over to the lagoon and fire it into the water— the target would be too close and the safety mechanism would prevent detonation.

Rasalom was out of sight, so he aimed at the bulkhead along the far side of the lagoon where he'd seen him go in. If he was on the surface, he'd be caught in the kill radius. If underwater . . . Jack had no idea.

He fired and was running toward the lagoon even as the bulkhead shattered. When he reached it, light from the burning garage lit the surface of the water. No sign of Rasalom. Dead on the bottom? Hiding below the surface?

He chambered a buckshot round and fired into the water. Twenty pellets of number four shot ripped into the surface. The last round sent twenty more.

Still no sign of anything moving.

He pulled his Glock. Spacing the slugs two feet apart

in a grid pattern, he emptied the magazine into the water. He replaced that with a fresh magazine and continued the pattern until he was clean out.

Still no sign of life or a body.

He checked his watch. Two and a half minutes of carnage. He still had a little time, but no more ordnance except for the Stinger—and he couldn't fire that into the water.

He knew he should leave but he couldn't. He had to be sure. He needed a final touch. But what?

Then he remembered a gas can he'd seen in the O'Donnell garage. As he ran back across the street he prayed it was full or near full. He'd dump it on the surface of the water, toss in a piece of burning wood from the garage, and *woomp!* Fire on the water.

He headed for the garage.

He broke the surface and gulped air. He'd known it was certain death—his head would be blown apart as soon as it appeared—but he could stay under no longer.

He braced for the attack but none came. Shuddering in the near-freezing water, he looked around. To his left the garage burned at the end of the lagoon. Directly ahead, above and beyond the bulkhead, the blazing house lit the night. Movement to his right drew his attention. A dozen feet away, the boat swung back and forth on a mooring rope, banging against the dock.

No one in sight on the dock or standing on the bulkhead. He appeared to be alone.

His whole body began to shake—from the cold, from the blood loss, and from the burns that covered most of his exposed skin. He almost gave in, almost allowed himself to succumb to his wounds and his hopeless position.

Or did he have a chance? Could his attackers have left him for dead?

He couldn't afford to allow himself to believe that. He had to assume they'd be back.

The flickering light from the garage flames revealed a ladder built into the bulkhead near the stern of the boat. He forced his shuddering muscles to move and kicked toward it. Focusing his remaining strength, he used his good hand to grip the side rail. His feet found a rung and he pulled himself half out of the water. Even at full strength, climbing the ladder with one hand would present a challenge. In his current condition it seemed insurmountable.

And then the boat recoiled on its rope and the stern bumped him, almost knocking him off the ladder. He managed to hang on.

The boat.

He released the ladder and swung his right arm over the transom. He found a handhold on the far side and clung for all his life. He swung his damaged arm over the edge and hooked the crook of his elbow there. The stump screamed with pain but he ignored it and kicked off the ladder. Slowly, painfully, he wriggled himself onto the transom, then tumbled over onto the deck.

He allowed himself a few seconds to lie there gasping, then struggled to his knees. The boat seemed to be secured by only a single line. He untied it and felt it begin to drift away from the dock . . . toward the bay.

This was it. This was his answer, his escape route. All he needed were a few moments and he'd drift out of the lagoon into the open water of the bay. Once there, he'd be beyond their reach. No one else out here had a boat.

The dark and the snow would swallow him and he'd be free. He'd—

The boat banged against something and lurched to a stop. He looked up and saw it scraping against the far bulkhead. The wind angled out of the lagoon but also across it, and was holding the boat against the bulkhead.

He was stuck.

No!

His attackers could return any minute. They'd find him and take their time using their guns to reduce him to ground meat.

He thought of climbing out and crawling into the brush, but they'd see the boat and guess what had happened. His best bet still was out on the water.

He crawled to the bridge and hauled himself onto the seat before the steering wheel. The keys were in the ignition.

Did he dare? He'd been fooled once.

But he had to think that his attackers wouldn't booby-trap both the car *and* the boat.

He realized he had no choice. He might die if he turned the key, but he would certainly die if he didn't.

Jack found the can in the garage and hefted it—damn. Just a tiny bit sloshing in the bottom. He—

—froze as he heard the faint sound of a diesel engine sputtering to life.

What the—?

The boat! Rasalom had reached the boat. Jack couldn't imagine how, but he knew how to stop it.

He grabbed the second Stinger and a BCU and raced back toward the dock, shoving the cooling unit into the grip as he ran. The boat's engine was roaring now, full throttle no doubt.

Jack arrived in time to catch a glimpse of its stern as it raced from the mouth of the lagoon into the open water of the bay. The snowy darkness swallowed it, leaving him no target.

Then he remembered he didn't need one. The Stinger was a heat seeker. All he had to do was fire it and it would find the boat and ram itself up its exhaust pipe.

He rested the launcher on his shoulder, aimed where he'd last seen the boat, and pulled the trigger. For maybe two seconds he followed the blazing yellow streak of the missile's rocket engine as it flashed across the water, just a few feet above the surface. Then impact. The explosion lit the night—high explosive plus whatever diesel fuel was in the tank. The swirling snow and mist enhanced the glow as Jack watched bits of flaming debris pinwheel and tumble in all directions—bits of Rasalom among them, he assumed. He hoped. He prayed.

The One is the None.

But was he?

He'd survived everything else Jack had thrown at him. Could he have survived that?

Jack had hit him with everything he had, but still he wasn't satisfied.

What would satisfy him?

Pumping Rasalom's lifeless body full of kerosene and watching it burn, adding more as needed, poking the burning flesh to make sure it was fully consumed, then taking the ashes up in a plane and scattering them over the ocean.

Yeah. Then he'd be satisfied.

But unless Rasalom's body washed up somewhere, he was going to have to make do with this.

He checked his watch. Four minutes gone. The neighborhood was due for lots of company—the flashing-light kind—real soon.

Time to clean up and move on.

His Glock brass had ejected into the water. The last 40mm buckshot empty remained in the thumper's chamber. He picked up the other casing and trotted back to the O'Donnell garage where he policed the HE empties. They all went into the Vic's trunk along with the Stinger launchers and the M-79.

A quick trip through the house to retrieve his Leica and the remotes. He'd worn gloves since the wipe-down, so no worry about prints.

At the five-minute mark he was backing out of the garage. He left the doors open to guarantee that Dawn's body would be found. He'd call later to identify her.

He made it to Route 27 without passing anyone and was halfway to Amagansett when the first police car screamed past going the other way. The road was slick and the Vic had rear-wheel drive, so he took it easy.

He called Gia.

"How's everything?"

"Fine. We're at Weezy's."

He felt like he'd been punched. *"What?* You and Vicky?"

"You sound surprised."

Surprised? Try shocked. The last people he wanted involved with that baby were Gia and Vicky. Dawn, Gilda, and Georges were dead because of that child. It was dangerous, it was bad luck, it was—

"How—?"

"Weezy called and said she needed help, so we came over."

Weezy called . . . Jack clenched his teeth. She should know better.

Or should she? She hadn't seen him sucking his mother's blood off his fingers. To her it was Dawn's baby—one weird little baby, but just a baby.

Was he overreacting? Could be.

He forced calm.

"How's the baby? Making that noise?"

"Not anymore. Vicky read to him and in ten minutes he was asleep. Are you okay?"

"Yeah. Safe and sound and on my way back. You're heading home?"

"Soon. You going to stop by?"

"Your place? Hope to. Gonna stop off and see Glaeken first."

"Be careful out there. I hear the roads are awful. What? Weezy wants to speak to you."

And he wanted to speak to her. Did he ever want to speak to her.

"Okay. Bye. Love ya."

"It's over?" Weezy said when she came on.

Jack stayed cool. The baby was asleep, Rasalom was dead, Gia and Vicky were okay and were headed home.

"Think so. Hope so."

"You're not sure?"

"Couldn't be. Circumstances wouldn't allow. I hit him with everything I had. I do believe he sleeps with the fishes."

"Let's hope. By the way, you know who I love?"

"Who?"

"Vicky. The little lady hath charms to soothe the q'qr breast."

Jack loved her too. More than life. That was why he wanted her far from that little monster.

"Yeah, Vicky's the best."

Jack ended the call then leaned back and sighed. What

was done was done. He just wished he could be sure Rasalom was done.

Uncertainty gnawed his gut all the way back to the city.

18. Ernst had been switching back and forth between the city and the Long Island stations, waiting for news of an incident from somewhere between the Hamptons and Montauk. Exactly what that incident might be, he had no idea, but he'd know it when he heard it.

He fairly leaped toward the screen when he heard an announcer mention a "live report from Nuckateague." A pretty woman reporter wearing a hooded parka stood in the swirling snow and spoke into a microphone while firefighters, lit by flashing lights from their trucks, milled back and forth before a large pile of smoking rubble.

"I tell you, Evan, it's like a war zone out here. A waterfront mansion in this quiet, well-to-do hamlet has been razed to the ground after reports of multiple explosions. The detached garage has also been reduced to ashes and the car within appears to have been ripped apart by a bomb. Take a look . . ."

Ernst stared in wonder as the camera panned across the scene. The Order had owned the property for decades. Ernst remembered spending a weekend there a few summers ago. How shocking to see what had become of it.

Jack, Jack, Jack . . . I do believe I underestimated you.

The reporter went on to mention the three bodies that had been found in a garage across the street—two women and a man, all murdered.

Georges and Gilda, no doubt. But who was the second woman?

Jack had taken no prisoners, apparently.

But where was the most important body? What had happened to the One? Had Jack destroyed him so completely that no trace remained? Were his ashes mixed with those of the house?

Ernst hoped so. For that would mean that the Change would be postponed indefinitely. Perhaps forever. Certainly for his own lifetime.

And his own lifetime was all that mattered.

19. Glaeken had given him a key to the elevator. Jack entered the darkened apartment, knowing he'd find him up. He was right. He spotted him by the big picture window, silhouetted against the glow of the snowy city.

Three and a half hours on the road to get here, dreading and anticipating this moment.

"Well?"

Glaeken didn't turn from the window.

"You're asking me if he lives?"

"Yes."

"You don't know?"

"I blew him up, set him on fire, and blew him up again. But I couldn't confirm the kill. What's left of him is somewhere on or under Gardiner's Bay."

Glaeken sighed. "He lives."

Jack dropped onto the couch and let his head drop back. "Shit."

"But barely. Just barely."

"What's that mean?"

Now Glaeken turned but Jack could not see his features. He imagined a pretty grim expression.

"Ever since his rebirth he has been a presence, a dissonant hum between my ears. That hum is still there, yet it has grown so faint in the past few hours that it hovers on the edge of perception. He is severely wounded, perhaps mortally so. He is dying."

"But he's not dead."

The silhouette shook its head. "No. Not yet."

Jack didn't know what more he could do. Be great if he knew someone in the Coast Guard. He could commandeer a cutter and go out in the storm with a harpoon, searching for what was left of Rasalom.

Yeah, right.

"Tell me the circumstances."

Jack recounted the progression of events during the four fateful minutes in Nuckateague.

Glaeken shook his head. "I don't see what else you could have done."

"I could have gotten more up close and more personal."

"And if you had, you might not be here describing your travails."

Jack banged the arm of the couch with a fist. "I don't know what else to do."

"We wait. From the sound of what you put him through, he must die soon. Unless . . ."

The last thing Jack wanted to hear right then was an *unless*.

"Unless what?"

"Unless someone helps him. But his two attendants are dead, and the storm is keeping everyone inside. Where could he find help?"

"He could wash up near the house and some rescue

worker could spot him and pull him out. Some CPR, some IV fluids, some hypothermia treatment, and some do-gooder could assure the end of life as we know it."

"What are the chances?"

"Who knows? I listened to the radio all the way in. Plenty of talk about the fire and the three bodies, but not a word about a survivor."

"Yet."

Jack nodded. "Let's turn on the TV and keep posted as to whether there's a sole survivor of this terrible tragedy. Because if there is, he's going to require a late-night consultation by Doctor Jack to finish the job."

20.   He opened his eyes again and saw the light. And once again he reassembled his scattered thoughts into a semi-coherent assessment of his situation.

He had washed up on an unknown shore. He lay upon snow-covered sand. A light shone somewhere ahead. He had been trying to reach it, crawling toward it. But every time he progressed a few feet, he passed out. And each attempt yielded less progress and briefer consciousness. But now something new.

Somewhere a dog barked.

The light went out . . .

. . . and came back on again. And something else. A vocal rumble nearby.

A dog, sniffing, panting, and growling. Would it attack? He could not defend himself against a sick kitten, let along a hungry dog. Never, not even during his darkest days trapped in the depths of the keep, had he felt this helpless.

And then a voice . . . one of the cattle . . . a cow . . . far away . . . or perhaps it only seemed far away.

"Rocky? Rocky, come back here this instant!"

He clung to the sound like a sailor to flotsam. He tried to speak but had no voice. He managed to raise his remaining hand, and that set the dog to barking again.

"What have you got out there, you dumb mutt?" the cow said. He sensed age in the voice. "Whatever it is, leave it alone and come inside before you catch your death."

No! Do not go in! Stay!

"Don't make me come out there!"

Yes! Come out! I beg you, come out! I will give you anything! I will seat you at my right hand after the Change if you will only bring me into your house!

He moved his hand again, precipitating a new round of near hysterical barking.

"I declare, you are the dumbest creature on Earth!" The voice . . . growing louder. "And I'm even dumber for coming out in this to get you. I should leave you out here, but you're so dumb you'd forget how to find the door! You'll probably—Mother of God! Is that—?"

He felt something nudge him. A toe? He raised his hand as he had before.

"Dear God, he's alive!"

He felt something tighten on his left arm. He assumed it was the cow's hands but he was too numb to feel anything beyond deep pressure.

"You're going to have to help me, mister," she said. "I'm assuming you don't know I'm on in years and don't see so well. You're dead weight and I can't move you on my own."

He pushed against the ground with his right hand

while she tugged on his left arm. Suddenly she released him and he dropped again.

"Dear God! Your hand! Did you lose your hand?"

He wanted to scream, *Isn't that obvious, you old idiot?*

Fortunately for him, he still had no voice. He could only grunt.

She grabbed him again, pulling on his truncated left arm while he dug his right hand into the semi-frozen snow and pushed toward the light.

21.

Plenty on the late-night news about the destruction and dead bodies out in Nuckateague, but nothing about a survivor.

Jack didn't know if that was good or not. If they found an unidentified man hovering near death, he'd know where to go and what to do to finish the job. If they didn't, it meant Rasalom was still out in the storm, burned, battered, barely breathing—and ready to breathe his last, Jack hoped.

He rose and grabbed his jacket. "I might as well head out."

"Stopping in to see your ladies?"

"Nah. Don't think I'm good company tonight."

"You need them."

"But they don't need me. Not like this."

Glaeken was staring at him. "Are you all right, Jack? I ask this knowing the answer."

"Well, if you know the answer, why are you asking?"

"Because I'm curious about the reason. I understand you're angry and disappointed and frustrated about tonight—"

"Do you? Can you? I threw every goddamn thing I had at him—everything short of a tactical nuke—and you tell me the son of a bitch is still breathing."

"You haven't failed yet. He still might—"

"Not knowing is driving me nuts."

"All the more reason to be with people who love you."

"They won't want to be with me very long. Even *I* don't want to be with me tonight. So rather than alienate them, I figure it's better I keep to myself."

The old man continued his annoying stare. "This isn't like you, Jack."

"Yeah? Well, I'm not feeling much like me lately."

"Oh?"

He looked at the finger he'd cut batting away the knife Georges had thrown. Pretty much completely healed now.

"I told you about the healing bit."

Glaeken nodded. "Not good news for either of us."

"Got that right." Glaeken on his way out and Jack being pushed someplace he didn't want to go. "But what's happening seems more than physical."

Another nod. "A certain . . . ruthlessness?"

"Right again."

"That's part of it. As your recuperative abilities increase, your empathy diminishes."

"So it's not just me."

"No. It's the Ally, or whatever infinitesimal fragment of it remains with this world. To be the Defender you must not only be physically resilient but you must have a singleness of purpose. As you've so painfully discovered, the Ally cares not a whit for us as individuals, only that we survive as a species to keep this corner of reality sentient."

" 'A spear has no branches.' " The phrase tasted bitter.

"Correct. Nor should said spear have any concern beyond hitting the target."

Jack shook his head. So that was why he'd considered setting out the shaped IEDs anyway, even if it meant sacrificing an innocent driver. And why he'd been kicking himself on the way home for not doing it.

"How do you fight that? How do you resist something that sneaks up on you and gets into your head and changes your perspective?"

Glaeken sighed. "With great difficulty. Because you don't feel it. You think it's right and natural. You think it's you. And in a way, it is. There's a darkness in all of us that will gladly use the end to justify any means."

"What you call 'darkness,' I call the brain."

"Ah, science. Stealing the mysteries from life."

"More like providing an antidote for magic."

"But 'darkness' is so much more picturesque, so much more evocative."

"You can't get much darker than the human brain. It's got no conscience. It wants what it wants when it wants it, but most of all it wants to survive, and will do whatever's necessary to preserve itself. But then there's the mind . . ."

"That which makes us sentient, which sees a bigger picture, a different perspective. You can't allow the darkness—or your brain—to overrule your mind." He shook his head. "But it's not easy. Back in the First Age, a number of us were chosen to lead the battle against the Seven—when Rasalom still counted himself in their number. Some of us succumbed to the influence, willing to sacrifice strings of innocent villages in order to win a single battle, becoming nearly indistinguishable from those we were fighting."

Jack thought of Glaeken's love for his wife and his continued devotion to her demented shell.

"You seemed to have succeeded."

"The best weapon is awareness. Knowing that your perspectives and values are being subverted forces you to question yourself. Preserve the real you early on, and that is the person who will prevail."

Jack slipped into his jacket. "I still don't want to subject anyone to my presence tonight."

Glaeken smiled. "See? You're winning the battle already."

"What about tonight's battle? You still sense him out there?"

Glaeken's smile faded as he nodded.

Shit.

Jack took the elevator down and trudged out into the storm. The falling snow muffled the sounds of the city. He'd garaged the car before coming to Glaeken's. The trunk had a special lock and he had the only keys. The Nuckateague evidence would be safe until he disposed of it.

A cab cruised by but he let it go. He lived twenty-some blocks from here. Might as well walk. To Julio's? Nah. Just home. He always had beer in the fridge.

He hoped the walk would tire him. Fat chance. He had a feeling he wouldn't sleep much tonight. Probably stay up listening to the radio for word of a survivor in Nuckateague.

Jack couldn't stand the fact that this wasn't over. It *had* to be over.

His phone rang. He checked the display: Gia.

"Hi. Home safe?"

"No. We've decided to spend the night at Weezy's."

No! He resisted an urge to shout into the phone.

"Bad idea."

A pause, then, *"Why do you say that?"*

"The farther you and Vicky are from that kid, the better."

"He's just a baby. And Vicky has such a great effect on him, we figured it would make things a whole lot easier for Weezy if we stayed."

Jack's turn to pause. Maybe it was okay if they stayed. He didn't see how anyone in the Order could connect Weezy with the baby. Still, he had a bad feeling about that child, that it was some sort of lightning rod for disaster.

"Stop over," Gia said.

"Maybe I'll do that."

Even though he wouldn't be good company, he wanted to stay close to Gia and Vicky. So he'd do more than stop by. If they were sleeping over, so would he.

22. After an endless series of heaves and lurches and lunges, the cow had managed to help slide him across her threshold into light and warmth. At least he assumed it was warm. He'd lost all feeling.

"Lord, you're all but frozen. I hope you don't mind, but I'm going to have to cut you out of those wet clothes. There's not much left to them anyway. Mostly charred rags."

During the next few minutes he felt himself rolled left and right as he assumed his tattered clothing was being ripped or cut away.

"Don't you worry about me staring at your bum or your privates. I got what they call wet AMD—macular degeneration. You're mostly a blur to me."

He wasn't worried about that. Survival was his concern.

She left him, then returned. He felt a blanket fall over him.

"You're gonna have to stay there on the rug for now, I'm afraid. No way we're gonna get you up on the couch. But this here's an electric blanket. It'll warm up shortly and start raising your temperature."

Good. Warmth. He'd thought he'd never be warm again.

"What happened to you? I heard an explosion and saw something light up out on the water. That you? Your boat blow up?"

Exactly what had happened, but he could not imagine how. He'd been free. The burning house had been a glow fading in his wake when something shot out of the darkness and struck the rear of the boat, hurling him through the air and into the water. He remembered nothing until he washed up on this shore.

"Well, whatever happened, you need a doctor and a hospital, especially for that hand. From what I can see it's all charred, and I guess that's good because it's not bleeding, but that stump's gonna need specialist care."

No! He was too weak. He'd be vulnerable in a hospital. Defenseless.

"But no way you're gonna get to one tonight. The phone's not working worth a damn, and even if it was, I don't see anyone coming out in this storm. So we're gonna have to ride it out together tonight and see what the morning brings. I'll get the boat out here as soon as it can make the trip."

He could not allow her to call for help, but how could he stop her? He fought to stay conscious, but it slipped away . . .

. . . until he felt himself rolled onto his side.

"Here," she was saying.

His head was propped on pillows or cushions. He

knew only that they were soft. He felt a straw pressed between his swollen lips.

"Drink some of that."

He drew on the straw. Hot salty liquid filled his mouth. He swallowed and greedily sucked more.

"I heated you up a can of chicken broth. Drink as much as you can. With the electric blanket cooking you on the outside and this working from the inside, we'll have you warmed up yet."

This cow . . . if he survived this, she would be rewarded.

He swallowed more and took a breath. He tried his voice. He had to know.

"Where . . . ?" was all he could manage. His voice sounded like sandpaper on concrete. He must have inhaled smoke, perhaps even a little flame.

"Oh, so you can speak. Well, your voice don't sound too good. Maybe you better save it. As for where you are—little place called Sadie's Island, in the middle of Gardiner's Bay. And me? I'm Sadie. Sadie Swick. I own this little hunk of rock and I'm its sole resident. And how about you? What are you called?"

What name to use? He'd had so many of them. He chose an old one at random.

"Roma," he croaked.

"Like the quarterback? Any relation?"

So many people had asked him those questions when he'd started using the name. He had no idea what they were talking about at first, but he'd soon learned.

"Rome-AH," he said.

"Like the city then. Got a first name?"

"Sal."

"A real Italian, ay? You don't look Italian, but then

I've known a bunch of Italians who don't. Welcome to Sadie's Island, Sal. Wish it could have been under better circumstances but . . ."

She talked on but her voice faded with his consciousness.

SUNDAY

I. The scream jolted Weezy from her sleep. A child's scream—not the baby's trademarked shriek. A little girl—

"Vicky!"

She jumped off the couch and ran for the bedroom. She'd given it to Gia and Vicky. The bedroom light came on almost immediately, and when Weezy arrived she found a terrified Vicky huddled against her shaken mother . . .

. . . and the baby standing at the edge of the bed, chewing on the sheet.

Vicky was babbling. "I-I-I opened my eyes and he was right in front of me, staring at me! I was so scared!"

Weezy couldn't blame the poor kid. She'd left a night light on in case Gia or Vicky had to find their way to the bathroom. She imagined Vicky opening her eyes and seeing that face just inches away.

Gia had her arms around her and gave her an extra squeeze. "It's okay, hon. He was just looking at you. He likes you."

"No! He bit me!"

She held up an index finger. Weezy stood near the foot of the bed, but even from there she could see reddened scrapes where his sharp little teeth had broken the skin.

Gia frowned as she examined it. "Well, now we've got a problem. Let's go clean that up."

"Should I wake Jack?" Weezy said.

He'd wanted to stay close by but Weezy had no room for him here—Gia, Vicky, and the baby maxed out her sleepover capacity—so he'd crashed across the hall on Dawn's couch.

Gia shook her head as she hustled Vicky toward the bathroom. "We can handle this. Let him sleep."

Weezy glanced at the bedside clock—*3:32*—and then stared at the baby. How on Earth had he gotten from the crib to the bedroom? As Vicky rounded the corner and disappeared, the baby screeched, then dropped to his hands and knees and began to crawl after her.

An infant . . . crawling . . . and biting.

What had she brought into her home?

2. "Breakfast time!" said the now-familiar voice.

He opened his eyes to daylight. The cow was back. She had awakened him periodically during the night to feed him warm broth. He wondered if she had set an alarm to rouse her to the task. No matter. He had gulped whatever she had offered, then returned to sleep.

Though he felt stronger—and certainly warmer—than he had last night, he remained terribly weak.

"Time to get something a little more solid into you."

He tried to raise himself to his elbows and gasped at the bolt of pain that shot up his left arm. He gaped at the charred stump of his wrist. He'd forgotten about his hand.

Slowly he became aware of pain all over his body.

The cow was talking again. She seemed to love to

talk. Not surprising. If she was as isolated as she had said, her only conversations would be with her dog and whoever she phoned.

What had she called herself? Last night was such a blur . . . Sadie, was it? Yes. Sadie.

She gestured toward her dog. "Rocky seems afraid of you. That's not like him. He usually adores people."

Idiot cow. You've taken in a pack animal that behaves according to a set of instincts honed by breeding and evolution. It adores nothing.

She pursed her lips and spoke to the dog in an inane tone. "Isn't that twue, Wocky-wocks. You're a good dog, aren't you, Wocky-wocks. Yes, you are."

Nauseated by this display of affection for a creature that was little more than a bundle of reflexes, he regarded the dog. The big brown mutt sat in the corner and stared at him. Animals tended to fear him, and that was just as well. He did not understand the concept of a pet and had not the slightest desire to own one.

When the Change came and food became scarce, pet owners' sickening anthropomorphisms would evaporate as they devoured their formerly beloved companions . . . those that did not devour them first.

But this mutt . . . had he watched like that all night?

The cow prattled on. "We cooked you some oatmeal, but made it real thin since we don't know how your digestion is doing. We put it in a cup."

" 'We'?" His voice was still harsh and faint.

"Sure. Rocky and me. We're the only ones here. And no, he didn't help cook the oatmeal. It's just the way I talk."

He nodded, hoping that would end her prattle. But no . . .

"If you can't drink it yourself, I'll spoon it into you.

But if I were you, I'd try the cup. With my eyes I'll probably miss your mouth more often than I'll hit it."

He took the cup and sipped the gruel. It went down easily.

"Ooh, look at your face," she said, leaning close to his left cheek. "It's all burned. Really bad."

That didn't surprise him. He was probably burned to varying degrees over most of his body.

She had her face close to the remnant of his wrist, not touching, but examining with her rheumy eyes. He disliked anyone being this close.

"Glasses?" he said.

"I got some—got a dozen pair, at least—but they're not worth a damn. With this wet AMD, I can't see a damn thing unless I get real close. And even then . . ."

His weakness left him no choice but to allow her to continue her inspection.

"I don't see any sign of infection yet, but it's coming. Can't get hurt like that and not get infected. We're going to have to get you to a doctor soon or—"

"No . . ."

"No arguing. You've got to have a doctor."

"No . . . please."

Words were agony.

"Why the hell not?"

"Later."

" 'Later'? That mean you'll explain later? Well, it better be a damn good explanation. But don't you worry about any of that now. The phone's still out and the storm's still going strong. So it's just you and me and Rocky for a while."

Good. That was good.

Now she was leaning close to the electric blanket that covered him, touching it here and there.

"Oh, dear. Look here. Some of your body burns have oozed through the blanket and dried. Ooh, it's going to be stuck to you. That's not good. I'll get another blanket and we'll try to ease that one off you."

He finished the oatmeal and put the cup down. With his remaining hand, he grasped the edge of the blanket and yanked it free of his skin. He gasped a few hissing breaths through clenched teeth as pain screamed through his body.

"Oh, dear God!" she cried, backing away. "Why would you go and do a thing like that? I could have taken it off you real easy like, without all that pain."

Didn't she know? Pain was good. Other people's pain was better, but even his own pain was better than none. Pain meant he was alive. Pain would stimulate his healing powers.

He handed her the soiled blanket and watched her hurry off to find a replacement. Then he lay back and closed his eyes. Sleep beckoned again. He answered the call.

3. Weezy placed the baby's sippy cup to his lips, and once more he turned his head away.

Gia had picked up a few of the cups last night on her run to a nearby CVS. He couldn't chew through the mouthpiece, which was good, but he kept rejecting them. Weezy didn't think the cup was the problem. More like its contents. Formula wasn't doing it for him.

At least he wasn't screeching, but his attachment to Vicky was a bit unsettling. The four of them sat at the kitchenette table, and as long as the little girl was present, he limited himself to baby noises. But God forbid she left his sight. He sat on Weezy's lap, but seemed largely unaware of her. He had eyes only for Vicky and watched her every move.

"Maybe he can't stomach formula," Weezy said.

What was she going to do? Dawn's child was unique—the closest thing this world had seen to his species in millennia. Well, except for the creature she and Jack had encountered as kids; she was convinced that had been a q'qr.

"Maybe he needs different food."

Gia sat across from her, sipping coffee. "We can try something solid when Jack gets back. I mean, he's got teeth."

Jack had risen, made a brief appearance—they hadn't told him about the biting incident yet—and gone out on a bagel run.

"Maybe we don't have to wait."

Weezy retrieved the loaf of bread she kept in the refrigerator—she didn't eat much bread—and tore a length of crust from a slice.

Gia took it and held it before the baby's mouth. He gave it a cross-eyed look, sniffed it, then chomped—but caught Gia's fingertip instead.

Gia dropped the crust and sucked on her finger. "Those little teeth are *sharp*."

As they watched, he reached out a stubby, black-nailed hand and wrapped it around the crust.

Gia shook her head. "Palm-grabbing already."

"What's that?"

"A crude form of grasping. Most babies can't do that till they're four months old."

The end of the crust was sticking out of his fist. He shoved it toward his mouth, missed, tried again, then made it on the third go. He bit off the end and chewed.

Gia's expression was full of wonder. "Feeding himself . . ."

But after only a few chews he spit it out, letting the mush drip down his chin.

"So much for bread," Gia said. She looked at her scraped fingertip. "Seems to like fingers, though."

"He's going to starve," Weezy said.

She felt responsible for Dawn's baby, for its survival. But this was no ordinary baby. Who did she turn to? She was pretty damn sure Dr. Spock's book had no sections on the care and feeding of q'qr babies.

Gia didn't look too concerned. "Usually that's not a problem with children, even with the fussiest. As a rule, if they get hungry enough, they'll eat. He'll—"

The buzzer for the downstairs entrance sounded.

Who could that be? Jack had a key. She carried the baby to the intercom and pressed the talk button.

"Hello?"

"It is I."

Weezy knew that voice, and the recognition startled her.

"Lady?"

What was she doing here? They'd left her in the Pine Barrens. Even better question: *How* had she gotten here?

"I wish to visit."

"Well, um, sure. Of course. Come up." She buzzed the door open. "Seven-C."

"I know where you are."

Well, of course she did.

Gia looked surprised. "The Lady . . . here?"

"You've met?"

Now she looked a little frazzled—Weezy had never imagined Gia's composure could slip. "Yes . . . and no."

Weezy cocked her head toward Vicky who was play-ing with the Band-Aid on her finger. "Does she . . . ?"

Gia shook her head. "No. Better that way. Gabby-gabby, if you get my drift."

Weezy got it. Better that Vicky knew nothing about the Lady's true nature, because she'd talk about her and everyone would think she was either lying or deluded.

A few moments later she arrived, looking perfectly dry and comfortable in her short-sleeved housedress, as if she'd stepped in from a balmy spring day instead of a winter storm that was still snowing and blowing.

Weezy felt a bit awkward introducing her as "The Lady," but Gia already knew who she was, and Vicky . . . Vicky seemed unaccountably in awe of her. She stared at the Lady like the baby stared at her.

"I believe we've met," Gia said softly.

The Lady nodded. "Yes, we have."

"Thank you. I know what you did . . . thank you."

"Would that I had been allowed to do more, but it was not possible."

Gia's throat worked. "I know that, but . . ." She glanced at Vicky. "Thank you."

Weezy had to ask. "How did you get here from the Pines?"

"I walked."

Gia blinked. "You *walked*? In this storm? From south Jersey?"

"I do not feel cold or rain or wind. And to be honest, I rode much of the way."

Weezy had a vision of the Lady walking along the side of Route 206 with her thumb out.

"Don't tell me you hitched a ride?"

"People are kind to an underdressed old woman caught in a snowstorm." She focused her attention on the baby in Weezy's arms. "You hold the reason for my visit. I wished to see him in person." She leaned in for a closer look. "Interesting."

The scene struck a discordant note in Weezy.

"But aren't you aware of everyone?"

"Only the sentient. Newborns aren't self-aware. And this creature, even when grown, will function mostly by instinct." The Lady leaned closer. "Where are the tentacles?"

"Tentacles?" Gia said.

"They appear to have been removed," Weezy said.

The Lady frowned. "Show me, please."

Weezy unsnapped his shirt and worked his left arm free. She raised it to expose the underarm area. While washing up the baby yesterday she'd looked for the tentacles and had found a healed but recent scar in each axilla.

"If you look closely you can see a little—ohmygod!"

Yesterday when she'd touched the scars she'd felt a little lump beneath each. Now this scar appeared to have split and something was protruding from it. Weezy remembered how Dawn had described the tentacles—"like slim little garter snakes." This was no more than an inch long, but that was what it looked like. Or maybe a rat tail. As she watched, it curved and straightened.

The Lady nodded, her expression impassive. "They are growing back."

Gia's face was ashen.

Vicky, who was out of the line of sight, said, "I have to go to the bathroom, Mom."

"Go ahead, sweetie." Gia's eyes were glued to the tentacle. "Go right ahead."

With Vicky out of sight, the baby began screeching. He fought Weezy as she tried to reinsert his arm in the sleeve, and struggled maniacally to break free from her grasp.

The screeches were almost nonstop.

Weezy felt ready to burst into tears. How was she going to handle this?

"This is not good," the Lady said, barely audible over the noise. "You cannot take care of him. As his tentacles regrow to their full length, they will be grabbing everything in sight. Your situation will soon become untenable."

Weezy had to admit the truth of that, but couldn't help feeling offended.

"Well, I can't just throw him out on the street or give him up for adoption."

She'd love to pass this torch, but to whom? Ideally someone who knew the care and feeding of q'qrs. No one alive today knew that.

The Lady stared at the baby. "Very little in this child is human. He houses more Otherness than humanity. And as such, he should be kept separate from humanity. I know you feel an obligation, a responsibility, but your greater responsibility is to humanity. You must continue your study of the *Compendium*."

Yes . . . the *Compendium*. No way she could concentrate on that or anything else with this screeching.

"She's right, Weezy," Gia said, wincing at a particularly loud shriek. The noise seemed to be causing her physical pain.

Weezy nodded. Only Vicky seemed able to quiet the baby and the girl couldn't stay with the baby every minute. She looked at the Lady.

"But who?"

"I will take him."

The Lady caring for a child . . . she wasn't even human. Then again, neither was the baby . . . not quite.

"How will you manage?"

"I know his needs. And I have my ways." She reached out and placed her palm on the baby's head. "Hush now. You've caused enough disturbance."

And miraculously, the baby quieted. He stopped struggling and stared at the Lady. Then he held his arms out to her. Weezy saw nothing else to do but hand him over. The Lady cradled him and he remained quiet, staring up at her face.

"If you will give me a blanket," she said, "I will take him to my home."

Some small part deep inside felt she was betraying Dawn, but the rest of her knew this was the best course—for her and for the child.

She went to his room and returned with the blanket from his crib.

The Lady wrapped him snugly and said, "You may visit any time you wish."

And then she walked out.

Weezy felt guilty at the flood of relief when the door closed.

Vicky returned then. "Where's the baby?"

"The Lady took him to her place, honey," Gia said. "He'll be happier there."

Vicky's expression said she was pretty happy herself.

Giving in to a need to move, Weezy wandered the room. As she passed the table where she'd left the *Compendium*, she noticed it was open. She knew she'd left it closed.

She looked at Vicky. "Were you looking through this?"

"That was me," Gia said. "Hope you don't mind."

Weezy stared at the open page.

"Was that okay?" Gia said.

Weezy shook herself. "What? Oh, yes. Of course. It's just that . . . is there any reason you left it open at this page?"

Gia approached and looked over her shoulder. "No. I just opened it at random. I was going to flip through but then you said coffee was ready. Why?"

"It's the same page Vicky opened to last night."

The Naming Ceremony page . . .

Odd. The page order in the *Compendium* was in constant flux—random, chaotic. Not impossible that it could open to the same page twice in a row, but the probability was low.

She closed the book, stepped back, and said, "Do me a favor and open it again—anywhere."

Gia gave her a puzzled expression, then shrugged and smiled. "I remember how this book used to drive Jack nuts. He could never find anything he wanted. I'll try near the beginning instead of the middle." She flipped it open and stared. "Well, I'll be."

Weezy checked it and felt a little tickle in her stomach. The Naming Ceremony page lay open.

She closed it again and motioned Vicky over.

"Hey, Vicks. Open this for me, will you? Any page you want."

"Sure."

She opened it near the middle . . . revealing the Naming Ceremony.

Gia glanced at Weezy. "Looks like this old book is trying to tell you something."

Tell me something? Ridiculous.

Or was it?

4. Ernst stormed up to the Lodge's second floor and found two Kickers replacing the door to one of the rooms. Ernst knew whose room.

"What is the meaning of this?"

"Just following orders," one of the Kickers said. "The boss told us to—"

"Where is he?"

The other jerked a thumb over his shoulder at the room. "Right inside."

Ernst raised his black, silver-headed cane. "Out of my way! Out!"

They scuttled to the sides, leaving him a clear path through the doorway.

After a number of days' absence, he'd returned to the Lodge and had been shocked to see its street façade defaced by a pair of steel window shutters on the second floor.

He stormed into the room and found Hank Thompson staring out one of those windows.

"The shutters must come down!"

Thompson smiled as he turned to face him. "Morning, Drexler. How're they hanging?"

He was goading. Thompson seemed to take inordinate pleasure in annoying him. Well, Ernst was already annoyed—*more* than annoyed.

"Remove those shutters immediately."

Thompson gave him a cold stare. "No."

"This is a historic building. You cannot deface it like this."

"What's defaced? These are primo roll-up hurricane shutters. Heaviest of the heavy duty. Watch."

He picked up a remote, pointed it at the nearest

window, and pressed a button. With a soft clatter, a ribbed steel sheet unrolled from the cylinder at the top and slid down the tracks attached to either side of the frame. He pointed the remote at the other window and the same happened, darkening the room.

He grinned. "Pretty neat, huh? And if there's a power failure, I've got a little gadget that lets me crank them up and down by hand."

"Have you gone mad? This is totally irrational. You're on the second floor. Someone would have to put up a ladder in full view of the street and the claque of your followers who drape themselves on the front steps."

Thompson's smile faltered. "What if what wants in isn't human? What if it flies through the air?"

Ernst stared at him. He *had* gone mad.

" 'It'?"

"The Kicker Man warned me. He hasn't led me wrong yet."

Was he talking about the Change? Had he had some sort of premonition and was preparing for it?

Ernst hoped he was wasting his time, hoped that Jack, the man Thompson hated so fiercely, had succeeded in stopping the One.

"So don't waste your breath telling me to undo this. It stays."

Ernst turned toward the new door. "And this?"

"Steel. With a big bar across it. The walls are stone, two feet thick on the outside, a foot on the inside." He looked around, nodding. "Yep, I'll be safe here."

Ernst saw no point in continuing the conversation, so he walked out.

Where was the One? Alive? Dead? He wished he could call Jack.

5. Jack turned away from the Lady's window and faced the occupants of the room. He'd taken Gia and Vicky home from Weezy's, then returned here.

"Storm's done. You're sure he's still alive?"

Both Glaeken and the Lady nodded from their customary places at the table. Weezy was in her place too, the *Compendium* open before her. And next to her, a new face: Eddie.

Under different circumstances, Jack would have been amused at his reaction to seeing Mrs. Clevenger alive and well, and finally meeting the mysterious "Mr. Foster." Even though Weezy had prepared him, he'd been awestruck.

Over in the corner, Dawn's baby, confined in a playpen, contentedly chewed on a bone—a freaking soup bone.

When Eddie had seen him he'd whispered a simple, "Jesus."

At least he hadn't done a Kramer.

Glaeken said, "And slowly, very slowly, growing stronger."

Not what Jack wanted to hear. A supernova of frustration blazed in his chest. He'd blown it. His original plan had been sabotaged—unintentionally, but sabotaged nonetheless—and he'd been forced to improvise. But he couldn't excuse himself. He'd blown it.

"I need to get back to Nuckateague."

"For what possible purpose?" Weezy said.

He glared at her. "Oh, I don't know. To toast some marshmallows over the ashes of Rasalom's mansion. What else?"

He was walking a thin line here and he didn't need anyone baiting him with stupid questions.

"I'm serious, Jack. You've seen the news. That whole area is crawling with state and local cops. Even Homeland Security is into the act. The Coast Guard found the wreckage of the cabin cruiser, so they're out on the water patrolling the bay, looking for bodies."

"But Rasalom is *not* a body. And he's *not* in the water. I don't care how resilient he is, he's saddled with a human body. It may be a special human body, but human muscle can't function in near-freezing water like they've got in that bay. Somehow he made it to shore—maybe somewhere along the South Fork, maybe Gardiner's Island, I don't know. But he's on land, and he's hurt, and he's hiding."

"I don't disagree," Weezy said. "And if he's findable, he'll be found. But not by you."

"Don't be so sure."

"Think, will you?" she snapped. "You'll be conspicuous as all hell out there. If you're poking through the bushes on land, the cops or DHS will want to know who you are and what you're doing there. If you somehow find a boat to take out, the Coast Guard will want to know the same things. If there's a chink anywhere in your ID you'll wind up in jail and completely out of the fight. Is that what you want?"

Of course it wasn't.

He forced a smile. "I hate it when you're right."

She continued her stare. "Funny. You didn't used to."

"I'm not exactly who I used to be."

"And you seem to be getting less like him every day."

Jack glanced at Glaeken and remembered what he'd said last night about the Ally.

The Ally wants a tool . . . a relentless tool.

He raised his hands in surrender. "Peace. You're right,

I'm wrong. I'm open to suggestions—anything but 'let's just sit back and see what happens.' *Anything* but that."

"All right," Weezy said. "Let's play a game."

"Weez . . ."

"No, I'm serious. And this is a serious game." She closed the *Compendium* and stood it up on its spine. "Guess which page it will open to when I let go of its covers."

Had she lost her mind?

"Weez . . ."

"I'm going to guess the page about the Otherness Naming Ceremony." She let the covers go and the book fell open. She looked down and said, "Well, well. What do you know: the Otherness Naming Ceremony. Let me try it again."

She did.

"How about that? The Otherness Naming Ceremony."

Jack moved around for a look. Sure enough. He recognized the page.

She called Eddie over and he got the same result.

Jack took the book from her and tried it himself: same page.

"What the—?"

He knew this book. Before Weezy had come back into his life and taken over the *Compendium*, he'd owned it, studied it—or at least tried to until its sequencing went on the fritz and pages began appearing in random order, anywhere they damn well pleased.

In all his time with the book it had never done anything like this.

"Since coming across that first reference on Wednesday I've been finding more and more mentions of the Other Naming Ceremony. Think about that: In all those months, not one reference till last week, then one after another, and now the book won't open to any other page."

"Another malfunction in its pagination?" Glaeken said.

"I showed it to Gia this morning and she said it looked like the book was trying to tell me something."

Jack laughed. "Yeah, but she was—"

"—joking, or at least half joking, sure. But it got me to thinking. *Could* it be trying to tell me something?"

"It's a book, Weez."

"But the *Compendium* isn't like any other book in the world, maybe not like any book ever made—and I emphasize *ever*. I've been studying it a long time. I've become attuned to it. It's kind of, well, almost interactive, and I'm wondering if maybe it's somehow become attuned to me."

Silence around the table.

Jack didn't know what to make of this. A book—even the most maddening and amazing book in the world—trying to tell them something? It didn't sit right. His instinct was to reject the idea out of hand. But Weezy had instincts too, and he'd learned to respect them.

Finally Glaeken cleared his throat. "What do you think it's trying to tell us?"

"That maybe what we talked about when I first showed you the page is a way to go."

Jack vaguely remembered. "Putting someone through the Naming Ceremony and giving him Rasalom's Other Name?"

She nodded. "That's it. '*No two humans may have the same Other Name. The First-named shall be powerless as long as the Second-named lives.*' That sounds pretty good to me. In fact that sounds like just what we're looking for."

Glaeken said, "You neglected the rest of it."

Weezy remedied that: " '*The First-named shall hear the Name within the Second and thus be able to resolve the duplication.*' "

Glaeken was nodding. "Which means the One will be powerless until he hunts down the usurper and wrings his neck. Which won't be very long if he can 'hear the name' within the unfortunate who has it."

As before, Jack was thinking that would be an excellent way to make Rasalom come to him, but he saw a couple of major problems.

"Aren't we getting ahead of ourselves?" He turned to the Lady. "Once again, I volunteer, but you're the only one who can perform the ceremony and you've already said you won't."

"It is a death sentence," she said, shaking her head.

He turned back to Weezy. "But even if we can change her mind, we don't know his Other Name."

Weezy looked at him, her expression intense. "I have an idea where we might—*might* be able to find it."

"I'm all ears. Where?"

"Under the Johnson Lodge."

The previous silence around the table had been baffled. This one felt more like stunned.

Finally Eddie said, "Johnson? *Our* Johnson?"

Jack said, "You mean those tunnels, that buried town?"

She nodded. "Remember we came across a big model of the Order's sigil down there, the one made out of the same black stuff as the little pyramid we found?"

Jack had a vague memory of it. He'd archived most of his childhood and pretty much everything else that had happened before his break with his past and arrival in New York. Most of what he could dredge up from their teenage venture into the dark region beneath the Lodge involved running from some bearlike creature they never saw clearly—what might have been the last q'qr—and trying to keep from drowning.

"What about it?"

"It was damaged, remember?"

He shook his head. "Sort of."

More like *hardly*. He remembered finding it and calling Weezy to take a look, but the details . . .

Looking frustrated, she pulled a pad and a pen from her backpack and began drawing. When finished she held it up for all to see.

"Here's the sigil as we know it. Check the outer border—the rows of boxes running between the points. Each row has seven boxes." She looked at Glaeken. "Didn't you tell me that each of the Seven's Other Names had seven characters?"

Glaeken nodded. "As do their taken, worldly names— like Rasalom. The original sigil belonged to the Seven. Seven points for the seven agents of the Otherness, interwoven to show a unity of purpose. Each of their public names was carved into the boxes of the great sigil that overlooked the hall where they would meet to draw up their plans for rule by the Otherness. After the Cataclysm, when the Seven and their schemes and their armies were no more, the Order adopted the sigil, but without the names."

"The great sigil is mentioned here," Weezy said, tapping the *Compendium*. "But so is another sigil—seven of them, in fact—all engraved with the Other Name of each of the Seven."

"I'd heard rumors of that back in the First Age," Glaeken said. "But I thought it was just wishful thinking on our part."

"Why?" Jack said.

"Knowing their Other Names would give us power over them."

Jack didn't get it. "What are we talking about here? It's just a name."

Glaeken shook his head. "The Conflict was out in the open back then. The laws of nature were different and could be bent in ways no longer possible. The things we could do in the First Age would be called magic now."

"Okay. I'll take your word for that. But that makes it all the less likely that they'd share this Other Name with anyone."

Glaeken gave a wry smile. "The Otherness did not cull the Seven from the cream of humanity. They were vicious and ruthless and without honor. Those of us fighting for the Ally were flawed in many ways—some fatally—but compared to the Seven, we were the First Age equivalent of choirboys."

"All the more reason not to let the Hank Thompsons and Ernst Drexlers of their day in on your closest secret."

"Ever hear of mutually assured destruction?" Weezy said.

Of course he had. "With nuclear weapons, yeah, but *names*?"

Glaeken was nodding. "It does make a sort of sense. If

one of them or even a pair of them went rogue, the others had the means to bring them into line or wipe them off the face of the Earth."

Weezy started erasing parts of her drawing.

"Okay, what if I told you we came upon a sigil, six feet high or so, and certain parts of it were missing?" She held up the edited drawing. "What if it looked like this."

"See?" she said. "Six of the seven borders have been removed. Only one remains—and that's got a name on it."

Glaeken leaned forward, keen interest sparking in his blue eyes. "What name?"

She leaned back. "I don't know. That's why I put little X's in the boxes."

Jack couldn't hide his shock. "You mean you forgot? You never forget anything."

"I doubt I ever knew, Jack." She closed her eyes. "I can see it there, leaning against the wall of the tunnel. It's covered with dust. You even rubbed off some of the dust to show me how it was made of the same black material as the pyramid. I can see that six of the borders are missing, and I have an impression of seven symbols on the remaining border, but for the life of me I can't remember what they are."

"That photographic memory of yours never failed before. Why now? Try."

Her eyes opened and flashed at him. "What do you think I'm doing right now? It's simply not there. You remember what it was like that night. We thought that door opened into some kind of floor safe but it was much bigger than that. It was dark down there, we had crummy little flashlights, I was nervous, and we were looking for a lost kid. So excuse me if I didn't pay a whole lot of attention to a dusty old sigil. I can't remember something if it never registered."

He realized he'd ticked her off. He hadn't meant to. He couldn't remember ever being so impatient. He also realized she was ticked at herself for not being able to remember it.

"Okay. Sorry. If that's the way it is, we'll just have to resign ourselves to not knowing."

"But we can find out," she said. "I mean, assuming the sigil is still there."

"If it is, it's got to be buried under a ton of mud from when the lake flooded in."

"Maybe, maybe not. I think we should go see."

"Where? Back to Johnson? What for?" He nodded to the Lady. "If no one's going to perform the ceremony, why bother?"

"We can worry about ceremonies later. Just knowing Rasalom's Other Name could be important. Don't you want to know it? Aren't you curious, even a little?"

"Not a bit."

"You won't go back?"

"No."

No way he was leaving for the wilds of New Jersey while Rasalom's heart was still ticking up here. If an opportunity arose to finish the job, Jack wanted to be ready to jump on it.

Where was that son of a bitch?

6. With the cow's help, Rasalom had struggled his way to the couch. She'd draped it with a sheet—the first step toward making him a bed, she promised—and he now sat upon it, wrapped in a blanket.

The effort had exhausted him. He hadn't felt this weak since Glaeken had trapped him in that wretched little castle in Romania. His lids felt heavy, and kept drifting closed, but he forced them open to concentrate on the television on the far side of the small room.

The woman had a satellite feed; she'd turned it on first thing this morning and left it running. He had a feeling she kept it on all day. Her only company besides her dog. Rasalom would have ignored it except the channel was updating what it called "the nightmare in Nuckateague." The mention of a triple murder associated with the "blitz-krieg assault" on the mansion had galvanized his attention.

Triple murder?

He assumed two of the dead to be Georges and Gilda, but who was the third? And then it struck him—the baby.

Oh, no . . . not the baby.

Despairing, he listened carefully, but the identities of the dead were being withheld pending notification of their families.

He had to get off this island . . .

Then again, what was the hurry? With the baby gone, he'd have to come up with a new plan.

Another concern arose: Did Glaeken know he had survived? The Glaeken of old could sense his presence in the world, just as Rasalom could always sense his. Had he lost that ability along with his immortality? If not, he knew that his scheme had failed. He might try another strike to finish the job. Rasalom's weakness and injuries left him painfully vulnerable out here.

He lifted the blanket and examined his naked body. The burns were still oozing, and that concerned him. Certainly his skin was further along in the healing process than an everyday human's, but he felt he should be doing better. The injuries had seriously weakened him.

He raised his left arm and stared at the stump of his wrist. More than weakened: maimed and mutilated. He could recover from the weakness, he could heal his wounds, but his left hand was gone forever.

Who did this to him?

Glaeken? Not personally, that was certain. Too old and feeble. How he had reveled in seeing him like that. He had not expected so bold a move—had not expected *any* move.

Killing Georges and Gilda and the baby . . . that was not like the old Glaeken. Rasalom had used his concern for "innocent" lives against him countless times. Perhaps the mortal Glaeken, with his clock winding down, had realized, like Rasalom, that no one was innocent.

And no one was supposed to know about the Nuckateague house. How had Glaeken found out? Did he have a source in the Order? That was the only answer. But who?

His Heir must have led the attack. An impressive assault, Rasalom had to admit. Only by the sheerest good fortune had he survived. If not for the presence of this island, if not for the wind and current that carried him here, he would have drowned. And even then, had it not been inhabited, he would have frozen solid on the beach out there.

The island's sole inhabitant, the cow, Sadie, bustled in carrying a plate and a glass of milk.

"Brunch! More like a real breakfast—bacon and fried eggs—but since it's after twelve we're going to call it brunch."

The communal "we" again.

"And since you've only got one hand, I put it between bread. So you've got a breakfast sandwich and some milk. Now, you may be saying to yourself, I want coffee, and maybe we'll get you some later, but right now you need nourishment to get your strength back and milk's got a lot more nourishment than coffee."

The chatter, the incessant chatter. Did she never tire of prattle?

She placed the plate and the glass on the table next to the couch and moved on to the window.

"Looks like the storm's finally giving up the ghost. About time, I say. About time." She turned and looked at him. "The phone should be working now. Time to get you some medical help."

"No!" he said. His voice was stronger now, but still raspy.

"You keep saying that, but you're not thinking straight. Those burns are going to get infected for sure and then you're going to be one sick puppy."

Infection was the least of his worries—his immune system would not allow it. But discovery . . . how was he going to stop her?

Perhaps the truth . . .

"You have been watching the television?"

"On and off. You've occupied a lot of my attention."

"You saw the fire in Nuckateague?"

Her eyes widened. "I surely did! Did you see what someone did to that house? I declare I've never seen any-thing like that in all my born . . ." Her voice trailed off as she stared at him. "You're not going to tell me . . . ?"

He nodded.

Her hand flew to her mouth. "Oh, dear God!"

He faked a sob. "They killed my family and were going to kill me but I managed to escape—though, as you can see . . . just barely."

"Oh, you poor man! Who were they?"

"I don't know." He had to improvise now . . . something lurid yet plausible. "Home invaders. I am a wealthy man. They thought I had a house full of valuables. They cut off my hand trying to get me to tell them where I had hidden all these supposed valuables. They did not want to hear the truth—that it was all in the city in a bank vault. When they finally were convinced, they became enraged and went on a murder rampage—my brother, my wife, and my baby boy."

"Oh, dear God!"

That would cover him should they identify the bodies.

"Then they left me for dead and blew up the house to destroy all evidence."

"Oh, you poor man!"

"That is why you cannot call for medical help. They believe I am dead and must go on believing that. I'll reward you well—"

"I don't need money. Got plenty of that. But it sounds like I should be calling the police instead of emergency services."

"No, I don't want to endanger you. If they learn I'm alive they might try to finish what they began. They will kill you too. They are merciless. You must keep my presence secret until I'm well enough to go to the police and ask for protective custody. Do you understand?"

She was nodding vigorously. "Yes. Yes, of course. When you're well enough, we'll put you aboard the boat and—"

"Boat?"

"The weekly boat out of Sag Harbor. How do you suppose I get mail and food and such? The boat stops every Tuesday. I'll just tell them you're a relative who's been staying here, recovering from some terrible accident. You can ride back to Sag Harbor and get in touch with the police there."

"Thank you. You are very kind."

"It's the least I can do after the terrible ordeal you've been through. I'll help you any way I can to get through this."

How easily gulled were these cattle. Especially the cows. Ruled by their emotions. Tell them a sad story and they were at your service.

"Now eat up." She took the sandwich plate and placed it in his lap. "Whether you're hungry or not, you need your strength."

Yes, that was true. But he was in no hurry to leave. Glaeken might or might not be aware of his survival. Even if so, he would not be able to pinpoint his location. Better to stay here until he was stronger—strong enough to transport himself from this lump of rock.

That would certainly not be by Tuesday.

MONDAY

I. *". . . more mysteries surrounding the deadly events in Nuckateague Saturday night. Police seem to be having as much trouble locating the owners of the house as they are tracking down the killers who demolished it with fire and explosives. The house appears to be owned by a corporation, which is in turn owned by an offshore holding company. The holding company is owned by yet another foreign corporation. Very confusing, very mysterious. As for the perpetrators, at this point in time the police still have no leads. A large black sedan was seen driving away from the scene, but whether or not it was connected to the devastation is anyone's guess."*

Rasalom suppressed a growl of annoyance. Those incompetents would never find the "perpetrators." He'd been watching this banal Long Island TV station all morning, hoping for word that progress had been made on tracking them down. A waste of time.

But then again, he had nothing but time while he healed.

He reached for the remote. He would have liked to turn off the TV while the cow was in the kitchen and be alone with his thoughts, but she'd only turn it on again when she returned. At least he could turn down the sound—especially when the talk was of Nuckateague.

He reduced it to a barely audible level, and was glad he had when he heard the announcer go on with the story.

"Progress has been made, however, in other aspects of the case, and a surprise was unearthed in identifying the three bodies found in a garage across the street from the fire. The owners of that garage are not involved, as they were out of state at the time of the incident. The youngest of the three victims turns out to be Dawn Pickering, whose name might sound familiar. She was in the news last year when she and her boyfriend disappeared after the death of her mother in Rego Park. Foul play was suspected. Still no sign of her boyfriend, but her connection to the house in Nuckateague is yet another mystery in the evolving story of this grisly, violent tragedy.

"In other news . . ."

Rasalom quickly changed the channel and leaned back, thinking.

Dawn . . . what was she doing there? How had she known about the house? She must have tracked the baby there. He doubted she could have done that on her own. She must have had help.

He was beginning to piece together a chain of events that could have led to the ambush when the announcer's words came back to him with a shock.

The youngest of the three victims turns out to be Dawn Pickering . . .

Youngest? What of the child? No mention of a dead infant, who certainly would have been the youngest of the three victims.

That meant the baby was alive. And that meant his plan was still viable.

But for how long?

A sudden urgency possessed him. This changed everything. He was certain his window of opportunity had not closed, but it could be shrinking by the moment. What had the cow said about a boat? Tomorrow? He could not wait until tomorrow. He needed to be back today.

He tried to rise from the couch.

"Here now!" she said, bustling into the room with a plate in her hand. "You need to visit the john again?"

The john . . . was there a more inane name for a bathroom facility?

He had suffered the indignities of having to allow the cow to assist him to the bathroom, his knees collapsing beneath him while she chattered to him in the tone she used to speak to her dog.

"Need . . . to leave."

He flopped back onto the couch, gasping from the effort.

"Leave? You're weak as a kitten. And even if you were strong enough to dance a jig, you still wouldn't be going anywhere today. The boat doesn't come till tomorrow, remember?"

"Can't wait."

"I know you want to get to the police as soon as you can and help them find those killers. If you can walk a few steps tomorrow, maybe we can help you out to the dock." As she looked over at her dog her voice took on that noxious tone. "Me and Wocky-wocks will come along and see you safely into town, won't we, doggy?"

The dog panted in the corner, beating its tail against the wall.

"Do you take him everywhere?"

"Of course I do." She continued the tone as she grinned idiotically at her pet. "Don't I, Wocky? Don't I? Cause you're a good dog, aren't you. You're Mommy's best boy, aren't you."

Rasalom rescinded his rash decision during the storm to reward her for saving him.

"So now," she said, resuming a normal tone, "you just sit back and eat this nice turkey sandwich I made you. That's the sort of thing that'll build you up and get your strength back."

She set the plate on his lap and looked around.

"Where's that remote?"

He pointed to it with his wrist stump. "There."

"Where?"

He remembered she could barely see. "Right next to me."

"Well, use it to turn up the sound, will you. I like to listen. Now go on and eat up. If you're getting on that boat tomorrow you're going to need all your strength."

She bustled back to the kitchen.

Yes, strength. He needed strength—but now, not later. He couldn't afford the time it would take for turkey sandwiches to do the job. He needed another form of nourishment, and here on this tiny island he was cut off from the emotions that could speed the process. The world out there writhed with a farrago of pain and fear and anger and grief, but he could access none of it from here. The population at this end of Long Island was thin this time of year, and the meager sustenance available was dampened by distance. Water further muted the effect.

He had only the cow close at hand, and he needed her.

He looked across the room at the dog, who stared back. But he didn't need her pet . . . her beloved pet.

Before he could do anything, he needed it closer. But the dog feared him. How to bring him within reach? And then he remembered the sandwich in his lap. Would the dumb animal's stomach overcome its distrust of the stranger in its home?

Let's see, shall we?

He pulled a piece of turkey from the sandwich and held it out, dangling it from his hand.

The dog's head shot up and rocked as it sniffed. But its body remained prone.

He waved the meat back and forth. Should he whisper its name? He didn't want the cow to hear, but decided to risk it. He was quite sure, however, that he could not bring himself to utter, "Wocky-wocks."

"Here, Rocky."

That was enough. The old dog pushed itself to its feet and ambled over, head down, tail giving a few tentative wags.

Rasalom slowly drew the meat back, enticing the animal closer and closer until he could lay his wrist stump on its back. Deep within the furry chest, he felt the heart beating.

He focused in on the beat.

And stopped it.

The animal stiffened, coughed once, and then its legs collapsed. It landed on the floor with a thump, shuddered, and did not move again.

Rasalom popped the piece of turkey into his mouth—after all, he needed it more than the dog.

Now . . . what was the cow's name?

"Sadie! I think something is wrong with your dog."

The cow rushed in. Her eyes darted to the corner where she'd left the dog, then to the still brown lump on the carpet before the couch.

"Rocky?" she said, her voice rich with anxiety.

When the lump did not respond, she bent and touched its flank.

"Rocky?" A delicious burst of fear accompanied the word.

When her fingers sent the message that no life lin-
gered in the inert flesh beneath them, she dropped to her
knees beside her companion and screamed.

"*Rockyyyyyyyyyyy!*"

Rasalom leaned back, closed his eyes, and bathed in the
cataract of grief and loss, absorbing it like a dry sponge,
feeding his needy cells, abating a hunger that could never
be fully assuaged.

Yessssss.

2. "I should move in here," Weezy said as she and
Eddie entered the Lady's apartment.

She placed the backpack with the *Compendium* on the
table.

The Lady smiled from her usual seat. "If you have no
place to stay, you are always welcome here. You know
that. I will not forget how you sat at my side that night."

Neither would Weezy. She'd been sure then that she
was seeing the last of the Lady.

She glanced over at Dawn's baby in his playpen. He
was chewing on a bone, just like yesterday.

"Where do you get the soup bones?"

"A local butcher delivers them."

"It looks raw," Eddie said, making a face.

"He prefers them that way. He wears them down to the
marrow. He likes the blood there."

Weezy remembered the blood she'd washed off his
face that first day. She'd assumed it was from his teeth.
Now she wondered . . .

She shook it off. It didn't bear thinking about.

"Do you know why Jack asked us here?"

The Lady shook her head. "He did not tell me."

"Nor me," Glaeken said as he entered and eased into his seat at the head of the table. "But he seemed . . . enthused."

Weezy could think of only one thing Jack had been enthused about lately.

"Then it must have something to do with killing Rasalom."

As if on cue, Jack entered.

"It does." He dropped his bomber jacket onto the remaining seat opposite Weezy but remained standing. "I think I've found a solution to the Other Naming Ceremony problem."

He seemed a different person from the surly grouch of yesterday's gathering. He appeared unable to sit still. He was psyched about something.

"Which problem?" Weezy said. "Not knowing the name, or no one to perform the ceremony?"

"The latter."

Weezy glanced at the Lady, then back to Jack. "You've found someone else who can read the small folks' writing?"

"No. But I think I can convince the Lady to perform it on me."

"I will not," she said with rock-solid finality.

"Give me a chance here. I've been up half the night thinking about this."

That would be Jack. Give him a problem to solve and he was like Dawn's baby with a bone: He'd gnaw it down to the marrow.

He turned to Weezy. "Could you read us that paragraph about the ceremony?"

"I don't need to read it."

"Okay. Would you recite it, please?"

Weezy pictured the page and began to read from it.

" '*No two humans may have the same Other Name. The First-named shall be powerless as long as the Second-named lives. The First-named shall hear the Name within the Second and thus be able to resolve the duplication.*'"

"Thanks," Jack said. "Now, the second half is the part that's causing the problem. The Lady here thinks it's a death sentence. I disagree."

The Lady said, "The One 'shall hear the Name' within you. That means, even if you never speak the Other Name you have been given, you will know it . . . it will be in your mind. He will hear it just as he hears 'Rasalom' whenever it is spoken. He will follow that name to you, wait until you are vulnerable, and slay you."

Jack held up a finger. "Ah, but what if I don't know the Other Name I'm given?"

"How can you not?" Weezy said. "You'll have to go through the ceremony."

He looked at the Lady. "Does the ceremony require me to say the name?"

She shook her head. "It does not."

"Well, then," he said, "what if I'm unconscious during the ceremony? Then I won't be aware of a word being said."

Weezy stared at him. She noticed Glaeken, the Lady, and Eddie doing the same. She voiced what she knew they were all thinking.

"Are you out of your mind?"

"Not at all." He began wandering around the table. "We can hire an anesthetist to put me under during the ceremony. I called Doc Hargus this morning and he said he could fix me up with one."

Weezy couldn't help it. "That's the craziest thing I've ever heard."

Jack glared at her. "Can I speak to you a minute? Alone? Outside?"

She hesitated, taken aback by his expression and the strange request. What couldn't they say in front of Eddie, Glaeken, and the Lady? But how could she refuse?

"Sure."

She followed him into the hall where he shut the door behind them and lowered his voice.

"Why are you so negative about this?"

"Because it's crazy, Jack."

"What's crazy about it? Look at the situation: Rasalom is down but not out. In fact, he's coming back and we don't know how to find him to finish the job. As soon as he's well enough, he's going to want payback. How long do you think it's going to take him to figure out I was behind the Nuckateague attack, if he hasn't already? That means he'll be coming after me anyway. So why not render him 'powerless' before he does? That will at least level the playing field."

"But we don't know what 'powerless' means. It could simply mean unable to bring about the Change. All his other advantages could very well remain intact."

"But at least he'll no longer be *the* One. There'll be two with his Other Name, and that's got to hamper him."

"I don't think that's going to change the Lady's mind."

"It might. But I'll never convince her with you constantly sniping at me."

"I'm sorry, Jack, but I've got to say what I feel, and I think it's a bad idea. What if you're wrong?"

"Even if I'm wrong, can we afford *not* to take the chance? If Rasalom finds a way to extinguish the Lady, this whole opportunity goes with her. The option of the Other Name is entirely off the table because there'll be no one to perform the ceremony."

Was this why he'd wanted to talk in private—didn't want to discuss the Lady's demise in front of her?

"But he's got nothing left to throw at her. If he did, he would have used it instead of trying that ambush."

Jack's mouth twisted. "That was just to test if she was still immune to Earthly harm."

"Which means if he had another option, he would have used it."

"I think Dawn's child might have been part of his plan."

Weezy's heart clenched. She'd had the same feeling but hadn't wanted to voice it.

"How could that baby be used against the Lady?"

He shook his head. "Wish I knew."

"Let's go back inside and ask the Lady herself."

As Weezy started toward the door, Jack gripped her arm. "You'll back me on the anesthesia?"

She didn't want any walls between Jack and her, but she couldn't get behind his plan.

"I think it's a terrible risk but I'm willing to compromise: I'll shut up and let you see if you can change her mind."

He gave a curt nod. "Fair enough."

Eddie gave her a what's-going-on? look when they returned.

Glaeken said, "Have you settled your disagreements?"

"We ironed out a few things," Weezy said, "but came up with an interesting question." She turned to the Lady and pointed to the baby. "Can you think of any way that child can be used against you?"

The Lady sat still a moment, then shook her head. "Not a one. Why do you ask?"

Jack stepped forward. "We're not sure. But consider what we know: We know the baby is brimming with the

Otherness. And we know that Rasalom protected Dawn throughout her pregnancy, then took the baby into hiding right after he was born. He's not the paternal sort and he's got a one-track mind that's fixed on the Change. He can't effect the Change with you around, so that means . . . ?"

Jack gave Weezy an expectant look, so she turned to the Lady and answered the implied question.

"He must think he can use the baby against you."

Glaeken said, "Your conclusion has a certain circumstantial logic to it, but in reality . . ." He shrugged. "The baby has a deep, strong Taint, but is not as full of the Otherness as a full-blown q'qr. The Lady was around when the world was full of q'qrs and they never posed a threat to her. Their blood may be from the Otherness, but they are creatures of the Earth and powerless against her. Maybe Rasalom thought he might eventually find a use for the baby against the Lady, but that is moot now."

The Lady nodded. "For now I have him."

Jack and Weezy stared at each other. She was sure Jack's suddenly troubled expression matched hers. She echoed Gia's question from the other night:

"Do you think this could have been his plan all along?"

After a long pause, Jack shook his head. "I can't see how getting caught in an exploding house and being set on fire and almost drowning and having a boat blown out from under you by a Stinger were part of his plan."

Eddie cleared his throat. "Speaking from an actuarial perspective, none of that eliminates the possibility that his original plan was to return the baby to Dawn."

"But Dawn is dead," Jack said.

"True. But isn't it true that this guy, this One, placed Dawn across the hall from Weezy? Which would place the baby, when returned to Dawn, in proximity to Weezy and, by extension, to the Lady." He pointed to the Lady, then to the baby. "If so, mission accomplished."

Weezy gave Jack a look. "Told you he'd bring a new perspective."

Jack glanced at the baby, then the Lady. "Jeez." Then at Eddie. "High or low probability?"

Eddie gave an uncomfortable shrug. "Wish I could say. I don't have enough data."

Weezy's mind whirled with all the possibilities and permutations of the situation. "I have to tell you, this is way confusing."

Glaeken said, "It is indeed. We don't know what the One's plans were for the baby, but Eddie, the Lady, and I came up with one of our own while you two were in conference."

Jack said, "What about my idea?"

"It has merit."

He dropped into his chair. "Well, that's a start."

"But it has serious flaws as well."

"Like?"

Glaeken leaned forward. "What if the anesthesia is just a tiny bit too light and you hear the name during the ceremony? Or what if your brain registers it and stores it even if your consciousness doesn't? What if you're wrong and you don't have to know the Other Name to allow Rasalom to 'hear' it within you? What if simply knowing you've been given his Other Name is enough?"

"A lot of what-ifs," Jack said.

"Then here's the ultimate what-if: If just one of those what-ifs is true, he will 'hear' the name within you. That means he will know where you are every minute of every day. You will never be able to surprise him again. But he will be able to surprise you. Knowing your whereabouts, he can bide his time, make his plans, and then strike when the time is right—for *him*."

Weezy could see that struck a nerve with Jack. The idea of someone knowing his whereabouts at all times was bad enough, but when that someone was Rasalom . . .

She was tempted to speak, but bit it back. She'd promised . . .

"You're our spear, Jack," Glaeken said. "I'd hate to think of you fitted with a locator."

Exactly.

Jack looked at the Lady. "So you won't do the naming ceremony."

"Not on you."

"Then who?" Jack said. "Glaeken?"

"That was a thought," the old man said. "I've got the least to lose, and if not for Magda, I wouldn't hesitate. But, even in her present state—or perhaps because of her present state—I can't desert my wife."

"Well, forget about Weezy," Jack said. "No way that's happening."

"No, not Weezy," Glaeken said. "Eddie volunteered—"

"No!" Weezy cried, her heart constricting.

He said, "I've lost my home, my business, and I've got no strings. I'm perfect, but—"

"But we came up with a better candidate," Glaeken said. "There is one more in the room you might consider."

Weezy had a sudden bad feeling about what was coming next. She slowly turned and looked at the baby, gnawing contentedly on its bone.

"Oh, no. You can't be serious."

3. During the time the cow had cried hysterically over her fallen pet, Rasalom felt the strength pouring into him. Even when her vocalizations ratcheted down to quaking sobs, the grief that poured from her remained considerable.

All for a dumb animal that was, in many other countries, considered an entrée.

"I'm terribly sorry for your loss," he said when she finally quieted.

She only moaned.

"My goodness," he said. "I hope it wasn't my fault."

Her head snapped up. "What do you mean?"

"Well, just before he died I gave him a piece of my turkey."

She sniffed. "You did?"

"Yes. I hope it didn't cause a reaction or anything. He wasn't allergic to turkey, was he?"

"No, he ate it all the time." She was staring at him, although he knew he was just a blur to her. "That turkey was to help you regain your strength, yet you gave him some?"

"Well, he seemed like such a sweet, loyal dog."

She began sobbing again.

Good . . . good. Keep it up. More. Give me more.

"I'm so happy that-that-that his last memory was of a stranger being kind to him."

His last memory? The cow was pathetic. That creature had been little more than a quadrupedal appetite.

She broke down again, bending over the dog, placing her cheek against its back.

As Rasalom drank, he lifted the blanket and examined his burns. Healing nicely now.

He closed his eyes and sighed as he feasted. Too bad he couldn't bring the dog back to life—just for a few minutes, just long enough to let her believe her pet was back from the dead—and then stop its heart again.

In his previous life he'd been so much more powerful. His very proximity could cause people to turn on each other, commit atrocities they would never dream of had he not entered their lives. He'd been able to make the dead move, walk, appear almost alive, even though they were not. But Glaeken had ended that life and Rasalom had been forced to wait until his rebirth to begin rebuilding his powers.

He was not yet powerful enough to make this carcass move. He could end a life, make a life a living hell, but he couldn't restore a life. Never could. Dead was dead.

At least until the Change. After that, who knew?

4. Weezy had jumped from her seat and gone to the playpen. After recovering from his shock at what Glaeken was suggesting, Jack rose and joined her. He realized he should not have been surprised. Glaeken had wanted the child removed from the picture.

He put an arm around her shoulder as she stared down at the baby.

"I know how you felt about Dawn," he said, "so I've a pretty good idea what you're thinking."

"Do you?" Her voice carried an edge. "Putting an infant in danger. Really?"

"Listen. Yes, he's a baby, but that is why he will *not* be in danger: He's not sentient yet. With all that q'qr blood flowing through him, he will most likely never be sentient in the fully human sense. And that's the beauty part.

The ceremony can be performed on him and he'll have no cognizance of it. If he's even listening during the ceremony, which I doubt, he'll hear that name then and never again. He'll certainly never be called by that name. He'll have no idea that it's even a name. He'll hear it as background noise, just as he's hearing this conversation. It won't register in his conscious or subconscious. He'll never even know he's been through a ceremony."

"And yet," the Lady said, raising a finger, "if what Srem says is true, once that infant has gone through the Naming Ceremony, he will render the One powerless."

Weezy turned to Jack. "What do you think?"

He found he had no easy answer. And their decision here would have momentous impact.

"Let me think out loud here." He couldn't stand still so he wandered the room. "First off, am I right in saying the Lady won't perform the ceremony on anyone else?"

The Lady nodded. "Correct."

"And it's also a fact that if something happens to the Lady, no one else can perform the ceremony?"

He stopped and looked at Glaeken and the Lady. Both nodded.

Moving again, he said, "Now, because we're on terra incognita here, we can't say it's a fact, but it seems a good bet that of everyone in this room, maybe even the world, this little guy here has the best chance of safely taking on Rasalom's Other Name." He pointed to Eddie. "Actuarial opinion?"

Eddie glanced at Weezy, then away. "Given the information at hand, true."

Jack turned to Weezy but said nothing. After a long pause, she gave a reluctant shrug. "I suppose so."

"So, if we *do* do it, Rasalom will no longer be the One, rendering him 'powerless' to start the Change. Not being the One might also rob him of some of his extra-human abilities as well, making him easier to take down next time we get a crack at him. Realizing he's no longer the One has got to distract him, sending him searching for whoever else has his Other Name instead of plotting against the Lady. That search will bring him out in the open, making him an easier target."

Jack paused. He had to admit those were strong arguments.

"Okay," he went on. "If we *don't* do it, it's business as usual for Rasalom: He's still the One and once he heals up he can go to ground and redouble his efforts against the Lady with no worries." He looked Weezy in the eyes. "Considering what's at stake, the effect on billions of lives if Rasalom brings the Change, I don't see how we can *not* do it."

Jack watched her stare down at the baby as he scored the bone with his sharp little teeth. He thought of another child: Vicky. *She* was the child he cared about. And after what Jack had done to Rasalom the other night, he had no doubt that if or when he brought the Change, he'd reserve a special place in that particular hell for anyone Jack held dear.

Rasalom had to be stopped.

But he said nothing. He had to let Weezy work this through.

"With so much at stake," she finally said, shaking her head, "how can I object?"

He sighed. "Okay. It's settled then. That means we're looking at another trip to Johnson to find that sigil."

Her eyebrows rose. "Oh? Yesterday you refused to go."

"Yesterday we had no possible use for it. That's changed."

"Well, I'm set to go. I was getting ready to leave when you called."

"Alone?"

"No. Eddie offered to go with me."

He turned to Eddie. "You don't have to now."

"No, I want to go," he said. "I haven't been back in a while."

Jack shrugged. "Well, the more the merrier, I guess. I'll throw some stuff together and we'll leave this afternoon."

He had a strange feeling that a circle was closing: the three of them back in Johnson, back in the Lodge. Like old times.

Except the fate of the world hadn't hung in the balance then.

5. The cow had calmed herself somewhat, yet remained on the floor, kneeling next to her dead pet. Acceptance had lessened the flow of grief from a gushing cataract to a steady stream.

Was it enough?

He pulled off the blanket and pushed himself up. He straightened his knees and stood—swaying at first as the room rocked and tilted, but he quickly steadied himself.

"Dear God!" she said. "What are you doing?"

"I believe it's called 'standing.'"

"But you don't have any clothes!"

He looked down at his body. He had never understood modesty. Except for the rare occasions it furthered his plans, he had no interest in cattle as sexual partners—he had other appetites—and felt no more embarrassment standing naked before her than would a shepherd before his flock. And even had he suffered from a modicum of modesty, she couldn't see much of him anyway.

He was more interested in his wounds.

He lightly touched the burns. No more oozing, and new pink skin was maturing in the open areas.

"Sit yourself back down!" the cow said. "Before you fall down."

He ignored her and took a faltering step, and then another. The room swayed again, but he would *not* sit down. Not yet.

"Go ahead," she said. "Fall on your face. See if I care. But you're not going to stand there naked as a jaybird. I'll get you some clothes."

Clothes? Did she expect him to wear one of her housedresses?

She returned a moment later with green twill work pants and a flannel shirt.

"These belonged to my husband. They're old and musty and they'll be big on you, but they're better'n what you got on now. Don't know why I kept them. Well, yes, I do. I just couldn't bring myself to throw them out. He had his own closet, you know, and I've just sort of left it like it was and . . ."

Did this woman ever shut up?

He took the shirt from her as she rattled on. The lack of his left hand caused minimal difficulty in slipping into it, but the buttons were an obstacle. Not insurmountable, however. He managed to button one single-handedly and was working on a second when the cow leaned in close.

"Stop fooling with that and help me get you into these pants. Then we'll tend to your buttons."

He didn't want her helping him, but pants were going to be a problem with only one hand. Bracing himself on a table, he stepped into the legs and allowed her to pull them up and button them at his waist. Then she leaned close and began fastening his shirt buttons.

He could see now that once he was back on the mainland and settled in a new abode, he would have to engage someone to dress him. What were they called? A valet? A man's man? Whatever, it was painfully clear that he could not manage this alone.

He clenched his jaw at the indignity of it: the One needing help to dress himself.

Whoever had done this—and he was increasingly certain that the Heir was responsible—had rendered him dependent. He might not understand modesty, but he understood dignity. And he had been robbed of his—or at least a portion of it.

The Heir, the one called Jack, would pay. He would suffer. But those he loved would suffer first, and he would watch.

Suffering . . . he sensed less of it here. The cow's grief had abated. His sudden ability to stand and her assumption of a caregiver role had distracted her from her loss.

She needed a reminder.

"There," she said, straightening as she finished the last button. "Now you're decent."

"Do you want me to help you with your dog?"

"Oh, dear God. Rocky!" Sobbing, she turned and knelt beside the carcass again. "Oh, Wocky-wocks. I didn't forget about you. Honest, I didn't."

"Very sad," Rasalom said. "Has he been sickly?"

"No!" she wailed. "The vet said he was in great shape."

"Well, I suppose it was God's will then."

"No, not God's will! It can't be."

Rasalom shrugged. "Don't they say, 'The Lord giveth, the Lord taketh away'?"

"No!" Her voice rose. "God is a giver of life, not a taker. Satan is a destroyer of life. This wasn't God's work, this was Satan's!" She pounded a fist on the floor. "Satan-Satan-Satan!"

Anger mixed with the grief. Even better. He supped.

Rasalom hid a smile. The Judeo-Christian myths personifying what the cattle perceived as "evil" were no closer to the truth than the rest of the world's religions. He knew the true wellspring of those myths.

"Are you sure?"

"Yes! Satan did this!"

And so, in a way, she was right.

6.   The sun was low over the bare, snow-covered corn-fields and orchards by the time they reached Johnson.

"At least Burlington County hasn't been paved over yet," Eddie said.

He'd called shotgun—for old times' sake—and Jack drove. Weezy had been perfectly happy to have the back-seat to herself and the *Compendium*.

Eddie was exaggerating—plenty of green left, especially with the Pine Barrens sprawling to the east—but Jack got the point. An awful lot of strip malls lining these once pristine country roads.

"Take it slow on Quakerton Road," Eddie said.

"You mean Q'qr Town?" Weezy said.

"What?"

Jack smiled. "Long story."

Too long to tell.

"Anyway," Eddie said, "I want to see what's changed."

So Jack did just that. Why not? They weren't in any big hurry. They'd see what was what at the Lodge and

then find a place to spend the night. First thing tomorrow
they'd get started on finding that sigil. If it was still to be
found.

They crossed the bridge over Quaker Lake—or was
that Q'qr Lake?—into Old Town and turned toward the
two-story stucco box of the Lodge. Jack was surprised to
see a pair of pickup trucks parked in front.

Weezy leaned forward over the back of the front seat
and thrust her head between them.

"What's up? Remodeling, y'think?"

Not good, Jack thought as he parked next to the pick-
ups. He didn't want company.

As the three of them walked through the snow toward
the front door, Jack noticed how the place had gone to
seed a little. Not quite rundown, but not as pristine as he
remembered. The stucco showed small cracks here and
there, the paint needed freshening, the grass was trimmed
but the foundation plantings needed weeding.

As ever, the Order's sigil hung over the pillared front
entrance.

Jack noticed something new that hadn't been apparent
from a distance.

"Check out the second-floor windows."

Weezy looked up and frowned. "Only the first floor
used to be barred. Now the second?"

Eddie said, "Why would they do that?"

Jack couldn't tell if he was being facetious or not.

"Because they were broken into?"

Weezy smiled. "Could be . . . could be."

The trucks bothered Jack. Except for sporadic gatherings of the regional members, the Lodge typically remained vacant, often for weeks at a stretch. The only time in memory that anyone had lived there was when the white-suited Ernst Drexler and his assistant—whose name eluded Jack now—had moved in during a crisis involving the deaths of a number of the Order's local members . . . deaths precipitated by something Jack and Weezy had dug from a mound in the Pines.

Jack had been counting on that emptiness, because they were going to need time—maybe lots of it—alone in the building if they were to find the sigil.

He knocked and turned to Weezy as they waited.

"Remember the first time we knocked on this door?"

She nodded. "We were looking for help for that lost guy we found in the Pines."

That was the day he first met Ernst Drexler. He'd been fourteen and Drexler an adult. The dynamics of their first meeting had been dramatically different from their last.

No answer, so he knocked again. Still no response so he turned to Eddie.

"What's the secret password?"

Eddie blinked. "What?"

"That opens the door. You're a member of the Order. We expect you to know these things. Right, Weez?"

"Absolutely." She grinned and nudged her brother. " 'Open, Septimus,' or something like that, right?"

Eddie wasn't smiling as he shook his head. "What an idiot I was . . . a few weeks ago that might have been funny. But now . . . now I realize how little I knew about them."

"Well, at least your eyes were opened," Weezy said.

Jack nudged him. "And you still have your skin."

"But little else."

He felt bad for Eddie.

"Let's try the back."

As they walked around the side, Jack peeked through the bars on the first-floor windows and saw lights on. They turned the corner in time to see a man in dirt-smeared work clothes exiting the rear door lugging a jackhammer.

Jackhammer?

"Tearing the place down?" Jack said.

The guy seemed surprised to see them. "I'm pissed enough to do just that. You with AFSO?"

"AFSO?"

"Ancient Fraternal Septimus Order," Eddie muttered.

Oh, right.

"You mean the Order? I've done some work for them."

True enough—he'd been the groundskeeper here.

"You get paid?"

Jack nodded. "On time, to the dime. I get the feeling you've got a different story."

The guy gave Jack a narrow look. "What's it to you?"

"Maybe we can help."

The man shrugged and rested the jackhammer on the ground. "All right. This guy from the Order hired me to put together a crew and excavate a section of the basement."

"Excavate?"

"Yeah. Break through the floor and start digging."

"For China?"

"No, just until we found something."

"Like what?"

"He called it an 'artifact.'"

Weezy stepped closer, eyes narrowed. "What did he say it looked like?"

"Didn't. Said we'd know it when we saw it."

Jack said, "And what were you supposed to do when you found it?"

"Stop digging and call Kris."

Kris? Jack had heard Szeto's bully boys call him Kristof. And in the last hour of his life Szeto himself had mentioned a "special project."

The One comes to me now. In fact, he has engaged me for special project in your hometown. Isn't that interesting?

Yeah. Very interesting. This had to be it. But just to be sure . . .

"Black hair, likes leather, perpetual five-o'clock shadow?"

The guy's eyebrows rose. "You got it. You know the SOB? Where's he hiding?"

Another guy in work clothes came out the back door with a number of shovels over his shoulder. He gave them a sullen look, then nudged the other worker.

"You comin', Tommy?"

"Yeah. On my way."

Had to keep this guy talking.

"Kris . . ." Jack said, looking thoughtful as the second guy walked away. "Not sure at the moment. Haven't seen him since sometime last week. But I might be able to find out. Sounds like you have a problem with him."

"Yeah. Like getting paid. He gave me an advance and I hired the crew and we got started. But the second payment is way late and he ain't returning my calls."

And he never will, Jack thought.

"So you're calling it quits?"

"Till we get paid, yeah. If I don't get paid, I can't pay my crew. And we're not working for free."

Jack said, "I'll check around. If I see him, I'll tell him to give you a call."

The guy picked up his jackhammer. "Yeah, you do that. Meanwhile, I'm somewhere else."

"Well, good luck." Jack stepped toward the door. "I'm gonna take a look at what you've done."

"You can't go in there."

Jack kept moving. "Yeah, I can."

Tommy paused, then shrugged. "Whatever." He headed for his truck.

Weezy and Eddie followed Jack inside, through the mudroom that led to the small kitchen. Tommy had left lights on and, while the place wasn't exactly warm, the heat was on—most likely to keep the pipes from freezing.

The place had changed. The refrigerator looked relatively new but the stove seemed like an antique.

"Remember the tour Drexler gave us way back when?" Jack said.

Eddie shook his head. "Not *us*. Just you and Weez. The only time I was in here was that night you found Cody."

Jack wondered if Weezy had ever told him the real story of what had happened that night.

"This is as far as you got before you chickened out."

"I was scared of the Order then," he said, his voice low. "Wish I'd stayed scared."

They moved through a short hallway into the conference room where the chairs had been upended and placed on the long table in the center of the room. The sigil painted on the ceiling looked faded. Dying light through the barred windows picked up dust motes in the air.

"Where are the paintings?" Weezy said.

Portraits of past leaders of the Order had lined these walls; now only rectangular smudges remained.

Eddie looked around. "The place looks like it's been abandoned. Or put on the back burner."

Weezy said, "And that's strange, because it's the oldest Lodge in the Americas—or at least the site is."

Jack didn't care if they turned it into a whorehouse. Only the basement interested him.

He opened the cellar door and flipped the light switch. The space below lit up. Weezy stayed close behind him on the way down.

"Who's this Kris and is he looking for what I think he's looking for?"

"Kristof Szeto was one of the Order's enforcers."

"That guy you slammed with the truck door?" Eddie said.

"The same. Also the guy who put out the hits on Weezy last year. We had a run-in on Thursday and he told me he was working on a project in my hometown."

"'Run-in'?" Weezy said.

"Yeah."

"Would that 'run-in' be the reason he's not returning calls?"

"It would."

No reason to get into Drexler's involvement and administration of the coupe de grâce.

"Will he ever again return calls?"

"Not without a séance."

"Oh, brother," Eddie muttered.

Weezy sighed. "Before he lost the ability to return calls, did he perhaps say what this 'project' involved?"

"No, but he told me who had put him up to it: the One."

Weezy stumbled against his back. "*What*?"

"Exactly."

"The One? But what—?"

"That's all I know."

The basement had changed too. Last they'd seen it, the space had been piled high with antique furniture. Now it lay empty except for scattered chunks of broken concrete and three six-foot piles of freshly dug earth.

Weezy clutched Jack's arm as they approached the dirt.

"Look at this. It can only mean . . . Jack, he's got to be looking for the altered sigil of the Seven."

"That's my guess too."

"But why?"

"Well, I'd be surprised if Rasalom didn't know we have the *Compendium*."

She frowned. "How could he?"

"Between what I heard from Thompson and Szeto and Drexler on Thursday night, they've been making connections between you and Eddie and me and my Tyleski identity. I'm sure Thompson mentioned somewhere along the way that Tyleski stole the *Compendium* from him and he wants it back. And I'm sure Drexler must have mentioned it to the R-man."

Weezy said, "And if he knows we have the *Compendium*, and knows the *Compendium* contains the Other Naming Ceremony . . ."

". . . then the last thing he wants any of us knowing is his Other Name," Jack added, nodding. A thought struck. "Could that be why he put Dawn across the hall from you?"

"To spy on me?"

"Or to steal the book."

Weezy looked offended. "She wouldn't! Tell me true, Jack. Do you really think she'd do something like that?"

"I'm reaching the point where, except for a very select few, I'm wondering if anyone is incapable of anything."

He caught her glare, so he added, "Oh, all right. I don't think she'd do that to you."

"Thank you. I like to think I'm a half decent judge of people."

"Well, then, does your judgment tell you why she was moved in there?"

"Eddie gave us a possible explanation."

Yeah, one that had made Jack very uncomfortable.

"I might have another," Eddie said. "Maybe the One had some way of influencing Dawn or tapping into what she knew."

Jack stopped and stared at him. Weezy did the same.

Eddie looked embarrassed. "Hey, just tossing it off. This guy is supposed to be more than human and I—"

"No-no," Jack said. "It's not as crazy as it sounds. She lived in his house for most of her pregnancy. Maybe . . ."

Weezy said, "Well, if he knew I was studying and cross-referencing the *Compendium*, and he learned from Drexler that you and I had been in the buried town—"

"Wait!" Eddie said, waving his hand. "What buried town?"

"Long story."

"According to you they're *all* long stories."

"I'll tell you later."

"Why didn't anyone tell me before?"

Jack and Weezy replied in unison: "Because you were a blabbermouth."

And then they both cracked up.

Eddie wasn't laughing. "Real funny. A riot."

Jack turned and stepped to the edge of the deep hole in the basement floor. When the underground corridor below had flooded back in the eighties, a lot of silt must have washed in from the lake, collapsing side walls, burying everything.

"Ras must have decided the safest course was to dig up the special sigil and either destroy it or find a safer place for it. He assigned Szeto the job, Szeto hired Tommy and his crew, but Szeto became . . . incapacitated and couldn't follow through on paying the workers. So there's good news and bad news."

Weezy and Eddie joined him at the edge.

"What's the good news?" Weezy said.

"They didn't find it."

Eddie said, "I think I can guess the bad news."

"Right. We get some shovels and replace Tommy and company."

7. Rasalom barely recognized the face in the mirror. His right cheek and ear had been severely burned. They were healing but would remain scarred. The disfigurement did not matter in and of itself. He was not vain. And once the Change began and he was transformed, the scars and loss of a hand would not matter. He would be renewed.

But until then, these scars would attract attention. He did not like the idea of people staring.

Well, it would not be for long.

Then again, it might be a very long time if he did not locate that baby. He had to return to the mainland—now.

He left the bathroom and made his way through the front room, feeling stronger, and somewhat steadier on his feet, but still nowhere near who he had been forty-eight hours ago. He needed to lean on the furniture.

"Where are you going?" the cow said as he passed her.

She remained on the floor beside her dead dog, caressing the fur of its carcass. How long would she stay there? Until it rotted?

He didn't answer her. Instead he opened the front door and stepped outside. The air was icy but still, and the sky a speckled black dome. With so little light pollution here, he could make out the crowded stars and dust lanes of the Milky Way arching above him.

If his plans held, all this would change—day would become night, and the stars would mutate into new formations.

The South Fork of Long Island glowed faintly straight ahead and to his right. He raised his arms to each side, spreading them like wings. He stood swaying, a human cross, then willed himself to rise.

Nothing happened.

He tried harder, but remained earthbound.

Unease filtered through him. Was it because he was still so weak?

He lowered his arms and stared at the stump of his left wrist. Or had the loss of his hand affected his mastery over gravity? Through the years he'd used that mastery judiciously and with caution—it wouldn't do to be seen floating in the air—and had found it of limited use. An occasional convenience. But now, when he *needed* it, it had deserted him.

"What are you doing out there?" the cow called from behind him. "Come in here right now before you catch your death of cold."

No, he would not catch his death from a cold or any other infection. Viruses and bacteria had no chance against his immune system. But a too-low body temperature could stop his heart like anyone else's.

Perhaps it was just as well he couldn't lift in his

weakened condition. The ability might fail him while airborne. He needed more strength.

He could go back inside and begin slow work on the cow with a knife. No one would hear her screams as he fed on her agony and fear. But he saw no guarantee that would be enough. He would most likely have to take the boat back to the mainland anyway. That meant witnesses. And if evidence were found in the house, he would be subjected to the inconvenience of a police investigation.

All reasons why he rarely harmed anyone himself. So much better to induce someone else to commit an atrocity.

Patient . . . he must be patient.

He returned to the house.

8. "How much farther, do you think?" Eddie said, panting.

Jack and Eddie were both in the hole, digging their way east along the dirt-filled subterranean corridor. They'd fill buckets with the excavated dirt, which Weezy would pull up on ropes and dump into the basement.

Jack had driven down to Spurlin's Hardware and bought shovels, an aluminum ladder, lanterns, and the rest of the equipment. Then he'd picked up sandwiches and drinks at the Krauszer's down on 206.

"We should be getting close," Jack said. He looked back and up toward the hole in their ceiling and basement's floor. "What do you think, Weez?"

Her face appeared in the opening. "If memory serves—"

"And it usually does," Jack said.

"—you should have just a few more feet to go. If . . ." She hesitated.

"If what?"

"If the flood didn't wash it deeper into the passage."

Jack remembered the force of the water as it had surged against him back when they were teens. Quaker Lake lay to the west, just beyond the other end of the passage. That September, swollen by record September rains, it had broken into the passage, flooding it and nearly drowning Jack.

"If it moved even ten feet, we're sunk. We're going to have to find Tommy and company and pay them ourselves. No way the three of us can dig that far."

"We don't have the authority to do that," Eddie said. "This Szeto guy must have cleared it with the Council first. No way they're going to clear it for us."

"Who says they have to know? We can—"

"Hey, guys!" Weezy said in a hushed voice. "Quiet for just a minute."

Jack glanced at Eddie and they shut up. Finally Jack said, "What's up, Weez?"

Her voice filtered from above. "I swear I heard someone upstairs."

Jack didn't like that. He climbed the ladder and retrieved his Glock from his jacket pocket.

"Maybe Tommy came back," he said as he led the way upstairs.

Both the front and rear doors were locked, which meant nothing if someone had a key. But it had begun to rain about an hour ago and the floors inside the doors showed no trace of moisture.

"You're sure?" Jack said.

Weezy shrugged. "I'm not saying I heard some*one*,

but I know I heard some*thing*. Maybe just the building settling."

"I think it would have pretty much settled by now," Eddie said.

"It's got part of a buried town beneath it, so who says it will ever be fully settled?"

Eddie nodded. "Point to you."

"Just to be sure, I'm going to take a room-to-room look-see. Anyone want to come along?" Jack said.

They both volunteered.

The first floor was easy—only the kitchen, the conference room, the front room, and a few closets. All empty.

A different story upstairs: lots of small rooms—almost like a dorm—and crammed with the furniture that had once filled the basement. Took longer, but same result: empty.

"All clear," Jack said. "Back to digging?"

Eddie shook his head. "I've got to tell you, I thought I was in shape, but I'm bushed."

Weezy laughed. "I *know* I'm not in shape, so imagine how I feel."

Well, the hour was late, and Jack had to admit he was feeling a little sore himself. Working out wasn't the same as working.

"Okay, let's knock off and see if we can find a motel and crash for the night."

"And risk not being able to get back in?" Weezy said.

"We'll get back in."

She gestured around them. "Why don't we stay here? Heat, electricity, running water, lots of rooms, no linens, but we've got mattresses."

"I don't know," Eddie said.

"Come on. It'll be fun. Where else can we stay? The Lonely Pine Motel? These mattresses here are ancient but I bet they're better than the ones at the Lonely Pine."

Jack said, "I can't do anything in the morning without coffee."

"I'll run down to Krauszer's for you. Come on. I've got an alarm on my phone. I'll set it for an early start in the morning."

Well, why not? They were already trespassers. Might as well become squatters too.

"As long as I get my coffee."

TUESDAY

1. Weezy's voice woke him.

"Jack? Eddie?"

It echoed from down the hall and she sounded terrified.

He leaped up from the bare mattress and looked around in the dark. He was fully dressed except for his work boots. He'd rolled his jacket into a makeshift pillow. He felt around for the flashlight and the Glock he'd left on a bedside table.

They'd left a light on in the hall before calling it a night. What had happened to it?

"Guys!" she called again, her voice quavering. "Can you come here?"

"On my way," Jack said.

He found the flashlight and turned it on, then grabbed his Glock. Couldn't imagine why he'd need it but he preferred to have it with him rather than on the table.

The piles of upended chairs and bureaus and such scattered around the room cast weird shadows as he hurried toward his open door. He flipped the switch on the wall as he went by but the ceiling light didn't go on. Odd. It had worked before.

Light flashed in the hall, though, and it turned out to be Eddie with his own flashlight.

"Weezy?" Eddie said.

"I'm in here," she called from two doors down where she'd chosen to spend the night.

Jack reached the darkened room first. A flick of her wall switch proved that her light didn't work either, but Jack's flash beam found her wrapped in her coat and crouched on the bed, holding her unlit flashlight and looking terrified. He entered with Eddie close behind him.

"What's wrong?"

"Someone was here."

"Who? How?" Eddie said. "There's nobody here but us."

Jack couldn't argue with that. The windows were barred and they'd barricaded both downstairs doors before hitting the mattresses. Even someone with a key couldn't get in without making a terrible racket. Eddie tried her wall switch again—as dead as Jack's.

"Mine's dead too," Eddie said. "Seems we've lost power."

Jack held his pistol against his thigh as he flashed his beam around. Like every other room, lots of furniture stacked and bunched together, but no people.

"I'm telling you someone was in the room." Her voice rose in pitch. "He was standing over the bed and looking down at me."

"'He'?" Jack said. "What'd he look like?"

"Okay, it could have been a *she*, but it . . . I don't know . . . it felt like a *he*. I grabbed my flashlight but it's dead."

She hit the button and the beam shot across the room.

"It didn't work before." She turned it off and back on again. "I swear it didn't."

Jack said, "The place is empty except for us. It wasn't Eddie or me, so that leaves a nightmare."

"I wasn't dreaming. Believe me, I know when I'm dreaming. What time is it?"

Eddie pulled out his cell phone and pressed a button. Jack saw his puzzled frown in the glow from its display.

"No service. It worked fine before."

No service meant no time on the display. Jack hadn't yet become dependent on his phone for the time. He trained his flash beam on his watch, an old Seiko that refused to die.

"Two thirty-two," he said, then noticed the second hand wasn't moving. "Wait. I take that back. My watch has stopped."

Okay. This was getting weird.

Weezy's door *slammed* closed.

Jack jumped just like everyone else. Eddie was closest. He grabbed the knob, twisted, and pulled.

"It won't budge." His voice had developed a quaver.

Jack stepped over to help. "Maybe the two of us—"

"Jack? Eddie?" Weezy said. Her voice sounded strange.

Jack turned and saw her awed expression as she trained her flashlight beam across the room.

"Look."

He followed her beam and stepped back in shock when he saw two chairs on the ceiling.

"What the . . . ?" His mouth had gone dry.

Those chairs had been part of the furniture pile a moment ago. Now they were in the front corner of the room, resting on their sides against the ceiling.

"We're outta here," he said.

He and Eddie tried the heavy wooden door together but it wouldn't budge—wouldn't even rattle. Seemed like it had fused to the frame.

He crossed the room to the window and looked out. Beyond the wrought-iron bars, the frozen surface of

Quaker Lake reflected the streetlights of the sleeping town.

He tried to raise the sash but it wouldn't budge—either painted shut or fused like the door. He could break the glass but didn't see the point: They'd never get past the bars crisscrossing the opening.

"Hey, guys," Eddie said, his ear pressed against the door. "Somebody's out in the hall."

Jack joined him at the door. He heard movement outside to their right. Floorboards creaking, joists squealing in distress.

Someone? No, some*thing* was moving down the hall, something massive, coming their way.

"Stand back," Jack said, pulling Eddie with him.

The sounds of the walls, floor, and maybe even the ceiling of the hallway struggling to hold together grew louder and closer. Cracks zigzagged along the stucco walls of the room, the door bulged inward as if some monstrous weight were pressing against its far side. It didn't look like it could hold.

Jack looked around, spotted an open closet door, pointed.

"In there!"

He had no idea if it would protect them from whatever was out there, but he saw no other options.

Their flashlights—all three of them—died just before the room door slammed open.

Weezy screamed, Eddie shouted in terror. For want of anything better to do, Jack dropped to one knee and fired a half dozen quick shots at the doorway. The muzzle flashes revealed what looked like a glistening gray surface sliding past, oblivious to the bullets. Nothing appeared to be entering the room so Jack saved his rounds.

Maybe ten seconds later the sounds and the sense of

massive movement faded away, and their flashlights came on. All three beams zipped to the doorway.

"What the hell was *that*?" Eddie said.

Jack shook his head. "Not sure I want to know. But I do want to know what's going on here. Weezy—any ideas?"

"Right now I'm having a little trouble thinking about anything but getting out of here."

"I'm with you on that. The Lonely Pine Motel doesn't sound so bad now, does it."

"Sounds like paradise."

Glock held before him, Jack eased toward the gaping doorway and the darkness beyond it. Eddie came up beside him.

"God, that thing is loud," he whispered.

"The pistol?"

"Yeah. My ears are ringing."

So were Jack's.

"Never fired one?"

"Shot my share of rifles, but always outside."

Yeah, inside a small, closed room was a different ball game.

Jack poked his head through the doorway and flashed his beam quickly in both directions. Empty.

Except for the slime.

The walls, floor, and ceiling glistened with a mucousy substance, as if some giant slug had just passed.

"Come on, Weezy," Eddie said, stepping into the hall. "Let's get the hell—"

He slipped on the slime and would have gone down if Jack hadn't caught his arm.

"Steady, guy."

Eddie stepped back inside, wiping his shoe on the floor.

"Slippery as hell. We're going to have to be careful."

Weezy was reaching under her bed. "Let me get my backpack and—"

The door slammed shut again.

"Ah, jeez," Jack said. "Now what?"

A startling clatter from the corner of the room: The two chairs had fallen from the ceiling.

Jack pulled on the doorknob and the door swung open with no problem. The hall seemed even darker than before. His flash beam picked up no glistening mucus this time. In fact, it picked up nothing at all. The hallway was gone, and in its place . . .

Darkness.

A darkness so absolute it swallowed his flash beam.

"Okay, Jack," Eddie said. "What the hell is *that*?"

"Wish I knew."

He did know it made his gut crawl. He couldn't say why. Maybe it was the sense of *emptiness* in that blackness.

He backed up a step, reaching for the door to slam it closed, but the blackness didn't enter the room. It simply sat there, absorbing light. A return trip to the window showed the same tranquil scene as before. Nothing had changed out there, but what had happened in the hall? What was the darkness? What did it hide?

He returned to the doorway.

"Keep back, Jack," Weezy said.

He hardly needed to be told that. But as he approached he again sensed that *empty* feeling out there. He had a strange impression that the hallway wasn't simply hidden in the blackness, but was no longer there. A feeling that *nothing* was out there, not even light.

He handed Eddie his flash and stuck the Glock into his waistband. Then he grabbed a chair from the nearby pile of furniture.

"Jack?" Weezy said behind him. "What—?"

"Just a little experiment."

He tossed the chair through the doorway and then stepped back, listening . . . and listening.

Nothing.

It should have hit the hallway floor. But it didn't. If by some stretch of possibility that was gone, it should have landed on the first floor. But it didn't. After that, some clatter from the basement should have echoed up. But it didn't.

"Jack?" Eddie handed back the flashlight as he stepped up beside him and stared into the black. "What happened to the chair?"

"Not a clue. It could be still falling, for all I know."

The blackness was bottomless. Or effectively so.

Eddie was shaking his head. "No . . . no . . . shit like this doesn't happen. It's some kind of trick . . . an illusion."

He turned, grabbed another chair, and heaved it through the door.

The three of them stood in silence, listening.

No sound. Falling is silent.

Eddie backed away. "What have we got ourselves into?"

Shaken, Jack closed the door.

Eddie flicked the beam of his flashlight back and forth between Jack and Weezy. Hard to say which wobbled more: the beam or his voice. "And how can you two be so calm about it?"

"I've been living with these sorts of things for years now. And I've had more practice hiding it. And your sister's suspected this stuff since she was a kid."

Jack turned to Weezy. He didn't want to shine the light in her eyes, so he kept the beam trained on the mattress.

"Okay, Weez. You're the expert here. What's going on?"

"I-I don't know. I can make some guesses but—"

"Guess away. Please."

"Well, the *Compendium* says that the mortar used to build the Lodges is often mixed with some dirt from a nexus point."

"What's a nexus point?" Eddie said.

"Places around the globe where the barrier—sometimes called the Veil—between our world and the Otherness is very thin."

"There's one not too far from here," Jack said.

Weezy stared at him. "You know about that?"

"I used to hang with some piney kids in high school. They mentioned a 'bald spot' deep in the Pines where weird lights flashed at certain times and nothing ever grew—hence the name."

"Sounds like the nexus point."

"How long has all this been going on?" Eddie said.

Weezy looked at him. "Almost forever."

"But . . . it's practically in our backyard—or at least what *was* our backyard."

She shrugged. "Tried to tell you, but you wouldn't listen."

Jack remembered one of Eddie's favorite descriptors for his older sister: *crazy.*

"Well, I'm listening now. Black is black, remember? This can't happen every night. Why's it happening now?"

"Well, if you combine the nexus point dirt in the mortar, and a nexus point not too far away, with the proximity of an equinox, maybe . . . *ow!*"

She had been reaching into the backpack where she kept the *Compendium*. Now she snatched it away and shook it in the air.

Eddie stepped closer. "What happened?"

"The *Compendium*. It's hot."

Jack reached in and gave it a quick touch. Right. Hot. Hot enough to raise a blister if you tried to hold it.

"The book must be reacting to all this weirdness," she said.

Jack wondered about that. "Maybe it's triggering it."

Weezy nodded. "That could be. Take all those elements—the mortar, the proximity to the nexus point, the time in the sun's cycle—and they may not be enough. But add this relic of the First Age to the mix and . . . who knows?"

"Whatever the cause," he said, "we're stuck here."

"No!" Eddie said, going to the window. "We can't stay here! We've got to get out!"

Jack said, "Not gonna happen. But if we stick together and stay awake, we'll make it to morning."

Eddie leaned closer. "How can you be so sure this'll change by then?"

"Sunrise," Weezy said, nodding. "Sunrise will change everything. You'll see."

2. Sunrise.

Rasalom stood in the cow's kitchen and watched the sky turn bright orange above the watery horizon. By noon—if the storm hadn't changed the boat's schedule—it would arrive at her dock and he would be bound for the mainland.

Her phone service had returned last night and he'd put in a call to Szeto. He'd been satisfied with his performance in the probe against the Lady—proof beyond doubt that the *Fhinntmanchca* had not altered her invulnerability to Earthly assault. He seemed competent, ruthless, and enthusiastic—an excellent mélange of qualities—and so Rasalom had rewarded him with another assignment.

But Szeto had not answered, and had not returned the call despite a message to contact him immediately.

Rasalom sighed. He supposed he would have to call Drexler. He knew his anger at the man was unjustified. His behavior had been exemplary in procuring the Orsa and creating the *Fhinntmanchca*. Not his fault that it failed to eliminate the Lady. And he had achieved the seemingly impossible by bringing down the Internet, albeit briefly. But long enough to further bloody an already hemorrhaging noosphere.

And yet, the Lady persisted.

Rasalom did not understand how. He could only assume that she had somehow evolved to a point where she could exist independently of the noosphere.

Again, not Drexler's fault.

Yet Rasalom had vented his rage and frustration on the man, had been ready to tear him limb from limb. But he had restrained himself at the last moment. And now he was glad he had. Never discard a tool for which you might find future use.

He punched Drexler's number into the cow's phone.

"Hello?"

His tone was appropriately cautious. He would not recognize the number on his caller ID.

"Drexler, I have a task for you."

A few heartbeats of confused silence, then, *"Sir! Of course! What do you wish?"*

"I want you to meet me at the Water Street docks in Sag Harbor. Leave in plenty of time to reach the docks by noon and wait for me there."

He supposed he could have hired a cab, but he had no money, and even if he did, he did not want to be seen by any more people than absolutely necessary. Besides, Drexler's Bentley was very comfortable.

"Yes, sir. Immediately. I . . . we heard about the house. We thought—"

"We will discuss that in the car. For that reason you will leave your driver and come alone."

"Of course. I am very glad to hear from you. We feared the worst."

"Yes. I'm sure."

He hung up.

How pathetically eager to please. Right now Drexler would do anything, perhaps even rape his mother, to return to the good graces of the One. He and the other higher members of the Septimus Order who knew of the Otherness and the Change were under the impression they would be given special treatment once the Change began. Rasalom encouraged that belief. It made them willing participants in their own demise.

But only the One would change with the Change.

Or so *he* had been led to believe.

What if the Otherness had been toying with him all these millennia? While improbable, it was not impossible. This was not the first time he had confronted the possibility, but he had no way to answer the question, so he let it go. He would continue on this path. Divergence, after all this time, was unthinkable.

He heard the woman stirring in her room. Last night he had slipped in while she was sleeping and laid his hand on her head. Soon she would realize what he'd done to her.

"Oh, dear God! Dear *God*!"

There.

He heard the approach of her scurrying footsteps as she continued to cry out to her deity.

"Praise God! Praise him!"

She hurtled into the kitchen and skidded to a halt before him.

"I can see!" Tears coursed down her cheeks. "Dear God, I can see! It's a miracle!"

"You could see before," he said, maintaining a bland, unimpressed air. "You inspected my wounds many times and—"

"I could see blurry shapes and maybe a little more close up, but now I can really *see*! Everything is perfectly clear! It's a miracle!"

Her joy was nauseating.

"Whatever was afflicting you has cleared up. That is hardly divine intervention."

"Don't you understand? I had AMD and it's incurable. Now I can see. I call *that* a miracle!"

"As you wish."

Her gaze narrowed. "Are you an angel?"

He hadn't seen that one coming.

"A what?"

"An angel, sent here by God to test me?"

"That is perhaps the most ridiculous thing I have ever heard."

"No . . . it makes sense to me now. God washed you up on shore to see if I'd be a good Samaritan and take care of you. And I did. So then He took Rocky from me to test me further. But still I didn't reject Him. And so now I'm rewarded with my sight. Praise God!"

"Well, if I'm his angel, I wish he'd give me back my hand." He remembered his cover story and forced a sob. "Or even better . . . my family."

The cow added a sob of her own. "And I'd give up my sight if I could have Rocky back."

"Maybe God has a mission for you that requires sight."

She brightened. "You think so? I could be God's instrument . . . I could do His work."

"Yes. That would be wonderful."

She looked around and made a face. "Having sight has its disadvantages. Look at this mess. I couldn't see the dirt before. This place needs a good scrubbing."

As she bustled off, Rasalom could not help but smile at the cow's comment.

Having sight has its disadvantages . . .

She could not realize how true those words, for she would curse her sight and beg her god for return of her blindness when the horrors of the Change reached her little island.

3. Eddie rammed his shovel into the hard-packed dirt. "How long do we keep this up?"

"Digging?" Jack said, doing the same.

"Yeah. When do we reach the point where we say two shovels aren't cutting it and go hire some help?"

Jack stopped and stared at the wall of hard-packed earth before them.

Good question.

And one Eddie would ask before either Jack or Weezy. Eddie had never seen the altered sigil. He'd only heard talk about it, so it wasn't as real to him as to them. Jack could picture it right about here, leaning against the right-hand wall. But even if it hadn't washed away, it might have fallen to the floor.

Eddie would also ask because he still looked shaken by

last night's events. Jack wasn't untouched—he realized the danger they'd been in—and he was sure Weezy wasn't either, but they'd learned to expect the unexpected and inexplicable. Eddie was still a long way from that.

Even though sunrise had brought everything back to normal, just as Weezy had predicted, Jack could tell Eddie wanted out of here. Because even though the hallway and beyond had been restored at first light, the two chairs they'd tossed through the door were nowhere in sight. They'd gone Somewhere Else.

Jack wondered if that might be the same Somewhere Else his brother Tom had been taken. In truth, he didn't even know if his brother was alive. But if he was, and in the same Somewhere Else, at least now he had someplace to park his doughy butt.

But no matter what they found down here today, if they needed to stay over another night, they'd do it at the Lonely Pine Motel.

"Jack?" Eddie said. "The end point?"

"What?" He yanked himself back to the here and now. "Oh, sorry." He shook his head. "I'm not sure."

"Well, pick something. I need a target."

"Why?"

"I'm goal directed. It's the way my mind works. It needs an end point. Give me one."

Jack thought a moment, then shrugged. "Two more feet."

Didn't sound like much, but with a passage ten feet wide and eight feet high, that was 160 cubic feet of dirt. Eddie's daunted look said he realized that.

"And then what?"

"Then we call Tommy."

"Do we know his number?"

Jack smiled. Eddie was already preparing for defeat. Jack wasn't ready to concede yet.

"It was on the side of his truck."

He squinted at Jack. "You remember it?"

"No, but I'll bet your sister does."

"Sister does what?" Weezy said from behind them as she descended the ladder.

"Remember Tommy the excavator's phone number."

"Sure." She rattled it off as she slipped on her work gloves. "You giving up?"

"After two more feet," Eddie said.

Weezy took the shovel from her brother and gave Jack a semi-stern look.

"Is we gonna stand here jawboning or is we gonna move some dirt?"

Before Jack could answer, she drove her shovel into the wall of dirt—

And hit something that went *clink!*

They all froze.

Jack said, "Do that again."

She did, with the same result. Jack attacked the dirt in the area and within minutes a four-inch-wide expanse of gleaming black appeared.

"That look familiar?" he said.

"Does it ever." Weezy's smile was beatific as she turned to Eddie. "See? Same material as our little pyramid."

"So we've found it?"

"We have."

But they had a lot of digging left to do to free it from the earth.

4. Ernst jumped at the sound of a knock on the car window. He turned and saw some disfigured derelict peering at him through the rear passenger window.

Ernst waved him away. Probably wanted to wash the windshield or—

"Drexler, open the door."

That voice . . . he knew that—oh, no, it couldn't be! He looked closely and saw that it was.

The One.

He fumbled for the LOCK toggle. The buttons popped up and the One entered the rear of the car. Ernst gaped at him. The hair had been burned off the right side of his scalp; scars stippled his right cheek. And his hand . . . his left hand was—

"Close your mouth. You look foolish."

"Yes, sir. It's just that—"

"Someone tried very hard to kill me, Drexler. To make that attempt, they had to first find me. My presence at that house was supposed to be a secret."

Ernst tried to read his eyes, but as usual, that proved impossible. Those pools of black infinity revealed nothing. How much did he know?

"Your whereabouts was known only at the highest levels—and to Doctor Heinze, of course."

"Did that include you?"

Ernst swallowed. Best to stay close to the facts, if not the truth. He'd learned of the One's whereabouts through indirect means. No one could be aware that he'd known.

"No. I had no idea. The Council informed me only after the attack."

"I feel fear washing off you, Drexler. And while I find that enjoyable, I must ask: Are you guilty of something?"

"No-no. I'm simply afraid I'll be suspected of something of which I am innocent. We—the High Council and I—believe we have pieced together what happened. Doctor Heinze visited the baby on Friday. We believe the baby's mother—"

"Dawn Pickering—her body was found across the street."

"Correct. She was convinced that her baby was still alive, and we now believe she was following Doctor Heinze. We spoke to the doctor and he hadn't seen Dawn since he'd had her removed from his office last week. But we think she was following him and trailed him to Nuckateague."

The One looked troubled. "Sounds reasonable. It appears I underestimated that girl's determination."

"I assure you no one on our end let it slip. Gilda hadn't left the South Fork for a week and Georges only once to drive you to the airport. And no one could have followed you to Nuckateague because you weren't around."

Ernst would have loved to know where the One went on his jaunts but knew better than to ask.

"Doctor Heinze's visit might have led her to suspect her baby's presence, but not mine."

"If Dawn spotted either Georges or Gilda out there—and we believe she must have—it would be logical for her to assume that Mr. Osala was there too."

"But Dawn Pickering did not mount that assault."

He had a feeling the One knew the identity of his attacker—or had a pretty good idea who he was—but was testing Ernst in some way.

"No, of course not. My theory is that she informed Louise Myers—also known as Louise Connell—of the whereabouts of the baby."

"That requires a leap in logic."

Yes . . . definitely a test.

"Not so much, considering they lived across the hall from each other."

Ernst wanted to add: *Something you arranged*. But he dared not. He was still baffled by the move. Weeks ago the One had instructed him to find the Connell woman—find and no more. Absolutely no contact. Ernst had succeeded almost immediately, and shortly thereafter the One moved Dawn in across the hall. He must have had a reason for that, but Ernst could not fathom what it might be. Now was not the time to ask . . .

Or was it?

"Is that why you moved Dawn so close to the Connell woman? So they would meet?"

"That is not your concern."

Well, Ernst thought, glancing at the One's scars and the stump of his wrist where it rested in his lap, whatever your plan, it certainly backfired.

"As you wish."

"You knew the Connell woman as a youngster, Drexler. Do you think her capable of such an assault?"

"Louise Connell? No. A very determined young lady, but her weapon is her intellect. Her friend Jack, on the other hand . . . the one you were interested in . . . he's another story."

"Yes," the One said. "The Heir is quite another story."

Ernst jolted in his seat. He had never been struck by lightning, but this must be how it felt.

"Jack is the Heir?"

The One nodded. "Heir Apparent."

Now Ernst understood why the One had grilled him in such detail about his early experiences with Jack.

"I knew it!"

The singed remnants of the One's eyebrows lifted. "Did you, now?"

Watch it! Be careful here. Fabricate as little as possible.

"Well, I didn't *know*, exactly. But he visited me on Thursday night asking where he might find you."

"Really. For what purpose?"

Ernst's mouth was dry. "To kill you."

The One leaned back. "Interesting. And what did you tell him?"

"The truth: I had no idea where you were. He threatened me but became convinced I didn't know. In fact, I laughed in his face at the possibility that he could succeed in harming you."

Obviously, not such a laughing matter. Jack, you impress me more and more. But still . . . you failed.

Which put Ernst firmly back in the One's camp.

"He very nearly did. Why didn't you subdue him?"

"I tried but he was waiting for me when I entered my apartment and had disabled all my defenses." Time to stretch the truth. "But I did call Szeto—"

"Ah, yes. Szeto. Where is he?"

Yes . . . your beloved Szeto . . .

"Alerted by me, Szeto and two of his men captured Jack and brought him to a property the Order keeps on the West Side. Szeto wished to torture him for revenge, I wanted information from him—specifically, how he knew about you being the One. I had surmised he was involved with the Enemy but had no idea he was the Heir. When I got there, Szeto and his two men were dead and Jack was gone."

The One considered this. "Szeto did not strike me as the careless sort."

"Well, in this case he was. Perhaps because he was so full of rage at Jack for killing so many of his men, and for the brutal beating he had suffered at his hands just weeks ago." Ernst could not resist a final dig. "Szeto was competent, but I learned from my dealings with him that he suffered from an exalted estimation of his own abilities. If he had done his job, Jack would not have been around to attack you."

The One appeared to mull this. "Still, he proved useful on a number of fronts. I shall miss Szeto."

All but choking on the words, Ernst said, "We all will."

Another protracted silence, and then the One said, "Drive me to the city. And as we travel, I want you to call the Council and tell them to send someone over to the Connell woman's apartment—that is, if the Heir has left any to send."

"We still have a few."

"Tell them I want to know if she is there. If she is not, I want them to search her apartment for the *Compendium of Srem*."

Another jolt, albeit of much lower voltage. Louise Connell had the *Compendium*?

"Yes, sir. And if they find it?"

"If it is there, do not touch it. If it is not, they are to leave her apartment exactly as they found it and report back to you."

"As you wish," Ernst said and reached for the phone.

"And while that is under way, tell the Council to send some of the local members of that Johnson, New Jersey, Lodge over to the building to see what is going on. I want a report as soon as possible."

The Johnson Lodge? What could interest the One there?

"Right away. May I ask—?"

"You may not."

The One leaned back and closed his eyes. The hideous injuries aside, he looked haggard, exhausted. Ernst had never dreamed anything like this could happen. And yet it had.

He wondered what that ancient twisted mind was planning.

Of one thing he was certain . . . Ernst was quite glad he was not Jack.

5. Jack hacked away at the last layer of dirt packed around the gleaming black sigil where it leaned against the wall. Neither time, the flood, nor the encasing dirt had dulled its onyx finish.

Since the sigil measured a half dozen feet across, they'd decided to excavate a narrow passage in front of it, free it from the dirt, and drag it out. The passage allowed room for only one, so the three of them rotated between digging and hauling away the loosened earth.

Behind him, Eddie said, "Careful. Don't break it."

Jack bit back a retort that might have come out sharper than intended. Eddie had morphed into a pest. Yes, Jack understood that the Lodge creeped him out and he wanted the place in his rearview mirror ASAP, but he was beginning to micromanage. Maybe that expanded his comfort zone, but it set Jack's teeth on edge. Having dirt in his hair, his eyes, and down the back of his shirt didn't help.

So he said, "Not to worry, Fredo."

"Frodo?" he heard Eddie say to Weezy. "Why's he calling me Frodo?"

"I said 'Fredo,'" Jack called back. "And I'm getting in the mood to take you out on the lake for a little fishing."

"Fishing? What's he talking about?"

Jack heard Weezy laughing farther behind. "Never mind. And as for the stuff that sigil is made of, you can't even scratch it."

"Nice sentence structure," Jack said.

She laughed again. "Oh, now you're getting on *me*?"

"No," he said as the last bit of dirt fell away from the top point of the sigil. "Now I'm getting this thing out of here. Eddie, give me a hand and we'll see if we can shake it free."

Eddie slipped in beside him. Together they both got two-handed grips on the spokes of the sigil and began rocking it back and forth. Dirt rained on them as it became looser and looser.

"What *is* this thing made of?" Eddie said as they increased their efforts.

"Don't know . . . but it looks like the same stuff as our little pyramid back in the day, and that was virtually indestructible."

"It's called *tenathic*," Weezy said.

"Since when?"

"Since I read about it in the *Compendium*."

He remembered Professor Nakamura telling him and Weezy that the folks at U of P hadn't been able to identify the pyramid's shiny black compound, mainly because they hadn't been able to chip off a sample. Now he had a name for it: tenathic.

Finally it came free.

"Yeah!" Eddie shouted. "Yeah!"

"Okay. Let's try to roll it out of here."

They put their shoulders against the spokes, and Weezy pitched in by pulling on the free side, but the remaining section of the perimeter was jammed. Jack stepped up on one of the crosspieces and grabbed the perimeter. He could only vaguely make out the glyphs carved into the surface, but he could feel them against his palms. Something strange about them . . . something not right, but he couldn't say just what.

Well, right or not right, it needed freeing up, so he tightened his grip and threw his weight backward— once . . . twice . . .

It loosened up on the third try. He dropped back to the floor and put his shoulder against the sigil. The three of them resumed their effort to roll it.

"Watch out for that point," Jack told Weezy. "If this thing starts to move, it could—"

It moved and a point angled toward Weezy but she danced out of the way. Another couple of turns and it sat free in the passage. Dusting the dirt out of his hair, Jack stepped back with the others and stared at it.

Weezy said, "That has to be his Other name. Don't you think? Can it be anything else?"

Jack looked at her eager face. "It had better be. It's all we have."

After they'd discovered the sigil this morning, Weezy had brought her backpack down. As she stepped over to where she'd tied it to the ladder, Jack leaned in for a closer look. He couldn't say why it had felt so strange. But he recognized the glyphs.

"No doubt, Weez. Those are the same seven characters from the pyramids—the big and the little."

"Makes sense, doesn't it?" she said, pulling out her camera. "Each of the seven sides of the pyramid had one of these glyphs. Each of the Other Names is composed of the same seven glyphs, so, in a way, each member of the Seven had his name chiseled on the pyramid."

She fiddled with the lens as she returned, then leaned in next to Jack and flashed a photo. When she checked the display, she frowned.

"What's wrong?" Jack said as he and Eddie angled in on either side for a look.

"Blurred," Eddie said, then grunted. "Huh. Master of the Obvious."

"Maybe you've got some schmutz on the lens," Jack said.

Weezy gave him a cockeyed look. "Schmutz?"

"Abespeak for dirt. Enough of it down here."

Weezy checked the lens. "No. Clean. I always keep the lens cover on and—oh, crap."

"What?"

"Just remembered something."

She snapped another photo with the same result.

"Damn!" she said. "The pyramid wouldn't photograph either, remember?"

Now that she mentioned it . . .

"Right-right-right. Neither would the box it came in. And since this is the same material . . ."

Weezy returned to her backpack and traded her camera for a yellow pad and one of her Sharpies.

"That never stopped me from drawing them before."

Less than a minute later she displayed her work.

"I now present the One's Other Name."

$$\text{ɔ ヒ 入 ค た ꞁ ᖴ}$$

Jack made a quick comparison with the sigil: a damn near exact copy.

"We hope."

Her smile faltered. "Yeah . . . we hope."

"Whether it is or not," he said, "it's a beautiful name . . . so euphonious."

"Okay!" Eddie said, clapping his hands. "Our work here is done, so let's get the hell out."

Jack couldn't argue with that.

Eddie led the way up. Jack followed with Weezy's backpack, then helped her up to the basement level. He was about to unplug the spotlight they'd used below—he'd leave that and the shovels as a gift to the Lodge—when he heard footsteps on the basement stairs. He turned to see two men in suits step into the room from the stairwell.

"Who are you and what are you doing here?" said the one in the lead.

Jack had left his Glock in the backpack while he was digging. Neither of these two seemed to pose much of a threat but that didn't keep him from slipping his hand inside to find its comforting polymer composite.

"We were hired to excavate the subbasement."

"I know who was hired," the guy said, "and you aren't he."

Ooh . . . *you aren't he* . . . a grammarian.

Without missing a beat Jack changed the story: "The One told us to check out the work."

Both men frowned.

"The one what?" said the second.

Either they weren't high-ups or were pretending not to know. He bet on the former and figured it wouldn't hurt to keep them off balance by changing the subject.

He jerked his thumb at the opening in the floor. "We found an interesting variation on the Order's sigil down below."

Weezy was nodding. "Really interesting. Like nothing you've ever seen before."

The Order guys glanced at each other. Both looked dubious but finally the first said, "I'll go see." He pointed at Jack. "No games, all right?"

Jack put on a wounded look. "I assure you, this is not a joking matter."

He turned to the second. "Watch them."

He headed for the opening, descended the ladder, and was down maybe half a minute when his excited voice echoed up.

"Hey, Lee! Get down here. You've *got* to see this!"

Lee gave them a look as he approached the opening. "Don't go anywhere."

"As if," Jack said. "That's our find and don't you guys even think about stealing credit."

He waited for Lee to descend then stepped over to the opening. Both of them were out of sight, so he grabbed the ladder and quickly hauled it up.

Ignoring the cries of "Hey!" and "What the fuck?" from below, he signaled Weezy and Eddie to follow him up the stairs.

"Yeah," Eddie said. "Let's roll."

Jack glanced at him. *Let's roll*? Really?

Well, at least they had a name—whether the right name or not, no one could say, but the only name available. It would have to do.

But something about the glyphs and the feel of that sigil continued to gnaw at him.

6. Ernst ended the call and closed his phone. Just ahead, the Manhattan skyline loomed above the entrance to the Midtown Tunnel, while his impatient passenger waited behind.

They had heard from the Manhattan brothers who investigated the Connell woman's apartment. Neither she nor the *Compendium* had been in evidence.

And now word from New Jersey. Some of the information was puzzling, and even a little disturbing.

"That was from the brothers who checked the Johnson Lodge. They found two men and a woman in the basement. The woman's description fits Louise Connell. Descriptions of the men are vague, but they easily could have been Jack and the woman's brother."

"What were they doing?"

Here was the puzzling part.

"According to the brother I just spoke to, they were digging."

"Were they." A statement rather than a question.

"Yes. They appeared to have been digging in an excavation beneath the basement of the Lodge."

"That would put them in the ruins of the buried town."

The One had been very interested in the town when he had quizzed Ernst about Jack's boyhood.

"Yes. The brother told me that the High Council had authorized the dig and sent an emissary named Kristof Szeto to initiate it."

"Did they find anything?"

"Someone—they don't know whether it was Jack and his friends or the workers Szeto hired—but someone unearthed the large, damaged sigil that has been down there longer than the Lodge."

It had been largely forgotten over the years. Ernst hadn't thought about it in a long, long time—not since the 1980s when he'd researched the Johnson Lodge before visiting it. The sigil had been found in ancient times. The brothers back then had no use for a damaged symbol of the Order but did not feel right discarding such a relic. So they stored it away.

"Then we must assume the Heir saw it."

"No assumption necessary: He directed the brothers to it."

The One made no reply. He remained silent as they entered the Midtown Tunnel. Ernst glanced in the rearview mirror and saw him staring out the window, his expression unreadable.

"Does that particular sigil have a special significance?"

His voice seemed to come from far away. "It belonged to me back in the First Age."

Ernst stiffened in his seat. What a remarkable revelation. That explained the One's interest in it when Ernst had mentioned it during his quizzing about Jack.

"If only we'd known, it would have been displayed all these centuries in a place of honor."

"I am glad it wasn't. I had thought it lost forever." He seemed full of sudden determination as he leaned forward. "When we reach the city, turn downtown."

"Yes, sir."

Ernst knew better than to ask why. But then the One answered his question.

"I must feed."

7. " 'It may never happen, Weez,' " she said, quoting. " 'This may all be wasted time and chatter.' "

Jack, behind the wheel, stared straight ahead and said nothing as they cruised north on the New Jersey Turnpike. She'd called shotgun for the trip home. She was too rattled about what lay ahead to concentrate on the *Compendium*.

She studied Jack. He'd been strangely silent since leaving the Lodge. Something was bothering him. Endangering the baby? She doubted it. That was *her* worry.

"But, since it *is* going to happen," she added, "I guess it wasn't just wasted chatter. Not that I have veto power."

He glanced at her. "We all respect your feelings, Weez. There's just . . ."

". . . too much hanging in the balance," she said. "I know that. I just . . ."

". . . never believed the end justifies the means."

Behind them, Eddie laughed. "Are you two going to spend the entire trip finishing each other's sentences?"

They were, weren't they. Once again she was filled with such a longing for Jack. What was it? He wasn't handsome—not ugly, but a long way from a hot guy. He didn't radiate alpha masculinity; it might be there, but he hid anything that might draw attention.

But he was Jack, and he couldn't hide what he was from her. And she'd fallen for who he was.

They made a pretty good team too. Didn't he see that?

Well, maybe he did, but he didn't feel about her the way she felt about him. Not even close. How could he? To him, they were simply . . . buds—close as could be, with a history that went way, way back, but she didn't go beyond friend for him. He would never see her any other way, and that tore a hole in her heart.

After a couple of beats of awkward silence, Jack said, "In this case, I don't think the means are so terrible. The baby won't know he's got an Other name."

"I know. I've come to terms with it. The Lady won't perform the ceremony on anyone else, so that's the way it has to be."

Eddie said, "Why not give him a plain old American name right after the ceremony. That way he'll grow up answering to Tom or Dick or Harry or whatever."

"Assuming he grows up," Jack said.

Weezy frowned. "What do you mean?"

"Assuming we have the right name, assuming the *Compendium* has the right ceremony, and assuming the ceremony will do what we hope it will, we all just might see the summer."

The summer . . .

Jack was convinced—said he'd heard from multiple sources—that darkness waited in the spring. If Rasalom had his way, if they didn't find a way to stop him, there'd be no summer.

"If just one of those assumptions is wrong," he added, "then all this is for nothing."

She couldn't argue with his logic, but he seemed so negative lately.

"The *Compendium* hasn't let us down yet."

"But the name . . ."

Yes . . . the name. Everything hinged on the name belonging to Rasalom.

"We have to trust it's his Other Name."

"Trust? Trust whom? R?"

"Trust what we know about him from Glaeken—that he suffers from a monstrous case of hubris. The Seven served the Otherness, and one by one he eliminated them until only he remained. It fits perfectly with his personality that as he eliminated them he removed their Other names from his sigil—like crossing them off a list—until only his remained. And it makes sense that he kept that sigil as a souvenir of his triumph."

Jack shook his head. "But does it make sense that he left it in Johnson, New Jersey, where we could find it? Seems just a little too convenient."

"Now that you mention it," Eddie said. "It seems a *lot* too convenient."

"On the surface, yes, but 'too convenient' implies that someone put it there for us to find. Think about that. We first discovered that sigil when we were in our midteens. Rasalom was reborn just a few months before you. That means when you were fourteen, he was fourteen. Do you see him, at some time during his first fourteen years, hunting down his sigil, transporting it to Johnson, New Jersey, and somehow hiding it under the Lodge? And that's a big 'somehow' because the sigil would never fit through that trapdoor we found back then. 'Too convenient' requires an awful lot of assumptions, don't you think?"

Jack mulled that a moment, then gave a reluctant shrug. "Point taken. But I'm still uncomfortable with how convenient it turned out for us."

Weezy understood. That skepticism made Jack Jack, one of the reasons he had survived so long doing what he did. She doubted she could make him comfortable, but maybe she could make him less uncomfortable.

"I don't think he had anything to do with its presence in Johnson. But I'll bet the Order did. What do we know about the sigil? It's a relic of the First Age, which makes it about fifteen thousand years old. Because it's made of the virtually indestructible tenathic, it survived the Great Cataclysm that ended the First Age. Because it's a relic of that time, it was only natural that the Septimus Order—which adopted it as its seal—would have preserved it through the ages. Somehow it wound up in the Pine Barrens."

"It's that 'somehow' that bothers me. Even if it's not 'too convenient,' it's one helluva coincidence. And 'no more coincidences,' remember?"

"Well, we know from Glaeken that the Order settled in the Barrens and caged the last q'qr there—another leftover of the First Age. Is it such a stretch to believe that they'd bring along this ancient, damaged sigil too? Unless they've got some sort of Rosetta Stone, I'm sure they had no idea of the significance of the seven glyphs, or that it had once belonged to the One. But they kept it because it was an antique, a reminder of their salad days. It wound up in the town that was eventually buried, and they built the Lodge over it."

Jack's expression remained sour. "Just blocks from the home of the Heir."

"No, you've got it backward, Jack. Rasalom's sigil was brought to the Barrens long, long before you were born. Probably before the Pilgrims arrived. The sigil wasn't moved near you—you came to it. Do you know why your folks settled in Johnson?"

He shook his head. "Never occurred to me to ask. My folks got married in the fifties, and moved to Johnson after Kate was born. I have no idea why they chose Johnson. I'm pretty sure it was my dad's idea—he liked the idea of raising a family in a small town, away from all the crowding and problems of big-city life, and my mother tended to leave those decisions up to him. Wish he was alive so I could ask him."

"Well, I can see only three possibilities: He was either drawn there, pushed there, or just happened to stop there."

Jack grimaced. "I've been moved around the chessboard all my life. Maybe he was too."

"So maybe it's not a coincidence."

"Maybe it's not," he muttered.

He still didn't seem satisfied.

"What's wrong, Jack?"

Instead of answering, he pulled off the road into a service area and parked near the food court.

"We have to go back."

"What?" Eddie said. "No way. We're halfway home."

Weezy was baffled. "Go back for what?"

"I need to see that sigil again."

Eddie popped his seat belt loose and leaned forward. "But you won't *get* to see it again. As it was, we were lucky we weren't arrested for trespassing or breaking and entering. They'll be watching for us. We got what we came for. If we go back to that Lodge again we're sure to get arrested and that's the last thing we need."

For once she had to agree with her brother. As much as she hated to side against Jack . . .

"He's right, Jack. Risking arrest only plays into Rasalom's hands. We need to get this name to the Lady and put the Naming Ceremony behind us."

"Okay, maybe three of us can't go back, but one can."

"How?" Eddie said.

"Where the hell are we?"

"Exit Seven-A is ahead," Weezy said. "Route 195. Trenton, et cetera."

"Good. Gotta be a car rental place there. I'll rent something and drive back to Johnson while you continue on to the city."

He put the car back in gear and started moving again.

She said, "I don't get it, Jack. I just don't get it. What do you hope to find?"

"Nothing. I hope everything is just what we think it is. But I . . ." He shook his head. "I don't know."

"Give me something. Please."

"I just don't like the way everything is falling together so neatly. It feels orchestrated."

"Maybe it *is* orchestrated—but by the Ally."

"Yeah, well, you know how much I trust the Ally."

Weezy sighed. She had no comeback for that. She knew what the Ally had done to him. She didn't trust it either.

But she trusted Jack.

8. Ernst checked his watch again. Hours now since he'd dropped off the One.

The One had offered no explanation, simply directed him to an address in the East Twenties and walked into a brick-front office building. A brass plaque was affixed to the wall to the left of the door, but in the fading light Ernst could not read it from the street.

I must feed . . .

What was he feeding on in there?

Ernst had driven around the block a number of times until a parking space opened with a view of the entrance. He'd left the car and walked over to view the plaque close up.

MRP RENEWALS.

He could find nothing else to give any hint as to what was being renewed, so he returned to the car and called the Order's office in midtown. He asked the receptionist who answered to look up the organization.

After a short wait she said, "It appears to be a drug rehabilitation facility."

Ernst stared at the entrance. What possible need could the One have for a place like that?

He watched a few people straggle in and out—none of them looked like the clientele one would expect at a rehab center. Finally the One appeared. He walked to the curb and stood. Ernst started the car and pulled in before him.

Ernst got a brief look at him while the courtesy light was on and was nearly as shocked at his appearance now as he had been this morning. The wounded, haggard, exhausted, depleted man who had exited the car was gone, replaced by someone who looked healthy and rested.

Still scarred, yes, and still missing his left hand, but the scars seemed less prominent, his complexion had improved, and he seemed to have—was it possible?—filled out.

"Sir, you look . . ." He searched for the right word.

"Renewed?"

Yes. Exactly.

"May I ask—?"

"Not your concern, Drexler. Your immediate concern lies in retrieving the item I entrusted to you for safekeeping before the Internet fiasco. I assume you still have it."

"Yes. Of course."

"Then proceed."

Traffic was light and he made good time, pulling in front of his building fewer than fifteen minutes later.

"I will wait here."

Ernst hurried up to his apartment but entered cautiously. What if Jack waited inside? Not an irrational fear—it wouldn't be the first time. Ernst would have to choose sides right then and there: Tell Jack that his prey waited below, wounded and unsuspecting, or keep the One's confidence.

But his fear proved unfounded. His apartment was empty and he removed the rectangular box from beneath his bed without incident.

Ernst returned to the car and opened the rear door to hand it to the One, who took it awkwardly with his remaining hand. Then Ernst slipped back behind the wheel.

"One more stop," said the One.

Only one? And then what?

He gave Ernst an address in the West Eighties. Traffic was heavier there, and half an hour passed before he pulled in before a four-story brownstone. The One got out, carrying his package, and disappeared into the narrow alley running along the side.

What now? More *renewal*? How long would this take?

Not long at all. The One reappeared less than ten minutes later, still carrying that strange box under his arm. But instead of re-entering the car, he motioned Ernst to lower the window.

"You may go about your business. I have no further need of you tonight."

That came as both a relief and a disappointment. The One's presence was intensely discomfiting, but at least he knew where he was and what he was doing . . . although he had to confess he had no idea what the One had been up to since they'd arrived in Manhattan.

"But where are you going, where will you stay? You have no phone, no money. I will give you the use of my—"

"Not necessary. Events will reach a head in the next

few hours or days or . . . they will not. If they go our way, phones and money will be irrelevant. If they do not, you will hear from me."

With that he turned and began walking east. Where to? Central Park lay in that direction.

Ernst sat and watched him go, remembering his parting words.

If they go our way . . .

The One had said "*our* way." Did that mean that Ernst was back in the fold, that he'd be spared the tribulations of the Change? It certainly seemed so.

With a lightened heart, he put the car in gear and headed home.

Strange, how things worked. Had Ernst not sided with Jack last week, Szeto would still be alive. The One's remarks this morning had made it clear that he'd called Szeto first and, were he alive, Szeto would be ferrying the One around today instead of Ernst.

Always trust your instincts, he reminded himself. And right now his instincts told him to stay as far as possible from Jack.

9. Jack slowed his southward progress on 206 as he neared the light at Quakerton Road. The sun had sunk a while ago and darkness had settled. Eddie's BlackBerry had found an Enterprise car rental place but it had taken forever to reach it and do the paperwork. Jack figured he'd probably ruined John Tyleski's credit by abandoning his last rental on the South Fork, so he'd used a new credit card identity to rent a Pontiac G6. Not much of a car, but that wasn't a bad thing. It meant no one would pay much attention to it.

He let Eddie and Weezy keep the Crown Vic.

Was he doing the right thing, leaving Weezy and Eddie to go on alone? He wasn't comfortable with that but . . .

He shook his head. Maybe it was just him, but he couldn't shake the feeling that they were missing something . . . something that had to do with that sigil.

As he turned onto Quakerton he saw a pickup pull out onto 206 and head north. Looked familiar. That guy Tommy? What had he come back for? Something big, covered by a drape, sat on the bed of his truck. Most likely some of his equipment, but Jack had a feeling—

Enough with these damn feelings. Feelings-feelings-feelings. What the hell? They were driving him crazy. He needed *facts,* damn it.

He reached the Lodge, a pale blob against the darker trees behind it, and not a single light on inside. He parked a block down on the street and walked back. Old Town had fewer streetlights than the newer sections on the other side of the lake, and that was a good thing tonight. He'd taken his lock-pick set and bump keys from the Crown Vic and carried them now, along with a flashlight, plus one of Weezy's Sharpies and a pad, all in a small backpack slung over a shoulder.

He went straight to the back door. He'd noted the brand of the door lock before, so he had his Quickset bumps ready. The third one fit and in seconds he was in. Turning on his flashlight for only a second at a time for guidance, he found the basement door . . . leaning against a wall. The black rectangle of the doorway gaped before him.

His gut twisted. Not good.

Discarding all discretion, he turned on the basement lights and pelted down the stairs. The basement looked different, rearranged since they'd left. He fairly ran to the opening in the floor. The ladder had been pulled out and lay beside it. He lowered it back into the hole and descended.

No sign of the sigil.

Shit.

Heart pounding, Jack raced back up the ladder. The sigil was too big to hide, so the only explanation was they'd removed it. That guy Tommy had been leaving Johnson. Had he had the sigil in the back of his truck?

What was his phone number? Weezy had rattled it off. She'd know. But as he pulled out his phone to call her, he heard her voice in his head reciting the number. Instead of speed-dialing her, he punched in that number. After two rings he reached the voice mail:

"You've reached Thomas Mulliner Excavating and Land Clearing Service. Leave a number and we'll call you back as soon as possible."

Got him. Jack left his cell number, said he had to speak to him ASAP.

So, Tommy was one of the Mulliner clan. The Pinelands were full of them, going back to revolutionary times. Jack wasn't going to sit around waiting for a call back that might not come till morning. He had to find a Mulliner with an excavating business.

He punched in 4-1-1.

10. Rasalom rose through the darkness at the rear of Glaeken's building. He had fed well and was strong enough now to reassert his mastery over gravity.

The drug rehab center had served him well. He had identified certain centers—the ones that offered detox programs—as excellent feeding grounds. Not all detox programs were equal, however. The more high-tech centers, catering to the upper socioeconomic strata, performed rapid detox under general anesthesia, rendering their clients worthless for Rasalom's purposes.

The more run-of-the-mill centers, the ones that oversaw withdrawal from alcohol and opiates and other drugs the old-fashioned way, offered a veritable smorgasbord of pain, fear, and self-loathing. A couple of hours in proximity to a few addicts in varying stages of the process had replenished him.

He reached the fifth-floor level. He willed the window latch on the other side of the glass to rotate to the unlocked position. With the box pinned under his left arm, he used his right hand to lift the sash. He climbed into the apartment without fear of disturbing a tenant. That was the wonderful thing about Glaeken's building— only Glaeken and the Lady and a few others lived here.

He left the apartment and ascended the stairwell.

After the revelation of Glaeken's mortality, Rasalom had had no trouble locating him. He had then enlisted Szeto to find someone who could make certain modifications to the quarters below the Lady's.

He reached that floor and entered the bare apartment. Szeto had told him that the equipment had been hidden in a built-in cabinet. Rasalom laid the box before it. He opened the cabinet to reveal its electronic contents.

He could not help but marvel at this modern world. His body had matured in these times but his consciousness and the predominance of his reference points were anchored in vastly more primitive eras. Communication now was a wonder, astoundingly convenient—unless one wished to sever communications. And Rasalom so wished. But he'd had no idea how to accomplish that, so he had left it up to others.

The cabinet contained a metallic box with multiple

antennae jutting skyward. To its right lay a remote with a single button; to the left, a set of headphones.

He understood little of electronics and modern communications. He'd spent the decades since his rebirth trying to erase the Lady's presence through the arcane and traditional avenue of Opus Omega, and then the even more arcane *Fhinntmanchca*. When those failed—or, in the case of the *Fhinntmanchca*, only partially succeeded— he'd allowed Drexler to attack the Lady indirectly via modern electronics or cyberspace or whatever it was called. That too had failed, and so now he was compelled to launch a direct assault.

Perhaps compelled wasn't quite true. He was now *free* to take direct action, and he relished the opportunity.

Remembering Szeto's instructions, Rasalom found the power switch on the box and pressed it. Lights began to glow along the front. It made no sound, not even a hum, but Szeto had sworn it would render all cell phones in the top half of the building useless.

Rasalom picked up the remote. This was supposed to activate a switch that would block incoming calls to the landline phone connections in the building. He pressed the button.

He did not know how long he would have to wait here for his moment, or if his moment would ever come. But he would wait as long as it took. He had time.

He put on the headphones and listened . . .

11. Glaeken admitted them to the Lady's apartment. Weezy had called ahead from the road to tell him they would be there soon. The first thing upon entering, she went straight to the Lady and handed her the paper.

"What do you think? Is it a name?"

As the Lady took it, Weezy moved to her side and together they stared at the weird glyphs.

ꝺ ᴇ ʌ ᕤ ꝃ ᴍ ᴕ

After a moment the Lady nodded. "It has been so long since I have seen this form of writing. It has been dead for ages. But, yes, it is a name." She then made a sound like two grunts of different pitch connected by a click.

"That's a name?" Eddie said. He sounded as if he was suppressing a laugh.

The Lady looked up at him. "I believe that is what I said."

Weezy realized that Eddie wasn't used to the Lady's literal nature, so she jumped in.

"But is it *the* name—Rasalom's Other Name?"

The Lady shrugged. "Who is to say? I have no way of telling."

"But it came from the broken sigil," Eddie said. "It was written on the only remaining section of the border."

"And the sigil is made of tenathic," Weezy added.

Glaeken said, "If that's true, then it can only be from the First Age—the secret of forging it was lost in the Cataclysm. We have no choice but to proceed on the assumption this is his Other Name."

"But what if it's not?" Weezy said.

"We will never be sure until we try."

Weezy finally looked directly at the playpen. Since entering the apartment, she'd kept it in her peripheral vision. Now she had to confront the reality of burdening that baby with Rasalom's Other Name.

As ever, he sat in his space and gnawed a soup bone. He seemed perfectly content, oblivious to the role he was about to play in a cosmic drama. If Glaeken was right, his limited intelligence would allow him to remain oblivious. And that in turn would protect him.

She watched him and thought about how they were all pawns being moved around a cosmic game board. And now the pawns in this room were about to move him, bringing him into the game.

But hadn't he always been in play? Wasn't that what Jonah Stevens had in mind when he started designing his own strategy using his bloodline—a strategy aimed at producing a child that would supplant the One?

So, in a way, Jonah was going to get his wish: His grandchild was going to stop the One, though not in the way he'd intended.

"Even if it's not the One's Other Name," Eddie said, "we haven't lost anything, have we?"

Weezy looked from Glaeken to the Lady. "Have we?"

"The Other Naming Ceremony can be performed only once on the child. Once given an Other Name, it cannot be undone."

Weezy looked back to the baby. "So, he could wind up with an Other Name that has no power. Then what?"

Glaeken shrugged. "It is the only name we have. Unless you know of some other inscribed tenathic sigil somewhere, we must accept it as the only name we will ever have."

"We've got to go with it, Weez," Eddie said. "And the sooner the better, if you ask me."

She wasn't asking him. She shook her head. "I want to wait for Jack."

Eddie scowled. "He could be cooling his heels in a jail cell for all we know."

"Wait," Glaeken said. "Where *is* Jack? Why isn't he here?"

How did she explain? She wasn't sure herself.

"Something about the situation bothers him. He thinks it's too easy, too pat."

"I can't argue with him on that. But if the sigil is, as you say, made of tenathic, then it must be genuine."

"I agree, but he wanted another look at it."

"We were caught trespassing in the Lodge," Eddie said. "We were lucky we got away. Jack might not be so lucky a second time."

"You don't know Jack," she snapped, fully intending the double meaning.

Eddie sighed. "I do. Or at least I've been getting to know him. But nobody's perfect. I think it was risky going back."

"And don't you think the stakes merit some risk? We'll wait until we hear from Jack."

She didn't have the authority to say that, but she guessed enough of her determination shone through. No one argued.

12. Rasalom frowned. The Heir was absent. He had expected him there, wanted him there—*needed* him there.

The woman had just said he wanted another look at the sigil. Why? Did he suspect the truth? But how could he?

This was not going as planned. Rasalom had expected the woman, the one studying the *Compendium of Srem*, to be the problem. If anyone would have noticed inconsistencies, it should have been she. These electronic countermeasures had been put in place to block communication from her.

Rasalom was suddenly glad he'd had the foresight to order Drexler to remove the sigil from the Lodge. The question was, where was the Heir now? With the sigil gone, what could he be doing?

13.   Jack found the home of the Thomas Mulliner Excavating and Land Clearing Service at the end of a dark, twisty path in the woods off Carranza Road. His headlights picked up a clearing with a leaning shed, scattered backhoes and earth movers, and the Dodge pickup truck he'd seen earlier. He saw no sign of a house nearby, so he backed the little Pontiac around until the headlights were centered on the pickup, and left them on.

He left his car running and approached the pickup with fingers figuratively crossed. The draped object leaning in the bed was the right size. If only . . .

Using the rear bumper as a step, he hopped up into the bed and yanked the tarp free.

Yes!

The broken sigil gleamed in the headlights. He leaned in for another look at the glyphs carved into the black surface. Before leaving Weezy earlier, he'd asked her to draw him a duplicate of the glyphs she'd copied. He pulled it out and checked it again against the originals.

ꝺ Ɛ ʌ Ꝿ Ꞁ ꞃ Ɛ

A perfect copy. So why wasn't he satisfied? Why—?

A shadow moved into the edge of the light cone from the headlights and a voice said, "Hold it right there!" before Jack could move.

Shit.

He did a slow turn and saw a guy standing about ten feet away pointing a shotgun at his midsection. More than a silhouette—he stood far enough off to the side for the lights to reveal some features. Jack recognized Tommy Mulliner, holding what looked like a Mossberg over-under twelve gauge.

"The fuck you think you're doing here? Get your ass off my truck!"

"Just looking," Jack said as he sifted through ways to play this.

"Bullshit!"

"If I'd seen anyone around, I would've asked, but the place was deserted, so—"

"I know you. I seen you at the Lodge. You was trespassing there and now you're trespassing here. Get down."

Jack thought about that. The sigil was too important and he wasn't through with it. He couldn't go for his Glock without the Mossberg tearing a hole in him, so . . .

"No."

In the following seconds of stunned silence, he turned back to the sigil.

"*What?*" Tommy finally said.

"No. It's a simple word. Also known as uh-uh, non, nein, nyet, and that's a negatory."

"I'll blow your fucking head off!"

"Well, go ahead, Tommy. I'm here only to look, not steal, but you go ahead and do what you think you have to do. By the way, you related to Luke Mulliner, the guy who used to run the canoes at Quaker Lake?"

Another pause—Tommy probably hadn't expected a question about his family right after a death threat.

"Yeah. My uncle. What about him?"

Jack knelt beside the sigil and ran his hand over the

glyphs. Again that feeling of something not right, but he had to keep Tommy talking.

"Knew him when I was a kid living in Johnson."

"Easy to say."

"I know he had brothers named Matthew, Mark, and John. Their mother was into the Gospels. And you're Thomas. Another apostle. Doubting Thomas. You still doubting me, Tommy?"

"I'm doubting you've got your head on straight. Get off my truck or I shoot."

"Your family's related to Joe Mulliner, the Robin Hood of the Pines, right? Would old Joe approve of that?"

He ran his fingers over the glyphs, outlining their shapes.

"Old Joe was hung in the seventeen hundreds."

And then it hit Jack like a sucker punch to the gut.

"Oh, no."

He rose and turned toward Tommy. He didn't want that itchy trigger finger to twitch so he gave him a preview of what he was going to do.

"I'm getting off your truck and going to my car."

"Now you're talking."

Jack jumped to the ground and pulled open the passenger door. He found the pen Weezy had given him on the seat.

"And now I'm going back to the truck."

"No, you ain't!"

Tommy made the mistake of stepping in and trying to club Jack with the barrel. He wasn't experienced in this sort of thing and, before he knew it, the shotgun had changed hands.

Tommy raised his arms and cringed back as Jack pointed it his way.

"Hey, no! Don't!"

Jack lowered the weapon, saying, "Not here to hurt anyone or anything. I need about two minutes with that crazy black thing and then I'll be on my way."

He took the shotgun with him when he climbed back into the truck bed. He took out Weezy's drawing and laid the sheet over the glyphs, then began rubbing the pen over it. Gradually the writing began to appear. When he was finished he held the sheet up to the light. He leaped to his feet when his worst suspicions were confirmed.

ϽƐΛᏀ₭ᏁƐ
ᏀƐƐϽΛ₭Ꮑ

"Shit-shit-*shit*!"

The same glyphs but in a different order. An optical illusion. The visible glyphs weren't the same as the carved glyphs. A different name. Rasalom had hidden his true Other Name. Had all of the Seven done that, so that even if someone outside their circle found their sigils, he still wouldn't know their Other Names? Over five thousand fake variations remained, after all. Or had Rasalom been the only one?

Didn't matter. What did was the Lady using the wrong name in the Ceremony.

He had to tell them.

He opened the Mossberg's breech and pulled out the two shells, tossed them over his shoulder, then closed it. He laid it at the foot of the sigil and hopped down to the ground again. Without a word, he jumped into the car and slammed it into reverse.

"What the fuck's going on?" Tommy shouted as Jack

backed around. Jack heard him repeating, "What the fuck?" two or three times as he roared down the drive-way.

WTF, indeed.

14. When Jack turned back on to Carranza Road, he faced a straight shot back to 206, allowing him to make some quick calls. He speed-dialed Weezy's cell number but her voice mail picked up immediately. He tried two more times with the same result. Another post-crash cell dead zone? They were happening less frequently, but still happening.

Or had she turned off her phone? She wouldn't do that. Not unless they'd started the ceremony.

No-no-no. They wouldn't start without hearing from him. Or would they?

Feeling a little frantic, he dialed her home landline: no answer. No surprise there—she had to be at the Lady's—but he'd needed to give it a try. He dialed Glaeken's apart-ment. He'd no doubt be down in the Lady's place too, but he usually left a nurse with Magda. She'd answer and he could ask her to go downstairs and—

Glaeken's voice mail picked up immediately too.

He wanted to smash his phone against the steering wheel. What the hell was going on?

He gunned the car around the traffic circle onto Route 70 and headed west, weaving through the traffic, but care-fully. He faced a frustrating gauntlet of traffic lights be-tween him and the freeways, and he couldn't risk a cop stop for being too aggressive.

Every cell in his brain and body screamed at him to

stop that ceremony. But why? As if some part of his subconscious—the primitive crocodile hind brain perhaps—was sensing danger but unable to explain it to the higher centers.

All right . . . what did he know? Why this gnawing feeling that they'd been gamed?

It all centered around the Other Naming Ceremony. Where had that come from? Discovered by Weezy in the *Compendium of Srem*.

The *Compendium* . . . it kept opening to the Ceremony—so often that Gia had remarked that it seemed to be "trying to tell you something"—a quip they could have brushed off had it referred to any book other than the *Compendium*. Because the *Compendium* was *sui generis*, and its page order seemed to be in constant flux. It frustrated you by making it almost impossible to return to a page after you'd seen it. And yet here it was, opening to the same page time and again . . . the page about the Other Naming Ceremony.

Yes, it did seem to be "trying to tell you something."

But books don't have awareness, don't have a will. Not even the *Compendium*. At least not as far as anyone knew. Srem had used a long-lost technology to construct it, but Jack doubted she'd been able to imbue it with consciousness.

So that meant randomness or manipulation. He discarded randomness—first, because he couldn't buy it, and second, because if that was the case, he had nothing to worry about.

But the manipulation possibility bothered him. A lot.

Two sources for that: the Ally or the Otherness. If the Ally, no problem. It wanted to frustrate the Otherness as much as Jack and Glaeken.

But what if the Otherness was the source?

Jack's fingers tightened on the steering wheel as he remembered how the Order had put out a BOLO on Weezy a few weeks ago. Out of the blue. After months and months of disinterest—he now knew they'd been preoccupied with developing the Jihad virus—they suddenly wanted to locate Weezy. And according to Eddie, they'd found her.

But they did nothing. They left her alone. Or maybe not. Rasalom moved Dawn in across the hall. No one had yet to make sense of that. But Weezy discovered the Other Naming Ceremony shortly thereafter.

Connection?

Could Rasalom have sneaked in and altered the *Compendium*? Manipulated it to show the Ceremony page every time it was opened?

Jack stiffened in the seat. Could he have *added* the page? Neither Glaeken nor the Lady had ever heard of the Ceremony. Was it bogus? Could the words, written in the Small Folk tongue that only the Lady knew, have an effect that went beyond naming? Would the Lady's reciting them harm her?

His mind whirled with possibilities.

What if discovery of the Ceremony was meant to spark memories of the broken sigil and send Weezy and him back to Johnson to find it?

No, wait . . . Rasalom couldn't know they'd seen it . . .

Unless Drexler told him. Drexler had been living in the Lodge when they found it.

Jack tracked down Drexler's number in his phone history and hit SEND. When Drexler picked up, he wasted no time.

"This is Jack. Did the One ever ask about me?"

A heartbeat or two of hesitation, then, *"You flatter yourself."*

Not an answer.

"He never asked you about our interactions when I was a kid?"

"Why on Earth would he care?"

Still not an answer.

"Yes or no?"

"No. Never."

"Okay."

Jack ended the call.

Lying . . . Drexler was good at it. A good liar's reflexes when withholding info were to avoid getting caught in a lie, so he dodged a yes-or-no answer whenever possible—just as Drexler had done until pinned down. And Jack had sensed an instant's hesitation before the flat denial.

Pretty clear now that Drexler had been contacted by the wounded Rasalom, maybe even helped him. The One had survived and turned to Drexler, and so he'd switched sides again.

Why am I not surprised?

But it meant Drexler's denial was bullshit. Rasalom *had* quizzed him on what he knew of Jack's childhood.

The scenario took shape in Jack's head:

Rasalom, knowing Jack was the Heir, probed Drexler about his childhood and learned that he and Weezy had seen the broken sigil. That may or may not have been important to him at first.

He knew finding Jack would be nigh impossible, but the Order knew what Weezy looked like, so he told Drexler to find her and then do nothing more than watch her—because maybe she would lead them to the Heir.

Once Rasalom knew her location, he could have floated to her apartment windows, entered, and found the *Compendium*. He could have altered the book—

Wait. The Other Naming Ceremony didn't appear until after Dawn moved in. So . . .

He moved Dawn in across the hall—reason to be determined.

Then he changed the *Compendium* to keep opening to the Other Naming Ceremony—which he might well have added to the book.

Jack punched the steering wheel. And we played right into his hands. We remembered the name on the sigil, we went and found it, and now we're ready to perform the Other Naming Ceremony on a not quite human baby—

He almost hit a divider as the truth hit him.

That's it! That's why Dawn was moved in across the hall. So we'd go looking for the baby. Because the baby's such an obvious choice to take on Rasalom's Other Name.

Except it isn't his Other Name. It's bogus.

But what was all this supposed to accomplish?

Jack hadn't a clue, but he did know that, for whatever reason, Rasalom wanted the Lady to perform the Ceremony.

He called Weezy again, and again got her voice mail. Then he remembered Eddie. He'd probably be with Weezy, and even if not, he could run over and tell them to wait for him.

But Eddie's voice mail came on immediately as well.

Jack tossed the phone into the backseat—worthless piece of crap. Wait. Could be a local cell outage in the city, or was the Internet down again?

He retrieved it and called Gia. She picked up almost immediately.

"Is everything okay there?" he said. "The Internet and the phones?"

"Yes. I'm on the computer now. Why?"

"I'm not sure. Can't get hold of Weezy or Eddie."

"I thought they were with you."

"Long story. Are you going out at all tonight?"

"No plans. Schools are open tomorrow. Why?"

"Good. Stay in. Don't go anywhere."

"Should I be worried?"

"I don't know. Just . . . stay in. I'll call you later."

He cut the call and stepped on the gas. He didn't know what Rasalom was up to, but he knew he had to stop the Ceremony.

15. "It's been *two hours*, Weez," Eddie said. "We should have heard from him by now."

Eddie was really on her nerves with his constant bugging to start the Ceremony.

"How can we hear from him when our phones say 'no service'?"

"I believe we should get on with it," Glaeken said. "The One has regained his strength."

Weezy looked at him. "You're sure?"

He nodded. "I sense it. He's back in the city and he's damaged, but he is strong again."

"Where in the city?" Eddie said. He looked frightened.

Glaeken shrugged. "I've never been able to pinpoint his location. I know only that he is here."

"Weezy . . ." Eddie drew out her name. "If he's nearby and he finds out what we've got planned, no telling what he'll do."

"I told Jack we'd wait."

Eddie gave her a look. "Is that really what this is about?" He nodded at the baby. "Or are you just postponing the inevitable?"

Was that it? Was she delaying the Ceremony just because of the baby?

"Jack could be in jail, for all we know," Eddie added. "We've got to get this done."

"I agree," the Lady said. "We have all we need here to perform the Ceremony."

Weezy looked around the room. Looked like she was outvoted.

She sighed. "All right. Let's do it." She looked at the Lady. "What's the first step?"

"According to the *Compendium*, the baby must be seated on the lap of whoever recites the Ceremony. That would be me."

While Eddie pulled one of the wooden chairs away from the table, Weezy stepped to the playpen and lifted the baby. He loosed one of his ear-piercing shrieks as he lost his grip on his bone. Weezy quickly retrieved it for him and returned to where the Lady was seating herself on the chair. Weezy set the baby on her lap. The Lady faced him outward and wrapped her arms around him.

"Now . . . hold the *Compendium* before me so I can see the words . . ."

16. Perfect.

Rasalom removed the earphones and paused to marvel at how everything had fallen into place. His original plan had gone off track in seemingly disastrous directions, and yet somehow . . .

His original intent had been simply to locate Glaeken. He'd known for years the identity of the Heir, although not where he lived. The plan had hinged on one all-important assumption: that the Heir knew the where-abouts of Glaeken. If that were so, Rasalom could use Dawn's baby as a means to locate Glaeken through the Heir.

From his discussions with Drexler he'd known of the Connell woman's relationship to the Heir. So he had paired Dawn with the Connell woman, knowing the girl would be needy and would attach herself. He would even-tually allow Dawn—with the Connell woman's help—to find her way back to her baby. The Connell woman would show the q'qrlike child to the Heir. The Heir, if he knew Glaeken's whereabouts, would want him to see the child. And Rasalom would follow.

But the revelations in North Carolina had made all that unnecessary: Glaeken turned out to be an impotent mortal and no threat.

Which freed Rasalom to devote all his energies to eliminating the Lady.

That was when he realized that Dawn's baby could be used as a means to that very end.

Through the Connell woman, he had learned where the Heir lived—a bit of information crucial to the plan. Once he had established that, he entered her apartment while she was out and inserted a new page about the Other Naming Ceremony into the *Compendium*, arrang-ing for it to appear whenever the book was opened. The Connell woman couldn't help but find it, and couldn't help but bring it to Glaeken's attention. And to the Lady's as well, since she was the only living being—aside from Rasalom—who knew the Small Folk's language.

He had worded the page with caveats carefully tai-lored to leave the q'qrlike child as the only safe recipient of the Other Name.

The Heir and the Connell woman would go in search

of Rasalom's ancient sigil, would find what they'd believe was his Other Name, and the Lady would perform the Ceremony.

Everything had been working perfectly until the Heir's ferocious assault almost ruined everything.

Almost.

Because even though Rasalom had been maimed and had nearly lost his life, it had been worth it. The child had followed the path he'd originally set for it: straight to Glaeken and the Lady.

He went down on one knee and opened the case.

After all these millennia . . . time to end this.

17. Weezy held the *Compendium* open before the Lady while she in turn held the baby on her lap. The Lady was perhaps half a minute into the tongue-twisting, larynx-torturing vocalizations that made up the Ceremony when the apartment door slammed open.

Jack?

Weezy looked around in time to see a disfigured stranger emerge from the shadows behind Eddie who was himself in the midst of turning.

Time seemed to slow . . .

The stranger's arm blurred as he swung something through the air. Eddie's eyes widened and she watched in horror as his head tipped to the side and toppled free of his shoulders.

She screamed at the twin jets of red pumping from his neck stump as the stranger shoved him aside in his headlong rush into the room.

His eyes blazed in his scarred face . . . they fixed on her as he raised his right arm again.

A sword . . . he carried a sword . . .

She saw it arc toward her and instinctively raised the *Compendium* for protection. The blade bit into the metal of the cover and Weezy recognized the pitted blade of Jack's katana—the Gaijin Masamune—before it pulled free.

Another swing of the blade, lower this time. She tried to block it again but was too slow . . .

She felt it slice across her belly, parting the fabric of her shirt and the skin beneath as if they were paper . . .

No pain at first, and then a burst of staggering agony, deeper and more intense than she'd ever felt or imagined possible, as the point gouged through her intestines.

She dropped the book and slumped to her knees, doubling over as the stranger rushed by, raising the sword again.

From the corner of her eye she saw it ram through the baby and into the Lady.

The baby screamed, the Lady's mouth opened wide but no sound emerged as blue light began to glow where the blade pierced her chest.

Leaving the Lady and the baby skewered on the sword, the stranger released his grip and stepped back to watch.

The Lady's eyes rolled up in her head and she began to shudder as the blue glow grew brighter, spreading until it enveloped her and the baby, covering them like a second skin. The baby stopped shrieking, stopped moving as he began to press back against the Lady's chest and abdomen.

No . . . not press back . . . the baby was melting into the Lady . . . or the Lady was absorbing him. Weezy couldn't tell. But either way, the baby was disappearing into the Lady. And when he was gone, the Lady's shuddering became more violent. The feet of the chair legs beat a tattoo on the floor, then went silent as it began to rise into the air. The Lady's mouth hung open, emitting a long low moan as the enveloping blue glow brightened and brightened until it flashed with intolerable brilliance.

The sword bounced off the suddenly empty chair and both clattered to the floor.

The Lady and the baby . . .

Gone.

No, please, she couldn't be! No!

"At last!" the stranger said, his voice vibrant with triumph.

This had to be Rasalom . . . could only be Rasalom.

Through her blur of tears and haze of pain she saw him raise his arms and noticed his left hand was missing. That and the scars . . . Jack's work. But not enough.

Not enough.

"Done!" he cried.

Eddie . . . my poor Eddie . . . and the Lady . . .

She wanted to rear up and strangle this creature, this beast, but could do no more than topple to her side and curl into a ball of agony. She clutched her gushing wound and felt the slick tubes of her small intestine.

Rasalom turned and stepped closer.

"Thank you for making this possible," he said as he stood over her. "I doubt I could have done it without you."

What did he mean? She didn't understand, but the possibility that she was in any way responsible for what had happened in the last few seconds hurt her more deeply than any wound. She wanted to scream a denial, but had no strength for even a whisper.

She felt her life oozing away, the room dimming . . .

"A gut wound is soooo painful," he said, his tone

taunting. "As a reward for your help, I should let you die and end your agony, but I need it. And I need you alive."

He nudged her with the toe of his shoe. The room brightened, but her agony screamed on unabated. Why wouldn't he let her die?

She looked at the empty wooden chair. The Lady. He'd killed her. This was her third death, and that meant she was gone and couldn't come back.

The voice went on. "I only wish the Heir were here. I owe him. His presence would make my victory complete. But that will have to wait for another day. And that day is soon coming."

Wait . . . where was Glaeken? He'd been somewhere behind her when all this happened. Why hadn't he done anything, why was he silent?

Her question was answered when Rasalom stepped over her and addressed someone else.

"Well, what do you think, Glaeken. Enjoy the show? You may speak now."

18.   Glaeken felt his larynx loosen but his limbs remained locked.

He made no reply. He was too shocked to speak.

He stared with grief and dismay at Eddie's severed head, staring blindly into space, at the Lady's empty, toppled chair and the bloody sword beside it on the floor, and at Weezy's shuddering, huddled form next to it.

He and Rasalom had surprised each other numerous times through the millennia of their battle, but this was by far the most devastating blow ever dealt. It surpassed even Glaeken's imprisoning him in the keep.

As Rasalom stepped forward Glaeken took in the

scars on his face and the absence of his left hand. Jack must have come close . . . so close.

"What's that you say?" He leaned close, grinning. "I didn't catch it."

Still Glaeken said nothing. He had no defiance left.

Over . . . after all this time, it was finally over. A spark of relief flashed within but he doused it. Yes, he was tired of the endless struggle, exhausted from it, but he couldn't allow himself to welcome its end—not when the Otherness had won.

Weezy moaned, and now he had to speak.

"Let her go."

Rasalom shook his head. "Her agony is tasty, but I have another, more important reason to keep her alive."

"Jack?"

"The Heir . . . yes. I want him to find her like this, I want the agony of his loss, I want to feel his unfounded guilt that if only he'd been here things would have been different, when in truth, I'd have frozen him just like you."

Glaeken knew what would come next. "And then you'll kill us, slowly."

"Yes. As you know, I never forgive, never forget. But I'll save that pleasure for later. He has people he loves. One of them writhes in agony behind me, but there are others. The woman and child will go first, and slowly. And he will watch. Then he will go, even more slowly. And you will watch. Because he's your heir, and because you love him, don't you. Love him like a son."

Glaeken blinked in shock. He'd never seen their relationship in those terms, but now that he thought of it, yes . . . Jack was like a son.

"And after your son is dismembered, you'll watch your wife die."

He cringed at the thought, but took infinitesimal consolation in the fact that Magda's limited awareness would spare her the worst of it.

"But before her agonies begin, I will restore her mind."

"Impossible."

The grin broadened. "At this moment, yes. But I will transform during the Change, and in my new form I will be able to perform"—he spread the fingers of his remaining hand—"miracles. Remember: I never forgive, never forget. And I well remember how that bitch delayed my exit from the keep. If not for her, I would have escaped before you arrived, and everything would have been so different."

Now Glaeken could smile. "You did your damnedest, but she withstood everything you threw at her."

Glaeken remembered Magda's courage, how she'd stood like a lone Spartan with the gate of the keep as her Thermopylae.

"You will both pay for that. And she will be aware of every torment I inflict on her, and will know it is all because of you. That is perhaps the best part: When your loved ones begin to curse *you*—not me—as the cause of their agonies."

Glaeken didn't care about himself, but poor Magda . . .

"But none of this will take place," Rasalom went on, "until the Change is well under way. Before your personal agonies begin, I want you to have a front-row seat from your big windows upstairs as the reality you've protected for so long is transformed into something incomprehensible."

Glaeken shook his head. "Gloating becomes you."

"Why shouldn't I gloat? I manipulated you and your pathetic band like a maestro directs an orchestra. I'll even bet it was you who suggested that the baby carry my Other Name."

Glaeken realized with a dismay that the suggestion had indeed come from him.

"Am I so predictable?"

"Yes! You've always tried to avoid collateral damage, and dubbing a nearly mindless human-q'qr hybrid was the perfect solution. That helps me in so many ways. The Heir made the same mistake. If he'd concentrated all the massive firepower he'd assembled upon my car as I arrived, I would be cinders now and we wouldn't be having this conversation. I'm sure he considered it, just as I'm sure he discarded it for my driver's sake."

"We're trying to preserve this world, and those in it, and so we have different rules of engagement."

"And that is why I was always destined to win, Glaeken."

"We follow a code—"

"And where has it gotten you? You've lost everything— quite literally, *everything*."

He began to pace before Glaeken.

"Yes, I *should* gloat! When I learned of the Gaijin Masamune, I knew it had been repurposed from one of your blades, made of steel from a meteor. And then I learned of the heavily Tainted baby conceived as a result of my old protector and betrayer, Jonah Stevens. Suddenly I saw the possibilities. Nothing of this Earth can harm the Lady, but a sword made of steel not of this Earth could cut her. But would it kill her? Perhaps if coated with tainted blood that is not wholly of this Earth, it might very well inflict a third and final death upon her. And I was right. I was *right*!"

Glaeken realized that Rasalom had no one to celebrate with, so he was celebrating with Glaeken.

"It's over, Glaeken. You've lost. The Change is imminent now. Remember what I told you in North Carolina: It will begin in the heavens." He looked around, as if sniffing the air. "I should go. The Heir will be here soon."

"Afraid to face him?"

"Hardly." He turned and headed for the door. "But if he sees me he will be all rage, which will overcome the tastier, more delicate agonies he'll exude when he cradles one of the great loves of his life in his arms and watches helpless as she dies."

Jack loving Weezy . . . yes, Glaeken could see that, even if Jack couldn't.

Rasalom's cruelty was truly boundless.

As if to prove that, Rasalom turned at the door and added, "And you, Glaeken . . . until the Heir arrives, you will stay silent in that chair and watch the woman suffer and be able to do nothing to comfort her."

With that he was gone. Glaeken tried to move but could not, tried to call for help but could not.

He could only listen to Weezy's agonized moans and watch her writhe in pain . . .

19. The first thing Jack saw when he stepped off the elevator was the blood pooled outside the Lady's door. Heart in his mouth—he'd heard the expression, now he knew how it felt—he rushed forward and grabbed the doorknob. An instant of hesitation while his brain screamed *Don't let it be!* and then he pushed it open and—

Blood. So much blood. Where could it possibly come—?

And then he saw the headless corpse sprawled on the floor. And beside it a head with Eddie's face, so pale, the eyes so wide.

Jack's gorge rose. Eddie . . . innocuous Eddie who'd joined the Order just to network, who'd spent his days crunching numbers, who'd never harmed a soul in his life. Who would ever—?

But Jack knew who.

He stood transfixed, staring until a low moan shook him free and he looked around. There, farther into the room, another pool of blood, another form on the floor, back to him, huddled in the fetal position. It moved . . .

Weezy?

Oh, no!

He stepped past Eddie, slipping and almost falling in the sticky blood of their merging pools, and dropped to his knees beside her.

"Weezy! Weezy!"

Her eyes fluttered open. "Jack?" Her voice was barely a whisper. "That you? Can hardly see."

He looked down to where her hands clutched her abdomen, saw a loop of intestine between her bloody fingers.

"I'll get help."

He fumbled out his phone, punched in 9-1-1, then noticed "No Service" flashing on the display.

"Too late," she rasped. "The Lady . . ."

Jack looked around and spotted a katana next to a nearby wooden chair lying on its side. He recognized the Gaijin Masamune and his heart sank as he realized what had gone down here.

He spotted Glaeken sitting silent and immobile on the far side of the room, staring. Was he too—?

No. The old guy blinked. Jack knew what Rasalom had done to him. Jack had been frozen like that a couple of times himself.

He turned back to Weezy.

"I've got to get you out of here, find some help."

"No," she said. "Too late. I love you, Jack."

And then her eyes went blank and she stopped breathing.

"No! *No!*"

He rolled her onto her back and jammed his fingers against the side of her throat. No pulse. He parted her lips and blew into her mouth, then placed his palms one atop the other, and began thrusting against her chest.

"It's no use, I'm afraid," Glaeken said.

Jack glanced up and saw him approaching in a slow, stiff walk. Apparently he'd been released.

Jack felt a surge of blind anger. "Don't tell me what's no use!"

"She should have died some time ago, but he wouldn't let her. He kept her alive for you . . . so you would see her die."

"No." He kept pumping on her chest. "No!"

"I loved her too, Jack." Glaeken's voice was thick with pain. "But she has no blood left to pump."

When the inescapable truth of that simple statement penetrated, Jack stopped. He slumped forward and rested his face against her silent chest. Pressure built in his own chest until it burst free in an explosive sob.

She was gone. His Weezy was gone. Forever. The light of that brilliant, unique mind, snuffed out, never to shine again.

20. Rasalom closed his eyes and drank in the misery from above.

Ambrosia.

The strongest individuals provided the sweetest nectar when they broke. The Heir hadn't broken—it would take much more to crush that one—but he had been deeply gored, and his pain was a delight.

Glaeken's pain was a bonus. Rasalom hadn't realized what deep affection he'd harbored for the Connell woman.

And something else from Glaeken . . . defeat? Was his old nemesis giving up? That was even sweeter. But it would not let him off the hook. He had slain Rasalom twice, deprived him of half a millennium of freedom. He would suffer.

He caressed the stump of his left wrist. So would the Heir. He had much to answer for, and Rasalom knew how to break him. The woman and child he so adored . . . he would watch them slowly skinned alive—just for starters.

But until then, Rasalom would bide his time until the Otherness provided him with the seeds of Change. That would not happen until it was safe to proceed. The Lady's beacon of sentience had been extinguished, and so it was only a matter of time now until the Enemy realized that this sphere, a formerly valuable possession, had become worthless, and discarded it. When that happened, the Otherness would scoop it up and have its way.

Not long now. After all this time, not long at all . . .

21. Glaeken dropped heavily into a chair.

"The Lady's gone. We're done. He's won."

The words barely registered through the emotional storm whirling through Jack, but when they did, he raised his head from where he'd lain it on Weezy and stared at him.

Glaeken had changed since this morning. He'd lost something. A spark had died. He looked older than ever, and seemed to have shrunk. Something had gone out of him.

Something had gone out of Jack as well. Losing Kate and Dad to violence had been awful, but this . . . this was unbearable . . . unspeakable. And yet . . . his father and sister had been collateral damage. Not Weezy. She'd been an active participant in the war. She'd died in battle. And to concede defeat right after she'd sacrificed everything . . . was obscene.

"I don't want to hear that."

"We have to face it, Jack. It may take a week, it may take a month or two, but the Ally will soon realize that this corner of reality has stopped emanating a sentient signal, and it will abandon us. The Otherness will have a clear field, and humanity cannot stand long against it. It's too vast, too powerful. Without the counterbalance of the Ally, we're helpless."

Jack rose to his feet. Weezy's blood soaked his jeans from the knees down. His hands were caked with it.

"Fuck 'em both."

"I share the sentiment." Glaeken shook his head. "But it's like expecting a tiny anthill to survive against a human armed with gallons of insecticide."

Jack's grief burned away in a blast of fury. He stepped

over to the straight-backed chair and grabbed the Gaijin Masamune. He hefted the handle in a two-handed grip and inspected the bloody, pitted blade.

"Weezy's blood," he said. "And Eddie's."

"And the baby's," Glaeken said.

Of course . . . the baby's too.

He remembered the Lady's words when he'd asked her about the katana.

It might now be a weapon only for good, or only for evil. Or, like any blade, it might cut either way, depending on who wields it. But it will be used for something momentous.

She'd suggested he dump it in the ocean, but hadn't given him a good reason why.

. . . something momentous . . .

She'd been right about the momentous part.

. . . depending on who wields it . . .

Why hadn't he listened? Why hadn't he hopped on a boat right then, motored to the edge of the continental shelf, and dropped it off?

Maybe because the Lady had once told him there'd be no more coincidences in his life, so he'd assumed it was no coincidence that the sword had fallen into his hands. At the time it had seemed logical to assume he was expected to come up with a way to wield the blade against Rasalom.

Instead Rasalom had done the wielding, to disastrous effect . . . for momentous evil.

Contact with the katana now opened a door within him and darkness swirled free, filling him, seeking a victim. Glaeken was the only other living being in the room, and Jack almost turned on him. But at the last moment he found another target. With a wild cry Jack swung the blade at the chair. The otherworldly steel sliced through the wood of the ladder back and into the seat. Another swing and he'd cut the chair in half. It felt *good* to destroy.

He turned to Glaeken. "It's not over." The words grated through his clenched teeth.

But Glaeken was staring not at him but at the katana. He extended his hand. "Here. Let me see that."

He took the sword and held it before him, turning the bloody, pitted blade this way and that. A spark had returned to his eyes.

"Perhaps you're right. Perhaps it's not over."

"That's more like it."

But Jack's defiance had been all emotion. He had no idea how to proceed against the coming darkness. He looked at the remains of Weezy and Eddie and felt the fight start to leak out of him. He'd failed them. He'd failed everyone who had depended on him.

"You have a plan . . . ?"

"No, but I have an idea. We must locate certain people, certain objects, and a nonhuman being. We must gather them, and maybe, just maybe, we can fight back. But it is such a long shot, such a terribly long shot."

Jack felt a twinge of hope. "I'll take a terribly long shot any day over no shot. Tell me what you want me to do."

"Right now it is what I must do. I must search out who and what we need." He hefted the katana. "This is just one of the things I need. There are others. When I find them I will need you to help bring them together."

"Just say the word."

The spark grew in Glaeken's blue eyes. "We are going to fight, Jack. We may lose—in fact we most likely *will* lose—but before this is over, Rasalom will know he's been in a fight."

Jack turned and caught sight of Weezy again. Crushing grief washed the rest of the fight out of him.

"Yeah, well, whatever."

He knelt at her side again. He glanced over at Eddie—his head, his body . . . he'd have to do something with what was left of him. But right now . . .

He slipped his arms beneath Weezy.

"What are you doing?" Glaeken said.

The words slipped out. "Making her comfortable."

He wasn't sure what he meant. Just something to say. But he knew he couldn't leave her on the floor a moment longer.

He rose and carried her to one of the Lady's unused bedrooms—*all* unused, because she never slept. He positioned her on her back on a queen-size bed in the nearest room and pulled the spread over her, up to her breasts, covering her wound. He closed her eyelids. In the dark, with only the backwash of light from the living room around the corner, she could have been asleep.

He sat next to her as an emptiness yawned within him. She'd become such a part of his life since she'd reappeared last year, what was he going to do without her? A light had gone out. The world without Weezy . . . it wasn't right, it wasn't fair, it wasn't . . . *whole*.

His voice broke as he took her bloody hand in his and whispered, "Weezy."

A man who is something more than a man goes to the mountain and shouts his name.

Not "Rasalom." And not his birth name, the one his mother bestowed on him. He discarded that back in the First Age when the Otherness held more sway in this sphere. When he tapped into that mother lode of power and strangeness he took on a new name, an Other Name he had protected like a wolverine guarding her young. But the time for secrecy is past. He can now shout his Other Name anywhere and it will not matter.

From here atop Minya Konka, through a break in the clouds, much of what is now called China spreads out in the darkness nearly five miles below. His birthplace is not far from here. It is bitterly cold on the mountaintop. Gale-force winds shriek and howl as they swirl the frozen air about his naked body. He scarcely notices. The power within protects him, fed by the delicious woes of the world below.

The horizon brightens. Dawn does not break at this altitude—it shatters. He stares at the glint of fire sliding into view and focuses the power he has been storing during the months since the death of the Lady. Eons of frustration fall away as he finalizes the process to which he has devoted the ages of his existence. No gestures, no incantations, just elseness, Otherness, vomiting out of him, spreading out and up and around, seeping into the planet's crust, billowing into its atmosphere, saturating this locus in the multiverse.

Soon all shall be his. The Enemy has moved on. No one and nothing opposes him, no power on Earth or elsewhere can stop him. He drops to his knees, not in prayer but in relief, elation.

At last, after so many ages, it has begun.
Dawn will never be the same.

On May 17, the sun rises late.
And so it begins . . .

THE SECRET HISTORY OF THE WORLD

The preponderance of my work deals with a history of the world that remains undiscovered, unexplored, and unknown to most of humanity. Some of this secret history has been revealed in the Adversary Cycle, some in the Repairman Jack novels, and bits and pieces in other, seemingly unconnected works. Taken together, even these millions of words barely scratch the surface of what has been going on behind the scenes, hidden from the workaday world. I've listed them below in chronological order.

Note: "Year Zero" is the end of civilization as we know it; "Year Zero Minus One" is the year preceding it, etc.

The Past

"Demonsong" (prehistory)
"Aryans and Absinthe"** (1923–1924)
Black Wind (1926–1945)
The Keep (1941)
Reborn (February–March 1968)
"Dat-tay-vao"*** (March 1968)
Jack: Secret Histories (1983)
Jack: Secret Circles (1983)
Jack: Secret Vengeance (1983)

Year Zero Minus Three

Sibs (February)
"Faces"* (early summer)

The Tomb (summer)
"The Barrens"* (ends in September)
"A Day in the Life"* (October)
"The Long Way Home"****
Legacies (December)

Year Zero Minus Two
"Interlude at Duane's"** (April)
Conspiracies (April) (includes "Home Repairs")
All the Rage (May) (includes "The Last Rakosh")
Hosts (June)
The Haunted Air (August)
Gateways (September)
Crisscross (November)
Infernal (December)

Year Zero Minus One
Harbingers (January)
Bloodline (April)
By the Sword (May)
Ground Zero (July)
The Touch (ends in August)
The Peabody-Ozymandias Traveling Circus &
    Oddity Emporium (ends in September)
"Tenants"*

Year Zero
"Pelts"*
Reprisal (ends in February)
Fatal Error (February) (includes "The Wringer")
The Dark at the End (March)
Nightworld (May)

Reprisal will be back in print before long. The Secret History will end with the publication of a heavily revised *Nightworld* in 2012.

---

* available in *The Barrens and Others*
** available in *Aftershock & Others*
*** available in the 2009 reissue of *The Touch*
**** available in *Quick Fixes*

NIGHTWORLD

A REPAIRMAN JACK NOVEL
THE *NEW YORK TIMES* BESTSELLING SERIES

F. PAUL WILSON

This is the way the world ends…
not with a bang but a scream in the dark.

It begins at dawn, when the sun rises late. Then the
holes appear. The first forms in Central Park, in sight
of an apartment where Repairman Jack and a man as
old as time watch with growing dread. Gaping holes,
bottomless and empty…until sundown, when the first
unearthly, hungry creatures appear.

tor-forge.com

Hardcover • eBook